MEMORY CATCHER

A ZORDI WORLD
STANDALONE NOVEL

MEMORY CATCHER

MELISSA LAM

12 Bunnies Publishing

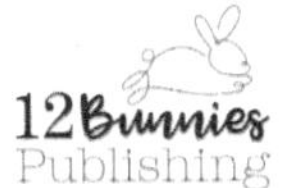

Editing, cover design, and proofreading by: Enchanted Ink Publishing
Author photo by: AB-Photography.us
Logo art by: A. Krause Studio

www.authormelissalam.com

Also by Melissa Lam

Zordi World Novels

Secrets Trilogy

Ordinary Secrets

Captured Immune

Scrubbed Mind

Standalone

Memory Catcher

Links to all books may be found on

www.authormelissalam.com

Contents

Playlist

Content Warning

If consuming spoilers makes your throat itchy and your eyes water like you've just sniffed a peanut, turn the page now!

But if you enjoy treating content warnings like dinner menus, here's what your hunky, curly-haired date is dishing out for you tonight:

- Chips and Salsa (with a side of bad decisions and zero regrets)
- **Violence** Ceviche (raw and cold, topped with cilantro, lime juice, and a dash of **murder**, **death** [including a child], and **off-page gun violence toward a baby**)
- **Explicit Sex** Asado (smoky cuts of beef and sausage *wink* slow cooked to perfection and served hot to keep you on the *edge*)
- **Kidnapping** Quesadilla (filled with cheese, **trafficking**, and a sprinkle of **on-page rape**)
- **Profanity** Fried Ice Cream (topped with cinnamon shit and chocolate fucks—I mean, fudge)

One

LIZ

"Fabulous dancing today!" I say to my class of twelve little girls in pink leotards. From the folding chair where I keep all my stuff, I grab my phone to turn down the gentle piano music playing over the ballroom speakers. The tune continues to play above me at a softer volume. "Huddle time!"

The girls' little feet pitter-patter across the wood floor until they cluster around me in a circle. The scents of their innocent souls waft toward me, all light and wholesome: honeycrisp apples, cotton candy, freshly picked flowers, and a variety of baked goods.

"Miss Hart?" One of the six-year-olds tilts her head up to look at me. She's the one whose soul smells like Fruity Pebbles.

I drop to my knees between her and the sweetheart who smells like a chocolate cake baking in an oven. "Yeah?"

"Are you giving us homework again?"

I rest my satin-gloved hands in my lap. Even around children, I have to wear gloves. I could probably take them off around this group, but I'm not willing to risk it. I never know what someone's past looks like, even at six and seven.

"Homework is good for you, remember?" I say in my

teacher's voice. "Daily practice is what turns a good dancer into a great one."

Two girls on the other side of our circle laugh as they play some sort of palm-slapping game. I clap my hands together in a rhythm. All the girls follow suit, and their chatter stills.

"Okay, Sprouters. Keep doing your stretches every day. I don't care if it's in the morning when you wake up, in the middle of the hallway at school, or at home before you go to bed. The important thing is . . ."

"That you practice," the girls say in unison.

I flash them a thumbs-up. "Fabulous. Your assignment for this week is to practice your pliés. Do three every day. If you do them after you do your daily stretches, in total, it shouldn't take more than ten minutes a day. And remember, when you do your pliés, your heels are to stay . . ."

"On the ground," my students say in unison.

"Yes!" I toss up my jazz hands. "Have a great rest of your week."

Another round of little feet scurry across the wood as the kids disperse to their cubbies to collect their backpacks. Then they rush out the ballroom door, taking their sugary scents with them. I wave at the parents through the large glass window. A few wave back with smiles.

Once the last kid is gone, I close the ballroom door. It squeals as it shuts, so loudly that I cringe.

Finally, for the first time today, I have a chance to take a deep breath. While teaching kids ballet is one of my favorite things to do, it also takes it out of me. Especially today, because I've barely had any sleep and my stomach has been growling for hours. It's angry at me for skipping breakfast and lunch.

I pull at each fingertip of my left glove before slipping it all the way off, then do the same with my right glove. They make a light *flop!* sound when I toss them onto my folding chair. Underneath it is my duffel bag, where I keep my water bottle.

I'm in the middle of gulping as much liquid as I can when the ballroom door squeals back open.

"Lordy lord," Dixie says. "We need to get some WD-40 on them hinges, don't we?"

I toss my water bottle back into my duffel bag, then rush to retrieve my gloves.

"Damn, Liz! You be lookin' like a yummy piece of lemon cake today." Dixie holds the door open for a gorgeous man to step in behind her. As her bright red heels click across the ballroom floor, the towering man's heavy work boots thump behind her.

I'm surprised Dixie allowed him in here with those muddy soles. She's got a thing about keeping her studio spotless. I'll bet the face of the man wearing those boots has something to do with it. I don't blame her either. The more he closes the distance between us, the more he's clearly an eleven on the scale of one to ten.

The second he gets within an arm's length of me, a little tingle activates in my chest. It's the zense telling me that another Zordinary human is near. That explains why I find this man so attractive. Zordis are naturally attracted to other Zordis.

People like us are born with a set of three powers each. We also typically have big eyes, straight teeth, and smooth skin. This guy has all that *and then some*. I feel the urge to ruffle my hands through his flawless blonde curls, just so he won't look so impeccable.

I can tell his zense is also tingling when he smiles at me with a knowing look.

"That's a cute dance skirt, Liz." Dixie's soul smells of freshly brewed coffee—dark roast with a single sugar cube.

In my black leotard and flowy yellow skirt, I give her a graceful twirl. "Thanks. I found it online!"

"Send me the link. I'll get one in red."

"Sure." I make a mental note to do that later, when I'm in

the comfort of my own home and can take off my gloves to use my phone.

Dixie gestures a newly manicured hand toward the hunk behind her. "This is Colton Finley. He just signed up for lessons. Guess who his new instructor is?"

I ignore her eyebrows waggling up and down as I tap my chin. "Hmm. Lemme take a wild guess. Me?"

Dixie places a hand over Colton's brawny shoulder. "See? Told ya you'd like her. Not only is she beautiful, but she's smart too!"

I roll my eyes as I pull the scrunchie out of my hair, letting my cherry-brown curls fall just past my shoulders. "Since you're introducing him to me, it would have taken *at least* a genius to figure that out."

"See? Beautiful, smart, *and* funny. She's the whole package. Colton, meet Liz Hart. She's single, ready to mingle, and I hear she's got a thing for bondage." Dixie winks, and I swear my face goes red. It takes a lot of self-control to not turn toward the big mirrors lining the walls to check if I am.

I've known Dixie for many years. With her perky tits and long legs, she could get married men with broken ankles to sign up for dance lessons. I'm used to her unique and strong personality. It's what I love most about her, but sometimes, people think Dixie's too much.

Not Colton. He simply chuckles and sticks his hand out. "Great to meet you, Liz."

His voice is deep and sultry, like the kind on a love song ballad. As I return his handshake, the scent of his soul floats toward me. It smells of the ocean breeze on a warm day— light and relaxing. He also smells like puppies. Lots and lots of cute little puppies.

"Nice to meet you too." My attention falls to his firm fore- arms. He's got the long sleeves of his Henley pushed up to his elbows, and the rest of his arms are practically bulging out of the confines of the dark green fabric. I force my eyes back up to his face. "And please don't trust a single word that leaves this woman's filthy mouth."

Colton smiles at me not only with his luscious lips but his eyes too—his deep hazel-green eyes that are surrounded by long lashes and adorable little wrinkles in the corners. "So are you saying you're *not* into bondage?"

I shoot Dixie a *see what you did?* look.

Colton's hands go up in surrender. "I don't mind either way. I was just bein' curious."

"I am *not* going to answer that," I say through a laugh. *Yeah, pretty sure my face is red.* I don't even need to glance into the mirrors to verify.

"Well, would you look at that?" Dixie grins, all smug. "Ten minutes ago, you was huffin' and puffin' about paying for them ballroom dance lessons you didn't want. Now after one look at ya dance teacher, who I told ya was a ten, you all of a sudden look *excited*."

Colton grins with a *what d'you want me to say?* shrug. "A man's allowed to change his mind." His cheeks turn pink.

I'm glad I'm not the only one changing colors. Leave it to Dixie to get me, a woman who rarely blushes, and this guy who looks like he could do fifty pull-ups no problem, to blush.

I imagine Colton lifting me into his beefy arms and carrying me to his bed. I'll bet he'd make it look like lifting a sack of feathers.

Internally, I slap myself. Did I just imagine my new dance student taking me to bed with him? I shouldn't do that. Not only because he'll be my student but because this guy is probably taken.

There aren't many men who willingly stroll into a dance studio alone and sign up for dance lessons. Especially not men at Colton's age. He's gotta be in his late twenties or early thirties. Guys his age are typically sent here by their girlfriends or wives.

Maybe he's engaged and his new fiancée has requested

that he take dance lessons. That way, when they dance at their wedding, he'll look like he knows what he's doing. That's a pretty common situation around here.

Damn. How the hell am I supposed to stay professional and keep my eyes off Colton's captivating face knowing he's got a fiancée back home? Then again, he blushed earlier when Dixie made it clear that I'm single. Maybe that means he is too.

Or maybe this is another Matt situation. *Oh, god. I hope not.* That'll be worse than if he's engaged.

I steal a long look at Colton's face until I conclude that I haven't met him before. I'd remember a face like that. Then again, I didn't recognize Matt when he came here asking for dance lessons either, and his face was also blessed by the gods.

Being reminded of Matt makes me sigh. That man did nothing for me except steer me away from ever dating my dance students and confirm that my body power is why I'm still single. Actually, my body power is the source of *all* my problems. It's why I don't have a family, why I have only one friend from the Zordi world, and why I'm the weirdo who's always wearing gloves.

On the bright side, my mind power and elemental power function normally. My mind can sense someone's soul and interpret it into a scent the same way other Soul Sniffers do. I can make water balls appear the same way other Hydros do too. Somehow, it was just the power in my hands that turned out *defective*.

Dixie's heels click toward the exit. "You two get acquainted. I'll be in my office if ya need me."

Once she's gone, I tear my eyes off Colton's delicious-looking forearms to rummage through my duffel bag. I'm not even looking for anything. I just need to be doing *something* with my hands.

I find my water bottle again and take a sip. "Which class did you join, Colton?"

The beautiful man hooks his thumbs into his denim pockets. "Uh, I didn't join a class. I signed up for private lessons."

An invisible red flag shoots into the air. This is exactly how the Matt situation started.

I play it cool. "Private lessons? On which night?"

"Thursdays. For six weeks. I don't start for another two though. Apparently, that was your soonest opening."

"Did you request me?" His answer to this question matters so much.

"Nah. I requested the first available private lessons. Dixie said you're it."

That woman, I swear. She intentionally pinned him with me. I know for a fact that two of the other teachers have open slots right now. "Do you have any background in dance?"

He shrugs. "Some."

I plop into a folding chair and untie my ballet shoes. "That's good. It can be helpful, but it's not necessary." I yawn and cover my mouth with a hand.

Colton snaps a finger and grunts. "Dammit. I did it again. Bored another woman so much, she's falling asleep right in front of me. Typical Thursday."

I finish my yawn, then let out a chuckle. "Sorry, I'm just super tired. Didn't get much sleep last night." That probably sounds odd to him, because Zordis rarely yawn and only need to sleep every other day. I'm a special case though. I have to sleep *every* night.

"Sounds like we're on the same sleep schedule. Last night was my night to sleep too."

"Fifty-percent of all Zordinaries are probably on the same sleep schedule."

He thinks about that for a second. "Hmm. I've never thought about it that way."

I toss my ballet shoes into my duffel, then pull out a pair of flats and slip into them. Then I zip up my bag and hoist it over my shoulder. "My current Thursday night couple canceled, so I'm done for the day. Do you have anything else you need to do here?"

"Nope. I'll walk you out."

As I stand, my heart thumps with more excitement than it should. He's just walking me out. It doesn't mean anything— if only my insides knew that.

Colton follows me as I switch off the ballroom lights. When I disconnect my phone from the Bluetooth speakers, the music stops. Then I close the squeaky door behind me.

Our footsteps echo through the wide hallways as we pass an empty ballroom. At the next ballroom, I wave at Abigail. She's in the middle of teaching the Budders, otherwise known as the middle schoolers. Usually, she waves back or blows me a kiss. Today, her jaw drops as her gaze locks onto the fine piece of ass beside me.

She mouths, "Oh my god!" then fans herself with a hand.

My lips curve into a smile as my attention slides up to Colton. He doesn't register that Abigail was gawking at him, because he's too busy gawking at me. His eyes dart the other way, but it's too late; I've already caught him staring. I don't think he was trying to look down my shirt or anything, but he was definitely staring at me.

As always, Dixie's office door is half open, so I peer in and wave goodbye.

With her desk phone pressed to her ear, she whispers, "See you Monday."

I whisper back, "See ya."

Colton props the front door open for me as we exit Dixie's Dance Studio. The late-afternoon sun burns low in the sky. As the heat kisses my skin, my body's natural equilibrium works to keep my internal temperature neutral. I have no doubt Colton's body is doing the same, especially since he's wearing a long-sleeve Henley. He either doesn't care about trying to look like an Ordinary, or he must not be from around here, because I don't know anyone who'd wear a thick shirt like that in Southern California. Not even in early January, like today. It's at least sixty-five degrees out right now.

"How long have you been dancing for?" Colton asks as we trek across the parking lot.

"Since I was little, and I've been an instructor since I was eighteen."

"Dixie told me you're the best she's got."

I hike my bag straps higher up my shoulder. "She says that about all the teachers."

"Maybe, but she means it about you." He gestures toward the vehicles around us. "Which one's yours?"

I point toward my car in the opposite corner. Dixie asks all the staff to park as far from the front door as we can. "The silver Malibu. You don't have to walk me all the way there though."

Colton keeps pace with me. "What kind of man would I be if I left a pretty woman to walk through a parking lot alone?"

Yep, this man is totally single. He's gotta be if he's talking to me like that. I pretend like he didn't call me *pretty* to avoid my cheeks going pink again. "It's still daylight. What could possibly happen?"

"Bad guys don't wait 'til the sun sets to commit crimes."

Playfully, I side-eye him. "Are you speaking from experience?"

He side-eyes me back. "Are you saying I look like a criminal?"

I hold my thumb and pointer finger up, leaving a little sliver of space between them. "Maybe like a small-time thief."

"Nah. If I'ma commit a crime, it's not gonna be petty burglaries. I'd go big or go home. Also, I'd make sure I don't leave a trail, so I can't get caught. And if the feds did catch me, they'd never find enough evidence to convict me."

"Wow. Sounds like you've thought this through."

He chuckles, shrugging one shoulder. "Ya know, sometimes when you're between jobs, you just start planning another bank heist while you wait to hear back from the applications."

I arch a brow. "*Another* bank heist? As in, it's not the first?"

"It's not the second either. Not that anyone would ever know that my heists were all done by me. I've made sure each job looks different. Used a different crew, different tactics, different timing. That way, they never connect the dots."

I squint at him. "I thought you were just playing around, but now I'm starting to believe you."

His face lights up with a laugh. "I'm just teasing, Liz. I wouldn't rob a bank. That's too flashy. Plus, there's potential to hurt innocent people. I'd rather rob a drug lord or something. At least then, I'm stealing from another criminal."

"The second I get home, I'm googling your name."

"Really? Give the fake criminal side of me a little more credit than that. Do you really think if I had a record under *Colton Finley* that I'd sign up for dance lessons with the same name?"

"Good point." I stop at the trunk of my car, then turn to face him. "So tell me, Colton Finley, if that is your real name, are you from the LA area?"

"No, Michigan. I'll only be here for a few months."

"What brings you to Los Angeles?"

"I'm a construction project manager. I'm assigned here for four months before they make me pack up and relocate somewhere else again."

My mind wastes no time conjuring up mental images of Colton shirtless with a tool belt hooked around his waist. I have no idea if he's got abs or not, but in my imagination, he does. I picture him wearing an orange hard hat and pounding a sledgehammer into a wall. His arm muscles ripple with each swing, and don't even get me started on his sexy back.

If I was smart, I'd tell Colton thanks for walking me to my

car and end the conversation now. Instead, I set my duffel bag on top of my trunk, then lean against my car.

Only five more minutes, I swear. "How long have you been in LA already?"

"Since last week."

"Where do you go next?"

"Dunno," he says with a shrug. "I'm flexible, so they just assign me wherever they need me. I don't normally know where I'm going 'til the week before."

"Sounds like you're an easy guy to work with."

He grunts. "You haven't seen me dance yet. You'll learn then that I'm not easy."

"You're probably not as bad as you think."

"Picture an elephant attempting the Electric Slide—while wearing roller blades. That'll be me."

"Wait." My eyebrows dip. "I thought you said you had some background in dance."

He sticks his hands into his pockets, not looking at me. "By *some*, I meant that I know the Cupid Shuffle. That's the extent of my dancing abilities."

I giggle like a little schoolgirl, because apparently, that's how I act around a man who could simply smile at a woman and make her fall to her knees. "Is that why you're taking private lessons? You wanna be able to say you know more than two dances?"

"Nah. I signed up 'cause my little sister told me that while I'm in LA, I should go out and meet new people. Somehow, she convinced me that signing up for dance lessons is a great way to do that."

"Um, forgive me for not understanding, but how is signing up for *private* dance lessons a great way to meet new people?"

He sucks in a breath through his teeth. "Technically, Chrissy told me to sign up for a dance *class*, but I wasn't about to embarrass myself in front of a group of strangers. I thought private lessons would be a good compromise. Little did I know, the teacher I'd get assigned to is hot as fuck, so in two weeks, when I embarrass myself in front of her, I'm hoping she'll ignore me when I shout curse words at my sister who won't be around to hear 'em."

First, he called me *pretty*. Now I'm *hot as fuck*. I can't decide which one I like more.

Colton continues as if he didn't just get my stomach to flutter. "Chrissy has this way of getting me to do whatever she wants. In my defense, though, she's been trying to get me to sign up for a dance class for over a year. Back then, I was in Florida for another project and I spent all my nonwork hours hiding in my apartment.

"Chrissy nagged at me for weeks for being antisocial. No matter what she said, I refused to sign up for a dance class, or cooking classes, or rock climbing, and I said *fuck no* to pottery. You name it, she suggested it. I guess after a whole year, she's finally broken me down."

"Or maybe you respect that your sister has your best interests in mind."

He rolls his eyes with a huff. "Nah. Really, I'm just a pushover when it comes to her."

"Don't play it off like that. You can admit that you love your sister so much that you allow her to talk you into doing things you don't want to."

His mouth lifts into a smile that brightens his hazel-green eyes again. "Now that I've met you, I'm thinking I should allow Chrissy to talk me into stuff more often."

I try, but no matter what I do, I can't stop a smile from forming on my lips. Quickly, I transform it into a playful glare. "Stop hitting on your new dance teacher."

"Is that not allowed?"

"I don't date my students."

"If you'd rather skip the dating thing and get right to the good stuff, I'd be down."

That makes me laugh. I smack his chest with the back of

my hand, only to realize I shouldn't have. His pecs are as firm as a brick wall, and now all I wanna do is graze my fingertips up and down his body. "You know what I meant. You're my student. We can't have a personal relationship like that, so stop flirting with me."

He sticks his finger into the air. "First of all, I'm not your student yet. And second, I'll only stop flirting with you if you stop flirting with me."

"I'm not flirting." *I totally was . . .*

"Maybe not with your words, but you were with your eyes. I saw the way they lit up when I called you pretty and hot as fuck."

"My eyes did *not* light up."

Dramatically, he presses a palm against his chest. "Oh, I'm sorry. I didn't realize that one of your powers lets you see your own eyes without a mirror."

I laugh again, then stop and straighten my back. "Stop it."

The studio door opens. Dixie strolls out with her clicky heels, rummaging through her purse as she makes her way across the parking lot. Her SUV is two down from my Malibu. When she glances up and spots Colton and me still here, a wide smirk spreads across her red lips.

She's about five cars away when she says, "Lookee what we have here! You guys just gonna hang out in the parking lot all night?"

"We were just about to leave," I say.

Colton's gaze whips to me. "We were?"

I tilt my head back to look up at him. "Yes, we were."

"But I wasn't done flirting yet."

Dixie's heels click past her SUV, then stop once she reaches us. I was hoping she'd simply get into her car and leave, but of course, she didn't. The three of us form a triangle as that stupid smirk on her face grows.

"Ya know, there's a cute Mexican place a few blocks from here." Dixie points down the road. "I imagine it'd be more fun to keep eye-fucking each other over some chips and salsa."

Colton's face breaks into a giant grin as his cheeks turn pink again.

I shoot Dixie a glare. "We were *not* eye-fucking each other."

She slumps her slender shoulders and places a hand over her hip. "Girl, lie to me one more time. I was watchin' you two from my office window since the moment you left the studio. Within the first minute, both of yous was mentally undressing each other."

"I was *not* mentally undressing him." *Unless picturing him shirtless with a sledgehammer counts.*

Dixie bats her long eyelashes up at Colton. She doesn't have to tilt her head back as much as I do. "Be honest, handsome. Was you mentally undressin' Liz?"

He doesn't miss a beat. "Hell yeah. At least six times now."

My jaw drops, and I backhand his chest again. Harder, this time. "Stop."

Dixie takes a few steps backward toward her car. "He's a cute one, Liz. Just do some research before you climb into bed with him. Don't wanna end up finding out he's another Matt Gaff." With that, she gets into her car and drives away.

I'm going to strangle her. What are the chances that Colton didn't hear that last part? I glance up at him. He stares back at me with a crumpled face. *Nope, no chance at all.*

Maybe he won't ask about it. He better not. It'll be a waste of his time, because there's no way I'm telling him about Matt Gaff. Doing so would mean I'd have to tell him about the other part of my life, which means he'd probably Google me. After that, he'd question me about my relationship with my best friend, Trey. If that doesn't chase him away, knowing the truth about my body power will. Sadly, that was how I finally got rid of Matt.

No matter what I said to that psycho, he refused to leave me alone. I told him I wasn't ready for a serious relationship. He said he could change my mind. I told him I don't have a family. He said we could start our own. We only went on one date—a date that ended with me running away. However, as soon as I told him that I'm *defective*, he became the one to run.

I guess if there's one positive to this shitty gift, it's being able to tell a psychotic man about it and know I'll never have to see him again. I don't want that to be the case with Colton, though, which is why the details of the Matt Gaff thing are staying sealed behind these lips.

"So, uh," Colton says, scratching the back of his head, "who's Matt Gaff?"

I groan as I dig through my duffel for my car keys—like I should have a while ago. "Nobody."

"Doesn't sound like nobody. Ex-boyfriend?"

I open my back door, then toss my bag onto the seat. "Ew. Not even close. Can you just pretend you didn't hear Dixie say that? Actually, can you just pretend that entire interaction with Dixie never happened?"

"Sure. I can forget that you were mentally undressing me . . . if you come out for tacos with me?"

I narrow my eyes at him, half playfully, half seriously. "Are you blackmailing me into getting dinner with you?"

"Nah. I wouldn't say blackmail. More like . . ." He purses his lips together and nods. "All right, yeah, I'm totally blackmailing you."

A laugh leaves my mouth, betraying me. If cute is what he was going for, it worked. "I don't date my students, remember?"

"I'm not your student yet, remember? Besides, who says this dinner thing has to be a date? Why can't we just go out as friends?" He smirks. "Friends who like to eye-fuck each other."

I shove him in the chest. *His hard, muscular chest.* "I was *not* eye-fucking you!"

"Okay, okay." Colton throws his arms up, palms forward. "Look, in all honesty, I'd love it if you joined me for dinner, but you don't have to. I travel a lot for work, so I'm pretty used to eating by myself. It's not a big deal."

"Are you trying to guilt-trip me now?"

He grins, and *wow*, is it beautiful. "Is it working?"

A growl from my stomach answers for me. I suppose tacos do sound good. "Do you mind if I eat in this? I didn't plan on going out tonight, so I didn't bring a change of clothes."

"You could wear nothing at all, and I'd still want you to come out with me." His cheeks redden. "Sorry, I didn't mean it like that. Not that I wouldn't enjoy watching you eat naked, 'cause I would. I just meant—Ah, fuck." He slaps a palm against his forehead as I burst out in giggles.

Best thing ever: He keeps going. "I'm sorry. Lemme start over. I just meant that I don't care what you wear. That's it. You look great in this whole black-tights-and-yellow-skirt thing. And with the matching gloves, you look like a cute little bumblebee. I mean, not that I think you're cute. I mean, well, you are. But I know some girls don't like to be called cute. They wanna be called beautiful or sexy. Which, I mean, you're both of those too. I just . . ." He slumps his shoulders and sighs deeply. "Shit. I dunno how to get myself outta this one."

I'm enjoying watching him struggle. "Are you done rambling now?"

He groans. "I hate that you didn't stop me. You didn't even try."

"I would have let you go on forever."

His gaze drops to the ground. "You got to see me embarrass myself, and we haven't even started the dance lessons yet."

Still chuckling, I open my backseat door again and dig through my duffel for my cross-body purse. Once I find it, I throw it over my shoulder, letting it hang at my hip. "Come on, Mr. Doesn't-know-when-to-shut-up. I'm so hungry I could eat, like, fifty tacos right now."

Two

COLTON

Taking risks—something I've gotten pretty damn good at.

Signing up for private dance lessons was a risk, especially because they cost as much as a kidney. I'm not sure if I'll even enjoy dancing. However, from the list of things Chrissy suggested—sorry, demanded—I sign up for to "get my ass outta the house," dancing sounded the least daunting. Since my sister is coming to visit next week, I either had to buy dance lessons now or get a lecture from her later.

Now that I've met my new drop-dead-gorgeous dance teacher, suddenly, I don't care how much money I just spent on ballroom dance lessons I never wanted.

Asking Liz to join me for dinner was another risk. I expected her to turn me down. Part of me wanted her to. Hearing her rejection would have gotten my inner wolf to chill the fuck out.

The moment I laid eyes on Liz, my wolf perked up inside me. He panted longingly at her, with his tongue hanging out and everything. He tried shifting his way out of me, just so he could mount her. My wolf hasn't acted like that about a woman in, well, ever. He gets excited about women, but never like *that*. And never after *one* glance.

While he's more thrilled about this dinner thing than I am, that doesn't mean I'm not glad Liz accepted my invitation. Despite my mouth going off like a nervous preteen's a minute ago, here she is, walking beside me toward a Mexican restaurant.

I can't believe I embarrassed myself in front of someone so beautiful. Since when do I ever ramble like that? Blaming my wolf is the best explanation I have for whatever that bull-shit was coming out of my mouth. He's all worked up about Liz, and it's getting me all worked up too.

I'm trying not to look over at her too much, but failing epically. She keeps catching me staring at her—because I can't help it. My wolf can't either. He's breathless inside me as he gawks at her big brown eyes, her smooth skin, and her curly hair. They're the type of curls that are loosely natural and frame her face perfectly.

I think she's part Hispanic. She looks it. I wish I could impress her with some Spanish skills, but I've forgotten every-thing I learned in high school. I can say *hola* and ask where the bathroom is. That's about it. Nothing impressive about that.

"Are you from LA?" I ask as our feet tread across the side-walk in sync.

"Chicago. I moved to LA when I was eighteen."

"By yourself?"

"Mm-hmm. Technically, I live in Pasadena now." One of her satin-gloved hands tucks a curl behind her ear.

Why does she wear gloves? I didn't miss the way she rushed to get them on when Dixie led me into the ballroom earlier. Does she wear gloves around everyone, or did she put them on because of me? "What made you move here by yourself?"

"I wanted to pursue a dance career." We stop at an inter-section, then Liz gives the pedestrian button a poke. "Dancing has been my dream since I was little."

"Mission accomplished. What's next? Are you planning to start your own studio someday?"

"Eh. I'm not into doing all the businessy stuff. I just wanna dance. Dixie does more computer work than dancing nowadays, which sounds awful to me."

The walk light flashes for us to cross the street. I let Liz go first before taking the side of her that faces the road.

"What about you, Colton? Are you planning to be in construction forever?"

"Nah. It pays decent, but it's hard work. I put up with a lot of stupidity. I guess that's what I get for having a job where all the men think they've got a bigger dick than the rest."

Liz laughs, and the sound of it gets my wolf to wag his tail. "What would you rather be doing?" she asks.

"I'd tell you, but it's lame."

"I won't judge."

"Promise?" I hold up my pinky finger, never pausing my steps.

She stares at it, hesitating. After a moment, she wraps her gloved pinky around my bare one. "I promise. No judging."

I hook a thumb into my pocket. "I've always wanted to be a detective."

"How is that lame?"

"Because it'll never happen."

"Says who?" She yawns, covering her mouth with a hand. That's the second time she's yawned now. I've never seen a Zordi yawn this much in such a short amount of time.

"I'm already thirty-one, Liz. Don't you think my window of time to go to school has closed? By the time I get a degree, all the people my age will have already gotten tons of field experience. No one's gonna hire me.

"Plus, there's no way I can get a degree without also working full-time, because ya know, a man's gotta eat. That means I'd have to do school on a part-time basis, which means it'll take me twice as long to finish."

"If you want it enough, you'll find a way to make it happen."

I purse my lips together. "Maybe that's it, then. Maybe I don't want it enough."

"Or maybe you've just let life get in the way and you've forgotten how much you want it."

"Hmm. Maybe." I think she's right. Many years ago, being a detective was all I could think about. Eventually, between working, taking care of my sick mother before she passed, and all the other shit in between, I've let that dream fade away. "Have you always been a deep thinker, Liz?"

She shrugs one shoulder. "I guess so."

"Since I'm hiring you as my dance teacher, do ya think I could hire you as my life coach too? Maybe you can give me some advice on how to fulfill my dreams."

Liz chuckles lightly. "Since I know nothing about how to become a detective, you might wanna look for a coach else-where. Besides, I'm already life-coaching one man, and he's more than I can handle."

I'm about to ask who that is, but we've arrived at the restaurant. I sprint ahead to get the door open for my special dinner guest.

"Thank you," Liz says as she strolls in.

The plump lady behind the counter gestures toward the many vacant tables around the large restaurant. A few booths are occupied by other patrons. Otherwise, it's mostly empty. "Pick anywhere you like."

I stare at Liz's long, sexy legs as she leads us toward a booth in the far back corner by the restrooms. It's the perfect table—away from the front door and everyone else. It's not until Liz sits down that I force my eyes off her and seat myself.

The plump lady drops some laminated menus in front of us. "I'll get you some water. Dinner specials are on the back."

After she walks away, I pretend to read the menu while my wolf paces inside me, anxious for Liz to pet him. The only times Liz has touched me were when we shook hands, when she backhanded my chest, and when we locked pinkies. There's no way my wolf is getting petted by her before me.

Sit the fuck down, I order him.

With a whine, he twirls in a circle before sinking down and resting his head over his hairy paws.

Better. Now stay.

The plump lady returns with two small plates, two glasses of water, and a basket of chips with a side of salsa. "Ready to order?"

"Sí." Liz hands her menu back to the lady as she says a bunch of words in Spanish that don't mean *Hello* or *Where's the bathroom?*

Since I haven't read a single word of this menu, I say, "Same," and hand it over.

The lady takes it, then disappears into the kitchen, shouting stuff in Spanish.

"You speak Spanish too?" Liz asks.

"Nope."

"Then how do you know what I ordered?"

"I don't, but I trust that you know what you're doing. Plus, I heard *tacos*, and that's good enough for me." I slide out of the booth. "I'ma go use el baño."

As I saunter away, my wolf whines.

We're coming right back, I tell him as if it'll help.

After I do my business, I wash my hands and splash some water over my face in an attempt to get my wolf under control. We've met plenty of pretty women before. Why does he have to choose *now* to get attached to someone? And after knowing her for . . . I check my watch. Half an hour? *Really, bro?*

Does he know something I don't? Animals have that animal instinct, after all. Either that or because we haven't been with a woman in a while, he's starved for attention.

When I return to the table, Liz is scrolling through her

phone. She tosses it back into her purse as I slide into my side of the booth. Then she slips her gloves back on like she's in a *how fast can you do it* competition.

If I had to guess, I'd say the gloves have something to do with her powers. I've heard of Premonitioners wearing gloves to protect their hands from accidentally seeing someone's future. Maybe that's Liz's body power. That could explain why she wears gloves.

"I hope you don't mind that I basically ate all the chips while you were gone." Liz nods toward the mostly empty chips basket. "I skipped breakfast and lunch today, so I'm famished. I've already ordered more chips though."

I scrutinize her through slits. "Please tell me you aren't one of those girls who thinks they're fat and starves themselves to lose weight."

"Oh no! Definitely not."

The little alarm in my temples that tells me when people are lying doesn't go off. I let out a breath of relief.

"I woke up late this morning because I didn't sleep well, so I rushed out the door. Then during my lunch break, a raging dance mom barged in and went off on Dixie about how her spoiled little princess wasn't getting one-on-one attention in class. I wasn't having it, so I stepped in to back Dixie. I'll never understand why people think they're entitled to private lessons without actually paying for private lessons. Anyway, by the time that angry mom left, my next class had already arrived. Then I taught classes up until I met you."

I dip a chip into the salsa, scooping up some tomatoes with it. "Why didn't you sleep well last night?"

She gives me a one-shoulder shrug. "I dunno."

This time, my internal alarm does go off with a little pinch in my temples. That's the third lie she's told me so far. First was when she claimed she hadn't been flirting with me. Second was when she denied mentally undressing me. And now this, saying she doesn't know why she didn't sleep well last night. I wish I would have felt the pinch when she said she hadn't been eye-fucking me. *Can't win 'em all.*

"Maybe you need a man around to exhaust you before bed. It could help you sleep better." I playfully waggle my eyebrows up and down.

She glares at me from behind her long lashes. "Stop it. You can't be talking to your dance teacher like that."

"Hey, right now, we're just two friends who like to mentally undress each other."

She throws her head back, groaning. I chuckle because she's adorable when I mess with her.

"You said you'd forget about that if I came out for tacos, remember?"

"Sorry." I don't mean it. "I'm just curious if you like what you pictured."

She pretends to zip her lips shut. "Not telling."

"Ha." I lean back into my booth, smirking. "So you admit you *were* mentally undressing me?"

"What? No." Her lie pinches my temples. "Okay, fine. Maybe I was, but it was only for a second."

I lean forward, resting my arms over the table. "What did you picture?"

"Oh, you know." She plays with the straw in her water glass, not meeting my eyes. "Just you with a tool belt, a hard hat, and your dirty jeans."

I let out a grunt. "There's nothin' spicy about that. That's exactly what I look like when I'm working."

"Do you work shirtless?"

A smile grows over my lips. "Is that what you pictured?"

"Maybe." She plays with her straw again. With another groan, she throws her head back. "Stop it."

"Stop what?"

"Getting me to flirt with you." She slides the glove off her right hand, placing it over her lap. Then she plucks a few chips from the basket and places them onto her small plate.

I admire her struggle to resist me. It's cute that she thinks she needs to. Highly unnecessary though. She can have me if she wants. She can have me *however* she wants.

My wolf nods his furry head and barks his agreement.

"Dixie told me you're single," I say.

Liz nods. "Yep."

"Then why can't we flirt a little? It's natural for two single people to flirt."

She pours some of our salsa onto her plate. "But we shouldn't."

"Says who?"

"Says me." She points at her chest with her ungloved hand.

"How old are you?"

"Twenty-six," she says easily. I like that she didn't do that thing women do where they make people guess, just to see if they'll answer with a lower number. That game is stupid, and I never win.

"Are you interested in men?"

"Yeah."

I stroke my chin. "Hmm . . ."

"Hmm, what?"

"I'm trying to figure out why you don't want to flirt with me. It's not because you're taken, too young, or a lesbian. My next question would be if you're not attracted to me, but I already know that answer 'cause you mentally undressed me earlier." I throw my hands into the air, letting them fall back onto my thighs. "I'm stumped."

"I told you already. I don't date my students."

"And I told you already, I'm not your student yet." I rest my arms over the table again. My wolf wants to be closer to her. "Answer me this, Liz: If I were to ask you out on a date before my first dance lesson, would you say yes?"

"No."

My lie-detecting pinch doesn't activate, making my wolf pout. *Sorry, bud. Me too.* "Why not?"

"Because you're *going* to be my dance student."

"But not for two weeks. Therefore, right now, I'm just a regular ol' guy. Let's say you and I met at a grocery store and you didn't know I was gonna be your student. We get to talking, I crack a few jokes, make you laugh, then ask you out. Would you say yes?"

She bites down on her bottom lip and squints her eyes a little, staring off into the distance. "What grocery store are we at?"

Not the response I expected. "Does it matter?"

"Yeah." She gives me a *duh* look.

"All right, fine." I scoop up some salsa with a chip and eat it as I think. Liz seems like she'd be the type of person who supports small businesses, so I say, "We're at one of those locally owned grocery stores."

"What's in your cart?" This woman is giving me a hard time on purpose.

I play along, curious to see where she's going with this. "First of all, I'd be carrying a basket 'cause I hate pushin' carts. Second, I'd probably have some ramen noodles, 'cause, ya know, single guy. Too lazy to cook for myself. I'd also have some shaving cream, a razor, and junk food like Scooby-Doo fruit snacks and baby Goldfish. Ya know, the manly stuff."

That gets her to laugh—so much that she snorts a little. *Too. Fucking. Cute.*

I continue, "Maybe some grapes and celery too. Only 'cause if I don't buy those things, I'll get lectured by my sister about not eating enough fruits and veggies."

Liz takes a sip of her water. "Is that it?"

"Yeah, that's probably good enough for one trip. Anything else and I'd have to get a cart."

"No condoms?" She sits back and pretzels her arms together, wearing a smirk.

She's testing me. *Smart move.*

No matter what I say, I'm going to fail. Say there aren't condoms in the basket and I'll look like a loser who knows his own hand pretty well. *Not far from the truth.*

Say I'm buying condoms and I'll look like a player. What's worse? Lonely loser or guy who can get a girl whenever he wants?

"Of course I have condoms," I say, going big or going home. "They're just under the ramen noodles so you don't see 'em. Who walks around with a basket of groceries with a hundred pack of Trojan on display?"

Her mouth pops open. "Hundred pack? Aren't you only here for four months?"

"Gotta keep my options open. If I get a twenty-four pack, that limits my options to twenty-four. Do the math. That's a number a lot less than one hundred."

"If you're only here for four months and get a hundred pack, that means you're having sex almost once a day. Considering you don't have a girlfriend, good luck finding a woman or women to keep up with those high demands."

I put my arms up, palms forward. "Hey, I never said anything about using *all* hundred condoms within the next four months. When I leave this city, I don't have to leave them behind. Besides, I was kidding. To be honest, I haven't been with a woman in over a year."

"Is that because of all your traveling?"

"That's part of it." If she had my mind power, she'd feel a pinch in her temples. Traveling has *nothing* to do with why I haven't been with a woman in over a year.

"Taco time!" The plump lady places two steaming plates of delicious-looking street tacos, Mexican rice, and refried beans between Liz and me.

A teenage boy behind the plump lady sets a full basket of chips and more salsa onto our table too.

"Gracias," Liz says as she slips out of her other glove. It joins the first one in her lap.

We take a moment to eat. I'm about to finish my first taco when I say, "If I don't show up to my dance lessons, does that still make me your student?"

Liz wipes her hands off on a napkin. "If you don't show up, Dixie won't be giving you a refund."

"That's okay. I wouldn't ask for one anyway."

"You would skip the expensive dance lessons you just signed up for if it meant we could go out?"

"Probably." *A thousand percent yes.*

"Please don't do that."

"I won't, but only 'cause you told me not to."

She finishes her first taco and grabs another. "If I told you to jump off a building, would you?"

"Depends. Are you standing at the bottom, naked?"

"Nooo." She giggles, and the sound of it gets my heart thumping.

My wolf perks up, panting at her.

Chill out, bud. Just let me do my thing. You'll get your turn. I clear my throat. "Then no, I wouldn't jump off the building."

"But you would jump if I was at the bottom, naked?"

"Most likely."

She rolls her eyes as she takes a bite of her beans. "Men."

"Speaking of men, who's Matt Gaff?"

"Not a chance."

Earlier when I asked if this Matt guy was her ex, she denied it and my internal alarm didn't go off. If Matt's not her ex-boyfriend, who is he?

"Your creepy stepbrother?"

"No," she says, swallowing her food. "And please stop guessing."

I want answers, but not enough to pry. Especially not when she looks so uncomfortable whenever I say the name *Matt.* So I change the subject. "Do you even have a brother?"

"No."

I scoop some rice into my mouth. "Sisters?"

"Yeah, but I don't count them. I usually just tell people I'm an only child."

"Hmm. Is that something I shouldn't ask about either?"

Silently, she nods. The way her gaze falls to the table tells me there's a lot of pain that comes with this sisters thing. My wolf whimpers for her. *I hate seeing her sad too, buddy.*

I make a mental list of all the things I want to know about Liz:

1. Why didn't she sleep well last night?
2. Who is Matt Gaff?
3. Why doesn't she count her sisters as sisters?
4. And most of all, why are those damn gloves in her lap so important?

I didn't miss that while I was in the bathroom, she ate chips straight out of the basket and then, once I came back, she strategically put the chips on her own plate. Is she afraid I'll accidentally touch her hands if we go for a chip at the same time?

I gesture toward her inner forearm. "Is your tattoo also on the list of things I can't ask about?"

"Nah, you can ask about this." She points at the palm-sized circle inked into her skin. Bright red flames intertwine with a wave of blue water, just below her inner elbow. "I got this about eight months ago. My best friend has a matching one shaped like a guitar."

"Matching tattoos? Jeez. You two must be close."

"We are," Liz says through a yawn. "Anyway, what about you? Is it just you and Chrissy? Are you guys close?"

"Yeah, it's just us. And with her high energy and constant need for adventure, Chrissy is like having five sisters. So one's enough. And yes, we are pretty close."

I'd never claim that my and Chrissy's childhood was the worst, but it definitely wasn't the best. We were both forced to be adults way sooner than we should have. That's just what happens when you've got a shit-ass dad and a mom who was too sick to work.

My love for Chrissy grew as I watched her take care of our slowly dying mother, when she should have been playing with Barbies or collecting Pokémon cards. Chrissy's love for me grew as she watched me go work any odd job I could find just to keep the lights on and the water running.

"Where does your sister live?" Liz asks.

"Back in Michigan. She's a veterinarian."

For the rest of our meal, we talk mostly about Chrissy. I don't mind, because my sister is my favorite person in the world, and Liz has begun to relax now that I'm not asking about her. I don't want to be the reason for that sad look in her eyes ever again.

When we finish eating, I pay the tab, even though Liz insists I don't. While she was too busy fumbling to get her gloves back on, I had already handed my card off to the lady.

Eventually, we get back on the sidewalk with the sun setting in the distance.

"Thanks again for paying the bill, but I am totally capable of paying for myself," Liz says.

"I'll let you get the tab next time, bumblebee."

She jerks her head back, smiling. "First off, what makes you think there's a next time? And second, bumblebee?"

"Yeah, you're cute like one, and you've got the right colors on, so it fits. You don't like it?"

"Hmm. Ask me again once I've heard it more. One time is not enough to come to a firm conclusion."

If she doesn't hate the nickname right away, that's a good sign. "So are you saying there won't be a next time?"

"I dunno. I just think it's funny that you assume there will be."

"I didn't assume. I just hoped." We keep strolling a few more steps before I ask, "Did you have a good time with me?"

She shrugs nonchalantly.

"Really? You're gonna play it off like that? Like this wasn't the highlight of your day?"

"It wasn't."

The pinch in my temples makes my wolf wag his tail.

If I had a tail, I'd wag it too. "Well, this was definitely the highlight of *my* day. Although before this, I was working around sweaty, mouthy men on a construction site. Not that hard to beat."

Since Zordinaries don't sweat, the Ordinary guys at work give me lots of shit for "not working as hard" as they do. I do work hard. My body's natural equilibrium just keeps me from showing it. I can't tell them that, though, because Ordinaries don't know they live among humans who can do things they've only ever seen as CGI.

Liz glances up at me with a curiosity in her eyes I haven't seen yet. It only adds to her cuteness. "Can I ask you something without you getting offended?"

"Depends. Are you about to accuse me of being a small-time thief again?" I'm winning the game of making her smile a lot.

"Did that offend you?"

"Of course! Look at me. I'm totally a *big*-time thief."

Liz rolls her eyes, but she still laughs, shaking her head.

"All right, bumblebee. Ask your question."

"Are you normally this flirty?"

"Are you trying to figure out if you're special or just one of many?"

She shrugs. "Maybe."

"Honestly, yeah, I can be a flirt sometimes. With you, I've been laying it on a little thicker. Can you blame me though? I just spent the last hour and a half with the prettiest woman in LA."

She lets out a little snort. "If you think I'm the prettiest, you haven't seen enough of this city yet."

"Don't want to. Don't need to. I could lay eyes on tens of thousands of women in this city and they wouldn't hold a candle up to my bumblebee."

Liz's brows arch. "Oh, so I'm *your* bumblebee now?"

"Does anyone else call you that?"

"A minute ago, *no one* was calling me that."

"Good." I beam, sticking my nose into the air. "Only I'm allowed to call you that."

"Since when do you get to make up rules about what people call me?"

We stop at an intersection, and I press the walk button. "Since you made up rules about not dating your students."

"Those are legit rules."

"Maybe they're legit *bumblebee* rules, but they're not Dixie rules. She practically threw us at each other today. When I walked in asking for dance lessons, she elevator-eyed me and said, 'Ooo, do I have the perfect instructor for you.' " I imitate Dixie's sassy voice almost perfectly.

When Dixie told me that all her teachers were fully booked and that the first available lessons were with a Liz Hart, I felt the pinch in my temples. I didn't question it because I was curious as to why she would lie about something like that. After one look at Liz, I wasn't mad about it. Not even a little.

"Oh my god." Liz slaps a gloved palm against her forehead. "I can totally hear her saying that. Dixie is always trying to set me up with someone. If it's not her brother, it's her neighbor or a random clerk she met at a store. Once, she tried to set me up with her uncle. She said that his daughter and I being the same age shouldn't matter."

"Dixie's a character, isn't she?"

"Hell yeah, but that's why I love her."

We arrive back at Liz's car too soon. My wolf wants to keep hearing her voice. *So do I, buddy.*

I can't remember the last time I had such natural conversations with someone. Talking with Liz feels easy—and right. I don't think there's anything I wouldn't want to talk about with this woman—well, except for the *one* thing.

Anyway, I want to ask Liz for her number, but I doubt she'll give it to me. She'll probably say something like, *I don't give my number to my students.*

I'd love to get dinner with her again too. Maybe we could hang out some more this weekend. *Or tomorrow.* Then again, I probably shouldn't push her. She hesitated to come out with me tonight. This could have been just a one-time blessing.

"Got any plans this weekend?" I ask when we stop at her car, and she turns to face me. We haven't even separated yet, and my wolf's already whining.

"A few."

"Anything fun?"

"I've got a friend staying over tonight until Sunday. We might go bowling. What about you?"

I stick my hands into my pockets. "I work all weekend. When I'm done for the day, I'll probably just sit in my apartment and binge the entire third season of *Friends* while I stuff my face with a family-size bag of Doritos."

Liz's face lights up. "That's the best season! My favorite episode is the one where Ross and Rachel take a break. Oh! And the one where they all go on that ski trip."

"Wow. You might be a bigger *Friends* fan than me."

She grins proudly. "I've seen all ten seasons, like, six times now."

"If you get bored over the weekend, you're welcome to come to my place and watch it with me." I lock my gaze onto her, waiting for her reaction.

My wolf grunts a little when she shakes her head.

"Thanks, but my friend who's staying over keeps me pretty

busy." A buzzing sound comes from her purse. She pulls out her phone. "Speak of the devil." She taps the screen, then holds the phone to her ear. "Hey, T. Yeah, I was just getting something to eat."

I can't make out exactly what words are being said on the other end. All I can hear is that it's a deep male voice.

My wolf shoots onto all fours and perks his ears as if it'll help him hear better. He can only hear what I can, so I don't know why he's acting like that. *Calm down, bud.*

"I'll be home soon." Liz pauses, then rolls her eyes. "Yes, you can eat my leftovers. I told you already, just help yourself to anything in my house. Okay, I'll see you in a bit. Bye."

I don't even wait for her to hang up. "Was that your sleep-over friend?"

"Yeah." She slides her phone back into her purse.

"You didn't mention that your friend was male."

"You didn't ask." She shrugs like it's no big deal, and it makes my wolf restless inside me.

Thankfully, the human side of me is better at controlling himself. "I guess I just assumed it was a female. Is he also single?"

"Yes. Very."

I let out a little *hmm*.

Liz smiles with a hint of a smirk. "Are you . . . *jealous?*"

I clear my throat a little, kicking a rock on the ground. "Of course not."

"Suuure." Liz lets out a laugh, patting my chest.

My entire body ignites with a deep fire inside me, yearning for her to touch me again. The flames don't fade even as she unlocks her car and opens the driver's door.

"See ya in two weeks, Colton."

I step back, offering her a wave. "See ya next time, bumblebee."

As she drives away, my wolf tries to claw his way out of me to chase after her.

Three

COLTON

The baggage claim area of LAX buzzes with people rolling their suitcases behind them. A rapid clacking of heels comes from behind me, and I spin around just as the zense prickles in my chest. Long blonde curls attack my face as my sister launches herself at me. I barely have enough time to catch her. She grasps onto me so tight, someone would have to use a crowbar to pry her off.

"It's only been three weeks," I say as I plant Chrissy's feet back onto the floor. She keeps her arms wrapped around my torso and her face buried in my chest. "We've gone way longer without seeing each other."

I might be playing it off like it's no big deal, but I've probably missed Chrissy more than she's missed me.

My wolf's tail is perked and wagging. He nudges me to let him out so he can lick her face. *Later, buddy. Be patient.*

"Three weeks feels like three years," she says into my shirt. I'm seven years older than Chrissy, and a hell of a lot taller, so the top of her head barely reaches my collarbone.

"How was your flight?" I ask when she finally releases me from her death grip.

"The big guy next to me wouldn't stop snoring." She

shoves her giant tote bag at me. Instinctively, I grab it and hoist it over my shoulder. "The guy across the aisle from me was pretty cute though. We flirted the whole time, and he asked for my number when the plane landed."

"Did you give it to him?"

"Nah, he was an Ordi." Chrissy's just as much of a flirt as I am. Maybe more. The difference between us is that I only flirt with Zordis. She extends her attention out to Ordinaries, even though it's against Zordi laws for us to be with them.

Relationships with Ordinaries risk the exposure of our hidden world. We're allowed to be friends with Ordinaries, but that's it. No dating, and especially no sexual activities.

I gesture toward the parking garage, where I've parked my truck. "You ready to get some food? I'm starving."

"We've gotta get my bag first."

I point at the huge tote thing hanging over my shoulder. "What the hell is this?"

"My carry-on. I brought a suitcase too."

Of course she did. With a sigh, I follow her toward the many rotating carousels of luggage.

Per my luck, Chrissy's suitcase is the last one to come around. When it does, it's half open, with some of her clothes spilling out.

"Seriously?" Chrissy scowls.

I set her giant bag down to heave her even gianter pink suitcase off the conveyor belt. On the inside is a printed note from TSA. I skim it, then toss it aside. "Looks like your bag was searched and they had a hard time getting everything back in."

Chrissy huffs, then drops to her knees to reorganize her things.

For a few minutes, I wait patiently.

When we hit the ten-minute mark, I lose my patience. "You done yet?"

"Chill out, Cole. I'm checking to make sure everything's here."

"Ya know you're only staying for two nights, right? Why do you need all this stuff?"

"Options, Cole, options! I've never been to LA. What if I meet someone hot and he wants to take me out? Depending on what he wants to do, I could need a cocktail dress or casual jeans. And don't even get me started on the correct footwear."

I put on my best *big brother, no bullshit* face. "Nuh-uh. Not happening. You're not going out on any dates while you're here. You came to visit *me*, not pick up some guy. And besides, if someone did ask you out, you know you'd force me to take you shopping for something new."

She grins up at me with a spark in her eyes. "Does that mean we're going shopping?"

I shake my head, sighing. "Can ya just get your shit together so we can eat? My wolf's gettin' antsy."

"Tell him to settle the fuck down. I'm almost done." A moment later, Chrissy flips the top of her suitcase down, then comes the sweet sound of the zipper.

Finally!

After I toss Chrissy's bags onto the backseat of my pickup truck, we join the extensive line of traffic leaving the airport.

The sun hangs low in the sky, reminding me I should have eaten at least two hours ago. Usually, I eat right after work. Today, I got stuck working late, so instead of grabbing a quick snack somewhere like I had planned, I rushed to the airport to grab my sister.

"What place did you decide on for dinner?" I step on the gas to speed past some old fella driving like he's got an open bowl of soup sitting on his lap.

"It's called the Soul House. Google says it's the best place in downtown LA for live music and good food."

"Downtown LA? Seriously? You couldn't have picked an

easier place to get to? It's a Friday night. That area's gonna be packed."

"Come on, Cole. It's my first night in the big city of Los Angeles. We have to go where the fun is!"

"What about the idea I suggested earlier?" Before Chrissy boarded her flight, I told her to pick out a place for dinner. Then I suggested that afterward, we go back to my apartment to watch a movie.

Knowing Chrissy, I figured it was a long shot to get her to stay in. However, I hoped she'd be tired from the plane ride and agree to it. The way she's laughing right now tells me I was an idiot for even suggesting we do anything inside my apartment.

"Did you really think I was gonna watch the extended cut of *The Lord of the Rings* with you on my first night in Los Angeles?"

I let out a long sigh as I hold out my phone. "Type that Soul House place into my GPS."

Chrissy happily snatches my device and plugs it in. Seconds later, a blue line appears on my truck's dashboard. The ETA says sixty-some torturing minutes. And with LA traffic, who knows how accurate that is.

My wolf whines as my belly rumbles.

I feel ya, bud. I press my foot harder against the gas. The faster we get there, the faster we can eat.

The sun's almost all the way down by the time I catch sight of a glowing THE SOUL HOUSE sign.

"Hell no, Chrissy. We are *not* eating here."

"Why not?"

We're stopped at a red light as I gesture a hand out the windshield toward the long-ass line wrapped around the building. "It'll be *hours* before we can get a table."

"Obviously, if there's a line, that means this place is good."

"I'm dying of hunger. I'm not tryna wait in a long line, let alone a short one. I want food now."

"Please, Cole?" She pouts, sticking out her bottom lip.

I turn my head so I can't see her. "Nope. Start googling another place. That pouty shit isn't gonna work on me."

"Pretty please?"

Two minutes later, I'm handing my keys to a valet dude, then Chrissy and I join the back of the long-ass line I never wanted to stand in. Stupidly, my wolf perks up. He thinks this means we're eating soon. We're not, but I don't have the heart to tell him.

About ten people up the line stands a colossally tall, dark-skinned man. His black shirt features the word CREW printed in big white block letters. With a device, he scans everyone's phones or papers, then he stamps the back of their hands.

"Looks like we need a ticket for the show." I don't try to hide my excitement. This means we can go elsewhere.

My overly outgoing sister takes the liberty of tapping the shoulder of the young Asian woman in front of us. The woman twists around, as do her three friends.

"Hi." Chrissy waves at them with a smile. "Do we need a ticket to get in?"

The woman nods. "Yep. And if you don't have one yet, I can almost guarantee you won't get one now. These shows are usually sold out weeks to months in advance. We got our tickets back in October."

"Oh, shucks," I say extra sarcastically. "Looks like we'll have to go somewhere else."

Chrissy's shoulders slump, and I hate seeing her so disappointed.

"Tickets, please." The big guy with the CREW T-shirt holds out his ticket-scanning device. It beeps as it scans all the phones of the Asian woman and her friends. He stamps the back of their hands, then steps up to us. "Tickets?"

"Is tonight's show sold out?" Chrissy asks.

The name tag attached to the big guy's shirt says REGGIE.

"Regular seats are sold out. I've got two VIP tickets left if you're interested."

I'm about to tell the man no thanks until Chrissy pipes up. "How much?"

"One-fifty each. Includes VIP seating, one drink, an entrée, and a meet and greet with the band after the show. Meet and greet includes a backstage hangout session, a signed photo of you with the band, and a digital download of their first original album."

Chrissy slaps my shoulder. "What are you waiting for, Cole? Pay the man."

I gape at her. "Seriously?"

"I'll pay you back. Please?" She puts her hands together like she's praying.

I sigh as I dig my wallet out of my back pocket. "Don't bother. This'll be my treat."

She jumps up and down, clapping her hands together. "Yay! You're the best big brother ever." Still jumping, she circles her arms around my torso and gives me a tight squeeze.

And just like that, the three hundred dollars I'm about to drop is already worth it.

Once Reggie finishes running my card through his device, he passes Chrissy and me each a lanyard with laminated tags hanging off the ends. Under the letters VIP are the words *Flames in the Night*. The word *flames* is on fire. I'm assuming that's the band's name. Sadly, I can't tell what type of music they play from the name or their logo. Hopefully it's not boring.

"Follow me," Reggie says.

I don't move. "Where we goin'?"

"You're VIPs now. This is the regular ticket line. VIPs have already been let in. So come on."

Beaming and without hesitation, Chrissy follows the man. I follow her.

Inside the dimly lit restaurant, Reggie shows us to a small

table three rows from the stage. All of the front-row tables are occupied by people eating food and sipping drinks. Suddenly, this VIP thing doesn't seem so bad.

Upbeat music blares from the speakers. On the stage, three more guys in CREW shirts set up microphones while Chrissy and I get seated.

A waitress appears before I even have a chance to pick up the menu. "I know y'all just sat down, so I can come back, but if you know what you wanna drink, I can get that goin' for ya."

"Yes, please," I say as I scan the menu. "I'll have an old-fashioned and . . . an order of the buffalo wings."

"Great." The waitress turns to Chrissy. "And you?"

"Whatever fruity cocktail you'd recommend and . . ." She skims the appetizers list. "The truffle fries, please."

"Perfect. Be back soon."

The restaurant door opens, then tons of feet thunder inside.

"Looks like the regular ticket holders are being let in." Chrissy flashes me a big smirk. "Aren't you glad we got VIP tickets to avoid all that chaos?"

My attention glazes over the many people filling the tables behind us. "I'm gladder now that I've got wings on the way."

Chrissy rolls her eyes. "You've got such a one-track mind. Could you at least *try* to enjoy being out? The second I fly back to Michigan, you can return to your lonely little apartment and sulk about whatever it is you've been sulking about for the past year."

I haven't told Chrissy about what happened because I refuse to talk to anyone about it. I hate that she even knows anything happened at all and that she brings it up constantly.

It's not that I think Chrissy will disown me if she knows what I did. It's not that I think she'll be disappointed either. It's that I can't burden her or anyone else with the gory details of my worst mistake.

After the incident, I wanted to crawl into a dark cave and stay there until I withered away. The only reason I didn't was Chrissy. With our dad leaving to find a new mate and Mom passing away from zancer, I couldn't leave her too. So I kept going—for her.

She doesn't approve of my version of living, which is to hide in my apartment whenever I'm not at work, but at least I'm living, right?

"I'll be more fun to be around once I've eaten," I say. "Promise."

"I'll believe it when I see it." Chrissy thunks her elbow over the table, then sets her chin into her palm. "Anyway, did you sign up for those dance classes like I told you to?"

"Sort of."

"Sort of?"

"Yeah." I scratch the back of my head. "I sort of, um, signed up for six weeks of private lessons instead."

"What? That's not what I suggested at all."

I lean back into my chair. "Well, I thought about it after we talked, and I didn't wanna make a fool of myself in front of a bunch of strangers."

"Cole, how are you supposed to find a girl if you don't put yourself out there? You're thirty-one. That's like a-hundred-and-thirty-one in wolf years. Most wolves your age have mated by now and have a little pack of baby wolves running around."

I scoff, mostly because that's something our mother would have said. "I don't know how you think showing off my lack of dancing skills will land me a girl. Besides, didn't you say the point is for me to meet new *people*? Not to find a girl."

"I only said that because if I sold it as an idea to get you a date, you wouldn't have done it. Also, you didn't have to choose dance. I also suggested rock climbing and theater."

"I'm a land animal, sis. We hate heights. And theater is

worse than dance. I can't act, nor would I want to do it in front of an audience. You know how much I hate attention."

Our waitress returns in record time with our drinks. I take my first sip as Chrissy picks up a table tent from behind a battery-operated candle.

She reads the advertisement aloud. "Flames in the Night. Every Friday and Saturday. For tickets and the live show schedule for Sundays through Thursdays, visit our website." She holds the sign up to my face. "They look like an awesome group."

I offer the sign a lazy glance. "Yeah, they look cool."

As Chrissy places the sign back onto the table, I snatch it back up as if it'll grow feet and run away.

My wolf jolts onto his paws. He saw it too.

I gape at the band's photo with my mouth open. Right there, under the band's flaming logo, is a picture of five people. I don't recognize any of them except for the curly-haired woman wearing yellow gloves. Her smile in the photo lights up my insides the same way it did when I first met her a week ago.

Four

COLTON

"Sommethin' ya like?" Chrissy has a wide shit-eating grin plastered over her lips.

I ignore it and point at Liz's face in the band's photo. "That's my new dance teacher."

"What?" Chrissy snatches the table sign from me.

"Liz didn't tell me she was in a band." Actually, Liz barely told me anything about herself at all. That doesn't mean I haven't spent the last week constantly thinking about her.

"She's gorgeous. Is she one of us?"

"Yes, and stop that."

Not listening to me, Chrissy continues to wiggle her eyebrows up and down. "What are the odds, Cole? This has to mean something."

"It doesn't mean anything. It just means my dance teacher is also in a band."

"A band that we have VIP passes to meet tonight!" She rubs her hands together, squealing. "Ah! This is gonna be great! How did Goldilocks react to her?"

Chrissy's been calling my wolf *Goldilocks* since the moment she could form sentences. As a kid, I hated it because it implied that my wolf isn't the badass I like to think he is.

Sadly, Chrissy's stupid name for him has grown on me, so I allow it.

If I tell Chrissy exactly how my wolf reacted to Liz, she'll go nuts. Instead, I say, "Liz is pretty. He reacted the same way he usually does to pretty women."

Chrissy shoves my shoulder. "Whatever. I don't believe that for a second. I bet Goldilocks wanted to mount her the moment he saw her."

Sometimes, I hate how well my sister knows my wolf.

The stage lights flash as a drumbeat echoes over the speakers, saving me from having to respond. My heart thrashes at the idea of seeing Liz again. Inside me, my wolf howls with enthusiasm.

"Welcome to the Soul House!" a peppy female voice booms over the speakers. "Please put your hands together for tonight's opening performers, the Pinkzanites."

The crowd erupts into cheers as a diverse group of four young women steps out from behind the black curtain and into the spotlights. None of them are Liz. I didn't think about there being an opening act.

My wolf spins in a circle before flopping back down with a huff.

We'll see her soon, buddy.

After a few songs, my buffalo wings arrive. Chrissy and I order our entrées, then I promptly dig into my spicy goodness. Because she's the best little sister a man could have, Chrissy offers me some of her truffle fries. I don't hesitate to accept and offer her some of my wings.

The Pinkzanites perform an upbeat show complete with in-sync dance moves and a hell of a lot of hair flipping. Some of the crowd look like they've come solely for the openers. They're wearing shirts with the girl band's faces on them and are shrieking like wild animals.

When the opening act finishes their set, the house lights turn on, then the stage becomes empty again. My heart jumps around, imitating my wolf. He knows it's almost time to see Liz.

"Cedarwood salmon." Our waitress sets a steaming plate in front of Chrissy. Then she sets a plate in front of me. "Filet mignon, rare, with a side of asparagus. Anything else for you two?"

"No, thank you." I pick up my fork, practically drooling over my meal.

As I eat, a bunch of people in CREW shirts appear on stage to get some instruments set up.

My plate is almost clear when a heavy drumbeat thumps over the speakers, and the crowd goes wild again. A familiar voice bellows over the beat—Liz's voice.

My wolf pops up onto all fours and pants with his tongue out.

"Like a sunrise on the darkest day or a shining star within the black sky, you'll always see us because we are . . . Flames in the Night!"

A countdown plays as the crowd chants along. It seems to be the cool thing to do, so I join in. "Five! Four! Three! Two! One!"

The lights bounce and flicker as, one by one, the band members from the picture pop out from behind the black curtain. A dark-skinned man twirling drumsticks around his fingers appears first. Following him is a pale woman with firetruck-red hair. After her comes a slender Asian man with a bass guitar strapped over his shoulder.

The next person to appear makes my breath hitch. She waves at the crowd with a microphone in her satin-gloved hand. Her gloves are black tonight, not yellow. Under her black leather jacket is a bright yellow tank top that shows off her pierced belly button. I didn't realize I was attracted to pierced belly buttons—until right now.

My wolf pants at Liz with hearts in his eyes. I don't bother telling him to calm down, because I'm no better. I'm already weighing the consequences of jumping onto the stage, hoisting Liz over my shoulder, and taking her home with me so I can rip all her clothes off just to see if she's pierced anywhere else. Since there are three large men standing on each side of the stage wearing black shirts with SECURITY printed across their chests, I suppose I'll stay in my seat.

A guitar riff plays over the speakers as the last band member joins the stage. Clearly, he's the reason why all these women are here, because the audience explodes with high-pitched screams.

For the next two hours, my wolf and I watch Liz perform, in awe. Not once do we take our attention off her. She might as well be performing alone, because to us, she is. Liz shines with every note she sings and every sway of her hips she throws in. I could watch her perform for days.

Like how my time with Liz last week ended too soon, the show does too. My wolf groans when she disappears behind that black curtain and the lights flip on.

"That was amazing!" Chrissy's been screaming at the top of her lungs this whole time. Whenever a song ended, she was the first to clap and cheer. She sang along to every cover song they played and waved her hands in the air whenever prompted. She grabs my arm. "Come on, Cole. It's time for the meet and greet."

We're the last to join the VIP line of about thirty others. Reggie is going around, handing everyone a slip of paper.

When he gets to us, he says, "You're number twelve. When you get backstage, the band will be off to the side, taking photos and signing autographs." He points to the slip of paper he just handed to Chrissy. "When this number is called, and *only* when this number is called, you may head to the photo area. Approach the band out of turn and you'll be asked to leave. Got it?"

Chrissy and I nod in unison.

With a thumbs-up, Reggie says, "There will be a bar and

table games to keep you entertained. Merch table will be to your right when you walk in. Once all the groups have met the band, there's typically another half hour left. Feel free to leave whenever you want, but at that time, the band will go around to hang out with whoever's still here. Any questions?"

I shake my head. "Nope. Thanks."

The last thing I expected from this meet and greet was a backstage party. But that's exactly what we walk into when the doors open to a large room with upbeat music, colorful lights, and pool tables.

I don't care about anything in the room except for the alluring woman standing in the back. She's chatting with her band near a white backdrop. Bright photography lights shine over the five of them.

The lead singer, who I've learned is named Trey, steps up behind Liz and places a hand over her shoulder. She spins around on her heel, then he bends to whisper something into her ear. My stomach drops as she slips her hand into his. Her *bare* hand. And she keeps it there.

I thought she was single.

My wolf growls through his teeth. The way Liz and Trey just intertwined their fingers looked so natural. It's as if they hold hands like that all the time. *Do they?* I keep staring at them as they talk, hopelessly waiting for their hands to separate. They don't, and my wolf continues to growl.

That's when I see it: Trey's tattoo. The one with bright red flames and blueish waves of water shaped like a guitar. The one that matches the circular tattoo on Liz's inner forearm.

My wolf's growl jumps up two notches on the aggression scale. I had assumed that Liz's matching tattoo friend was a woman. I don't know how I feel about being wrong.

Trey leans in toward Liz's ear again. He says something that makes her throw her head back with a laugh. My wolf stops growling only to bark like he's seen the mailman. No one can hear him besides me, so I don't know why he's being so loud.

Settle down, bro.

My wolf ignores me and keeps barking.

"Group one!" a voice says over the speakers.

Finally, Liz pulls her hand out of Trey's and slips her palms into a pair of satin gloves from her back pocket.

My wolf stops barking and goes back to growling—with all his teeth showing.

"Goldilocks is going batshit crazy, isn't he?"

My attention shifts to my sister. "Huh?"

"I saw the way you just looked at Liz holding hands with her bandmate. Human Colton may be able to keep it together, but I'll bet anything your wolf wants to eat that guy alive."

Playfully, I narrow my eyes at her. "How do you know him so well?"

"We've spent a lot of time together."

"Speaking of which, when we get to my place tonight, I'll have to shift. He needs to get out, and he really wants to see you."

My wolf stops growling, only to nod and paw toward Chrissy.

"I want to see him too." She pats my chest and speaks to it. "Hang in there, Goldilocks. I promise to give you lots of pets tonight."

My wolf springs upward and spins in a few circles.

Chrissy takes my arm and drags me toward the bar. "Let's get a drink."

With icy-cold refreshments in hand, I trail her to one of the pool tables, where two guys are racking up a new game.

"Can we join you?" Chrissy asks them.

Both men glance up. Their gazes start at Chrissy's face, then drop to her chest—and stay there. Suddenly, I realize how low-cut her shirt is and how high her denim shorts ride up her thighs.

I'm tempted to tear my Henley over my head to slip it over her. It'll probably cover more of her legs than those stupid shorts. She'll give me hell if I do that though. Instead, I glare at the tall white guy, who's licking his lips as he eyes my little sister.

We're close enough to them that if they were Zordis, I would've felt the zense by now. Since my chest isn't tingling, I shouldn't get too worked up. Still, I don't like how this guy is looking at my sister like she's a fucking snack.

"Grab a cue." The tall white guy points a finger toward the rack of sticks attached to the wall.

I follow Chrissy there and say under my breath, "Since when do you play pool?"

She grins at me. "Since there were two cute guys playing it."

"Remember what I said at the airport? No dates."

"Relax, Cole. It's just a game." She plucks the shortest stick off the wall for herself, then hands me the tallest one. Leaning in to me, she whispers, "And I swear to all the wolf gods, if you get overprotective big brother wolflike on me, I'ma tell Liz that you used to cut holes into your stuffed animals to practice on."

My face screws together. "I never did that."

"That's not what I'm gonna tell her."

I shoot Chrissy a dirty look, but it does nothing to intimidate her. She simply heads back to the pool table—with a smirk.

"I'm Ted." The tall white guy offers his hand to Chrissy.

"Wesley," the Asian one says.

Chrissy takes a moment to shake their hands. "I'm Chrissy. This is my brother, Colton."

The second she says *brother*, Ted's eyes light up.

My wolf snarls at him.

Human me plays it cool, and thank fuck I'm in control,

because if it was up to my wolf, he would have started a brawl by now.

While Chrissy takes a lap around the pool table, she asks questions about the rules. Wesley answers her many questions, keeping his attention on the table, where it should be. I can't say the same for Ted.

Once all the rules are settled and the balls are broken, Wesley takes his first turn. He hits the white ball into a striped one that rolls across the green and sinks straight into a pocket.

Wesley rounds the end of the table and sets up his cue again. He misses. "Your turn, Chrissy."

I glare at Ted as Chrissy bends over the table and effortlessly aims her cue. She pulls it back a couple times before releasing it. The cue ball flies into a striped ball that rolls straight into a solid. It sinks precisely into the pocket.

The guys drop their jaws.

I do too. *What the hell was that?*

Wesley throws his arms into the air. "I thought you didn't know how to play."

A sly smirk spreads across Chrissy's lips as her eyes scan the table for her next shot. "I never said that."

"Then what was with all the questions?"

"I was just making sure we were playing by the same rules. You *assumed* I didn't know how to play."

Hold on. I'm her goddamn brother, and *I* didn't even know she plays.

Chrissy bends over the table again and positions her fingers over the green. When she releases the cue, the cue ball sinks another solid. For the rest of the game, she makes it clear she's no stranger to billiards.

Any chance I get, I steal glances at Liz. Her fans are keeping her busy with pictures and autographs, so I don't think she knows I'm here yet. I admire the way she pays full attention to whoever is in front of her.

"Group ten!" someone calls over the speakers a while later.

"Good game," Wesley says as he re-racks the balls. "Another?"

"How 'bout another drink first?" Ted offers Chrissy his hand to put hers in. "Can I buy you one?"

"Sure!" My sister sets her cue down, then puts her hand in Ted's.

My wolf glares holes into Ted's back as they head toward the bar.

"Your sister's really good at pool." Wesley plucks the balls out of the pockets, rolling them onto the green.

I lift my old-fashioned to my lips for another sip. It's almost gone. "I'd like to say I taught her, but considering she threw me off her team after my second turn, that's obviously not the case."

I turn my attention back to Chrissy just in time to witness her slap Ted in the face. He jolts backward, cupping his cheek. With the loud music pumping over the speakers, I can't hear what he shouts at her. All I catch is the shape of his lips, and I'd know the shape of those words anywhere: *What the fuck?*

My wolf growls as a scowling Chrissy stomps across the room toward me.

Wesley groans under his breath. "Not again."

"What happened?" I ask when Chrissy returns to my side.

"That pervert just grabbed my ass."

My wolf snarls through his teeth.

Human me isn't as reactive. I also know Chrissy well. She doesn't need me for this.

I down the last of my drink, then set the glass on a table, adding to its collection of other empty glasses. "Looks like you took good care of him."

Wesley steps forward with an apologetic hand over his chest. "Chrissy, I'm so sorry. Ted chugged a few beers before we got here and a few more during the show. I know that's no excuse. He's just a jackass when he's drunk."

"You don't have to apologize," Chrissy says. "You're not the one who just tried to feel me up."

"Do you wanna leave?" I ask, even though I'd rather stay to see Liz. But I won't do that if Chrissy feels uncomfortable here.

Before she can respond, Ted has the audacity to show back up in her breathing space. "Come on, sweetheart. Was that really necessary?" He even has the nerve to put his hand over her shoulder. At least, he *tries* to.

Chrissy smacks his hand away before he can touch her. "Don't you dare."

"Settle down, you feisty little girl. It was just a joke. Let's just try to have a good time, 'kay?" Stupidly, he tries to put his arm around her again.

I'm about to push him away, but Wesley beats me to it.

He steps in between Ted and Chrissy, getting all up in Ted's face. "Back off, bro. She doesn't want you to touch her."

Ted flashes his friend a nasty look. "Who's side are you on?"

Wesley puts his arms up in surrender. "Just keep your hands off her."

"Stay the fuck outta my business."

I see it coming a mile away, so I grab Chrissy's arm and pull her toward me just as Drunk Ted shoves Wesley in the chest, making him fall back into the pool table.

Wesley regains his composure, then balls his fists together. "Don't start with me again, man. You know I'll end it before you can."

Clearly, Ted is dumber than a rock, because instead of backing off, he shoves Wesley again. "Fuck you!"

Instinctively, I pull Chrissy back by her waist and step in front of her like a shield. Ted aims a punch at Wesley's face. Sure, the drunk man is taller and slightly bigger, but Wesley seems to know what he's doing. He ducks, then heaves his fist straight into Ted's gut. The drunk man keels over in pain, clutching his stomach, and I'm not sorry for him at all.

Drunk Ted is about to throw another punch at poor Wesley when I grab Ted by his shirt and yank him back. "Chill out, man."

Again, the dude is not smart. He shoves me away, then swings at my face. I catch his fist in midair before punching him in the side of his head with my other hand. Is it fair to punch a drunk guy when I've only had two drinks? Probably not, but he felt up my sister, so . . .

I think about throwing another punch, just as big ol' Reggie appears out of nowhere with his booming voice.

"Stop!"

Five

LIZ

"**F**uck you!" someone shouts from across the room.

The next thing I know, a fight has broken out while a muscular man pulls a beautiful blonde behind him. I've only met the man once, but I'd recognize him anywhere, even from the back. *It's those arms.*

Colton punches some guy in the head just as our security manager rushes over there.

"Stop!" Reggie shouts.

"What just happened?" Trey asks.

"I dunno, but I know that guy," I say as Reggie and some other crew members escort two men, Colton, and his blonde date out the back door. "The one with the curly blonde hair."

"You do?"

"Yeah. I'm gonna go see what's goin' on."

Trey grabs my gloved hand as I step away. "Um, we're kinda in the middle of something." He points toward the group of girls we just finished taking pictures with.

"Those ladies came to meet you, T, not me. I won't be long."

I exit the back door into the cool night's air as Reggie

shouts at the tall guy Colton punched. "Get outta here, ya dimwit!"

Huffing under his breath, the tall guy stumbles away.

"Dammit," an Asian man says with a groan. "I rode with him here."

The blonde woman puts her hand over Colton's shoulder. "We'll give you a ride home, won't we, Cole?"

"That's okay," the Asian man says. "I can call an Uber—something Ted *should* be doing. Knowing him, he's probably off to the next closest bar."

"No need to call an Uber, man," Colton says. "We'll get ya home."

The comfortable way this woman touches Colton tells me this isn't her first time doing it. Why does that make my stomach sink and my heart so heavy? Did Colton lie when he told me he's single? But why would he lie, then show up to my meet and greet with someone? Is he trying to rub it in my face that I can't have him?

"Y'all ready to head back inside?" Reggie asks.

"Yes, sir." Colton flips around, then stops when our eyes lock. "Liz." My name sounds breathless leaving his lips.

"Colton."

"W-what are you doing out here?"

"I came to see what all the commotion was about."

Reggie gives me two thumbs-up. "Everything's handled, Liz. No need to worry." He types in the code for the back door. The keypad beeps, then he heaves the heavy door open. "Ladies first."

We all shuffle inside as group eleven gets called over the speakers.

"That was supposed to be me and Ted," the Asian man says.

"Cole and I are group twelve." The blonde turns to me. She's close enough now that the zense is tickling my chest and

I can smell her soul. Sweet strawberries and a hint of mint. "Is it cool if the three of us come together?"

I nod. "Of course."

When we reach the white backdrop, the blonde gives all my bandmates a hug, offering each person a compliment based on something she saw them do on stage. Not only is she beautiful, but she has a good soul and she's nice as hell. *Colton's got a good one.*

As she hugs me, she says, "Nice to finally meet you. I'm Chrissy."

The tornado in my stomach instantly settles. Colton told me his sister lives in Michigan. It never crossed my mind that this could be her. They don't look alike. Well, except for the curly blonde hair. I guess I can see the resemblance now.

I offer her a genuine smile. "I'm Liz."

"I know. *You're* the girl Cole's been yapping about all night."

My heart skips a beat. "He's been talking about me?"

"*Talking* isn't the best word for it. More like drooling."

"Was not," Colton says. "My sister likes to make up stories. Don't you, Chrissy?"

She scoffs, chuckling. "I could have filled a gallon-size bucket with all the drool rolling down your chin."

My bandmates laugh as Colton slaps a big hand over his sister's shoulder, wrenching her behind him. "Your turn's over, loser." With his arms out, he pulls me in for a hug. The scent of clean ocean water and puppies covers me like a soft, warm blanket.

He whispers into my ear. "You look amazing, bumblebee." His breath kisses my skin, making a shiver run down my neck, all the way to my ass.

I try not to let it show on my face how much his closeness affects me. "Thank you. You look fabulous too."

I wish he wouldn't, but he releases me from his tight grasp. "I had no idea you were famous."

"I'm not."

"You have a Wikipedia page. Pretty sure that classifies you as famous."

So much for him not finding out about the other part of my life.

Before I can say anything else, Trey chimes in. "Are we ready for pictures?"

After all the photos are taken, printed, signed, and in the hands of their owners, the band separates to mingle with the fans still hanging around. Chrissy and the Asian man, who I now know as Wesley, head straight to the bar.

Without me having to ask, Colton follows me to the sectional couch and takes a seat right next to me. My heart thrashes because I still can't believe he's here. He looks even more handsome than the last time I saw him. Crazy how that's even possible.

"Sorry 'bout my sister." Colton sets his signed photo onto the coffee table in front of us. "She likes to embarrass me, and she's really good at it."

"No need to apologize. She's harmless."

He scoffs. "To you."

"How long is she visiting for?"

"Two nights. Her plane just landed a few hours ago."

I rest an arm over the back of the couch. "Are you planning to take her anywhere fun?"

"Nah. Chrissy's not the type you make plans for. She's the type who makes the plans and everyone else just follows."

"Was it her plan to come here tonight?"

"Yeah, but not 'cause she knew you'd be here. She found this place through Google. It wasn't until she had conned me into buying last-minute VIP passes and we'd sat at our table when I realized *you* were in the band."

My brow furrows. "Wait . . . you bought VIP tickets to meet a band you've never heard of?"

Colton shrugs and chuckles a little. "Reggie said the tickets included food. Besides, I told ya I'm a pushover when it comes to my sister. That little brat can get me to do anything."

I tear my gaze off Colton's thick chest to find Chrissy skipping toward us. Wesley is only a few steps behind her, walking like a normal person.

What Chrissy looks like now must be what I look like to Trey. He always says I have a lot of happy energy and that he doesn't understand where it comes from. I don't tell him how hard I have to force myself to look and act happy all the time. I have to; otherwise, all these painful memories living inside my head would eat me up alive.

"Coley Cole Cole!" Chrissy sings, waving her photo in the air.

Colton doesn't take his stare off me as he says in a low monotone, "Whaaat?"

"Did you ask her yet?"

He still doesn't look at her. "Ask who what?"

"Liz, if she wanted to join us for late-night ice cream."

He finally looks at her, making a crumpled face. "Huh?"

"Remember? We made plans to get dessert after this, and you said you wanted to see if Liz could join us."

His face crumples more. "Whoever you had this conversation with, it wasn't me."

Chrissy shoves his shoulder, and it barely moves him. "You're such a snooze fest. At least play along." She flashes me a gorgeous smile. "Liz, would you please make Colton's night by joining us for ice cream?"

"What about Wesley?" Colton asks. "Aren't we taking him home?"

"I've already asked him. He's down for ice cream."

Colton rubs the back of his neck. "Chrissy, I don't think Liz wants to go out after she's just performed a two-hour show and did a bunch of meet and greets."

"Actually"—I stick up a gloved finger—"I'd love to."

Chrissy squeals, clapping her hands together. "Yay! Let's

finish our drinks, then go!" She takes Wesley by his arm, leading him back to the bar.

Colton turns to me. "Liz, please don't feel obligated to come out with us."

Everything in me tells me this is a bad idea. I shouldn't be spending time with my soon-to-be dance student I'm hopelessly attracted to. Still, I waggle a finger in his face. "Hey, now. Don't uninvite me. If there's ice cream involved, I'm in."

When the meet and greet ends, Colton, Chrissy, and Wesley stash their photos behind the mini bar to pick up later, then we head out the back door together.

Under the dark sky, Chrissy loops her arm through Wesley's as we stroll down the sidewalk. I keep pace with Colton, who's walking kinda slow. So slow that we end up about twenty steps behind his sister. Now that I think about it, he's probably being slow on purpose. Like how he purposely positions himself on my side that's closer to the road. Both gestures make me want to squeeze him like he's a golden retriever.

"Chrissy is full of life, isn't she?" I readjust my cross-body purse so that it hangs on the side Colton's not on. I feel closer to him when there isn't anything between us.

Colton huffs under his breath. "That's an understatement. Her element is Earth with an emphasis on lightning. You know how energetic those people can be."

People with the Earth element can form rock balls or lightning balls. Never both. It's the same as people with the Water element. They can form water balls or ice balls. Never both. There isn't a scientific study that explains why our elemental powers work that way, just like how there isn't an explanation as to why my body power works the terrible way it does.

I tuck some curls behind my ear. "There's nothing wrong with having high energy."

"True." Carefully, Colton steps around a homeless man sleeping on the ground before coming back to my side. The brief stench of cigarettes and stinky gym socks attacks my nose, and it's not from the man's soul. "I asked Chrissy to have a low-key night watching movies with me. Apparently, that's too much to ask."

Playfully, I narrow my eyes at him. "Are you saying you'd rather be doing that than hanging out with me?"

"Hell no, but if I'ma be hanging out with you, I'd want to be with *only* you. Not while babysitting my little sister and some Ordi guy she just met."

Earlier, Wesley's scent came to me like sweet pears and citrus. "Wesley's a good person. You don't have to worry about him."

"You know him?"

"No."

"Are you a Mind Reader?"

"No."

Colton side-eyes me. "Then how do you know he's a good person?"

I shrug a shoulder. "Just look at him. His demeanor and the way he talks says enough."

"Looks can be deceiving, Liz."

I'll never know what it's like to have to guess if someone's good or bad. That's not to say that good people can't do bad things or that bad people can't do good things. With my mind power, I just have a better idea than most of what intentions to expect from someone. "I have no doubts that Chrissy will put Wesley in his place if he tries to wrong her."

Colton chuckles, nodding. "Yep, that's Chrissy. I can be protective of her, but most of the time, she doesn't need me. Even when she was a kid, she could handle herself. Once, when she was eleven and I was eighteen, she came home crying. Some kid stole her bike while she was on the swings at a park. She chased him down for a few blocks before losing her breath.

"After she finished having her cry, she changed into better

shoes. Then she said something about recognizing the boy from her school bus and having an idea of where he lived. Then, without asking for help, she left.

"An hour later, she came back with her bike and some Pop-Tarts. I don't know what happened, but every day for several months, whenever she got home from school, she had a snack in hand. I'm pretty sure she zapped that boy with a lightning ball, then kicked his ass and threatened to tell his friends about it if he didn't pay her in Fruit Roll-ups and Hostess cakes."

I nod my approval. "Like I said, no doubts."

We step around a group of three homeless guys holding cups out. Up ahead, Chrissy and Wesley turn a corner. They don't even bother looking back to see if we're still trailing them.

"Sooo, Liz . . ."

I peer up at the beautiful specimen next to me. "Sooo what?"

"What's *your* element?"

I jut my head back. "What makes you think I'm gonna tell you?"

His gaze tightens on me. "Are you one of those women who likes to keep their powers a secret so they can seem mysterious?"

"You know that, like, eighty-five percent of Zordis don't like to reveal their powers up front, right?"

"I didn't ask you to tell me about your mind or body power. Just your element."

In our culture, talking about which element you have is pretty normal because we all have one of four: Fire, Earth, Water, or Air. However, openly talking about our other two powers isn't common.

There are hundreds of different powers out there, and they're passed down through genetics. Since some people have powers that are viewed as invasive or dangerous, that information is only shared amongst close friends and family.

My mind power of smelling souls isn't viewed as invasive or dangerous. And unlike my body power, it's actually useful. Touching someone's hands to get a vision of their most traumatic memory is not. A gift like that will *never* come in handy. That's why I call it a curse rather than a gift. Especially because whenever I sleep, the painful memories I've caught over the years always replay in my head.

That's why I can never stay asleep for long and why I have to sleep every night, like an Ordinary. It's also why I wake up screaming more nights than not. Why I have to wear these stupid gloves. Why my so-called family treats me like I'm a diseased and deformed animal. Why other Zordis view me as *defective*. And why I'm not telling Colton what my gifts are.

"Eighty-five percent of Zordis, huh?" he says. "I suppose I'm not a part of your made-up statistic. I'll tell you my powers if you tell me yours."

I scoff. "It's not a made-up statistic."

"Come on, bumblebee. Don't you know that, like, ninety-eight percent of all spoken statistics are made up on the spot?"

"Including yours."

He smiles, shaking his head with his nose in the air. "Nuh-uh. My statistics are facts."

I roll my eyes, making sure he sees it. "Even if I was comfortable sharing my powers with you, I wouldn't wanna do it while we're walking."

He freezes where he's at, right in the middle of the sidewalk. "Better?"

I don't bother looking back. I just keep going as I say over my shoulder, "You know what I mean. This isn't a conversation we should have out in public."

He catches up to me and hooks a thumb behind him. "We could go back to my place if you'd like."

The possibility of that excites me more than it should. *Everything* about this man excites me more than it should.

"If I had to guess," he says, "I'd say your element is either Fire or Water, based on your tattoo. And whichever element you have, Trey has the other."

That's highly observant of him—and accurate too. "Guess all you want, but I'm still not telling."

We turn the same corner Chrissy did. Up ahead, she and Wesley have stopped outside a club with music booming from the inside. Two guys with arm muscles the size of my head are stationed outside the double doors propped open.

I toy with the strap of my purse. "Are they planning to go in there?"

Colton shrugs. "Looks like it."

"Hey!" Chrissy calls with a hand cupping her mouth. "You guys got your IDs?"

I fidget with the fingertips of my gloves.

Colton eyes me. "Something wrong?"

"Um, I thought we were getting ice cream."

"Me too. Welcome to life with Chrissy. It's always an adventure."

When we catch up to her, she and Wesley are in the middle of putting their IDs away. I'm too far away to smell the souls of the people inside the club, but I can only imagine it's the same as the first and only time I've been in a club. Some people smelled of fresh soap and clean linens. Others smelled like sewage and animal feces. Unfortunately, the bad scents always overpower the good ones.

"Do you guys wanna dance for a bit?" Chrissy asks.

"It's free admission," Wesley adds. "Chrissy told me to say that, by the way. She said it'd be a deal breaker for Colton if there was a charge."

Chrissy backhands Wesley's arm. "You could have left that part out."

Colton turns to me. "I'm down if you are."

I tug my gloves higher up my wrists. "Um, I'm not good at dancing."

"What? You're a *dance* teacher."

"Club dancing isn't the same as ballroom, jazz, or ballet." I prepare myself to decline again because this is a hard no for me. Last time, I couldn't take the nasty stench of all those bad souls in one tight place. I ended up puking in the bathroom. My girlfriends thought it was the alcohol, and I didn't correct them.

"You guys go ahead," Colton says.

Without missing a beat, Chrissy grabs Wesley's arm. "Okay, bye!"

Seconds later, they have run through the doors and are disappearing within the blinking strobe lights.

I'm still fidgeting with my gloves. "Are you sure this is okay? Isn't the point of Chrissy coming to visit you that you spend time with her? If you wanna go dance, I'm happy to—"

Colton throws a hand up. "Don't even finish that sentence. I wanted to have you to myself without babysitting my little sister, remember? This is my wish come true. Besides, Chrissy had plans to ditch me for the first cute guy she met since before she got on that plane today."

That makes me feel a little better.

Side by side, we continue down the sidewalk. I wait until we can't hear the club music to ask, "Do you still wanna get ice cream?"

"Sure, but aren't they all closed by now?" He checks his watch. "It's almost midnight."

"There's an ice cream place about four blocks from here. I thought it was the one Chrissy was headed to since they're open 'til one."

"Cool. Lead the way."

A group of giggly young women in tight black dresses step around us as we pass them. Their makeup looks precise, and all their hair is set in perfect loose curls. When I glance up at

Colton, I expect him to be checking them out. Instead, he's checking *me* out.

He tears his gaze away, then clears his throat. "So, um, tell me about your band."

Gosh, he's cute. "What would you like to know?"

"How long have you guys been playing together?"

I squint my eyes as I think. "Over six years now."

"How did it start?"

"Trey and Kevin started it after they met in a guitar store. They found Marcus, our drummer, through Kevin's brother. Emmy, our pianist, joined soon after. I was added last."

"How'd they get so lucky to find you?"

It amazes me how this man can twist everything into a compliment. "Around the same time they were starting the band, Trey was taking dance lessons, and he became my partner for a dance competition. Between our rehearsals, he found out that I can sing. I sing to myself a lot while I'm in the ballroom because the acoustics are amazing.

"Anyway, he asked me to join his band, and I said yes. Honestly, I didn't think it would become such a big thing. I thought it'd just be a fun way to play music with some great people. Now we've released two original albums, lots of cover albums, gone on two sold-out tours, and we play at the Soul House every weekend. My band is like my family now."

Really, they're my *only* family. The family I was born into doesn't give a shit about me, so I'm lucky to have found some people who do.

Colton and I reach an intersection. We look both ways before crossing it.

"So Trey was your dance student?" he asks.

"No, he was Dixie's. She knew I was looking for a partner to enter the competition with and recommended him to me."

"I was about to say, I thought you didn't date your dance students."

I already know the answer but ask anyway. "What makes you think Trey and I dated?"

"Oh, um, during the opening act, Chrissy and I got curious about your band, so we did some googling. At first, we just wanted to know what kind of music you play and how big you guys are. Then we came across some articles about how you and Trey used to date. Or still are. I'm not sure which it is."

I roll my eyes. This is exactly why I didn't want Colton finding out about me. "Just so you know, all of those articles are lies. We've never dated. Our fans and the media just like to pin us together because it creates headlines that sell. Unfortunately, drama is what grabs people's attention.

"Once, someone snapped a photo of Trey and me hanging out at a beach. The caption said something about how we secretly got married and were honeymooning in Fiji. Not only were we at the Santa Monica beach here in California, but I didn't even know Fiji was a place. I thought it was just expensive water."

Colton's shoulders relax as a smile grows over his cheeks. "I'm glad to hear that. Now I don't have to fight him for you."

My cheeks heat as the smile on my face grows to match his. Colton fighting for me? The idea that any man would fight for me makes me swoony. It's quite a change from what I'm used to: men who run away.

I don't acknowledge Colton's comment because by next week, he's going to be my dance student. "Sometimes, I can understand why our fans like to ship Trey and I. We're pretty close, and we don't pretend not to be just because people like to spread rumors about us. Our band manager loves it. I swear, she purposely feeds into the drama, because it gives the band extra attention. I suppose from a business standpoint, it's a positive."

We continue talking about my band until we arrive outside a bright pink building with a glowing ice cream sign on top.

There's a line of people coming out the door, snaking around the building. Along the curb and on outdoor benches sit some people who've already gotten their ice cream.

It takes a while, but once Colton and I finally get our desserts, we find an empty spot along the street curb to sit. I'm barely two bites into my chocolate brownie delight when someone gasps from behind me.

"Is that Liz Hart?"

Instinctively, I turn around.

A girl screams, clasping a hand against her face. "It *is* Liz Hart!" Still screaming, she shoves her ice cream cup at her boyfriend and bolts toward me. Four girls from her group rush over too.

I stick my plastic spoon into my ice cream, then hand it to Colton. I take my purse off and offer it to him too. He accepts both without question as I offer him an apologetic smile. "This will only take a minute."

Apparently, I lied. It doesn't take a minute. While I smile for photos with the screamer and her girlfriends, a small crowd forms around me. Some ask who I am while the girls spew out facts about my band. From what I catch, they seem to be pretty big fans and attended tonight's show. Other patrons join the crowd, just to see what the commotion is about. Whether they know who I am or not, they stick their phones in front of my face to snap a selfie with me anyway.

I chat with the girls for a bit as they ask me a bunch of questions, mostly about Trey.

"Did Trey move to New York because you broke up with him?"

I answer with a calm "No, we've never dated."

"So it's not true that you and Trey got married and honeymooned in Fiji?"

"Nope, that's completely made up."

Another girl pipes up from the back. "Is he single then?"

"Yes."

A ten-year-old boy, who I'm positive doesn't have a clue who I am, asks for a picture. I step away from the girls for his mother to snap our photo.

"Thank you," he says politely.

"You're wel—"

A deep voice cuts me off. "Is that Trey Grant?"

The screamer girl whips her head around. "Where?"

Colton appears at my side and points down the street. "I just saw him go around that corner."

The screamer and her friends shriek as they sprint down the sidewalk. Some people in the crowd follow them.

The wind is knocked out of me as Colton hoists me over his shoulder and dashes the opposite way. It takes me a second to realize what he's doing. I giggle as he turns a corner and the ice cream parlor is no longer in sight.

Six

LIZ

We're about two blocks from the large crowd when I pat Colton's shoulder. "You can let me down now."

"You sure? Someone might have followed us."

I scan the empty sidewalk. "It's clear. Everyone's too busy chasing after the invisible Trey Grant."

Colton sets me back onto my feet, then draws my purse off his shoulder and offers it back to me. Then he hands me my ice cream cup.

I accept it. It's a little soupy now, but still good. "There's no way you just pulled that off and still managed to save my ice cream."

He shrugs nonchalantly. "Can't waste good ice cream."

I begin strolling the sidewalk, and Colton follows me. "That was clever of you, Mr. Finley. If your construction career doesn't work out, you should consider becoming a bodyguard."

He beams. "Where do I apply?"

"I dunno, but I'm sure there's some website out there."

"No. I mean, where do I apply to be *your* bodyguard?"

I chuckle, shaking my head. "A crowd like that doesn't

happen often enough for me to justify hiring personal security. Actually, a crowd like that has never happened to me—not when I'm by myself, anyway. It's only when I'm with Trey or the rest of the band."

"I'll be your bodyguard for free."

I eat a scoop of my ice cream and smile up at him. "I'll let you know when there's an opening."

When I finish my dessert, Colton takes my cup and spoon from me, then shuffles ahead to throw them into a garbage can. He returns to my side as I stop at an intersection. "Where to now, bumblebee?"

It's official, I like the nickname. "Let's just walk around and see where it takes us."

"Sure. I'll follow you."

After we pass some blocks of businesses closed for the night and countless homeless men sleeping on benches, we end up at a small park featuring a giant fountain. The water sprays upward in a beautiful arrangement of arcs and falls. Circular lights at the bottom of the fountain illuminate a layer of scattered coins.

"You wanna make a wish?" Colton asks.

"Do you have any coins? Because I don't."

He digs through his pockets and comes up empty-handed. "Me neither."

"That's okay."

"No, we can't give up that easily. People drop coins all the time. Maybe we can find one lying around."

Together, we scour the area. We look in the grass, in the flower beds, and under the trees. Colton even gets on his hands and knees to search under the park benches.

I'm on the other side of the fountain when I call out to him. "What are the chances of us actually finding a coin in the dark?"

He scoffs with attitude. "Much higher if you'd actually help me."

An idea pops into my head. I march over to the flower garden and sift through the rocks until I find two of the most coin-size rocks there are. From behind me comes the scent of the ocean breeze and a litter of puppies.

"Did ya find one?" Colton peers over my shoulder. His breath on my neck sends a tingle down my spine.

Ignoring the butterflies in my stomach, I twist around and hold out the rocks in my gloves. "Let's use these."

He flashes me an *are you serious?* look. "Liz, the fountain fairies who grant our wishes will laugh at us for throwing these in there. They don't accept payment for their magic with mere rocks. They need *real* money."

"Fountain fairies?" I laugh because I've never heard of such a thing. Still, I play along. "Maybe we can trick them into thinking these are quarters."

"They're not stupid." He takes the rocks from me and chucks them over his shoulder. Then he holds out his hand for me to take. "Come on. I've got an idea—one that's not an insult to the fairies' intelligence."

I stare at his outstretched hand. Holding hands with a person is something I've never had the opportunity to fully enjoy. Not without seeing their most traumatic memories at least a hundred times first. I've always wanted to know what it's like to not have to think about something as simple as this —something most people take for granted.

Colton scrutinizes me as I debate what to do. The problem is that holding hands has always led to the guy asking me to take my gloves off. When I refuse, that always leads to him asking why. If I ever feel comfortable enough to tell the truth, that's when he disappears.

I'm not ready for Colton to disappear. Not yet. I'm enjoying his company too much. So I loop my arm through his the way Chrissy did with Wesley earlier. My fingers wrap around his hard bicep as I offer him a smile. He doesn't move.

He only stares at me—probably debating whether or not to ask me why I didn't take his hand.

Silently, I stare back, begging him not to question it. Talking about my powers ruins everything. I don't want this night to be ruined. Especially not when it's been this good.

As if he heard my plea, he breaks our stare and leads me away from the park.

"So what's your grand idea?" I ask, desperate to fill the silence.

"You'll see."

I keep holding on to Colton's arm as we head down a block. It's not until we're steps away from a homeless guy sleeping on a bench when I catch on to what he's doing. The homeless guy has a cup of coins tucked under his arm.

"No," I whisper-yell, tugging Colton back. "You can't steal from the homeless."

Colton releases himself from my grasp and screws his face together. "Steal? What kind of man do you think I am? I'm a big-time thief, remember? Stealing from this guy is too small and petty for me."

"Then what are you—"

Colton squats and pokes the sleeping guy in the arm. "Sir?"

I slap a palm over my forehead. "Oh, lord."

Colton pokes the man again. "Sir?"

The homeless guy jerks upright. "Huh? No. I ain't movin'. I was here first."

"Sorry to wake you. I was just wondering if you had any quarters I could trade you some cash for?"

After rubbing his eyes, the man nods. From his cup, he digs out four quarters. "How many d'ya need?"

"Two is fine."

With dirt-stained hands, the guy drops his quarters into Colton's outstretched palm. Colton pulls out his wallet and hands the guy two twenties. "Thanks, man."

The homeless guy gapes at the cash. "For real?"

"Yep. I apologize again for waking you. Have a good night."

With the coins in his pocket, Colton sticks his elbow out for me to take. This time, I don't hesitate to accept.

Back at the fountain, he hands me a quarter. "Do you know what you wanna wish for?"

"Not yet."

"Well, I know what I want, so I'll go first." He turns to face away from the fountain. With his eyes closed, he sucks in a deep breath and lets it out. Then he tosses the quarter over his shoulder. It lands in the water with a little *plop!*

"All right. I know what I wanna wish for now." I close my eyes, and I'm about to throw my coin in when Colton gasps.

"Stop! What are you doing?"

I pop one eye open. "About to make a wish?"

"Like that? Liz, you can't *face* the fountain. You've gotta throw it behind you like I did."

"Where is that rule posted?"

"It's not, but everyone knows the fountain fairies only grant wishes that are thrown backward. Don't you ever watch movies?"

With an eye roll, I turn to face the trees. "Better?"

He gestures a hand toward the water. "You may proceed."

Closing my eyes again, I silently repeat my wish in my head, then chuck the coin behind me. It hits the water with a *plop!*

I open my eyes to find Colton watching me intently.

"What'd ya wish for?" he asks.

"I can't tell you. Then it won't come true."

He makes a loud *pfft* sound. "Says who?"

"Say the same invisible fountain fairies who made up the rule that you've gotta throw the coin backward." I lower my voice to mock him. "Don't you ever watch movies?"

An amused smirk spreads across his lips. "I'll tell you my wish if you tell me yours."

"That line didn't work earlier when you asked me to reveal my powers. Do you really think it's gonna work now?"

He crosses his arms over his chest. "For the record, I didn't ask you to reveal your powers. Just your element."

"Either way, I'm not telling you what my powers are, nor am I telling you my wish."

He huffs, tightening his gaze on me. "Are you driving me crazy on purpose?"

I point at my chest. "*I'm* driving you crazy?"

"Extremely."

Considering there's nothing secretive about my wish, I suppose I am keeping it from him just to taunt him. I can't help it though; he's cute when we're flirting.

Oh, fuck. I'm in deep trouble. How am I supposed to keep from flirting with him during his dance lessons?

Seven

❧

COLTON

Typically, I show up to everything right on time. Today, I showed up to my first dance lesson almost twenty minutes early. If there was a chance I'd get some extra time with Liz, I wasn't gonna miss it. Unfortunately, she teaches a class of little girls right before my session.

Outside Liz's ballroom, I lean against a wall, fiddling with the bright yellow gift bag in my hands. I look out of place within all the moms waiting for their daughters to finish dancing. Some of the women are on the benches, reading books or scrolling through their phones. Others practically have their noses pressed against the glass, as if making sure Liz is doing her job right. I have no doubt she is.

Music plays from the other side of the glass while Liz counts off beats. If I really wanted to, I could watch her through the glass too. However, I don't wanna be *that* guy. Also, I'm a grown-ass man. Someone might question why I'm staring at a class of little girls in leotards.

My wolf whines inside me. He doesn't understand why we're not seizing this opportunity to see Liz outside of our imagination.

Human me looks her up on YouTube every chance I get:

while I'm brushing my teeth, on my lunch breaks, when I'm having dinner by myself. Last night, as I lay in bed watching a video of her singing an acoustic cover of a Taylor Swift song, I realized I have a problem. I'm skating the line between being curious and becoming obsessed.

Liz didn't seem thrilled about Chrissy and me googling her. There's no way she'll find out I've watched every single YouTube video her band has ever released—in a matter of six days. Actually, it was more like four days, and I've spent the past two rewatching my favorites.

Behind me, the ballroom music lowers to a background level.

"Fabulous job today, Sprouters!" Liz says.

My wolf readies into an upright stance as if *he's* the one who's about to dance with her.

A minute later, the ballroom door opens and a bunch of little girls rush out. I wait until the last one has left before I step into the ballroom. I'm barely past the door frame when I stop. Liz is facing the other way, singing to herself as she slips her gloves off and drops them onto a folding chair. I'm mesmerized by her soft singing voice and the way she moves so angelically. From her duffel bag, she digs out a water bottle. Only then does she stop singing. My wolf and I can't take our stares off her as she chugs the liquid.

When she turns and finds me standing in the doorway, she jumps a little. I take that as my cue to enter. She stands her water bottle on top of the folding chair, then seizes her gloves. I slow my eager march into a leisure saunter to give her some extra time. I still don't know why she needs gloves, but they seem important to her, because once they're on, her shoulders relax.

"How long have you been standing there?" she asks.

"Not long." I hold the gift bag out to her.

She doesn't acknowledge it. Instead, she glares at me with a hand on her hip.

I take a step back. "What?"

"Where are your dress clothes, mister?"

I drop my shoulders with a groan. "I'm sorry, okay? I already got a lecture from Dixie on the way in. She told me jeans would do for now. I went to the store last week, but they didn't have anything in my size. I've got a few dress shirts, some shoes, and a couple of nice pants on order. They should arrive by next week."

"Hmm. I guess that's an acceptable excuse. But next week, Mr. Finley, I expect to see you in dress clothes."

The way she calls me Mr. Finley makes me want to push her up against these mirrors and attack her neck with my tongue.

My wolf pants like he wants to do the same.

Not before I get to. I hold the gift bag out to Liz again.

Finally, she accepts it. "What's this?"

"It's for you."

A bright smile lifts her cheeks. "You got me something?"

"Yeah. Open it."

She digs past the black and yellow tissue paper, then pulls out a notebook and a pen. Her entire face explodes into a wide grin. "It's got bumblebees on it."

"Yeah. I saw these at a store and thought of you, so I had to get 'em." *Lie.* I went on a special shopping trip with the sole purpose of finding something to give to her today. "You mentioned during your show that you write songs with your band. What's better for a bumblebee than a bumblebee-themed notebook and pen to write with?"

She shoves the items back into the gift bag and sets it onto her chair, then launches herself at me. Instinctively, I wrap my arms around her. My fingers splay across her back as I breathe in her sweet scent. She doesn't smell like anything in particular, just clean, good, and like my bumblebee.

My wolf howls, pawing at her to pet him. I almost pity

him because he's not able to feel Liz against his body like I am right now. *Wait your turn.*

"Thank you, Colton," Liz says into my neck. Her breath on me sends all my blood down to my dick.

I'm speechless. I didn't get her a gift with hopes that she'd hug me—not that I'm complaining. Now that I know this is her reaction, I'll be sure to buy her things more often. If I get the opportunity to hug her more in the future, and if they always feel like this, I'm in danger.

I don't wanna let her go. I don't even release her until she pulls away first. Even then, my hands itch to grab her again. When I don't, my wolf whimpers and pouts.

Liz claps her gloved hands together. "Okay, are you ready for your first lesson?"

"Lay it on me."

Dancing is no joke. The people in those YouTube videos I looked up earlier made it look easy-peasy. Newsflash: It's not.

By the end of my lesson, not only do my feet ache, but so do my calves, and my thighs, and my back, and my, well, everything. Even my toes. I didn't even know *toes* could get so sore.

I must be doing something wrong, because Liz seems unbothered by the physical torture she's putting me through. She's doing every move alongside me, and that's *after* she just taught a full day of classes. While she looks as graceful as a feather floating through the air, I look like I'm walking barefoot across a bed of needles.

Despite all that, Liz only has good things to say. "You did fabulous for someone who only knows the Cupid Shuffle. Maybe next time we can warm up with the Chicken Dance."

"Hell no." I collapse into a folding chair, panting. "The Chicken Dance has *waaay* too many steps for me. Between all the arm flapping and hand clapping, I get lost."

Liz giggles so adorably, it gets my wolf to whip his tail around. He's been highly alert and attentive this past hour, which is the opposite of how he usually is. Most of the time, he's just chilling inside me or taking a nap.

"Do you have another class after me?" I ask, trying not to breathe so heavily.

"Nope. You're my last one on Thursdays."

"Got any plans tonight?" I try not to sound too eager about the possibility of having tacos with her again.

"I do."

My wolf slumps inside me.

I try not to slump too. "What're you doin'?"

"Going on a date with this hot guy I met yesterday."

My heart plummets all the way to my stomach. Then I feel the pinch in my temples. I smile and narrow my eyes at her. "What are you *really* doing?"

She pops her mouth open. "Am I *that* bad of a liar?"

"Yeah." *Also, I'm a living, breathing lie detector.*

If Liz wanted to share her powers with me, I would have shared my powers with her by now. Despite what the Zordi norm is, I don't try to hide that I'm a Detector. I prefer telling people because it forces them to be more honest around me, which helps me avoid that little pinch. I suppose with Liz, this might be my only way of learning more about her since she keeps so much of herself behind closed doors.

"I've never been good at lying." Liz drops into the chair next to mine and pulls at her shoelaces.

"So?" I circle a hand in the air. "What are you *really* doing tonight?"

"Would it kill you not to know?"

I think about playing it cool, then ditch the idea. "Yeah, kinda."

She slips her feet out of her dance shoes and into a pair of flats. "I've got a friend sleeping over tonight. We're gonna have an *Iron Man* marathon."

"Is this the same *male* friend from two weeks ago?"

"Yep."

"Is he gay?" *Please say yes. Please say yes.*

She chuckles low in her chest. "Not one bit."

I grunt when my internal pinch never comes.

Liz shoves me in the arm. "What's with the stink face?"

"I dunno. I'm just not fond of the idea that you've got a straight male friend who sleeps over at your place all the time."

"He doesn't sleep over *all the time*. Just every Thursday, Friday, and Saturday."

My eyes bulge. "Every?"

"Yep."

I don't feel the pinch, which makes my wolf growl a bit. "Who is he, and how can I replace him?"

"You can't. He's irreplaceable."

I lean back into my chair as my wolf half whimpers, half snarls. "Damn. I've never even met this guy, and I already don't like him."

Liz shoves her gift bag and the rest of her things into her duffel bag, then zips it up and stands with her stuff over her shoulder. "Actually, you have met him. It's Trey."

I gape up at her, not ready to leave the comfort of this chair yet. "As in Trey Grant? The guy you secretly married and went honeymooning with in Fiji? That Trey?"

"The one and only."

I purse my lips to the side. "Hmm."

She arches a brow at me. "Hmm?"

"Yeah. Hmm."

"What's so *hmm*?"

I cross my arms over my chest, shaking my leg up and down. After a sigh, I say, "Let me put it this way, bumblebee: You're beautiful. Absolutely fucking gorgeous. And I don't mean just physically.

"I've only met you three times, but I've liked you since that very first day we mentally undressed each other in the parking lot. I liked you even more after watching you perform on a stage and after we made wishes together at that fountain. Then today, spending this past hour with you has only confirmed how much I like you."

She circles her wrist in the air. "But?"

"But what?"

"Isn't there a *but* at the end of all that?"

I shake my head. "No buts. I just wanted to verbalize to you that I really like you, just in case you haven't caught on yet. Maybe you can think about that while you're with Trey tonight, watching movies about a billionaire inventing metal clothing in a cave with a box of scraps."

Liz scrutinizes me. I can't tell what thoughts are running through her head. Whatever they are, they make her drop her duffel bag at her feet and plant back down in her chair. "Can I ask you something?"

My wolf stretches his tongue out toward her, trying to lick her face.

Again, thank fuck I'm the one in control. "Sure."

"On a scale of one to ten, how much does it bother you that Trey sleeps over?"

"Depends. Where does he sleep?"

"In my bed."

No pinch. "Where do *you* sleep?"

"In my bed."

Still no pinch. I jerk back. "You guys sleep in the *same* bed?"

"Yep." She never takes her gaze off me, like she's gauging my reaction. Like she's testing me.

I want nothing more than to pass this test. "Are you guys, like, friends with benefits?"

"Nope."

I wait for the pinch to come. It doesn't. The heavy weight in my chest lightens as my wolf settles down. "And there's really *nothing* going on between you two?"

"Nope. Nothing physical. Nothing romantic. We really are just best friends."

No pinch. Finally, I smile at her. "All right, cool."

"You believe me?"

"Yeah," I say easily.

"Just like that?"

"Yep. Just like that."

"Wow." She lets out a breath. "I can't tell you how many guys I've met who have more or less demanded I drop Trey from my life. And that was even before he and I began sharing a bed."

"I would never ask you to drop him." And I mean it. If Trey really is that important to her, which he seems to be, it would be awful of me to ask her to do that.

"Good, because it would never happen. I love Trey more than anyone else in this world. I know it's not normal to cuddle and sleep in the same bed with a guy who's not your boyfriend, but that's what I love about my relationship with Trey. I love that we can do stuff like that, and it doesn't mean anything."

"Well, shit. I didn't know you *cuddle* with him too." Sarcastically, I say, "That changes everything."

Liz's face falls. My sarcasm got lost on her. I almost feel bad for saying what I said, except seeing her reaction confirms she's got a little flame for me too. The only question now is if I can stoke that little flame into a raging fire.

My wolf grins, showing all his teeth. He likes that idea.

With two gentle fingers, I lift Liz's chin until her eyes meet mine. "I was kidding, bumblebee. Knowing that you cuddle with Trey doesn't change anything."

"It doesn't?"

"Nah. I still like you as much as I did before. Maybe more now 'cause you were honest with me. Do I understand the relationship you've got with Trey? No. Do I accept that you've got it? Sure. Do I still wanna pin you up against these mirrors and kiss you 'til you're breathless? Fuck yeah."

A lustful look crosses Liz's eyes. Even though I really fucking want to, I hold myself back from actually grabbing her face and planting my lips against hers.

My wolf tries to claw his way out of me so he can kiss her himself. He's trying so hard that my body hums the way it always does right before a shift.

Stop it, buddy. Not right now.

My wolf whimpers as he settles onto his hind legs and pouts. Only then does my body stop humming.

I'm pretty sure if I allowed him to take over right now, he wouldn't shift back for a while. He's been craving Liz more than I have, and that's dangerous. Who knows when he'd let me return? Could be hours. Could be days.

Also, I can't shift in the middle of a dance studio. There are Ordinaries in the other rooms. And unless Liz is also a Shifter, which I highly doubt, she would probably freak out.

Shifters have a terrible reputation within the Zordi community. We're known as uncontrollable and dangerous. With me, those labels are only true to those who pose a threat to the people I care about. Sadly, my list is just Liz and Chrissy.

Liz stands and picks up her bag. "You're not allowed to kiss me."

"Why not?" At the same time she does, I say her answer out loud.

"I don't date my students." She rolls her eyes. "Why ask when you already know the answer?"

"We don't have to date. We can just be friends who kiss. Kind of like your thing with Trey. Friends who cuddle. Our version is just a step above that."

She pauses to think, then her eyes turn to slits. "Am I going crazy, or did that actually make sense?"

My wolf perks up with hope.

I do too. "Does that mean you're considering it?"

She doesn't miss a beat. "No. We can't."

I get to my feet, towering over her. Our bodies are barely a fist apart. I lower my voice, and it comes out all husky. "You can fight this all you want, bumblebee, but there's no denying there's a spark between us. I feel it, and I know you do too. Why else would you try so hard to resist me?"

I throw my arms up in surrender and take a step back. "But hey, I respect that you want to keep our relationship professional while I'm your student. So for the next five weeks, I'll back off." I lift a finger into the air. "However, the second my last session is over, I'm asking you out. By then, you won't have this student-teacher excuse to hide behind anymore."

Speechless, she blinks up at me as she processes my words. I blink right back. I'll be damned if I'm the first to break our little stare-down, so I hold her gaze.

She opens her mouth, about to say something, then shuts it.

She opens her mouth again, then stops.

Another blink.

Then, without a single word, she huffs and stomps out the door.

Inside me, my wolf chases after her, fighting to be near her.

Eight

COLTON

As requested, I show up to my second dance lesson in nice dress clothes: black fitted pants, a pale-yellow button-up, and some fancy-ass shoes. I don't normally wear yellow—or fancy things—but since yellow seems to be Liz's favorite color, I'm willing to step outside my comfort zone.

Liz's mouth parts when her eyes land on me sauntering into the ballroom. "No."

I stop and glance down at my clothes. *Did I forget something?* "No, what?"

She sets her water bottle onto a chair and shakes her head. "You can't be wearing that."

"Excuse me? Last week, you gave me shit for not wearing fancy clothes. Now you're telling me I can't?"

"It's not the clo—I mean . . ." She sucks in a breath and lets it out with a groan. "Could you at least roll your sleeves down?"

"But I like 'em rolled up."

"I'm not gonna be able to concentrate with your forearms taunting me like that. So please, roll them down."

My lips curve into a slow smile. "Oh, I see now. It's not the

clothes you have a problem with. It's how good I look in them."
I push the sleeves higher up my arms to expose more skin.
Then I close the distance between us.

"Stop!" She laughs and presses a gloved hand against my
chest.

I take her in by her waist and walk her backward until her
plump ass plants against the mirror. Her breath hitches as I
press my other hand against the mirror to cage her in. Then I
tilt my head and lean in until our noses almost touch.

"Do you like me in fancy clothes, bumblebee? Say the
word, and I'll go buy more."

She pants a little as she stares at my mouth. Her gaze
slides up to my eyes, then back to my mouth again. My tongue
skates against my bottom lip, waiting for any sign that she
wants this as much as I do. The second I see that sign, I'm
going in. I won't be gentle either. I'm going to kiss this woman
until her knees give out.

Liz clears her throat, then her words come out in a whisper. "You said you'd back off, remember?"

Oh, fuck. I did say that last week, didn't I?

With a sigh, I drop my hand from the mirror and take a
giant step back. "I'm sorry, Liz. I totally forgot."

We behave much better at my third dance lesson—
we as in my wolf and I. Not once do I give in to
my urges, except for my urge to make Liz laugh.
Whenever I do, whether it's by doing something stupid or
cracking a lame joke, my wolf pants at the sound of her
happiness, but he never tries to force a shift on me.

It's hard to leave her at the end of the night. My hour with
her always seems to disappear too quickly. By the time she
shuts off the music and begins taking off her dance shoes, I
feel like I've just walked through the door.

. . .

One of these days, my time with Liz won't feel so short, but my fourth dance lesson with her is not that day. I can't believe I'm already over halfway through my dance sessions. I'm picking it up pretty well. No, I'm not ready to go on *Dancing with the Stars*, but I've stopped stepping on Liz's feet, so that's a positive.

Liz does things to me. Things I can't explain. In the middle of my fifth lesson with her, I say something to make her laugh so hard, she grabs onto my shoulder to keep from buckling to the floor. I take it as an opportunity to put my arms around her waist, and *fuuuck*. Her body in my hands is the only thing I can think about all night and for the rest of the week as I wait to see her again.

For someone who had a shit day at work, I sure am happy the instant I hear Liz's voice. One look at her, and I forget about all the guys who pissed me off on the construction site.

I enter the ballroom for my final lesson to find Liz wearing that yellow skirt again. The one she wore on the first day we met. The one she looks adorable in. The one that I want to rip off her so I can lick her naked body.

My wolf barks his approval. He's been getting antsy on all the long days we have to go without seeing Liz. Whenever he gets tired of pacing around inside me, he settles down and rests his head over his paws with a sad look on his face. I understand, because lately, I've been feeling the same way. My life is either the one hour I'm with Liz or the many torturous hours I'm not.

Like my lessons before, my final one ends too quickly.

Liz turns down the music and plops into a folding chair. "You've improved a ton."

I take the chair next to hers. "Thanks. I've got the best teacher." This woman amazes me. I'm gasping for air while she looks like she could go climb a mountain, no problem.

"You should continue to practice at home. If you keep up with it, you could really perfect those few steps you struggle with."

"Are you gonna come over to practice with me?"

She doesn't look up from untying her dance shoes. "I don't do house calls."

"How 'bout I just make you dinner instead?"

She still doesn't look at me as she stuffs her shoes into her duffel bag and slips into a pair of flats. "I've already got plans tonight."

Internally, I groan, because I know exactly *who* those plans are with. I'm a little jealous of Trey. And when I say a *little*, I mean a fuck ton.

After every dance lesson, I always ask Liz what her evening plans are. Every time, she reminds me that Trey is sleeping over. She wasn't lying when she said that he comes over *every* Thursday and stays through the weekend.

"We don't have to do dinner tonight," I say, trying to keep it cool. "How 'bout another night?"

Finally, she makes eye contact with me while fidgeting with the fingertips of her gloves. She doesn't say anything, but I can see those gears turning in her head.

"Don't give me that look. I told you the second my last session was over, I'd be asking you out. You knew this was coming. You should give me some credit for waiting almost fifteen whole seconds."

She forces a small smile onto her lips—those full pink lips I've been dying to taste. "Thanks for the offer, Colton, but I can't accept."

Seriously? What's a man gotta do to win this girl over? I

suck in a deep breath and let it out. "Okay. If you're gonna turn me down, could you at least tell me why?" *Because I know you want this as much as I do.*

She fidgets with her gloves again, looking anywhere but at me. I give her some time to think. When she takes too long, I tilt her chin up with my knuckle. Her head moves willingly.

The look in her eyes makes me want to hold her. I'd recognize that look anywhere. It's fear. But of what? I'm not going to hurt her. I think she knows that. Maybe her fear has more to do with herself than me. Or maybe it has to do with Trey. My wolf snarls at the thought of him. Neither of us likes that guy.

Liz backs away from me. "I'm sorry, Colton. I don't have a reason for saying no. Not one I know how to put into words."

I drop my arms to my sides in defeat. "Okay."

"Okay? That's it?"

"Yeah." I shrug, pretending this doesn't sting. That look in her eyes tells me she's not ready for something with me yet, and I'm not gonna stand around begging. Sure, I waited six weeks for this, but if she needs more time, that's fine. I can wait a little longer.

My wolf pouts. Clearly, he can't wait another minute.

Without asking, I pull Liz in for a hug. She comes willingly, and I'm glad. I'm not sure how my wolf would have taken it if she had pushed us away—not that she even knows she'd be pushing him away. I squeeze her tight, then speak into the top of her curls.

"See ya next time, bumblebee." It's the line I've been saying after every dance lesson.

She probably thinks I'm saying that like how people casually say *See ya later.* Most of the time, it means *bye for now.* When I say *See ya next time,* what I really mean is *See ya next week.*

Nine

LIZ

Colton left a few minutes ago, and his sweet cologne is still lingering in the ballroom. It's like he made sure to leave something behind to torture me with. It's working. I've either just made the right choice or the biggest mistake of my life.

This past month and a half with Colton has been like taking a mini-vacation once a week. I spent all of our dance lessons ogling him, and I can't count how many times he made me laugh so hard, my cheeks hurt. Or how many times I stared at his lips, willing him to kiss me while also hoping he wouldn't.

Like the gentleman he is, he never did. He always kept his hands where they should be and made good on his word to keep our relationship professional—except for the one time he pinned me against the mirror. I almost gave in to him then. Our lips were so close, and it would have been so easy. It took a lot of self-control to remind him to back off instead of tearing his dress shirt off like I wanted to.

I knew he was going to ask me out today. That didn't make turning him down any easier. I'd already decided two weeks ago that I won't date him. I can't. He hasn't asked me about my gloves yet, but he will. They always do, because I don't get to live like a normal human.

I can't name a single person—Zordi or Ordi—who has to wear gloves or anyone who can't stay asleep for longer than three hours. Zordis can't dream, but the terrifying memories that replay in my head are what I imagine nightmares are like. And I get them *every* night.

Plus, sometimes when I'm not careful and accidentally catch another traumatic memory, I shut down for days. It's hard to function like a normal human after seeing such horrific things—everything from sexual assault by fathers to physical beatings from mothers, to an angry spouse shooting an innocent baby out of spite, and all the other shit in between.

Normal people don't have to deal with things like that. If someone gets involved with me, they'll have to deal with those things too. No one has ever wanted to, and even though Colton seems like a great guy, he'll run. They always do.

It's happened so many times now that I'm used to it. It's always gutted me, but with Colton, it'll destroy me. I can't risk that. Besides, he's leaving LA in two months. I'm saving us both the trouble.

I wait in the empty ballroom for a few more minutes, giving Colton time to get into his car and leave. This way, I won't have to awkwardly run into him in the parking lot.

Eventually, I pack up my stuff, turn off the studio lights, and head out.

He's probably bad in bed anyway, I tell myself as I drag my feet down the hall. I almost laugh out loud. By how quickly that man picked up dancing, I have no doubts he's fabulous in bed.

He's probably . . . I groan internally. I can't even think of anything he *could* be bad at. He's probably frickin' perfect.

Did I just make a huge mistake? I still don't know.

Dixie's office door is shut when I pass it. *What the hell?* That woman never shuts her door, not even when she's on the phone.

I knock on the wood. "Dixie?"

She answers from the other side. "Come in, babe."

I open the door, then freeze. From her big leather office chair, my boss sports a shit-eating grin. On the other side of her well-organized desk is Colton. He, too, is smiling up at me, albeit a little less enthusiastically.

"What's up, Liz?" Dixie asks nonchalantly.

"Um, I was just wondering why your door was shut. I wanted to make sure you were okay."

"Colton closed it when he came in here. He doesn't know I like to keep it open."

I furrow my brow at him. "Why are you still here?"

He doesn't get a chance to answer, because Dixie perks up and speaks first. "You must have made a good impression on him, Liz. He's signing up for another six weeks of lessons."

I gasp. "What?"

Dixie points at her laptop screen. "I was just about to pull up your openings to see which time slot he wanted to claim."

I glare down at him. He smirks up at me. This man, this *impossible* man, knows exactly what he's doing.

I'm not having it. "Could I talk to you, Mr. Finley? Outside?"

A little too eagerly, he pops up from his chair and follows me out the front doors.

The warm sun shines above us as I drop my duffel bag onto the hard ground and cross my arms together. "What the hell do you think you're doing?"

"I'm not sure what you mean."

The nerve of this guy. He feigns ignorance and shoves his hands into the pockets of his dress pants. My attention latches on to his taut forearms. *Damn him for always rolling up his sleeves.*

Ignoring the muscular distraction, I shoot him a cold scowl. "Why are you signing up for more dance lessons?"

"Because my teacher told me that with more practice, I could perfect those few steps I've been struggling with." He grins at me like he's innocent. I'm not sure why. We both know he's not.

"Your teacher told you to practice at *home*, not here."

"Why would I do it at home when I can do it here with my pretty little bumblebee?"

I ignore the cute way he just said my nickname. "Seriously? You're really gonna do this to me?"

He steps back with a hand over his heart. "Why do you say that like I'm threatening to blast you with a fireball? I'm just signing up for more dance. There's no crime in that."

"You were supposed to walk away and never come back."

"Ouch. Is that really what you want?"

"Yes."

The man has the au-fucking-dacity to laugh. He even smirks at me. "You're a shit liar."

"Okay, fine. Maybe that's not what I want, but it's for the best."

"Best for what?"

"For you. For me." I point at his chest, then mine.

His arms cross over his front as his face goes hard. "You don't know what's best for me."

"Yes, I do."

"Do not."

"Do too. I know enough to know it's not me."

"Bullshit." He uncrosses his arms only to gesture with them as he talks. "Every moment I've spent with you has been absolutely amazing. I don't think I've ever been so happy, which is crazy stupid, because I only get you for an hour a week. Except for last week when you allowed me to walk you out and we stood in the parking lot talking for all of ten minutes. Those ten minutes were the highlight of my night."

They were the highlight of mine too. I've made it a point not to let him walk me out after his lessons. I needed to avoid standing by my car, talking with him until the sun comes up, because that's exactly what would happen if I allowed it.

Every week, I've made up some excuse to talk to Dixie or run to the bathroom. Last week, I caved. I accepted his offer to walk me out, and it only took ten minutes in the parking lot for me to realize it was a mistake. Only ten minutes with him, and I was seconds away from mauling him with my mouth.

"Look, bumblebee. I know you aren't ready yet, and that's okay. But until you are, I'm gonna take more dance lessons, because otherwise, I don't get to fucking see you. And if I haven't made it clear already, seeing you makes me happy."

Seeing him makes me happy too. Actually, it's the one thing I look forward to every week. Well, besides seeing my best friend.

Colton continues, "So if I have to buy expensive ballroom lessons just to have one hour with you every week, I'ma do it. And I'ma keep doing it until you come home with me, let me make you dinner, then let me kiss you until you're panting my name."

Oh, fuck. I want that. All of it. The hours with him. The going home with him. The having dinner with him. The kissing. The panting. I've imagined doing all that with him since the day we met.

With a firm hand, Colton cups the side of my face. My breaths get short as I stare up at him. He speaks in a low voice. "I'm gonna ask you again, Liz. I know the answer, but I'm gonna ask anyway, just in case you've changed your mind in the past sixty seconds. Will you come to my place for dinner?"

Yes! Take me home with you! My rejection comes out breathy. "No."

He blinks at me before releasing me from his warm grasp. "Okay."

My skin feels cold where his hand used to be. Without another word, he disappears back inside the studio.

I run after him and step in front of Dixie's office before he can enter it. "What are you doing?"

"I'ma go finish signing up for those dance lessons."

"Seriously?"

"Yeah, seriously. What part of *if I don't take dance lessons, then I don't get to fucking see you* don't you understand?"

I hold my arms straight out to my sides, blocking the doorway. "I won't let you do this."

He slumps his shoulders, giving me a look that says, *We both know that won't stop me.* "Listen, Liz. If you can look me in the eyes and tell me *honestly* that you don't have feelings for me, then I'll stop. I'll walk outta here, and you'll never have to see me again."

"I don't have feelings for you," I say in the sternest tone I can.

He blinks for a moment, then his entire face lights up with a grin. "Liar."

As if I'm thin air, he barrels straight past me and into Dixie's office.

The guest chair squeaks a little as he drops into it. "Did you get Liz's openings pulled up yet?"

Dixie turns her laptop around and points at the screen. "Yep. Her open slots are here in green."

"No!" I rush to slam her laptop shut. The noise makes Dixie jolt back a little. "I refuse to be his teacher. If he wants dance lessons that bad, give him to someone else. Abigail has tons of openings."

Colton spins his chair around to face me with a hint of a smirk on his lips. "Sorry, Dixie, I'm not available during any of Abigail's times."

"Then look through Meredith's list. Or Olivia's. Hell, assign him to Stephen or Cory for all I care. Just anyone but me."

Colton never takes his eyes off me. "Sorry, Dixie. I'm not

available during Meredith's times. Or Olivia's. Or Stephen's. Or Cory's. I'm only available during Liz's times."

I stomp my foot because acting like a child is what this man is making me resort to. "Why are you being so impossible?"

He stabs his chest with a finger. "Me? *I'm* being impossible?"

"Yes!" I glance at Dixie with a *help me out* look.

She throws her skinny arms into the air. "Don't look at me, babe. If I was you, I woulda dropped my panties the moment he said he wanted to take me home and make me pant his name. Actually, by now, I woulda knocked everything off this desk so he could bend me over it. Forget going home."

Colton laughs, and I smack his arm. He barely flinches. I can't believe Dixie is taking his side. She and I are *always* on the same team.

She continues, "By the way, when you guys have heated discussions outside, y'all should speak louder. I had to crack my window open just to be able to catch everything, and you know how I feel about opening them windows when the air is on."

Colton's still chuckling as he turns in his chair to face Dixie. "Are Liz's Thursdays still open?"

Dixie smiles at him as if I'm not standing right the fuck here. "Yes, sir."

"I'll take 'em."

She reopens her laptop, then types on it. "Same payment method as last time?"

"Yep."

"Great. I'll just need to verify the last four digits and the three numbers on the back."

Colton digs his wallet out of his back pocket, then hands Dixie his card.

The second she starts typing again, I throw my hands up. "Fine! I give up."

They both whip their heads my way, grinning.

"You give up?" Colton asks.

"Yeah. I'll do it. I'll have dinner with you." I hold a finger up. "But that's it! I'm not promising you any of that other stuff. And it's only *one* dinner. And only if you promise not to sign up for any more dance lessons."

Colton shoots out of his chair and scoops me into his arms. He spins me around in a circle before letting me slide down his front. My heart races as my feet return to the floor. I want so badly to rip these stupid gloves off so I can feel his skin.

His fingers splay over the small of my back, keeping me pressed against his body. "Can we do dinner tonight?"

I'm in no rush to pull away. "I told you already. I have plans."

"Cancel 'em."

"I can't." If my plans weren't with Trey, I totally would.

"Tomorrow?"

"Can't. I perform with my band every Friday and Saturday."

"Sunday, then?"

"Yes. Sunday night, I'm free."

"Perfect!" He licks his lips as he stares at mine. I will him to kiss me. My mouth tingles with the mere thought of it. At the same time, I silently plead for him not to. I have a feeling it'll be enchanting, and that'll only make it harder for me to keep resisting him.

"Oh my god." Dixie groans from behind me. "Will you guys just make babies already?"

Colton grins at her as he releases me. "Thanks for your help, by the way. You were right."

Dixie beams with her nose in the air. "I always am."

I squint at them. "Right about what?"

Chuckling, Colton scratches the back of his head. "Um, I walked in here, confessing to Dixie that I didn't know what to do about you. She was the one who came up with this grand idea to make a big show of signing up for more dance lessons, which I totally would have if you still wanted to deny this thing between us."

I gape at my boss, who I thought was my friend. "You were scheming against me?"

"Not *against* you, babe. I did this *for* you. Besides, I'm running a business. It's my job to get people to sign up again." Dixie winks at Colton. "I told ya the closed door would work."

Ten

LIZ

"Who is he?" Trey asks as he climbs into my bed. We just finished having dinner and watching *The Hunger Games* in my living room. Trey doesn't keep up with pop culture, so it was his first time watching it. We recently finished watching all the Disney canon movies together because he had only ever seen *The Lion King.* I think that's so odd but understandable coming from someone who didn't grow up with a TV.

"Huh?" I glance up from my phone, still smiling from the text I just read.

"Who's the guy you've been texting all night with that permanent grin on your face?"

I plug my phone in, then set it on top of my nightstand. "Sorry, T. I shouldn't be on my phone this much."

Trey props a pillow behind him, then leans against it. "I don't mind. I like seeing you smile and sensing your happiness."

Ever since Trey lost his soul mate, happiness has been scarce for him. Being an Empath, he has the power to sense other people's happiness, but it's never the same as feeling it for himself.

I round the end of my bed as I head toward my master bathroom. "His name's Colton. He's my dance student."

"I thought you wrote off dating your dance students after Madman Matt?"

I burst into a laugh. I forgot that's what Trey calls him. *Very fitting.* "Technically, Colton's not my dance student anymore. His last session was today."

"And now you're dating him?"

"Not really." In my bathroom, I grab my electric toothbrush off its charging port and squirt some toothpaste onto the bristles. "We're gonna have dinner on Sunday, but I don't plan on seeing him again after that."

"Why not?" Trey asks from my bed.

I brush for a moment, then spit into the sink and talk to the mirror. "He's leaving the city in two months."

"So?"

"Sooo, it won't work out." I return my toothbrush to my mouth.

Trey shuffles to get under the covers. "Has he asked about your gloves yet?"

"No." *Thank god.* If Colton had asked and I had told him the truth, there's no way he'd still want dinner with me.

"How long have you known him?"

I spit again. "Two months."

"And he hasn't asked yet?"

"Nope."

"Interesting."

I finish brushing my teeth, turn the bathroom light off, then join Trey sitting on my bed. "Yeah, most people would have asked by now."

"Do you know what his mind or body powers are?"

"No. I haven't asked. It's not fair to ask him when I'm not willing to share mine. I've got a guess for his element though. His soul smells like the ocean breeze. He's either an Aero or a

Hydro. I think he's an Aero, though, because his ocean scent smells light, like I'm standing *near* the ocean, not in it."

I like that my mind power allows me to guess a Zordi's element based on their soul's scent. The second I got within two steps of Trey, I knew he was a Pyro, and that he was a good person. Trey's soul smells like roasted marshmallows over a campfire and a burning candle—more specifically, the wick of the candle. Pyros with bad souls smell like singed human hair or burnt popcorn mixed with gasoline.

"At least you don't have to worry about him turning out like Rodrigo," Trey says.

Oh, shit. I forgot I lied to Trey about that guy. I suppose it's been long enough, I should tell him the truth. "Um, I have a confession. Rodrigo didn't break up with me because I'm a Hydro and he's a Pyro. Me having the dominant element over his had nothing to do with it."

"But I thought you said—"

"I know what I said. I lied because I knew if I told you the real reason why he left me, you'd hunt him down."

Rodrigo and I lasted eleven months, the longest romantic relationship I've ever had. Kinda sad for being twenty-six. We broke up over two years ago, and the sting of it still eats at me. The day he ended things, I showed up at Trey's house for comfort. Even though I downplayed how it happened, Trey still offered to beat him up for me.

"So," Trey says as his eyes narrow, "what's the *real* reason he left you?"

"I fell asleep at his house."

"Fuck. Really?" Trey stares at me for a beat before accepting that I'm dead serious. "How did he react?"

"Oh, ya know," I say to my bare hands resting in my lap, "he freaked out. Started asking me a bunch of questions. I told him that the nightmares happen every time I sleep. He blew up at me for hiding it from him for so long. He told me there was something seriously wrong with me because Zordis don't dream.

"I tried explaining that technically, the nightmares aren't dreams and that they're someone's traumatic memory replaying in my head. That only made things worse. He told me I needed to check myself into a mental hospital for *defective* Zordis."

"Nooo." Trey slaps a palm over his chest. "He really used the D word?"

In a secret world of people who are all gorgeous and illnesses are few and far between, having anything abnormal means being shunned. Not all Zordis discriminate against other Zordis who have issues, but most do. It's why I don't have any Zordi friends besides Trey. Some people go as far as saying that Zordis who have issues should be eradicated so we can't reproduce more *defective* people.

Thankfully, Trey has never judged me. He grew up with his own experiences of feeling like an outcast, so he understands what it's like to be different.

Trey lets out a little grunt. "You're right. If you had told me that back then, I one hundred percent would have slaughtered him."

I drag the blankets higher up my body. "And that's exactly why I lied to you."

"Your lie probably kept me from going to z-prison."

"You're welcome. Now, can you get the curtains and the lights for us?"

Trey waves his hands at the window. My curtains slide together with a *zip!* Then he points at my light switch, and the room goes dark.

Sometimes, I wish I had telekinesis too. It makes life simpler. Although if I had a choice, I would have taken *any* body power over the nightmare-inducing one in my hands.

Why couldn't I have been a *normal* Memory Catcher? I met one once. She could think of any memory she'd want to see, touch someone's hands, and that person's memory would play out in her head like a movie. It's kind of like being a Seer who can get visions of the future on demand, but for the past.

If I was a normal Memory Catcher, no one would call me *defective*. If I was a normal Memory Catcher, I wouldn't have to see other people's trauma every night. I wouldn't have a fear of touching other people's hands. I wouldn't have been abandoned by my family. And most of all, I wouldn't have so much trouble getting a boyfriend to stay. I'd just be . . . normal.

Trey and I get comfortable under the covers, then he opens his arms for me. Enthusiastically, I accept his invitation and nuzzle my head into the crook of his shoulder. He wraps one arm around me, resting it over my hip as I lay my palm over his hard stomach and let out a long sigh. I've been looking forward to this all week. Only with Trey holding me at night do the nightmares stay away. Neither of us know how or why that is, and I don't question it.

We also don't know how one day, three years ago, I stopped seeing Trey's most traumatic memory. During the years before that, every time our hands connected, I'd see the final moments seven-year-old Trey had with his parents before they were murdered.

I'd hear his mom yell out in pain as a violent man straddled her and pounded his fist into her cheek. I'd see his dad bleeding from the long, open gash down his face. I'd see his dad throw little Trey out the window and hear Trey screaming for them. Lastly, I'd see the explosion that ultimately took his parents' lives.

Then one day, our hands touched and I saw nothing. I've been seeing nothing ever since. I don't know how or why this nothingness has happened with Trey and only Trey, but again, I don't question it.

There are still so many things about Zordis that even the highest level of zoctors can't explain. No one knows why we can't dream. No one knows why some Zordis are only born with one or two powers instead of three, or why some are born with no powers at all. Whatever the cause is for my curse, I'm just grateful for Trey and that because of him, I can get some reprieve from it.

"T-Bear?" I say into the darkness. It's been quiet for a while.

"Hmm?"

I yawn, and he patiently waits for me to finish. "Do you think it's weird that we sleep in the same bed?"

He thinks for a moment. "It doesn't *feel* weird."

"Has it ever?"

"No."

"Not even the first time?"

"Nope," he says easily. "Why do you ask?"

"I told Colton that we sleep in the same bed."

Trey chuckles, and it rumbles against my palm. "Damn, Liz. Are you purposely trying to get this man to run before he even has the chance to find out about your powers?"

"I was trying to gauge his reaction."

"Hold on. He knows we share a bed and still wants to have dinner with you?"

I'm just as surprised as Trey is. "I explained that there's nothing romantic between us, and he actually believed me. I even told him that we cuddle."

"Like just casually during movies, or in bed?"

"I didn't specify, but the way I said it implied that we cuddle in bed."

"Damn. And this guy *still* wants to see you?"

"Mm-hmm." Now that I think about it, Colton might be a hidden gem. Most guys would have moved on by now.

"You might wanna keep him around, Liz. If some girl told me shit like that, I wouldn't give her the time of day."

"And that would make you exactly like every other guy I've ever been with. If my boyfriends don't leave me over finding out about my trauma-inducing body power, they usually do once they read some stupid article about us online. Or they get an ego trip over the fact that I can't touch anyone's hands but yours."

Trey drapes his hand over mine, giving me a comforting squeeze. Like always, my mind is blank. No flashback. No blood. No explosion. Nothing.

The first time I accidentally touched his hand, we were rehearsing for my dance competition. It was a light graze, but that's all it takes. I saw his parents getting blown up, then burst into tears. Trey yelled at me for invading his privacy. That memory torments him, and he never wants to talk about it, let alone share it. He stormed out of the studio without any intention of ever seeing me again.

Through some coaxing, I convinced him to come back and talk to me. That night, we bonded over our troubles. He told me about his terrible childhood, and I told him about my curse and how it affects me. He listened to me without passing any judgment.

For the first time ever, I had found a Zordi who didn't look at me like I was a freak. Trey doesn't see me as someone who belongs in a mental hospital or someone who's a disgrace to the Zordi world or their family. He sees me as a warrior, and he makes me feel like one too.

Trey will never know how much he means to me or how much of a positive impact he's made on my life. I try to tell him sometimes, but the words never carry as much meaning as I want them to. Also, he hates when I get sappy, so he always stops me before I can fully verbalize how much I appreciate him.

Trey keeps his hand over mine as he speaks toward the ceiling. "Do you think that one day, when you find your soul mate, you'll be able to touch his bare hands too?"

"I'm not sure." *But I hope so.* "I don't think it would happen right away. I have a feeling it'd only happen after I'd seen his most traumatic memory as many times as I had to see yours."

"Are you willing to do that?"

"Good question." I ponder it for a few moments, then say, "I guess it depends on the memory."

"Wouldn't it be worth it though? To spend the rest of your life with a man without wearing gloves around him?"

"Yeah, but what if I spend many, many years seeing his worst memory only to find out this fluke in my curse only works with you?"

"That's possible, but also, you touched my hands and saw my past over and over again for more than three years without any inclination that it would ever stop."

"I did that because you were the first and only person who's ever accepted me for the way I am. Around you, I didn't feel like I had to hide behind a pair of gloves."

"Yes, and when you find your soul mate, I think it'd be worth it for you to try the same with them, especially knowing it *could* stop. You deserve to have more than one person in your life you can stand to hold hands with—bare. And who knows? Maybe they'll become someone who can ward off your night terrors too."

I tilt my head back to see him. I can barely make out his facial features in the dark. "Are you trying to get out of cuddling with me?"

"Nah. I just think you deserve more than the hand you've been dealt."

"If anyone's been dealt a shitty hand, T, it's you."

For most of my life, I've looked at other people with envy: Envy that they can walk around without the chains of trauma weighing them down. Envy that they can do simple things like shake hands with someone without getting asked about their gloves. Envy that they can fall asleep without waking up two or three hours later, screaming and shaking. Sometimes, I wish

I could trade lives with those people. The only person I wouldn't trade lives with is Trey.

From seeing his parents murdered, to growing up with an abusive relative, to losing his soul mate, Trey's been through the worst of it. And that's saying something, because I've seen plenty of people's worsts.

About two years ago, Trey met his soul mate. Something that separates Zordi humans from Ordi humans is that when our soul mate is in danger, our bodies will tell us. We get a sickening sense in the pit of our stomachs that comes with nausea like you've been on a roller coaster for days and headaches that pound so hard, you can barely open your eyes. There's also coughing fits, numb limbs, and, sometimes, vomiting. That sense is called the *glimmer*, and Trey felt it on multiple occasions whenever Arella was in danger.

Unfortunately, Arella is an Ordinary, and since the zovernment doesn't allow our kind to be with Ordinaries, they erased him from her memories. Then the Scrubbers erased the existence of Trey and Arella's relationship from everyone's memories but his.

Even I don't remember them being together. I've heard lots of stories from Trey though. Apparently, Arella and I were pretty good friends. We bonded over our love of boy bands and laughed about the stupid things Trey said.

I feel awful for him. To fall in love with someone, only for them to forget you exist? Now *that's* a curse. Trey spent a while trying to convince her that she knew him, but there's no convincing someone of that when there's zero proof and the rest of the world doesn't remember it either.

Eventually, Trey did the only thing he could: He let her go. He quit the band, moved across the country, and spiraled into the broken shell of a man he is today.

He turned to heavy z-drugs and alcohol for a while until I forced him to quit. It's been a year and a half since he sobered up, and within that time, he's been healing. It's slow, but he's finally acting like a human again. He returned to the band, and he's writing songs again. Recently, he's even started to laugh again.

We have an agreement that if he ever feels the need to get high or drunk, he has to call me. Then it's my job to talk him off the ledge. Every time he's called, I've helped him stay sober. At least that's what he tells me.

"T?"

He squeezes my hand like I've startled him. "Yeah?"

"I'm proud of you."

"For what?"

"For how far you've come. There are still moments when I'll catch you staring off into space with that gloomy look in your eyes like you're thinking about her, but I also see you trying to move forward, and that makes me happy."

He lets out a light scoff. "I'm glad one of us is happy."

"Are you saying you aren't? Like not even a little bit?"

"Eh. Not really. Thanks to you, I've been living in all my raw misery."

I've never had a drug or alcohol addiction, so I don't know what it's like to have to fight that battle, but I can't imagine it's easy. "How often would you say you think about doing drugs again?"

"Every damn day."

My stomach knots. He didn't even hesitate. "How often a day? Like once? Twice?"

"More than that."

"Three times?"

"Liz," he says through a long sigh, "I'm not telling you a number, because you won't like it."

Well, excuse me for asking. "I'm just surprised, because I thought we had a pact. You said you'd call me whenever you felt the urge. You don't call me every day."

"I only ever call you when the urge gets *really* bad."

"How do you handle it the rest of the time?"

He shrugs the shoulder I'm not lying on. "I've been going to therapy like you told me to. I go for walks a lot. I've been trying meditation too."

I hesitate to ask this, because I already know the answer, but I like plugging it in occasionally with the hopes that he'll say yes. "Have you considered moving back to LA?"

"You know I can't do that."

"Do you think you ever will?" It would save him from buying all those plane tickets every week. He's in LA more days of the week than he's in New York.

"Only if she moved out of the state."

Trey and I have this unspoken rule that we never say Arella's name out loud. Sometimes I slip up, and his entire body stiffens like he's been whacked in the back with a metal rod. I try to avoid that at all costs because simply hearing her name can cause him to spiral into a pit of wallowing that takes him days to climb out of. Whenever we talk about her now, we'll simply say *she* or *her* and we both know who the other is referring to.

Trey continues, "Besides, I already sold my house. Where would I live?"

"You could move in with me. I've got an extra bedroom. Not that you'd be sleeping in it." I can already see the headlines: *Trey and Liz from Flames in the Night officially move in together.* Our fans would go nuts.

"Move in with you?" Trey chuckles. "Why? So you can constantly babysit me?"

"I don't babysit you."

"Liz, you're only a few suburbs away from her, and I'm here every Thursday through Sunday. You know how often I think about driving by her apartment just so I can catch a glimpse of her. Why else do you refuse to leave me alone for more than an hour? I'm pretty sure that qualifies as babysitting."

"That's because of that one time I went over to Emmy's

for barely three hours, and you had thrown your motorcycle keys onto my roof."

"To keep myself from going to see her," he says defensively. "And don't question my methods, because it worked. I locked myself in your bedroom until you came back."

"We spent half an hour scouring my roof in the dark before we found your keys. I was convinced you'd thrown them so far, they were on my neighbor's roof."

He snickers. "Me too."

The room goes quiet.

Minutes later, I break the silence again. "Colton asked me to go over for dinner tonight."

"Why didn't you?"

I make a *duh* face, even though he can't see it. "Because I can't leave you alone for that long."

"I woulda been fine."

"Really?"

He clears his throat. "I guess I could have gone over to Kevin's for a bit, just to be safe."

"See?"

Trey lets go of my hand to scratch an itch, then his hand comes right back to intertwine with mine. "Can I give you some advice, Liz?"

"Sure."

"When you see Colton on Sunday, don't tell him any more stuff about us. With all the details you've already let out, the fact that he still wants to see you tells me he could be a good one. I'd hate to watch you push him away before he has the chance to know how great of a person you are."

I let out a chuckle. "So in other words, I should avoid telling him that your hands are the only ones I can touch without gloves on?"

"Yes. One hundred percent do not tell him that."

"If he asks about it, I'm telling him. I've tried hiding it before, and that's never worked. I think I'm gonna try the *ripping off the Band-Aid* method from now on. At least then, I won't have to waste my time."

He sighs deeply. "You can do whatever you want, but I'm just saying I think you should give this guy a chance. You never know. Maybe he'll turn out to be the first man who's cool with never touching your hands. Or better, he'll be someone you let in, like you did for me."

Eleven

COLTON

"Daffodils?" Liz says when I open my apartment door.

My chest tingles from her nearness—both from the zense and the fact that she's really here. Her reddish-brown curls drape flawlessly over her shoulders. They're the type of curls that only happen with hot tools and an investment of time. I would know. Chrissy has long curly hair too, and I've had to wait plenty of hours for her to be "ready."

I'll never understand why curly-haired girls curl their hair more. Chrissy says it's to "tame the curls," but whenever she comes out after a long time of hogging the bathroom, she always looks the same.

Liz doesn't. She looks extra gorgeous right now, and it's flattering that she did it for me.

I hold out the bouquet of daffodils. Liz accepts them into her yellow-gloved hands that match the flowers. "I got these for you because they're your favorite color. The lady at the store said daffodils symbolize new beginnings, and that's what tonight is."

"A new beginning of what?"

"Ya know, us," I say, pointing between our chests.

She chuckles in a flirty yet patronizing way. "Sounds like you've got high hopes for tonight, Mr. Finley."

My insides flutter whenever she calls me that. I don't care that it's pathetic. I could listen to her call me Mr. Finley all night. "I've been waiting too long for this. So yeah, you bet your ass I've got high hopes."

I wave for Liz to step inside. She does, slips her feet out of her heels, then plops her purse onto the kitchen counter.

"For the daffodils," I say, offering her a glass of water to put the flowers in. I should have thought about buying a vase. *Oh well.* Too late now.

Beep! Beep! Beep! I press the off button on the oven. Steam flies out of the appliance as I open its door. With some silicone mitts on, I drag the sheet pan out.

Liz's eyes bulge at the large filet of salmon. "Wow. That looks amazing. I thought you weren't a good cook?"

"I never said that. All I said was that I'm too lazy to cook for myself."

She leans her elbows onto the counter, watching my every move as I shut the oven door and toss the mitts aside. "Does your company pay for your living arrangements?"

"Mostly."

"Do you always get a fully furnished apartment to yourself?"

I toss some precut romaine lettuce into a large bowl, then mix it with the Caesar dressing. "Depends on how long the stay is. If I'm working on a project for only a week or two, sometimes they'll book me a hotel room. But yes, I always get my own place."

That's also because I told my boss that I'll refuse any job where I have to share a room with someone. Sometimes I shift at night to let my wolf out. If I stay a human for too long, he gets antsy and will force a shift on me. If I'm not careful, he could do it in the middle of a crowded mall—and that's a one-way trip to z-prison. The zovernment doesn't take exposure cases lightly.

I plate the salmon and salad, then make a show of zesting some lemon over the fish. Liz giggles at the ridiculous way I do it like I'm the host of a popular cooking show.

From a pot on the stove, I scoop some mashed potatoes onto our plates. Then I place our full dishes onto the already set table. With a lighter, I fire up the candles that I also purchased this afternoon and set those onto the table too. Some soft piano music sways through the air from my Bluetooth speaker sitting on the counter. This is a playlist I curated last night, just for Liz.

She beams as I pull out a chair for her. "You went all out. I hope this wasn't too much trouble."

I grab the cup of daffodils off the counter and arrange it near the candles. "You're worth it."

After I pour the wine, I sit in my chair and lean back to admire my work. The table looks like something from one of those cheesy romance movies Chrissy always makes me watch with her, but the smile painted over Liz's cheeks tells me she likes it. Silently, I thank my sister for making me watch all those lame movies. Maybe she was training me for this very moment the whole time.

Liz picks up her fork and takes her first bite of the salmon. When her eyes light up, my wolf and I mentally high-five each other. "Mmm. This is amazing!"

My wolf bounces around inside me. He's got higher hopes for tonight than I do. He's expecting me to let him out so he can finally meet Liz. I doubt that'll happen, though, because this is Liz. I'll be lucky if she stays for more than just dinner.

We fall into easy conversation. I tease her. She laughs. She teases me back. It's been like this over our texts too—the ones we've been exchanging all weekend, almost nonstop. The only time she leaves me hanging is when she's working. She even texts me when she's with Trey—at a slower rate, but still, it makes me happy that she doesn't completely ignore me when she's with him.

Eventually, I've got a full belly as I push my empty plate forward. Then I turn to give Liz a crumpled look. "What do you mean, you like pineapple on your pizza?"

She eats the last bite of her salad. "It's my favorite topping."

"Like *just* pineapple?"

"No, usually with pepperoni. Sometimes ham or bacon."

"Ew."

"Hey, don't yuck my yum." She takes a sip of her white wine, playfully glaring at me, and it's adorable. "Have you ever tried pineapple on your pizza?"

"Once, and it was enough for me to know it's nasty. It's a fruit. Fruit doesn't belong on pizza. Would you put strawberries on your pizza?"

"No, but that's different."

"Nah. It's the same damn thing."

I stand to take our plates to the sink. Liz follows me, and together, we clean the kitchen. Not once does it feel awkward. We work naturally, as if we do this together every night.

When I hand her a wet towel, she takes it straight to the table, knowing exactly what I want her to do with it. When she hands me some dirty cookware, I rinse it off, then place it into the dishwasher. If this was our nightly routine, I wouldn't mind.

Once everything is clean, I grab our wine bottle and our half-empty glasses, then head into the living room. Without me having to ask her, Liz comes with.

On the coffee table, I set our glasses down and pour more wine into Liz's.

She aims a narrow gaze at me, smiling. "Are you trying to get me drunk, Mr. Finley?"

I swear, if she keeps calling me that, I'm gonna have to

make her Mrs. Finley so I can keep hearing her call me that for the rest of my life.

With his snout in the air, my wolf howls his approval. I'm glad he likes her as much as I do. I've heard of some Shifters whose animals hate their human's partners. I can only imagine how tough that internal battle is. I would rather have to constantly ask my excited wolf to settle down around Liz than have to ask him to accept her.

"Drunk? No. Tipsy enough to stop holding back and let me kiss you? Maybe." I smirk, hoping she'll take it as an invitation to jump me.

Unfortunately, she doesn't. She just shakes her head and giggles as we settle onto the couch together.

I'm relieved that she's not trying to leave right away. More so, it doesn't seem like she's ready to leave at all. No, I don't expect Liz and me to dive into a serious relationship tonight, but I wouldn't refuse it if that's what she asked for.

Half an hour later, I've got Liz laughing so hard, she almost spits out her wine. My wolf wags his tail, barely taking his eyes off her. I'm not sure who's enjoying this more, me or him.

Liz's glass is almost empty again. "She did *not* say that."

"Hell yeah she did." I pour myself more wine.

"I don't believe you. Why would Dixie tell you that I like it rough? How would that have come up in conversation?"

"You know that woman better than I do. She doesn't strike me as someone with a filter."

Liz scoffs. "She's not."

"It was right before my second dance lesson. You were still teaching your class of little girls. I stopped by Dixie's office to say hi. She looked up at me and said"—I put on my best Dixie impression—"'Mmm-mmm-mmm. You lookin' extra yummy today, Colton. Better be careful walking into Liz's ballroom like that. Wouldn't want the mirrors to break.'"

Liz half gasps, half laughs. "No way."

"Yes way. Naturally, I asked her why they'd break. She said, 'Liz likes it rough. I'd bet anything you do too. If y'all gon' be gettin' it on in my ballroom, just be careful of the mirrors. They be expensive.' "

"Oh lord." Liz slaps a gloved palm over her forehead. "Dixie would totally say something like that."

"I couldn't make this up if I tried. She then proceeded to tell me how, if that happened, I'd be living out Matt's fantasies."

Liz's glass stops a fingertip from her lips. "Say what?"

"You know . . . Matt. The guy you so desperately don't want me to know about."

Liz's face goes pale as she sets her wineglass onto the coffee table. "What the hell did she tell you?"

"Nothing really," I say with a nonchalant shrug. "Just that he was a stalker fan of yours and that he researched you until he found out where you worked. And how he signed up for private lessons just to get you alone with him."

"Is that it?"

I shrug again. "Well, she might have also mentioned that you went on a date with him, not knowing he was a stalker."

"That's it?"

"She might have mentioned that you went home with him too."

"And?"

"Um, I think she said something about a Liz Hart shrine?"

Liz's jaw drops as she gasps. "I'm gonna kill her."

I slash a hand through the air. "Don't worry 'bout it, bumblebee. Now I understand why you're so against dating your students."

"Colton, that man was a wackadoo! We first met when he came to a meet and greet. Apparently, I complimented his hair, and he took that to mean I was interested. I say *apparently* because I don't remember meeting him. I didn't even recognize him when he became my dance student three months later.

"After his fourth lesson, he asked me out. I said yes, not knowing he'd been stalking me the whole time. I swear to you, during dinner, the guy was a completely normal gentleman. It wasn't until he brought me home and showed me his shrine when I freaked out. He literally said he thought the shrine would *impress* me. He knew things about me—things that aren't on the internet. He had stuff in his house that he dug out of my trash bin. My *trash bin*. I literally ran out the door, screaming.

"Two days later, he showed up to his lesson as if nothing had happened. When I refused to teach him, he stormed into Dixie's office, demanding that she, as my boss, force me to have sex with him. Because, ya know, all bosses have that power."

"Shit." I rub the back of my neck. "Dixie didn't tell me that part. What did she do?"

"She called the cops, of course! He left before they got there, and I haven't seen him since. For months, I was too afraid to go anywhere alone. I almost filed a restraining order."

This Matt guy is lucky I wasn't around when that shit happened. I would have made sure he couldn't walk anywhere —ever.

To change the subject, I say, "You wanna know what else Dixie told me?"

Liz throws her arms up, letting them drop onto the couch. "That's it. You and Dixie are no longer allowed to speak to each other. What the hell did she say?"

"When I was in her office, about to sign up for another round of lessons, she mentioned that you have a thing for blonde guys."

"She did not." Scrutinizing me, Liz picks up her wineglass and takes a long sip. We both know Dixie totally did.

"She said your celebrity crush is Chris Hemsworth."

"True, but who doesn't have a crush on Chris Hemsworth?"

I rake a hand through my blonde curls, flashing her my best smolder. "Have you ever noticed the color of *my* hair?"

"Eh, I'm too busy looking at your open fly."

I wait a second. The pinch doesn't come. *That only means one thing.* I glance down. Sure enough, my zipper is wide open. My forest-green boxer briefs are in plain sight. Liz giggles as I yank up my zipper.

I glower at her. "How long has it been like that?"

"Ever since you came back from the bathroom in the middle of dinner."

"And you waited until *now* to tell me?"

"Sorry, not sorry." She giggles some more, making my wolf hop around in happy circles.

I stare at her, admiring how much her face lights up when she's laughing. "Have I told you yet how beautiful you look tonight?"

"Yes, you told me twice during dinner, then once again while we did the dishes."

"Well, I'ma say it again. You look fucking beautiful."

Her eyes widen as she presses a hand to her chest. "Oh, earlier I was just beautiful. Now I'm *fucking* beautiful? What changed in the last half hour?"

"Nothing. You just seem to get more beautiful every minute I'm with you."

Her lips curve into a slow smile as her eyes meet mine. Then her gaze falls to stare at my mouth. She does this a lot. Sometimes, I think she's wondering what it'd be like to kiss me. At least, I *hope* that's what she's wondering about. She doesn't have to wonder, though, because I'm more than willing to show her.

Her tongue peeks out, licking her lips. I lick mine too.

My wolf pants, willing me to lean in to her, so I do.

Tenderly, I cup her cheek, pressing my fingertips against the back of her neck. My heart thrashes as my wolf pants harder. I lean in some more, going as slow as possible to give her the opportunity to stop me. When she doesn't, I close my eyes and go for it.

A firm hand slaps against my chest, stopping my lips barely a breath from hers. I don't move forward. I don't back off either, and she doesn't drop her hand.

My voice comes out in a husky whisper. "I thought you wanted me to kiss you."

She responds in a whisper back. "I did."

No pinch. I'm officially confused. "Then why did you stop me?"

"Because we shouldn't."

"Why not?"

"Because . . ." She bites her lip, chewing it a little. "Then we won't stop."

My mouth spreads into a wide smile. "I'm okay with that." I pull her toward me. Our lips graze just before she pulls back.

"Colton, please don't." Her hand slides down my chest and into her lap. Then she plays with the fingertips of her gloves.

My wolf whines as he sits on his hind legs and huffs.

Me too, buddy.

"Okay." My hand falls from her face, hitting the couch with a light thud. I rest my other arm over the back of the couch, then offer her a fake smile.

She gapes at me. "Okay? That's it?"

"Yeah? What d'you expect?"

"I dunno. I guess I expected you to try again."

"Do you want me to?" If she's playing mind games with me, I'm not having it. Being a Detector, I value the truth more than anyone. I don't wanna have to guess what she wants or have to play stupid games to find out. I'd rather she just tell me.

Liz doesn't look at me. "It's not that I don't want you to kiss me. It's just best for you if we don't."

I let out a frustrated scoff. "There you go again, acting like you know what's best for me."

"I do."

"That's what *you* think."

She picks up her wineglass and finishes the rest of it. The glass clinks against the table as she sets it back down. "You're leaving the city in two months."

"And?"

"That means we either start something now and end it in two months or we don't start anything at all."

My brows dip heavily. "What makes you think we'd have to end things when I leave?"

"I don't do long distance."

"Have you ever tried?"

"Yes. Three times. And it's not for me."

I gulp down the rest of my wine, then set my empty glass next to hers. "How about this? If, in two months, we decide we want to keep going, I'll quit my job."

"What? Why would you do that?"

"I'm not attached to my position. Especially not if it's the thing keeping me away from you."

"You would quit your career just to be with me?" Her lips part as she gapes at me. I don't like the *Is this boy crazy?* look in her eyes. I may sound crazy, but I'm not. Being with her makes perfect sense. Sticking with a career I never even wanted doesn't.

"Yes," I say with a shameless nod. "In a heartbeat."

"What would you do instead?"

"I have tons of job experience. Someone will hire me somewhere."

She rolls her eyes, making me feel like I'm being ridiculous. "You would drop your career for a girl you've only known for two months?"

"Technically, by then, I'd know you for four months. And yes, I would, but not for *any* girl. I'd only do it for you."

"You're insane. You're telling me that you'd rearrange your life just for me."

I don't have much to rearrange. I don't have a home, because I bounce around from project to project. My only family is Chrissy, and she's already used to having to travel to see me. What do I have to rearrange?

Liz continues, "You're almost up there with Matt."

"Hell no." I put my hand up, palm forward. "Don't compare me to that fuckwad. He came after you with the idea that he could live out some weird fantasy with a woman he became obsessed with over the internet. I had no clue who you were when we met. And now I'm crazy about you."

"You barely know me."

"That's not true. I know lots about you. I know that you're beautiful, inside and out. You're an amazing dancer and singer. I know you can shake that sexy little ass of yours on a stage and get a whole crowd of men to drool over you—me included." *My wolf too.*

She rolls her eyes again, and it's starting to drive me up the fucking wall. I don't mind that she does it when we're flirting, but to hell with it when we're arguing. "Anyone can know those things about me. All they have to do is google my name."

I straighten my back. "Can Google tell people that you have a sleep disorder? Or that the real reason you left Chicago has more to do with your sisters than it does with pursuing a dance career? Or that you hide your body power behind a pair of satin gloves?"

With each thing I list off about her, her eyes grow wide. I don't have proof of any of those things. They're just educated guesses. Judging by her reaction, I got something right.

"I—I wear gloves because I'm afraid of germs."

I don't need to hear her stutter or feel the pinch to know

she's lying. The pinch comes anyway. "I'll pretend to believe you, only because I don't need to know the truth behind your gloves to know that I want you—want this." I point between her chest and mine.

"Well, I don't." She pushes off the couch, then marches into the kitchen.

The pinch in my temples aches more than normal. My wolf smiles with me.

It's not until Liz has thrown her purse strap over her shoulder that I realize what she's doing.

I shoot off the couch. "Liz, no. Please don't leave."

"Thanks again for dinner, Colton. It was the best salmon I've ever had." She slides a foot into one of her heels.

I dash to stand between her and the door with my arms up in surrender. "Please, Liz. Let's talk about this."

She slides her other foot into her other heel. "Good night, Colton."

"Bumblebee . . ."

She gestures for me to move aside.

I don't. "Look, I'm really sorry. I didn't mean to hit a nerve. I just wanted you to know that you don't have to hide things from me. Sure, it's not normal for Zordis to have sleep disorders, but that doesn't change the way I feel about you."

"I—" She stares at her feet. "I don't have a sleep disorder."

The lack of my internal pinch makes me feel like an asshole. A sleep disorder was the only explanation I could come up with as to why she yawns all the time. Now that I think about it, she hasn't yawned once tonight. That's a change from the three or four times she usually yawns during our dance lessons. "Well, whatever it is that causes you not to sleep well, I don't care."

"That's what everyone says until they find out the truth." Without another word, she marches past me, opens my door, then slams it shut behind her.

The silence in this apartment has never been louder.

My wolf paws at me, urging me to chase after our highly frustrating and confusing woman.

Don't worry, bud. I'm not about to let her go that easily.

I snatch my apartment keys off the counter, then rush out the door. I don't even bother putting shoes on.

Liz is already way down the long hallway when I shout, "Wait! Please!"

She doesn't wait. Instead, she dashes away faster, disappearing around the corner toward the elevators.

When I catch up to her, the *down* button is already lit. "Listen, I know that you're ambidextrous. You hold your fork with your right hand, but you write with your left. I know that you are the type of person who would make a wish at a fountain to benefit someone else over yourself. I know that you were excited to see me tonight, because you spent extra time on your hair."

She jabs the *down* button a few more times as if the elevator can't get here fast enough. It stings that she's in such a hurry to get away from me. "Why are you telling me all this?" she asks.

"Because I want you to know that I see more than just the things you don't want me to see. I see your inner beauty and your strength. I see that you've fought battles, and forgive me if I'm wrong, but I see that you're still fighting them."

She doesn't confirm it. She doesn't deny it either. She just keeps jabbing the *down* button.

"Liz, this is gonna sound insane, because technically, we've only been on one date, but I'm ready, baby."

"For what?"

"To fight those battles with you. I don't even know what they are, but I'm suited up, and I'm ready for war."

Ding! The elevator in the corner opens its doors, inviting her in. She rushes to accept the invitation, presses the ground button, then turns to me. "I'm sorry, Colton, but this is a battle I have to fight on my own."

My wolf barks at me to jump into the elevator with her. The hard look on Liz's face tells me that's a bad idea. Our eyes lock as the elevator doors slide shut.

Then down,

down,

down it goes,

taking Liz and all the hopes I had for tonight with it.

Back in my apartment, I blow out the candles. Smoke rises from their wicks. The daffodils stare back at me, reminding me she didn't take them with her. *So much for a new beginning.*

I don't know how tonight could have gone any worse. Inside, my wolf barks at me like *How could you be such an idiot?* We both waited two months for this date, and I ruined it in two hours.

Maybe I shouldn't have vocalized my theories about her. Maybe I should have asked her about them first and let her explain them herself. The problem is, whenever I've casually brought up these topics, she's told me they're off-limits. I'm not supposed to ask her about Matt, her sisters, or her powers.

What I was trying to tell her tonight is that I'll accept her, scars, family issues, disturbing past, and all. If she could just let me in, I could be the one who makes her feel accepted in all ways. She just needs to give me the chance to do it.

I slump onto the couch, lay my head over the armrest, then stare at the ceiling. *What now?* Do I call her? Text her? Should I wait a day or two first? There's no way I'm letting her end things like that. So, one thousand percent, yes, I will be contacting her. It's just a matter of when.

Knock. Knock.

My wolf leaps up onto all fours.

Is it her? I spring onto my feet too, and rush to the door.

I yank it open to find Liz standing there with her eyebrows drawn together.

"Colton." My name leaves her mouth like a plea. Like she's begging for me to hold her. To comfort her. To tell her that everything's gonna be okay.

I keep my hand on the doorknob. I won't reach for her, no matter how badly I want to. She either needs to ask for it or come to me first. I'm done with her shoving me away. "Bumblebee."

She takes a moment to find her words. Whatever she has to say, I'm willing to wait for it. I'm just happy she's back.

"You scare me," she says so softly, I barely hear it.

Those aren't words I like, but it's a start. I keep my tone gentle. "How so?"

"You . . . you pay attention to me. You ask questions. Good ones. About stuff I don't want to talk about. While you don't force me to give you answers, you still put the pieces together in your head and come to conclusions that are mostly right."

"Because I want to know you, Liz. I want to know everything about you."

"And that's what scares me."

It's taking everything in me not to grab her and tell her she doesn't have to be afraid. She has no reason to be. She's safe with me. I'll do whatever I can to make her feel like her battles are hills instead of mountains. I'll climb them with her. Hell, I'll *carry* her over a hundred goddamn mountains if that's what it takes for her to overcome them. I just need her to let me in.

"Why don't you want me to know you? Why does that scare you so much?"

She pretends to be fascinated by the hallway's carpet pattern.

When she takes too long to answer, I ask, "Are you afraid I'll hurt you?"

"I've been hurt plenty before. I'm used to it now."

That makes me want to hunt down every single person who's ever hurt her and hurt them myself. "But are you afraid that *I'll* hurt you? Like I'll be just like the rest of them?"

"You won't be. You'll be worse."

I take offense at that. "What makes you think so?"

"I don't think so. I know so." She fidgets with the fingertips of her gloves. I almost reach to stop her, then remember I don't want to touch her until she touches me first. "There are things you don't know about me, Colton."

"There are things you don't know about me too."

"My things are bad."

"So are mine." *Probably worse than yours.*

"Mine will make you run away from me."

"Same." I vowed to myself that I would never speak of what happened last year to anyone, but for some reason, I want to tell Liz—only if she's willing to trade her bad stuff for mine. All I hope is that she won't judge me.

Finally, she locks her eyes with mine. "I don't get to live the way most Zordis do. Once you see that, you won't want me anymore. I'm just saving you the trouble of falling for me only to realize it was a waste of time."

"It's too late, baby. I've already fallen for you."

She glares at me, her voice going sharp. "Don't say that."

"I will say it, 'cause it's the truth. I've been falling for you since the moment I saw you. And I've fallen more for you every week since."

"Stop."

I don't. "Every time you laugh, my stomach does this little flippy thing. Every time you touch me, my skin heats up. Every time you say my name, my heart thrashes against my chest."

"Stop."

"I want you, Liz. So badly that nothing you tell me will change how I feel about you."

"You don't know what you'd be getting yourself into."

This woman is impossible. What do I need to say to her to convince her that I'm in this for real and nothing she can say will change my mind?

I suck in a deep breath, then let it out with a grunt. "Why'd you come back? If you're not here to apologize for getting my hopes up, only to leave me hanging, then why did you come back?"

"I wanted to ask you to stop pursuing me. I had a feeling you'd keep trying, so I just wanted to make it clear that you shouldn't."

I shake my head at her. "You're being selfish."

She drops her jaw with a scoff. "How am *I* being selfish? I'm doing what's best for you."

"It's selfish of you to make this decision for me and to lie to yourself about why you're doing it. You're not doing what's best for me. You're doing what you think is best for *you*. You think I'll hurt you worse than the others? Why? Because you think I'll run away like they did? How do you know that, when you haven't even given me the chance to?"

I let her process that. As expected, she doesn't respond. She knows I'm right.

So I keep going. "I can't live the rest of my life wondering what this could have been, Liz. I think we could have something *really* beautiful, if only you'd stop pushing me away. I'm in love with you. Deeply, crazily in love with you. And you know what? I think you're in love with me too."

"I'm not."

The pinch in my temples makes my lips spread into a wide smirk. Fuck my self-imposed rule of waiting for her to come to me first. I'm done waiting. I seize her face in my hands and plant a hard kiss against her lips. Her body stiffens as she lets out a little gasp. My lips keep going, coaxing hers to open.

When her lips finally part, I suck in a breath and kiss her harder. My body ignites with the blazing fire she sparks inside me every time she's close. Keeping one hand around her head, I slide my other palm down her back, stopping just before her ass. I jerk her body in to mine, making her tits smash against my chest. The feeling of it gets my cock to harden. It's ready for her. *So fucking ready.*

A sexy moan escapes her lips as I push my tongue into her mouth. Her hands claw at my shirt, begging me to come closer. *No problem, baby.*

As I step backward into my apartment, I drag her with me. Then I slam the door shut before crashing her back into it. Her eyes are dazed as she grabs my neck, heaving my lips back to hers. I go enthusiastically, wanting—needing—every inch of our bodies to connect.

Careful not to touch her hands, I seize her forearms and trap them against the door above her head. I keep them there with one hand as my other arm wraps around her back, pulling her closer.

Our lips move against each other's like they're meant to, like the natural way a calm ocean slides against a sandy beach. Of all the times I imagined kissing Liz, I never imagined it like this. So desperate. So heated. So fucking passionate.

I adjust my cock so it sits more comfortably in my jeans. Then I press my length into her thigh, making her ass thud against the door. She lets out a sexy whimper over my mouth. The sound of it only makes my cock harden more.

I plant kisses down her neck, sucking in her soft skin. She rolls her head back to give me more access, and I'm living for it. This is exactly how I want her—melting at my touch, not pushing me away.

"Colton," she whispers, all seductive and breathless. She releases her arms from my imprisonment above her head, only to press them against my chest.

"No," I say, my voice rough. "Stop it."

"Stop what?"

"Thinking." I plant my lips against hers, and she lets me in again. "Let me kiss you, baby," I say over her mouth. "If this is all you want right now, that's fine, but stop resisting this flame between us."

Her lips part as she stares at my chest with her eyebrows pressed together. She can't look at me as she says, "But what if I get burned?"

I grab her by her chin and force her eyes to meet mine. "I'd burn the entire world down before I ever burn you."

Twelve

COLTON

I don't know how I'm doing it. I've been able to convince Liz to come over every night she's not with her band. By convince, I mean that I simply ask, and she comes eagerly. What am I suddenly doing right? It's almost too easy compared to how hard it was before.

Our routine is, we eat the dinner I make for her, then migrate to my couch and make out until she has to leave. We do some talking, but mostly, it's just us enjoying the taste of each other's lips.

After our frenzied first kiss, she's been adamant that we take this slow. That's why the farthest we've physically gotten is getting shirtless. She's let me suck on her tits, but otherwise, our pants have stayed on. It's torture, and I crave seeing her naked, but I won't pressure her into having sex with me. I have plans to be with this woman for a while, so there's no need to rush. In a way, I'm enjoying the wait. It's giving me time to savor her. At least, that's what I tell myself as I jerk myself dry the second she's out the door.

Sometimes I don't even make it to the bedroom. I just brace a palm against the back of the door and rub my throbbing cock as hard as I can until I cum. The whole time, I just imagine fucking Liz against the door while she screams my name.

I haven't gone this slow with a woman since high school. I got engaged to my high school sweetheart, Hallie, and ever since I broke off the engagement, the most I've had are flings and one-night stands. Neither of those is what I want with Liz, so if she wants to take it slow, then we'll take it slow. Eventually, though, I plan to eat her out until she begs me to—

"Thanks again for dinner," Liz says as she stands to take her plate to the sink.

I force my mind off the dirty things I was imagining, then stand to bring my empty plate to the sink too. "I'm glad it turned out all right. I've never made Cornish game hens before."

"It was delicious."

"Not as delicious as your lips will be for dessert." I give her a wink.

After we get the kitchen cleaned up, I take my dessert to the couch and waste no time getting our mouths to dance together. Liz doesn't seem to mind, as she tears her shirt over her head and tosses her bra somewhere behind her. The bra thumps onto the carpet as she climbs on top of me and straddles my thighs.

I'm practically drooling as I marvel at her plump breasts. I cup them with both hands and admire how well they fit in my palms. "Damn, baby. Have I told you yet how amazing your tits are?"

She giggles. "You've told me every time you've had your mouth on them."

"You know what? I forgot what they taste like. You should remind me."

Without hesitation, she leans forward until one of her nipples is in my mouth. I twirl my tongue around her nipple, then suck it in and bask in the sweet taste of her skin. She arches her head back and lets out a breathy moan toward the ceiling.

I've had plenty of nipples in my mouth before. None have ever tasted this good. Liz's tits are more mouthwatering than a five-course meal at a fancy restaurant.

Because I don't want her other nipple to feel neglected, I leave the one I've been sucking on and take in the other. Liz's gloved hands grip the back of my hair as she releases a seductive sigh. Simply hearing it gets my dick to harden more than it already was.

"You're killing me, bumblebee," I say against her chest. "I want you so bad."

"I want you too," she says softly.

I lean up to give her a kiss on the lips. "Then why can't we have each other?"

"Because we can't."

"Are you on z-birth control?"

"Yes."

Another kiss. "Then why can't we?"

"We just can't."

Internally, I groan. That's her way of saying she's still not ready. I won't push her on that, but . . . "Could you at least touch me?"

"I am touching you."

"With your bare hands."

Her body stiffens in my grasp. "I can't."

"Why not?"

"Because I can't touch anyone."

I lean back as her lie pinches my temples. I didn't need my mind power to know she's lying. Instead of calling her out on it right away, I give her a chance to tell me the truth. "No one? You can't touch a single person?"

"Nope."

Another pinch. Well, if she's not gonna confess . . . "I know you can touch Trey."

Her face contorts, then she pushes herself off me to sit on the next cushion. "How do you know that?"

"During your meet and greet thing, I saw you hold hands with him. *Bare* hands."

"Well, he's the only person I *can* touch."

I wait for the pinch. When it doesn't come, I scowl. "Why?"

"I don't wanna talk about this anymore."

I let out an exasperated breath. *Of course she doesn't.* "Okay."

"Okay? That's it?"

I toss a hand into the air. "Why are you always so surprised when I don't press for more?"

"Because everyone does. They always have questions, and they never stop until I answer them."

I laugh humorlessly. "I'm not gonna lie, I've got questions. Tons of 'em. But if you don't wanna tell me right now, I can wait."

"You'll be waiting forever, then, because I'm never telling you."

I freeze. "Never?"

"Never," she says firmly. "I mean, maybe if we got married or something."

"Does Trey know the truth?"

A nod.

My face creases into hard lines. "How come he gets to know without putting a ring on you, but I don't?"

"That's just the way it is."

I rake a hand through my curls. "You know, Liz, you told me there's nothing going on between you two, and I believe you. But that doesn't mean it doesn't bother me that he's the only person you can touch and knows why."

She toys with the fingertips of the very things causing this heated discussion. "I understand if this makes you not want me anymore."

"I still want you," I say, not missing a beat.

Her eyes flick up to meet mine. "Really?"

"Really," I say with a firm nod.

She stares at me with her mouth agape. "How do you still want me after knowing the only hands I can touch are Trey's?"

"Wait. Is it just *hands* you can't touch? Or is it any skin at all?"

"Just hands."

A little hope sparks in my chest. "We can work with that. You can take your gloves off, and I'll just make sure not to touch your hands."

"Too risky. I've tried that before, and it's never worked. Accidents happen, and it only takes a second for it to be bad."

My natural instinct is to ask, *For what to be bad?* but I know she won't answer that. Instead, I ask, "Are you a Vamp?"

Vamps can suck the energy out of people until they're an inch away from death. Shifters have a bad rep, but Vamps have it worse. Maybe Liz is afraid she'll accidentally hurt me or that I'll judge her for being an energy stealer.

"I'm not a Vamp."

No pinch. That's good. "Do you have an instant death touch?"

She shakes her head.

"Yes or no, baby?" Lies need to be spoken for my gift to work.

"No. My touch won't kill you."

No pinch. "Will it hurt me at all?"

"No."

I lean forward to peck her cheek. When I pull back, I say, "Then I'm okay with you touching my hands."

She groans from the back of her throat. "You don't understand."

I huff. "Because you won't explain it to me."

Liz slides off the couch and plucks her bra off the floor.

Her words come out rough as she hooks it back on. "Do you think I *want* to live like this? Do you think I enjoy being forced to wear gloves when all I want is to feel your skin? Do you think I like that Trey is the only person I can bear to hold hands with? Living like this isn't ideal, okay?

"I can't explain it to you because every time I have explained it to someone, they've left. The only person who hasn't is Trey, and that's only because he's my best friend, not my boyfriend. If he was in your shoes, getting naked with me, and I told him I couldn't touch him, he'd leave too."

The mental image of Liz getting naked with Trey eats at me. It's been years since Hallie and I separated, and now that situation is coming back to haunt me.

Liz returns to the couch fully dressed again. She sits with her legs in a pretzel. "I really like you, Colton. Like, so much that it scares me. That's why I don't want to tell you. Not yet. If you run too, it'll break me."

"I'm not gonna run." I mean that with all my heart.

"That's what you say now. That's what they always say." She hikes her gloves higher up her wrists, glaring at them with resentment. "If you don't think you can handle not knowing why I have to wear these things, maybe we should end this now. You know, before we get in too deep and I won't be able to recover from it."

I grab her face and kiss her lips. Hopefully, through this, she can *feel* how much I mean my next words. When I let her go, I keep my forehead against hers. "I'm not running, Liz. You need to stop thinking I will. And stop trying to end things with me too. I fucking hate it."

She whispers, "I'm sorry."

"Look, I can accept that you're not ready to tell me about your gloves, but eventually, you'll have to. If this thing between us is going to continue, I need to understand you. I can't do that unless you let me. Maybe you're not in too deep yet, but *I* am."

Thirteen

COLTON

It's finally Sunday again. Because of Liz's busy weekend schedule, I've gone a whole two days without seeing her. I don't know who's more excited that she's here for dinner, me or my wolf. He's hoping tonight will be *his* night. I don't have the heart to tell him it probably won't be. Liz isn't at that level with me yet, so my wolf's just gonna have to be patient.

I'm pulling some roasted veggies out of the oven as Liz mixes the salad. I didn't have to ask her to; she simply saw the salad kit on the counter and began putting it together.

Little things like this make me wonder how I stayed with Hallie for so long. With her, I was used to doing everything myself. If I ever asked her to contribute, she'd either refuse or do it half-assedly with long sighs full of attitude the whole time.

I set the sheet pan of vegetables onto the stovetop, then turn the oven off with a *beep!* "Is it possible for me to sign up for your Thursday nights to ensure that no one else takes them? I like that you get to come over right after your little girls' class."

"I'd ask if you'd really spend your hard-earned money on

something like that, but I already know the answer." Liz flashes me an eye roll. I catch that hint of a smile though. "Anyway, there's no need. I already asked Dixie to close off my Thursday nights after my Sprouters."

"You did?"

"Yep. And her response was, 'I will if you tell me how big he is.' Then she asked if your girth is closer to a banana or an English cucumber."

I adore Dixie. That woman never ceases to amuse me. "And?"

Liz smirks. "I said you were more like string cheese."

I tear the oven mitt off my hand and chuck it at her. "You haven't even seen it."

She giggles, making my wolf perk up. "I wasn't gonna tell Dixie that. Do you know what she'd say?"

"Something along the lines of how crazy you are for not letting me bang you against the mirrors on day one?"

"Exactly."

"I agree with her."

Liz plucks the oven mitt off the floor and throws it back at me. It hits my chest and falls again.

Chuckling, I bring down two plates from the cabinet. "I've got a surprise for you after we eat."

"What kind of surprise?"

"The kind that's waiting for you in the bedroom."

"Eh. I won't be hungry for any string cheese after all this." She gestures toward the abundance of food I'm shoveling onto our plates.

I stop dishing up just to shoot her a glare. "Compare my dick to string cheese one more time, and I'm gonna have to pull these jeans down to show you my eggplant."

She laughs as she hands me the salad bowl.

My wolf jumps around as if *he's* the one planning to get naked with Liz tonight.

After we finish eating, I ask my beautiful woman to close

her eyes. Then I take her by her gloved hands and lead her to my bedroom.

"You keepin' your eyes shut?" I ask.

"Yes."

No pinch. Just to be sure, I wave a hand in front of her face. She doesn't react.

Once she's standing at the edge of my bed, I say, "All right. Open your eyes."

She does, then furrows her brow at the items lying on the mattress. "What's all this?"

"Options." I point at each one. "Depending on how kinky you wanna get. Satin gloves in my size so you can take yours off. Handcuffs so you can ensure my hands stay away from yours. And these are bed straps. They go beneath the mattress, then come up to tie my wrists down."

She side-eyes me. "Did you already have all this?"

"Nah. I bought these earlier today. It took me a while too. I didn't realize how many different types of straps there are to choose from."

She picks up the handcuffs and spins them around her finger. "I wouldn't know. I've never tried bondage."

"But Dixie said you're into it." *And my internal alarm didn't go off.*

"I like the idea, but that doesn't mean I've ever done it."

"We don't have to try any of these tonight if you don't want to, but which of these would make you feel the most comfortable to take your gloves off?"

I don't see it coming. Liz throws herself at me, circling her arms around my torso. "You're adorable."

I return her hug. "Adorable? Thanks, but I'm not trying to be adorable. I'm trying to be naughty."

"You're both. Now strip down and put those gloves on. I'm about to suck you off so hard, you're gonna beg to come in my mouth."

My eyes widen as my dick instantly hardens. "No need to ask me twice."

Within seconds, my clothes are tossed all over the bedroom floor. Liz helps me get the black satin gloves on, then she cuffs my wrists together. With the metal securely on, she shoves me into the mattress and barely waits for me to get comfortable before she climbs over me and straddles my hips. I'm not complaining. Her eagerness only excites me more.

"Keep your arms above your head," she orders.

I obey as her willing captive. My cock stands tall for her, ready to accept whatever she's so enthusiastically about to give.

She pinches the middle fingertip of her glove, then pulls it off. It flops onto the floor behind her. Then she does the same with her second glove. Her fingernails feature a shiny coat of black nail polish. It's a shame no one ever gets to see it.

Tenderly, her fingertips trace up the ridges of my abs. Her touch leaves a trail of heat on my skin as she makes her way to my pecs. My cock twitches, growing harder with each second she puts me under her spell.

Actually, let's be real. This woman's had me under her spell since the moment I saw her. Somehow, my wolf knew she was a good one. I should trust his animal instinct from now on.

Liz leans down, pressing her lips against mine. I groan into her mouth as she tangles her fingers with my hair. Her nails dig into my scalp, making me writhe beneath her. Now that I've felt her bare hands against me, I can never go back.

Suddenly, she stops. "What did I say about your arms, Mr. Finley?"

"Oh, sorry." I raise my arms back over my head. I didn't realize they'd lowered themselves. I'm too captivated by Liz right now to control my body.

"Better," she says with a fire in her eyes I've never seen before.

I'm ready. I'm so fucking ready to take the heat. *Light me up, baby.*

Liz kisses her way down my neck, my chest, then my abs. The lower she goes, the more my cock jerks, begging for her to kiss it too.

She must hear my silent plea, because she takes my length into her hands, squeezing my base. Then she strokes me. Up and down, soft then hard.

I shut my eyes, taking in the pleasure I've been waiting so long for. The sounds that leave my mouth are almost inhuman. I groan, and grunt, and beg for her not to stop.

"I won't, baby," she says, stroking me into a rhythm. "Just keep making those sounds."

"Liz," I pant. "Oh, god. It's so good."

She bends to graze her bottom lip over my wet tip. The sight of her down there like that . . . with her lips so close to my dick . . . looking up at me from behind her long black lashes. *Jesus.*

"I think I'm going to enjoy this more than you are," she says through a smile.

"Doubtful," I say gruffly.

She sucks the stickiness off my tip, then licks her way down my shaft. Up again, then back down. She's fucking teasing me. I hate it and love it at the same time.

Liz licks her lips in the most sensual way. "You ready, Mr. Finley?"

I nod, my mouth parted, my mind in a foggy daze. She's got such a hold on me, and I'm more than okay with it.

Finally, she lowers her mouth onto me, and I let out a sharp gasp. Inside, my wolf falls onto his back in submission. As Liz pulls back up, she circles her tongue around the head of my cock, then sucks me into submission as well.

"Holy shit, babe."

My words must encourage her, because she bobs her head

a little faster. Her hand moves up and down my shaft, along with her mouth.

I groan toward the ceiling as my eyes roll back. "Fuuuck."

She falls into a steady rhythm, occasionally glancing up at me as if making sure I'm still under her spell. *I am, baby. Just don't stop.*

I climb up a mountain of pleasure, lingering near the edge. I've never gotten here so fast. This woman, she's magical, I swear.

"Slow down, Liz, or I'm not gonna make it much longer."

She sits up and squeezes the base of my cock. "Don't come until I say so."

Jesus fucking Christ. During our dance lessons, she could get a little bossy sometimes. It turned me on then. Hearing her bossy now only makes me want to come faster. I didn't realize how much I liked being dominated in bed. It's always been the other way around.

She waits a moment before sliding her mouth over me again. I let out a deep groan as my cock disappears between her lips. While one of her hands moves up and down me in the same rhythm, her other hand massages my balls. This woman hasn't even finished me off yet, and it's already the best I've ever had.

Disobeying her orders, I bring my arms down to grab two fistfuls of her hair. She doesn't protest as I guide her where I need her.

"Fuck, baby. I'm sooo close."

"Not yet," she says with my tip between her lips.

"But I need to come."

"I said not yet." She squeezes my base again, torturing me.

I growl at her as I back off the edge a little. The break only lasts three seconds before she's back to sucking me toward an explosion.

"Babe," I hiss. "Please let me come."

"Not until I say so." She sucks me harder.

I moan, struggling to keep it down. "Please? I can't hold it back any longer."

She takes me deeper, then looks up at me. Her eyes seem to give me permission.

"Can I come now?"

With my cock still in her mouth, she nods.

It only takes a few more bobs of her head before I leap over the edge. I grunt toward the ceiling and screw my eyes shut as I blow my entire fucking load down her throat. Not once does she pull away. Not once does she stop stroking me. She simply sucks and swallows me until every last drop is gone.

Once the pleasure dwindles, my breathing slows and my weak limbs relax beneath her. She continues to gently stroke me as I soften in her hand.

I gape at her through half-closed eyes. "Damn."

"What?" She grins, knowing exactly what.

"That . . . was . . . amazing," I say between breaths.

"I know." With a smirk of satisfaction, she climbs off me and shuffles out the door. Down the hall, the bathroom faucet turns on.

A moment later, she's back, and I still haven't moved. My mind is a puddle.

"Once I catch my breath," I say, "it'll be your turn."

"My turn?" She bends to pick up her gloves.

"Yeah, baby. I've gotta return the favor. So get me outta these handcuffs and lay down."

Twenty minutes later, after a lot of fingering and the work of my tongue, Liz comes apart beneath me. Her body shudders as I continue to suck her clit into my mouth.

Eventually, her body relaxes and she pants with the same dazed look in her eyes I had earlier.

My wolf paws at me to let him out.

Not yet, buddy. Be patient.

There have been moments when I've almost told Liz that I'm a Shifter. I didn't because I'm waiting for her to ask me what my powers are first. Not once has she shown interest in what I may be. Sometimes I think she doesn't care, which makes me kinda sad. If she doesn't care what my powers are, does she care to know me at all?

Other times, I think she hasn't asked because she's afraid I'll ask her the same questions back. I can't imagine what powers she has that makes her think I'll run. There's nothing worse than being a Vamp or having an instant death touch, if that even is a thing. Besides, even if she was a Vamp, I'd still want her.

In the bathroom, Liz and I wash ourselves off. I keep myself at a distance to ensure our hands don't touch. Then she leaves so I can pee.

When I return to the bedroom, I pick up my gloves and slide them back on. "Take yours off, babe. I want you to stay naked. Fully naked."

Under the covers, we lie down together in our birthday suits. I love the way she drapes her leg over mine. What I love more is the way she traces her fingertips over my abs. Her *bare* fingertips. If I can appreciate feeling her bare hands over my skin this much, I can only imagine how much she appreciates being able to do it.

She hasn't said the words *I hate my gloves*, but I know she does. I see the hatred in her eyes every time she has to put them on. It's a battle she fights every moment of the day. I'm relieved she was willing to try the options I presented to her tonight. A part of me was afraid she'd refuse. I'll keep thinking of ways we can work around her fears if she continues to let me in. Tonight was a huge step for us—for her—and I'm already thrilled to take the next one.

"Will you stay the night?" I ask into her hair.

"I can't," she says softly.

"Why not?"

"It's Thursday. Trey's staying over."

Every time that man comes up, my wolf shows his teeth. I've only met Trey once. I shook his hand for all of two seconds before moving on to Liz, and somehow, I know more about him than I need to.

If Liz isn't telling me a story about something fun they did together, she's referencing something funny he said. Or she reminds me that she can't see me because she'll be with him.

"Hmm," I say, not hiding the disdain in my tone.

Liz tilts her head back to look at me. "What?"

"I'm not fond of the idea that my girlfriend's gonna leave my bed to jump into her own with another man."

She scowls. "It's not like that, and you know it."

That's the first time I've ever called Liz my girlfriend, and she didn't bat an eye at the word. We haven't talked about making this thing exclusive, but I'm assuming I'm the only person she's seeing. At least, I better be.

"Do you still cuddle with Trey now that we're together?"

She doesn't hesitate. "Yes."

I hope like hell for the pinch to come. It doesn't. I guess it's good that she's not trying to hide it. "Does he know you're my girlfriend?"

"Yes."

"And he's good with it?"

"Of course. Like I said before, there's nothing romantic between Trey and I. He's my best friend, nothing else. He even told me not to tell you that I can touch his hands and only his. He said he didn't want it to chase you off."

"Hmm. That doesn't make me hate him any less."

She sits up, clutching the sheet against her bare chest. "You hate Trey?"

I push myself up too, then lean against the headboard. "Maybe *strongly dislike* is a better term."

"You don't even know him."

"I know that he cuddles with my girl every weekend and

that he spends a shit-ton of time with you. I know that he gets to hold bare hands with you and that he knows more about you than I do. That's enough for me to have unfavorable feelings toward him."

Liz frowns at me so hard, her entire forehead wrinkles together. "Trey knows more about me because he's known me longer, and we only spend a lot of time together because of the band. If it wasn't for that, I'd barely get to see him."

"But why does he sleep over at your house? And why *every* weekend?"

She pulls the sheet up higher, tucking it under her arms. "He lives in New York. He flies in every Thursday evening so we can do our band stuff on Fridays and Saturdays. He usually leaves on Sunday, then comes back on Thursday to do it all over again."

"Oh. I didn't realize he doesn't live in LA. I thought he was just sleeping over for shits and giggles. I guess that makes sense as to why he stays at your house, but why does he have to sleep in your bed?"

"I only have one bed." She flashes me a *duh* face, like I should've already known that answer, even though I've never been to her house.

"Don't you have a couch?"

"Trey sleeps in my bed because *I* want him to, not because he wants to. If he had a choice, he'd probably prefer not to."

If she's trying to comfort me, she's doing a shit job. "Wait, you *want* him to cuddle with you? Even after we've just cuddled?"

"You and I could cuddle for months straight and I'd still need to have that with Trey."

I jerk my head back. "Hold up. Now you *need* to cuddle with him? It's not just a *want*?"

She nods firmly. "Yes. It's a need."

No pinch, and it gets my wolf to snarl. "Will you die if he doesn't cuddle with you every weekend?"

"Well, I won't die, but it's not ideal."

I grunt as my eyes turn to slits. "Does this have anything to do with your powers that you're so secretive about?"

"Kind of."

No pinch, so that means yes. "Have you ever thought that maybe if you explained it to me, I could be the one who cuddles you instead of him?"

"It doesn't work that way."

"Does he have a gift that combats yours? Is that also why you can touch his hands and not mine?"

Liz pretzels her arms over her chest. "Is Trey gonna be a problem for us?"

I scoff, and I don't care that it sounds condescending. "He already is."

"He's only a problem because you're *making* him a problem."

"I wouldn't have to make him a problem if he didn't get privileges with you that I don't."

Jumping off the bed, Liz scrambles to find her clothes. She barely looks at her bra before hooking it around herself.

"Have you ever kissed him?" I ask, still heated.

"Not on the lips."

"Where the fuck have you kissed him?"

She shoves her legs into her panties, then does the same with her leggings. "I kiss his cheek sometimes, and he'll kiss my forehead or my hands. It's not in a romantic way. Just in a caring, comforting way."

Comforting or not, I don't like it. "Have you ever seen each other naked?"

"No."

When the pinch doesn't come, I let out a breath. Then I slide off the bed to get dressed.

"Look, Colton. This isn't a conversation I've never had before. I know where this is going, and I won't hold it against you for walking away. Just don't think for even a second that I would push Trey out of my life to be with you."

I pluck my boxers off the floor. "I'm not asking you to push him away. Honestly, it's not even your relationship with him that bothers me. It's that you're choosing to leave me in the dark about you. And since he knows the answers I don't, he gets to have privileges with you that I can't. I just wish you'd let me in so I can understand."

Fully dressed now, she slips her gloves on. "You can't understand. No one does. Not even Trey. Not fully, anyway. Unless you have the same exact struggle I have, you can't understand."

I've only got my boxers and jeans back on when I grab her and force her against my bare front. She comes willingly, and I'm glad for it. My arms squeeze around her so tight, she lets out a wheezy breath.

"Do you turn into a hairy bloodthirsty swamp monster at night?" I ask.

She laughs into my chest. "Is that really where your mind just went?"

"It's the only thing I might run away from. Even then, it's a *might*. I think I could tame your monster. Maybe scratch her behind the ear to get her to submit."

She laughs again, pulling back so I can see her face lighting up. "No, I don't turn into a bloodthirsty swamp monster at night."

"Hey, you forgot the hairy part. Does that mean you transform into a *hairless* bloodthirsty swamp monster?"

"No, I don't turn into a monster at all."

No pinch, but even if my internal alarm had gone off, I'd still want this woman.

Fourteen

LIZ

"Didn't I tell you not to tell him that?" Trey looks up at me from behind a Chinese takeout box. Since I've been eating at Colton's, I don't have much for groceries or leftovers, so Trey picked up some dinner for himself before coming here.

I hop up onto my kitchen counter to get a full view of Trey at my dining table. "Technically, you *advised* me not to."

"Advice that you ignored. How did he react?"

"He bought himself a pair of satin gloves, some handcuffs, and bed straps."

Trey squints at me, then his mouth pops open with an *Oh, I get it* look. "Smart man."

"Yeah, but then he got ticked off when I wouldn't stay over."

"Did you tell him why you can't?" Trey lifts the lo mein back to his face, shoveling some of it into his mouth with chopsticks.

"Of course not. He also made a big deal about how I still cuddle with you."

"Why the hell would you tell him that?"

I cross one ankle over the other. "Well, I wasn't gonna lie."

Trey takes another bite of his noodles, then says with his mouthful, "So are you two good now?"

"I think so. He said he still wants me, but I think it's only a matter of time before all of this builds up inside him and he decides it's not worth it anymore."

"Eh, if he's as smart as you say he is, he won't be that stupid. He's made it this far, so he's gotta know you're worth *something*."

My gaze falls to the floor. "I guess."

"Give him a chance, Liz. Who knows? Maybe soon, you'll be comfortable enough with him to tell him about your body power."

I pick at my fingernails. "What if I tell him I'm defective and he doesn't want me anymore?"

Trey glares at me. I knew it was coming. "Quit calling yourself defective. The correct term is *restricted*."

"Yeah, but who actually uses the more politically correct word? Did the kids at your Zordi school ever say *restricted* over defective?"

"It doesn't matter if they did or didn't. What I'm saying is if you keep calling yourself defective, you'll think you are, and you're not. You have a *restriction* in your power, not a defect."

I roll my eyes as he goes back to eating. "Either way, you know how normal Zordis are around *restricted* Zordis. They're like how normal Ordis are around people with intellectual challenges. They forget how to be human. They look down at them and assume those people are just stupid. What if Colton does that with me?"

"Then I'll beat his face in."

"Trey!" I gasp, half appalled, half laughing.

"Kidding." He sets down his noodles to pick up the box of fried rice. "Sorta."

I let him eat a couple of bites before saying, "I think I'm in love with him."

"I know you are."

"How?"

"I can sense it." He scoops up some more rice before switching back to the noodles. "Even if I wasn't an Empath, I'd still know. You walk around more smiley than usual. Plus, you never shut up about him."

"Sorry. I don't mean to talk about him so much. He's just all I can think about."

"It's cool. I like seeing you happy. It reminds me of how happy I used to be when I was with *her*." Trey's eyes soften the way they always do whenever he mentions Arella. One day, I hope to see that broken light in his eyes shine brightly. For as long as I've known him, he's never had a light that fully shines, but it's never been this dim either.

"Do you think you'd want to get lunch with Colton and me before you fly back home?"

Trey's face crinkles. "Why?"

"Maybe if he got to know you, he'd hate you less."

"I don't give a shit if he hates me. His opinion of me matters as much as the bullshit that accumulates in my belly button."

"Well, it matters to me. You're the most important person in my life, T-Bear. If Colton's gonna be around for a while, or even longer, I need him to like you. If he doesn't, my relationship with him won't work."

Trey finishes his noodles while he thinks. "Have you run this idea by him yet?"

"Nope. I just thought of it now."

"Do you wanna know my real thoughts or the ones I should say as your best friend?"

"Both."

"All right." He sticks his chopsticks into the empty noodle box, then sets it down. "My real thought is fuck him. I'm not gonna waste my time having lunch with someone just to get them to like me."

"Okay." I roll my eyes, huffing. "What's your answer as my best friend?"

"If you really want this lunch thing to work, you can't sell it to him as an *If you don't like Trey, we can't be together* kind of thing. Make it casual, like it's no big deal. If he's in, then I'm in."

"I can do that." I nod, pursing my lips together. Then I shoot him a glare. "But you've gotta promise you'll be on your best behavior."

He jerks his head back. "What's that supposed to mean?"

"Don't say or do anything to purposely get him to not like you."

"Two things. First, *you're* the one who's been saying all sorts of shit to get him to not like me. I haven't even met the guy, and somehow, he already hates me. And second, I'm not promising any type of behavior. If I have to drag that man outside by his ears and threaten to rip his guts out through his asshole if he hurts you, I will."

I scoot my butt toward the edge of the counter. "Actually, you have met him. He was at our meet and greet with his sister about two months ago."

"Don't remember him."

"You should. He was the blonde guy who punched that drunk dude that Reggie escorted out. Remember how I told you that I knew him?"

Trey thinks for a moment, then his eyes widen. "Oh! That guy? Damn. It's taken you *this* long to tell me I've already met him? This whole time I pictured you with some rough-looking construction worker with a beard."

"Why a beard?"

He shrugs. "I dunno. I just always picture construction workers with tanned skin, tattoos, and scruffy beards."

"Well, Colton's a clean-shaven man with wavy blonde hair, no tattoos, and a really big . . ." I wiggle my eyebrows up and down.

Trey's face contorts. "Ew. Fucking gross, Liz. I could have gone forever and a decade without knowing that."

I burst into laughter. "I was gonna say he has a really big dog."

"Bullshit. You've talked about him enough now for me to know the man doesn't own a dog."

Three days later, I spot my sexy man waiting for me outside an Italian restaurant. He's got his hands in his jeans pockets, reading the menu displayed outside.

Trey and I have just parked his motorcycle down the road. When Colton sees me, his face lights up. I leave Trey's side to run to him. He catches me in his muscular arms, spins me around, then presses a firm kiss against my lips.

When I try to pull back, he yanks me back for more. It doesn't escape me what he's doing. His kiss feels more primal and territorial than anything. I don't care. If he feels the need to claim me in front of Trey, I'll let him.

"Hey, bumblebee," he says when he finally releases me.

"Did you get it all out of your system?"

"Not even close." He looks up behind me, then around. "Where'd he go?"

I gesture toward the restaurant. "Inside. Don't worry. I'm sure he saw your little show."

"Hope so," Colton says under his breath.

I take his hand, then lead him into the restaurant. Trey's already got a booth in the corner.

After a firm handshake full of testosterone between the guys, we all sit and read our menus. I pretend to look mine over while casually glancing up at the boys. While Trey is actually trying to decide what he wants to eat, Colton keeps flicking his gaze over to me.

Under the table, I place a hand over his knee, giving him a reassuring squeeze. When I pull back, he grabs my hand and places it over his thigh. I take the hint and leave it there.

When our waitress brings us some waters, we tell her we're ready to order. After she leaves with our meal requests, I figure it's time to get these kids to get along.

"Trey's traveled around the states about as much as you have, Colton." I turn to my man. "What's been your favorite place to visit?"

Colton drapes his arm over the back of our booth. "I've only traveled for work. Most of the time, I don't get to pick where I go, and because I'm working, I don't get to explore it too much. If I had to pick a favorite, I'd say Utah. They have some really beautiful state parks there."

Trey folds his hands together over the table. "How long have you been working in construction?"

"Since I was twenty-two. I'm thirty-one now. So that's what, nine years?"

"What made you choose construction?"

Colton rubs a hand behind his neck. "Honestly, I just needed the money. Construction's easy to get into. When I was sixteen, my mom got really sick, so someone had to pay the bills. My sister was only nine, and my dad had already left us, so it was up to me."

My jaw drops. "Your dad left you?"

"Yeah," he says with a nonchalant shrug. "Technically, he left all of us."

"What a piece of shit," Trey says.

I lean over the table to smack his arm. "Trey!"

"What?" He feigns innocence. "Any man who leaves their family hanging, no matter what the reason, is a piece of shit."

Colton nods. "You're right. My dad is a piece of shit. His reason for leaving us was pretty selfish too. I haven't spoken to him since. Not that he's tried to reach out or anything."

Why has Colton never mentioned this? It seems to affect him more than he's showing. To be a teenager and have to support your mom and sister? That must have been hard.

"You said your mom got sick?" Trey asks.

"Zancer," Colton says. "She lost the battle four years ago."

I blanch. "What? You never told me that."

"You never asked."

We haven't talked much about Colton's family outside of Chrissy. We haven't talked about my family either, but that's because I avoid the topic. However, I feel like if my dad left for invalid reasons and my mom died of something so rare, I might have mentioned something by now.

"What kind of zancer was it?" Trey asks, because apparently, he's better at finding out stuff about my boyfriend than I am.

"The kind that made her powers go haywire. She was a Stretcher. Could stretch her limbs out fifty-some feet. With the illness, she couldn't control when her limbs stretched out or when they retracted back in. It'd take hours, sometimes days, for her body to return to normal. That's why she couldn't work. Can you imagine what an Ordinary would think if they saw that? Eventually, her body just stopped coming back together."

"That sucks," Trey says. "I assume you took care of her while she was sick?"

Colton takes a sip of his water. "It was mostly Chrissy, since I had to work. Sometimes my ex-fiancée would help, but getting her to be productive was like pulling teeth."

"Wait!" I gape at him. "You were engaged?"

He nods impassively, like this wasn't something I should've known by now. "Yeah. For three years."

My eyes bulge. "Three years? You never told me that."

"You never asked."

Sure, but it's not like he's tried to tell me. Now that I think about it, neither of us have talked about our past relationships. Not that I really want to tell him about mine. He knows all he needs to know: Everyone left, end of story.

Trey chuckles. "Jeez, Liz. Do you know anything about your boyfriend at all?"

I scoff. "Apparently not. You don't have a kid somewhere, do you?"

Colton laughs, and it makes my shoulders ease. "No. If I did, I definitely would have mentioned *that* by now."

I fidget with the fingertips of my gloves. "Can I ask why your engagement ended, or is this a conversation we should have in private?"

"I'm fine talking about it. Hallie and I ended because I found out she slept with her best friend. Ya know, the guy she told me not to worry about. It was only one time, and she said it was just a moment of heat, but I wasn't having it." He eyes me and Trey to gauge our reaction. Trey doesn't react.

All I can get out is "Oh, I'm sorry."

Now I feel bad. Colton should've told me this was a sensitive situation for him. I would have held back on telling him so much about my relationship with Trey.

Colton lifts a shoulder, making an *eh* face. "I'm over it now. Honestly, she wasn't that great of a person anyway. She had no talents, unless you wanna count scrolling social media all day and being a negative bitch as talents.

"She barely worked, too, always hopping from one job to the next, until eventually, no one wanted to hire her. She was known for having a strong track record for quitting on the spot whenever she didn't get her way."

"Why did you stay with her for so long?" I ask.

"Dumb reasons, but mostly, she was dependent on me. With me, she had a place to live and food to eat. I didn't have the heart to kick her out because her family didn't want her around either, and there was a part of me that believed I could fix her.

"Once I found out about her infidelity, I figured she could go live with her best friend and spend his money instead. So she did and got pregnant three months later. They got married shortly after the baby was born. Got pregnant again. Now they're divorced. Poor man pays a lot of child support. From what I've heard, she still refuses to get a job."

"Sounds like ya lucked out to me," Trey says. "And you've hit the jackpot with Liz. She's got tons of talents. Singer, songwriter, dancer, choreographer, my personal life coach, and she's always Miss Positive."

Colton leans over to kiss my temple. "I did hit the jackpot, didn't I?"

The rest of our lunch goes smoothly. I don't know why I was so nervous about this. Halfway through our meals, the boys start talking about baseball, and it dominates the rest of the conversation. I enjoy seeing them get along. Toward the end, it even looks like they're, dare I say it . . . bonding.

When the waitress comes by with the check, Trey offers to pay the whole bill.

"I can get it," Colton says, digging out his wallet.

Trey's already got his card out and is handing it to the waitress. Once she leaves with it, he says, "Too late."

I place a hand over Colton's forearm. "Trey's got a thing about never letting anyone spend money on him."

"Why's that?" Colton asks.

The air goes quiet as I glance at Trey, then back at Colton. Colton's eyes flick between Trey and me while Trey simply glares at me. The next thing I know, we're all just staring at each other.

Trey knows what I want to say. If it was just the two of us, I'd say it out loud, but he and Colton don't know each other like that yet.

Instead, I say, "It's just a thing of his. He's working on it."

Trey rolls his eyes, shaking his head. "Liz thinks she's Freud and tries to explain all of my behaviors by connecting them to my childhood. She thinks that because I grew up feeling worthless, I don't think I deserve for others to spend their money on me. While there is *some* truth to that, sometimes I really do just wanna treat people to lunch."

"T, it's not a treat when you do it *every* time we go out."

Also, whenever I buy him anything, he always accepts it with a look on his face like he doesn't know how to feel. He wasn't given much when he was a kid. Nothing for his birthdays. Nothing on Christmases. He was barely given clothes to wear. This man deserves so much, and he refuses to believe it.

After I say bye to my best friend and he heads toward the airport on his motorcycle, I loop my arm through Colton's and let him lead me to his truck.

"So?" I say, grinning.

"So what?" He knows what.

"I think that went well."

"Yeah. Trey's an all right guy."

I make a *ha* sound. "An all right guy? Come on. Once you two started talking about baseball, you didn't even try to pretend like I was there."

"Okay, okay. Toward the end, I kinda liked him. I can see by the way he looks at you that he cares about you, but not in a way I should be concerned about."

I beam and give his arm a squeeze. "Yay! That's exactly what I wanted you to see."

Back at Colton's place, I've barely kicked my shoes off before he lifts me into his brawny arms. My back hits the couch with a light thud.

I don't resist. Not one bit. In fact, as he straddles my body, I plant a gloved hand against each side of his face and pull his mouth to mine.

He doesn't resist me either as he presses hard, desperate kisses against my lips. "I've wanted you under me since the moment I saw you running toward me today."

"I'm surprised you lasted through lunch."

"If it was just us, I might have snuck under that tablecloth and eaten you out as my appetizer."

I imagine that happening and let out a soft moan of desire. "Remind me to only take you to restaurants that have tablecloths from now on."

Colton nips at the side of my neck, then sucks on my skin. Sparks shoot down my spine. "You taste like sweet honey and heaven, ya know that?"

"And you taste like . . . actually, I forgot." I lean back to smirk at him, then take a handful of his balls, giving them a light squeeze. "Do you want to remind me?"

He releases a husky grunt. "Say no more."

Within seconds, Colton has torn his shorts and briefs off. He throws them across the living room, then yanks his shirt over his head and tosses it somewhere near the TV.

I take a lingering look at his abs, admiring the little trail of hair leading down to his already thick and veiny erection. "Have I told you yet how impressed I am that you can get this hard this fast?"

"It doesn't take much when it's you, baby. You just look at me, and I'm instantly ready." His eyes grow dark as his voice deepens. "Now be a good girl and get naked for me. I may have missed out on an appetizer, but I'm desperate for some dessert."

I didn't realize that hearing him call me a good girl would

spark so much submission inside me. Without hesitation, I tear my shirt off, then the rest of my clothes, leaving only my gloves on.

Colton takes a moment to admire my body the way I did with his. His stare begins at my tits, then moves downward until his eyes stop at the main prize. He sucks his bottom lip into his mouth and bites down on it. "You're the sexiest woman I've ever known, Liz. There's no doubt about it."

"And you—"

He drops his mouth over my nipple, and suddenly, I can't talk anymore. The pleasure sends my eyes rolling back. My throat releases a guttural moan toward the ceiling.

Colton takes a handful of my other breast into his palm and massages my nipple between his fingers. "I'm obsessed with your tits, baby. They were made for me."

He trails kisses down my belly until his face hovers between my legs. He looks like he's about to take me into his mouth—until he slides farther down and peppers more kisses against my inner thigh.

I groan from the anticipation. "Are you teasing me on purpose?"

He looks up, grinning like a devil, and I take it as a *yes*. I'm about to protest and beg for him to lick me when his fingers find my clit and he rubs it in gentle little circles. Then his mouth returns to my chest. As he flicks my nipple with his tongue, his fingers never stop rubbing me. I practically melt beneath him.

I've never been with a man who has prioritized my pleasure like this before. Typically, the foreplay is no more than thirty seconds—if there's any at all. With Colton, our entire relationship has felt like weeks of foreplay.

Suddenly, I'm questioning why I ever thought it was a good idea to push him away. I thought resisting this fire between us would save us from getting burned. Turns out, he's exactly what I needed. Colton makes me feel safe from the horrific pasts that live in my head. He also makes me feel accepted for who I am. No, he doesn't know all the dirty details yet, but I'm getting the feeling that even if he did, he'd still be here. More importantly, I'm beginning to feel like I can tell him about me.

Something he said on our first date has been repeating in my mind: *"Liz, this is gonna sound insane, because technically, we've only been on one date, but I'm ready, baby."*

"For what?" I asked as I jabbed the *down* button for the elevator over and over.

"To fight those battles with you. I don't even know what they are, but I'm suited up, and I'm ready for war."

Is it naive of me to believe he meant that? Am I too blinded by my strong feelings for him to see that he'll end up leaving me, just like the others?

Colton's mouth leaves my breast only to immediately find my clit. I press on the back of his head to force him harder into me. As his tongue licks me into submission, I conclude that I don't care if I'm being naive or blind. This man makes me happy, and if it ends up being short-lived, so be it. At least I was happy for a little while. I can allow myself that, right?

So for now, I'll enjoy the moment without thinking about the what-ifs. I'll fall into Colton with trust that he'll stay when he finds out about me. I'll even put faith in him that he'll not only accept me but will become someone who can keep the night terrors away. That's asking for a lot, I know, but I'm done holding back. With Colton, I'm ready to go all in and dive headfirst, consequences be damned.

"Hold on a second," I say, and it makes him pop his head up. His lips are shiny with wetness, and it's the hottest he's ever looked. "Wasn't it *me* who needed to be reminded of how *you* taste?"

Colton's eyes glaze over as I shove him off me and climb on top of him. He rests his head on the arm of the couch.

"Keep your hands up," I order.

Without hesitation, my good boy obeys and intertwines his fingers together behind his neck. Only then do I feel comfortable enough to take my gloves off with full confidence that Colton will do everything in his power to not touch me.

My liberated hands grip the base of his hard cock. I feel the urge to take every inch of him into my mouth, but since he teased me earlier, I'm going to return the favor first.

So I start at his base and slowly drag my tongue up his shaft until I get to the stickiness at the tip. Making full eye contact with him, I lick him clean.

"Mmm. I remember how you taste now."

Colton shakes his head at me. "I know what you're doing, you naughty girl."

"And what's that?" I say as I lick him again from his base to his tip.

"You're teasing me."

I grin seductively. "Don't you like it?"

"It's torture."

I continue torturing him, making every drag of my tongue up and down his shaft better than the last. He writhes beneath me, groaning my name in a throaty voice.

When I take the entire head of his dick into my mouth, he gasps. I circle my tongue around his soft skin as he screws his eyes shut like he can barely take it. He probably can't—which only means I'm going to give him more.

Eagerly, I bob my mouth up and down, stroking him with my hands at the same time.

"Fuuuck," he says, his leg shaking. I don't think I've ever made a man shake his leg before. "You make it so hard to hold back."

"You better hold it back. I plan to ride you until you beg me to stop."

His mouth pops open, then he gapes at me through half-closed eyes. "Please tell me you're serious, because I don't know if I can take any more teases."

I think about it for all of two seconds before saying, "Yeah, I'm serious." And I mean it. I'm ready to take this to the next level. My body was ready the moment I laid eyes on him. I just needed my heart to get there too.

Even though this has been a big step for me in the past, with Colton, it doesn't feel that way. It feels natural to want this with him, and I have an inkling that it'll feel just as natural to have him inside me.

All of a sudden, the world tips as my back hits the couch cushions and Colton's on top of me again.

My eyebrows dip. "What are you doing? I said I was going to ride you."

"I'm gonna make you come first. Then I want to fuck your come. Only once I've had my fill of you will I let you ride me." He plucks my gloves off the coffee table and sets them on my chest. "Put those back on while I lick you to an orgasm."

He wants to lick me to an orgasm and I didn't even have to ask? *Hell yeah.* I return my gloves to my hands without protest.

Colton wastes no time. The second my gloves are on, he dips down and sucks my clit into his mouth. My mind instantly turns to mush. How does he know exactly where to put his tongue and how much pressure to use?

This man doesn't treat me like I'm a dessert. No, no. He treats my pussy like it's an all-you-can-eat buffet, burying his face between my thighs and getting the entire surface of his tongue to make contact with my skin.

I arch my head back, gripping the top of his hair to guide him higher up my clit. The way he practically punishes me with his mouth is making me lose all my coherent thoughts. I couldn't tell him what one plus one is, even if I wanted to.

Just when I think it can't get any better, he slides a finger inside me. He goes in and out, until he sticks another finger in and finds my G-spot.

"Colton," I moan as he circles his fingers against the sensitive area. "Oh my god."

He lifts his head up to stare at me. "I love seeing you like this. So satisfied. So vulnerable. And I love being the one to do this to you."

I try to think of a response but can't. All I can do is let out breathless whimpers.

Colton returns his mouth to my clit while his fingers relentlessly bring me near my climax. I shut my eyes and give in to the sensations. His touch carries me up an ocean wave of pleasure that keeps rising higher and higher.

Between breathless sighs, I manage to say, "I'm so close."

Suddenly, he pulls his fingers out.

My wave of pleasure falls as I open my eyes to gape at the cause. "Why'd you stop?"

"I don't want you to come yet. Not until I give you permission to."

"What?" I give him an *Are you crazy?* look. "I didn't sign up for this."

He grins up at me wickedly. "Don't like the taste of your own medicine, huh?"

"Not one bit." I'd rather be the one edging, not the one being edged. "Resume, please. And don't stop this time."

Still grinning, Colton returns his fingers to where they're supposed to be. He rubs my G-spot for only a few seconds before I'm back on top of that wave again. My labored breaths are the only sounds in the living room as he works my orgasm out of me.

Like the good boy I want him to be, Colton doesn't tease me anymore. He barely even comes up for air. He acts as if I'll punish him if he takes his lips off my clit—and I would. For him, breathing is not allowed. His only job right now is to keep eating me like he's a starving animal.

As my climax nears, my breaths get shorter. "Don't stop. I'm so close."

Colton obeys, licking me and fingering my G-spot until the ripples of bliss finally take over my body. I throw my head back into the couch and moan as the waves of pleasure crash over me, drowning me.

Colton doesn't stop licking me until my body relaxes and my arms go limp. Then he grins up at me, all proud of himself. As he should be. That was one of the most powerful orgasms I've ever had.

"Turn around and get on your knees," he orders in a husky voice. "I'm gonna take you from behind."

My legs feel like Jell-O, but I manage to turn and hold myself up with my palms against the arm of the couch. Behind me, Colton plants a hand on my hip, then slides his thick erection up and down my damp opening.

I gasp when he shoves it in. No warning or anything. He stills, waiting for me to adjust to his size. It feels so good that my arms give out and I collapse to my elbows.

"Fuck, Liz. You're so tight." He pulls back, then pumps his cock in deeper.

I let out an uncontrollable half moan, half whimper. I've never been fucked after an orgasm before. I didn't realize how sensitive I would be.

In a steady rhythm, he moves inside me. Every inch of him sliding in and out against my inner walls makes me lose more of my mind. It's such a snug fit, I can feel exactly where his thick head is. It's good to know I was right. This does feel natural with him. He fills me up like our bodies were molded to fit perfectly together.

"Get back on your hands for me," he says.

I do as I'm told and am rewarded by him cupping my tits. He massages them in his palms as he continues thrusting in and out of me.

"These nipples belong to me now, okay?" He rolls them between his thumbs and fingers.

"Okay," I say, panting.

One of his hands leaves a breast to rub my clit. "And this belongs to me too."

I moan out a breathless "Okay."

"This ass is also mine." He gives my butt cheek a light slap.

"Yes, sir." I swear, I'm melting right now. No one has ever been this possessive of me before. Or at all, really. It's so fucking hot. I've never felt so wanted.

Colton leans forward to nip my shoulder and whisper into my ear, "Say it, baby. Say you belong to me."

"I belong to you."

"Louder."

"I belong to you!"

"One more time so my neighbors can hear you through the walls."

This time, I scream it. "I belong to you!"

My eyes are closed, but I can feel him grinning. "Good girl. Now hold on tight. I'm about to fuck you so hard, you won't be able to walk tomorrow."

He slaps a hand against each side of my hips and holds me still as he relentlessly rams his cock in and out of me. The sounds we make can only be described as feral need. He grunts out his pleasure with each thrust, over and over.

I fall back onto my elbows again, barely able to hold myself up. This man is no longer trying to give me pleasure. Now he's taking it for himself, and I wouldn't have it any other way. We started off as two people making love to each other. Now we're two people who have a basic human need and are filling it.

"Fuuuck, baby. You feel so good." He grunts as our bodies slap together so loud, it practically echoes against his apartment walls. "Oh, fuck. I'm gonna come." Before I can stop him, he pulls out and moans a string of *fucks* as he jerks himself empty all over my back.

After his breaths slow and he lets go of his cock, he sinks

backward into the couch with a dazed look in his eyes. My legs are still tingly as I wobble toward the TV. I pluck his shirt off the carpet, then use it to wipe myself clean.

"That was absolutely amazing," he says between heavy pants.

Grinning, I climb on top of him and straddle his legs.

His eyes go wide. "What are you—"

"I told you already that I want to ride you until you beg me to stop. Since you decided to be a naughty boy and didn't let me do that, I'm going to punish you for it. Now keep your hands behind your head, because I'm going to take my gloves off and stroke you until you're ready for me again."

His mouth falls half open as he nods submissively. Then he locks his hands together behind his neck. "Punish me, baby."

Fifteen

COLTON

Some might say I'm jumping the gun, but I don't give a fuck. The way I feel about Liz isn't going to change in a month. That's why over my lunch break, I give my boss a call.

He's not thrilled to hear my news. "Tell me you're jokin', Finley. You're the best man I've got. You can't just dip out on me."

The construction site is quiet. The machines aren't running because everyone is on their lunch break. Many of the guys are over by the crane, basking in the shade, sharing some pizzas. I'm sitting on a cinder block with a half-eaten sandwich in my hand from a deli down the block. "Sorry, boss, but I'm not joking. After this project, I'm done."

He sighs, and I can picture him running a hand along the top of his bald head. "Gotta say, I ain't seen this comin'."

"I didn't see it comin' either."

"Then why you quittin' on me? Did one of the guys give ya a hard time? Just give me their name."

"Nah, boss. It's nothin' like that. I, uh, met a girl here."

His tone softens. "Jesus, Finley. I thought maybe you was offered somethin' better somewhere else. I was ready to up your salary. Now you tellin' me there's a girl involved? I can't compete with that. I ain't your type."

I chuckle lightly. "No, you're not." And now that I've met Liz, no one's my type. If I can't have her, I don't want anyone.

"If I'm able to pull some strings and get you somethin' permanent in LA, would you stay with the company?"

I take a bite of my sandwich as I think. Through a half-full mouth, I say, "I'd consider it."

"All right. Lemme see what I can do. Good-working men like you are hard to come by. I ain't lettin' you go that easily."

"Thanks, boss. Let me know what you can find out. And also, now that I know you coulda upped my salary this whole time, I'm expecting it with whatever new position you can get me."

"You got it!"

The second we hang up, I rest my sandwich on my lap so I can type out a message to Liz.

Hey bumblebee. Great news! I just called my boss to tell him that I'm resigning after this project. After our conversation last night about how I could be leaving the city soon, I decided it's not what I want. Staying here in Los Angeles with you sounds like a better plan. Think you can help me find an apartment near your place?

I eat the rest of my sandwich while I wait for her reply. She hasn't texted me back all day. Typically, it's the first thing she does in the morning.

Yesterday, after Liz made good on her word to ride me until I begged her to stop, I asked her to stay the night. I just couldn't bear the thought of her leaving. Having that woman next to me is all I want, to the point that I feel like I need to be breathing the same air as her to think properly. No matter what I said to convince her to stay, she wasn't having it.

I'll admit, I was pretty pushy about it, and things were still a little heated when I dropped her off at home. I realize now that I shouldn't have been so insistent. She's not still upset about that, is she?

I finish the last bite of my sandwich, then crumple up the paper it was wrapped in and drop it in my lap to throw away later. On my phone, I type out a message to Chrissy.

> Hey! Guess what? I've decided to stay in LA to be with Liz. Gonna look for an apartment soon. Wanna come down to visit? I can cover your plane ticket this time.

Within seconds, my phone buzzes over and over. I don't need to read the screen to know who's calling.

I answer it with a drawn out "Heeey."

Chrissy shrieks into my ear. "Oh my god, Cole! This is so exciting! Are you excited? 'Cause I'm excited! Of course I wanna come visit!"

I wish I knew where Chrissy gets all her energy from. I'd bottle it, sell it, and make billions. "When do you wanna come?"

"How about whenever you get your new apartment? I wanna help you pick out furniture!"

"That sounds great."

She shrieks again. "You'll need stuff like cookware, bedding, and decorations, right? Are you gonna let me decorate your place however I want? Oh, wait! Could Liz and I do it together? Does she like shopping? I bet she does."

Now that I think about it, I don't know if Liz likes shopping or not. If she does, it's probably not as much as Chrissy. "Having you two decorate my apartment sounds awesome. I'll ask Liz tonight and see what she thinks."

"Yay! This must mean things are pretty serious between you two. Has she met Goldilocks yet?"

"Not yet." A wave of nausea hits me just as my stomach rumbles. Suddenly, my chest aches like someone's slugged me with a baseball bat. Inside, my wolf pops up with his ears perked. "Sorry, Chrissy, I've gotta go. Can I call you later?"

"Sure. I leave work around five."

"Cool. I'll call you then." I hang up, then clutch my belly as I run toward the porta-potties. I lock myself in one and heave my lunch into the hole. The smell of my vomit falling into the hole makes me gag. *What the fuck was in that sandwich?*

Eventually, I finish vomiting and step back out under the sun. My temples are throbbing like I've heard a thousand lies in under a minute, and my mouth tastes disgusting. Sadly, I don't have any z-meds or a toothbrush.

I check my watch. My lunch break is over. There's no time to make a trip to—

One of the construction workers smacks a palm over my back. "You good, Finley? You're lookin' kinda pale."

My voice comes out rough. "I'm okay."

"Cool. We need ya to look over somethin' real quick."

"Lead the way." Gravel crunches beneath my shoes as I trudge behind the guy toward the crane. I spend a few minutes answering the group's questions. When I'm done, I head straight back to the porta-potty.

Forty-some minutes later, I'm still a train wreck. I haven't thrown up again, but I feel like I will. Inside, my wolf is half whining, half barking, and I don't know why. My illnesses never affect him. Why is it now?

My phone vibrates in my pocket. I drag it out, expecting it to be Liz. It's not. The name flashing on my phone is Theo.

My stomach tightens with knots, and this time, it's not because of the sandwich. Theo hasn't called me in so long, I could have sworn he'd lost my number by now. *Kinda wish he had.* Whatever he's calling about, I want nothing to do with it.

Eventually, my phone stops buzzing. I'm about to put it back into my pocket when it buzzes again. Surprise, surprise, it's Theo.

I don't answer. When I told him last year that I was done, I fucking meant it.

The call goes to voicemail, and this time, he leaves one. Against my better judgment, I listen to it.

His voice sounds panicky. "Hey, Jamie. It's Theo. Call me back ASAP. Life-or-death situation."

I haven't been called Jamie in over a year. Hearing it again feels foreign.

Life-or-death situation. Everything's a life-or-death situation with that guy. I mean, he's usually not wrong, but still.

To call back or to not call back? That is the question.

If I call him back, he's probably gonna tell me he's about to work his biggest mission yet and he needs my help. I'm gonna tell him no. He's gonna tell me some sad sob story about whoever's in trouble. I'll get suckered into helping, then he'll think my arms are wide open again. Well, they're not, and—

My phone buzzes. It's Theo calling again. *Seriously?* With a long sigh, I step away from the construction noise as much as I can to answer it. "Hello?"

"Jamie?"

"Yeah. What's up?"

"They took her. My wife, Chloe. They fucking took her."

I press the phone harder against my ear to hear better. "Wait. Slow down, man. Who took her?"

"Jamal West."

I stop breathing at the sound of that name. My wolf snaps his teeth, barking so loudly, I can barely hear myself talk. "But he's dead."

"I know. This is his brothers' doing. They're trying to get back at us for what we did to Jamal last year. Somehow, they found me, found out where I live, and they took Chloe. Thank fuck the twins were at school at the time. I can't imagine what would have happened to them too."

"How do you know it's the West family behind this?"

"Because they left a note. It's not signed or anything, but after I read it, I had a good fucking guess. Then I checked my home security cameras, and it confirmed my suspicions."

"What did the note say?"

Theo clears his throat. "It says, 'To exact revenge for your family is not only a right, it is an absolute duty.' "

Shit. There's only one family I can think of who'd be vindictive enough to do this.

"I called Andre. Raven is missing too. The same note was found. Now don't freak out, but Jamie, please tell me you don't have a woman."

"Oh, fuck." I hang up as my wolf barks, clawing at me. My body hums the way it always does right before I shift.

This is not the time, buddy. I suck in a deep breath and focus on staying in control. *We're in the middle of a fucking city. If you take over now, we'll get pounded.*

He doesn't listen to me. He's still barking, still clawing, and still making my body vibrate.

Stop. Just let me find Liz first. If the West family did take her, I promise you, I'll let you rip into every single one of them.

Within seconds, the pulsation in my limbs stops. He's still barking though.

I don't bother saying anything to anyone before running down the block to where my truck is parked. Once I'm behind the wheel and my tires are squealing their way down the road, I call Liz.

She doesn't pick up.

I call her again.

Nothing.

With one hand on the wheel, I use my other to google the number for Dixie's Dance Studio.

Dixie picks up right away. "Dixie's Dance. How can I—"

"Hey, it's Colton. Is Liz there?"

"No, and I've been calling her all day. She never misses her lessons."

"Fuck!" I slam my palm against the steering wheel.

"What's going—"

I hang up and turn my truck toward Pasadena. I've only been to Liz's place once. It was last night, and only to drop her off—in the dark. What I can recall is the general area and that she's got a cute welcome sign on her door. The only reason I even remember the sign is because I made a comment about how her sign had bumblebees on it. Can I find her house again?

This would be a good time to be a Teleporter, but unfortunately, I'm just a Shifter with a wolf inside me who's freaking the fuck out.

My heart thrashes with every wrong turn I take wandering around her neighborhood. Not remembering the exact location of her house is wasting time, but I've got a sinking feeling I'm already too late.

Eventually, I find Liz's place and silently thank her for having a memorable welcome sign, because all the houses in her neighborhood look the fucking same.

My truck comes to an abrupt, screeching stop in her driveway. I shove my door open and don't even bother closing it as I sprint to her front door.

Fuck. It's open. Liz doesn't seem like the type of person who forgets to shut their door.

For the first time, I step into Liz's home, into her silent living room. My wolf lets out a low growl as we make our way past the vacant couch and into the quiet kitchen. The first person we see who isn't Liz is meeting my wolf, no questions asked.

Unfortunately, we don't see anyone. Nothing looks out of place either. No messes on the floor. No signs of a struggle. And sadly, no Liz.

I open her sliding glass door and peer around the fenced-in backyard.

"Liz?"

As expected, no one answers. I slide the door shut and lock it, then head upstairs.

At the top is a long hallway. I head right and open the first door in sight. It's a closet stocked with clean towels and rolls of toilet paper. The second door reveals a small bedroom filled with storage tubs stacked on top of each other.

I rush down the other side of the hallway. Through a slightly open door is an unmade queen bed. On top of the comforter sits a piece of paper with one sentence printed on it.

TO EXACT REVENGE FOR YOUR FAMILY IS NOT ONLY A RIGHT, IT IS AN ABSOLUTE DUTY.

I collapse to the floor. *No, no, no!* This can't be happening. This can*not* be fucking happening. My arms and legs hum as my wolf growls. I close my eyes and steady my breaths until the vibration goes away. He snaps at me for fighting him.

I'm sorry, but I can't let you take control. Not right now.

We won't be able to get anywhere as a wolf. We need to stay in the mindset of a human for us to get Liz back. More importantly, I need to get back into the mindset of Jamie.

Once I've gathered myself, I drag my phone out of my pocket.

Theo picks up on the second ring. "Talk."

"She's gone. My girl is gone." With my phone on speaker, I race back to my truck. My tires squeal as I reverse out of Liz's driveway. I don't even know where I'm going.

"Did you get the same note?"

"Yeah. Do you know where they took her? Took them?"

Theo switches to his in-charge voice—the one I got used to hearing when we worked together. "I've been doing some digging this past hour. Looks like the Wests have a new mansion just outside of San Antonio, Texas. I've got a hunch that's where they've taken our women."

"A hunch? I'm gonna need something better than a fucking hunch, Theo. I need visual confirmation."

"Agreed. That's why I've already got a Speeder making his way there. He'll update me the second he's got any information. In the meantime, Andre and I are in the car, heading to Texas. The rest of the clan is on their way too, and I'm in the middle of setting up a place for us to meet."

Texas? How far of a drive is that from California? I turn toward the highway and step harder on the gas.

Theo continues, "Once I have a meeting location confirmed, I'll text it to you. There, we'll make a plan."

"Make a plan? Hell no. You're insane if you think I'm gonna waste time making a goddamn plan. I've already got one: Get in, get my girl, get out."

Theo huffs. "And this is why *you* don't call the shots, Jamie. We *need* a plan. Busting onto their turf without one is suicide. Trust me, I want to rescue Chloe just as much as you want to rescue your woman. However, the second we start acting on impulse, they'll win. We're gonna treat this like any other rescue mission, which means we need the whole team together first, then we're gonna formulate a plan."

I pick up my phone from my lap just to shout into it. "This isn't like any other rescue mission, asshole! This is my Liz we're talking about. Your Chloe. Andre's Raven. We need to save them!"

Images of the West brothers doing obscene things to Liz zip through my mind. Those images are quickly replaced with flashbacks of my last mission. I see the poor girl's blood drenching the floor and hear her screams all over again. My chest heaves unsteadily. I can't let that happen to Liz. I won't.

In a calm but firm tone, Theo says, "You're right, Jamie. This isn't like our past rescue missions, because this time, we're not leaving a single West alive."

Sixteen

COLTON

I'm pacing the airport, waiting for my flight to San Antonio, when my phone vibrates. It's a text from Theo.

We got visual confirmation. The Wests have
Chloe and Raven locked up in their mansion.
A third woman is with them. Curly reddish-
brown hair, about five-six, looks Latina. Is that
your girl?

I can barely breathe as I type a message back.

Unfortunately. Are they hurt?

My Speeder says they appear unharmed. Are
you on your way?

At the airport. Flight is boarding in twenty-
minutes.

Where are you coming from?

LAX.

I suppose that's faster than driving all twenty-some hours here. I have the address of where we're meeting. Send me an ETA when you land in TX.

In the middle of my four-hour flight, the old lady next to me gestures toward my shaking leg. It's probably been shaking since the minute I sat down.

"I get anxious about flying too," she says, then pulls out some minty gum from her purse. "This usually helps."

"Thanks." I accept a stick and violently smack on it until the plane finally lands.

The address Theo texted me is about an hour from the airport. I get a cab there and thank the universe for giving me a driver who isn't talkative. I'm not in the mood for conversation.

While he drives, he plays the radio at a soft volume. Meanwhile, I glare out the window at the darkening sky, hoping Liz is okay.

Since I've had a few hours to calm down, I've been able to admit to myself that Theo is right. If I want to get Liz back—alive—I need a team and a well-thought-out plan. My wolf still needs convincing though. He keeps pacing inside me, ready to rip some throats out.

When the cab driver drops me off outside a white ranch house at the end of a gravel road, the time on my phone reads 9:00 p.m. It's officially been eight hours since I found out Liz was taken, and it's already felt like days.

As I march toward the front door, I pass a bunch of cars parked by people who've been trained like I have. None of the cars are blocking the others, and each vehicle is facing the street, ready to peel out at any moment.

I can't believe I'm here right now. I thought this part of my life was over. Years ago, when Theo recruited me onto his team, one of the first things he said was "You can leave at any time, but understand that once you're in, you're never really out."

Back then, I didn't fully understand what he meant. Now I do.

Knock-knock.

A sweet-looking woman in her seventies answers the door. The zense in my chest tingles with her presence. She offers me a warm smile. "You must be Jamie."

I nod, still put off by the sound of my old codename. "Yeah, that's me."

"Come on in. I just made zoffee."

Since Zordi bodies process caffeine faster than Ordi bodies, we have special coffee with extra caffeine in it. I don't normally drink zoffee, but as I enter the house that smells of a fresh brew, a cup of it sounds delicious.

The old woman shuts the door behind me. Typically, I would take my shoes off in someone else's home, especially when it looks so clean. Since my body makes no effort to kick away my shoes, I can tell my mind is already snapping back into Jamie mode. Judging by the lack of footwear near the door, everyone else is also following the clan's rules.

I haven't thought about the car parking or shoes rule for over a year, and I hate how quickly it's all coming back to me. Even more, I hate how normal it feels. I spent a whole damn year trying to forget all this, and now it's as if my last mission was yesterday.

I follow the old woman into a huge kitchen, where a bunch of people are gathered around a wooden dining table big enough for ten. I recognize some of the faces as the zense prickles harder in my chest.

Theo's sitting at the head of the long table with his hands balled into fists. "It doesn't matter *how* they found us! What matters is that we focus on getting our wives back!"

The bulky Black man on the other side of the table springs up from his chair, slamming his palms against the wood. "It does matter, because however the fuck they did it, we need to make sure it never happens again. If they can find you and take your wife, who's to say they won't do that to the rest of us? And if we don't have a wife, who's to say they won't take our kids? Our dogs? The other members of our families?"

Theo keeps his tone cool yet firm. "Chill out, Lamonte. No one's gonna take your kid or dog, or your fucking grandma, for that matter, because we're ending this once and for all. I'll personally tear apart every man in the West family if it means protecting our loved ones."

Lamonte huffs and settles back into his chair as if to say he approves of that idea but he's still angry. The slender woman sitting next to him pats his shoulder, offering him an *It's gonna be okay* look. One side of her shoulder-length hair is dyed pink. The other side is a bright teal blue. The last time I saw Taryn, she had a pixie cut and it was purple.

Theo stands from his seat and approaches me with a half smile. "Jamie, it's good to see you again. Wish it was under different circumstances though."

I shake his outstretched hand. "Me too, man. Me too."

Theo slams a palm over my shoulder and turns to face the clan. "Everyone, this is Jamie. He used to be an inside man. Me, him, and Andre did all our missions together for what, three years? Four?"

"A little over five," I say.

Andre's chair makes a loud noise as he pushes himself away from the table. We embrace in a long man hug. "I've missed ya, Jamie. I really have."

I choke up a little as I pat his back. "Missed you too, bro."

Before I left the clan, Andre and I were like brothers. He was the hardest person for me to leave behind. Over the past year, we've texted a few times, but it's not the same.

Theo points at the guy he was just yelling at. "That's Lamonte. Inside man. He's the guy who replaced you, actually. And you remember Taryn, right? Our tech wizard."

With a piece of toast hanging out of her mouth, Taryn waves with a fully tattooed arm. The last time I saw her, she only had half a sleeve and it didn't have color yet.

Theo stretches his arm out toward the Indian woman next to Taryn. "That's Meera, our new disguise specialist who can always come on short notice. She's the best of the best."

Meera smiles and offers me a gentle wave. I return it with a head nod.

Theo gestures toward the Korean guy. "That's Elijah. Outside man. Did you ever get to meet him?"

"Yeah," I say. "Eli joined the clan about three months before I left."

"We used to hit the gay bars together," Eli says, grinning. "You were always a great wingman for me."

"Oh, that's right," Theo says, tapping his temple. "I remember now. Anyway, next to him is Zach. We just snagged him a few months ago, so I know you don't know him. He's an outside man. Specifically, a pilot."

"A pilot?" I say. "You've upgraded."

"You bet your ass we have. Our other guy you don't know is Keith. He works inside and outside. He's our Speeder keeping tabs on the mansion right now. Every fifteen minutes, he takes a lap around the place, getting as close as he can without getting caught, then he gives me an update. An hour ago, he said our women were moved to the basement, where he can no longer keep an eye on them. At the time, though, he said they still looked unharmed."

While that's good to hear, it does nothing to ease the tension in my gut. Why did the Wests move the ladies to the basement? What are they doing to my Liz down there?

The old woman behind me clears her throat.

Theo smacks a palm against his forehead. "Oh, sorry! Almost forgot about you, Betty." With a warm smile, Theo wraps an arm around the old woman's shoulders. She's almost three heads shorter than him. "This is Betty. She's a retired zoctor and an old friend of mine. It was nice of her to allow us to use her home."

"I made dinner for everyone, so help yourself." Betty gestures toward the mostly eaten lasagna sitting on the stove.

"No, thanks." I press a hand against my uneasy stomach. "Can't eat anything right now."

Theo shakes his head at me. "You know the rules, Jamie. You either eat or you're not allowed in. We can't have you hungry or low on energy. I can only assume you haven't eaten since I called, right?"

"Right," I say with a sigh.

"Exactly. So pick up a fuckin' plate and scoop up."

While I heat up some lasagna in the microwave, Theo returns to his seat at the head of the table and fills me in on the plan so far.

"The Wests are hosting a party tonight at two a.m. That's why they took our women. Now when I say *party*, you know what I mean, right?"

I swallow hard and nod. A West-style party? Featuring Liz? I'm pretty sure this is what the Ordinaries call a nightmare.

Theo continues, addressing the entire room. "A party like this typically starts with an hour of mingling. Then they put the women out on display for a half hour. After that, the auction starts, and each woman's first session is sold to the highest bidder."

I can't believe how nonchalantly Theo is talking about this —as if it's not *his* wife in there about to be auctioned off. I suppose after doing this for as long as he has, he's numb to it. I became numb to it after two years, but that was when we were saving innocent women I'd never met before. This time, it's the woman I love. If I were Theo, there's no way I'd be able to keep my cool.

Theo continues, "The only thing our team has agreed on so far is that the best time to infiltrate the mansion is during the party. With all the guests there, we'll be harder to spot and harder to kill on sight. Also, the Wests moved our ladies to the basement, which I assume is because they're harder to rescue from there. I have no doubt the girls are heavily chained and guarded behind bars."

I imagine Liz chained to the wall of a dark, cobweb-infested dungeon and a team of brawny men on the other side of the metal bars ready to take down anyone who tries to get too close. That mental image only makes me more anxious to finalize this plan so I can get her out of there as soon as possible.

Theo continues, "The plan is for us to become each woman's highest bidder. Once they're in the private rooms, they won't be behind bars anymore, nor will they be guarded. That's the best time for us to get them out alive and before any of those monsters can put their hands on them."

The microwave beeps, then I take out my steaming portion of lasagna. "That sounds like a good plan so far."

"Glad you agree, because it's the next part that none of us can agree on."

"Which is?"

"Oh, you know, the little stuff. Like how do we get an invitation? What's our backstory? How do we make sure we aren't caught before we have a chance to bid on our women? What happens if someone outbids us? Once we're in those private rooms, how do we actually get them out?"

"I see." I grab a fork, then sit in the empty chair between Eli and Andre.

"Whatever we do," Theo says, checking his watch, "we need to figure it out fast. The party starts in less than five hours, and the West mansion is two hours away."

For the next hour, all the men, including me, argue over every little detail of our plan. The problem is that whenever one guy suggests an idea, another one shoots it down. We can't agree on how much we're willing to risk. The only things we can agree on are that we can't risk our women's lives and we're not leaving the mansion until all the West men are bleeding from their necks.

After another hour, it's only the inside men and Meera in the kitchen. Everyone else has dispersed elsewhere to do their jobs. The guys have stopped arguing, and we finally have a plan.

While we've plotted, Meera's been hard at work, transforming us. Theo's no longer a pale-skinned guy with short brown hair. Now he's a bleached blonde with tanned skin, two eyebrow piercings, and a tattoo sleeve. His nose and lips look bigger too.

Andre, a skinny Black man in his late twenties, now looks like a middle-aged man with a little beer gut.

Lamonte also looks older, and the snake tattoos going up his neck have been covered up.

As for me, my blonde curls have been dyed black and cut short. My hazel-green eyes are now dark brown, and Meera put a bunch of prosthetics on my face to change my nose shape. After she's done blending the fake nose into my skin with some makeup, I steal a glance at myself in her tabletop mirror. "Wow." I don't recognize the reflection staring back at me. "It's crazy how a nose and some hair dye can change so much."

"Oh, I'm not even done yet," Meera says. "I've still gotta superglue this beard on you."

As soon as she finishes with my fake beard, the front door swings open. A second later, Eli and the pilot, whose name I can't remember, rush into the kitchen. They've got loads of bags hanging from their arms. Since most stores have already been closed for hours, I can only assume these things were swiped.

"We've got options!" the pilot says.

From the bags, I pick out the suit closest to my size. It's a little small, but it'll do. Theo, Andre, and Lamonte pick out their suits too, then we all get undressed, right in the kitchen. Because of Theo's rule of never taking anything personal into a mission, we take off everything we're wearing and put on new stuff—socks and boxers included.

A flash of pink and blue catches my eye as Taryn spins back around out of the kitchen. "Jesus fucking Christ, guys! Warn a woman. I just saw Lamonte's junk."

Lamonte chuckles. "Did ya like what you saw?"

Taryn laughs from the hallway. "Do most women like wrinkly prunes?"

After a loud *ha!*, Lamonte says, "Fuck you, Taryn. You're such a hoe."

"A hoe that your brother banged against his headboard last night." Her comment activates my internal pinch.

Lamonte laughs some more, then stops. "Wait, really?"

Theo, fully dressed in a brown suit, slips into a pair of matching dress shoes. "Whatcha got for us, Taryn? We're mostly decent now."

She reenters the kitchen with a laptop in hand. "Three things. First, I got the party invitation for you guys. However, it's not really an invitation. It's just a password you'll say to the guards when you get there. If they ask who invited you, you're gonna say Drew Sporder. He's a friend of the Wests and known for getting lots of people to these things. Apparently, the Wests pay a commission for this shit. Can you believe that? Anyway, lucky for us, Drew isn't coming tonight, so he won't be there to corroborate whether he knows you or not."

"Why isn't he attending anymore?" Theo asks.

Taryn grins. "He may or may not have gotten into a little accident on his way to the party."

"What kind of accident?"

"Oh, ya know. His car might have gotten hacked into and then auto-driven him off the highway, into a pole." Taryn puts a hand up in surrender. "No one was hurt besides him and, well, the other three men in his car."

"Great job."

"Thanks. Second thing: Keith was able to help me get into the Wests' security system."

I perk up as I continue tying the laces of my dress shoes. "Are you able to see the girls?"

"Sadly, no. The Wests only have security cameras around the outdoors and guest areas. Their private areas are unmonitored."

I let out a sigh. All I want is confirmation that Liz is okay.

"Last thing is your earpieces. I've got them all hooked to the same communication line and ready for insertion." Taryn circles the room, handing a pea-size circular device to each of the inside men. "Let Meera put them in for you. She's good at concealing them in the canal and making them stay."

Once Meera finishes gluing everyone's earpieces in, Theo says, "Let's leave in ten." Then he heads into the living room with Taryn and her laptop.

I go hunting for the bathroom to have one last piss.

When I come back out, Andre's waiting for me in the hallway. "Hey, bro," he says.

"Hey."

"So, uh, how long you been with your girl?"

"Only a few weeks." The short amount of time I've spent with Liz doesn't fully encapsulate the deep feelings I have for her.

"Damn. I'm sorry."

"Yeah, me too." Desperate to talk about anything other than Liz, I say, "I'm happy to know you and Raven finally tied the knot."

"Thanks. Five months ago. Small wedding. Just our families and closest friends. Theo was there too. Lamonte was my best man."

I swallow hard. I'll bet anything that if I hadn't left last year, Andre and I would still be tight and I would have been his best man.

Whenever I had vacation time, I'd spend half of it with Chrissy and the other half with Andre. Between projects, I'd live with him, and we'd head to the gym together every morning. His mom loved me so much, she'd invite me over for their family barbecues before she'd even invite Andre.

When I made the tough decision to leave the clan, I hated that Andre didn't get mad at me. He was more sad than anything, which made it worse. He just kept saying he understood and that if I ever needed him, he'd be there.

His mom was furious though. Andre and I told her we'd had a falling out, even though it's far from the truth. She tried to shun him from the family until we "made up." Sadly, she will never know the real reason behind why I stopped coming over. Explaining the real story required explaining that her son and I were part of a rescue group where we went by different names and risked our lives on the regular to save women from sex crimes. The number one rule of being in Theo's clan is that the only person in our lives who knows the truth is our partner.

"She's pregnant," Andre says under his breath.

My body stills. "What?"

"Yeah." He swallows hard, glaring holes into the hallway floor. "Four months along now."

I slap a hand over his shoulder and look him square in the eyes. "We're gonna get her outta there, man. You bet your ass on it."

"We better." He offers me a weak smile. "You know, she's been asking me about leaving the clan once our baby is born. I told her I would. After this, I don't think I'll be waiting for the baby."

"Understandable."

"I feel guilty, though, ya know? Like I'm being selfish."

I shake my head firmly. "Never feel selfish for putting your family first."

"How did Theo take it when you told him you were done?"

I shrug. "He wasn't happy, but he also understood. He never made me feel like a dick for it either. You know what he always says."

"Yeah, yeah." Andre rolls his eyes. "No one's forcing us to be here, and we can leave at any time. Easier said than done. How can I leave, knowing there are innocent women out there being captured, sold, abused, and used as playthings? Besides, Theo's like family to me now."

I give his shoulder a reassuring squeeze. "Look, just because I left the clan and everything that came with it doesn't mean you have to too. You and Theo could still stay in touch."

"I guess, but how can I ever look him in the eyes knowing I could be helping him save all these innocent women and I'm choosing not to?"

I'm surprised that Andre's questioning this decision to put Raven first. He's always made it clear that Raven is his everything. Theo and I used to tease him for how much that woman had him wrapped around her finger. Andre never cared. He embraced it. He knows he's whipped, and he's proud of it. Good men like him are hard to come by.

Footsteps thump from around the corner, then Theo joins Andre and me in the hallway. "You guys ready?"

We nod. I've *been* ready.

"Great. I have one last pep talk for you boys before we go in. Each of you have done this enough now to know that no matter how much we plan, something can and will go wrong. If for any reason we get in there and your woman is already dead, injured, or whatever, you can*not* lose it and blow our cover. If all three of them are dead, then you have my full permission to tear apart everyone in sight. Otherwise, you need to stay under control." Theo points a hard stare at me. "I'm talking mostly to you, soldier wolf."

Inside, my wolf growls. While Chrissy describes my wolf

as playful and submissive, Theo says my wolf is a fierce and relentless warrior. I'm glad my wolf knows when to be which. Theo wouldn't have recruited me onto his team if my wolf was a pansy in battle the way he is around Chrissy. That's part of the reason why my dad left us: Having a submissive wolf son and a daughter who didn't gain the Shifter gene made him want to mate elsewhere.

"I'll keep him under control," I say.

Theo gives me a skeptical look. "You sure?"

I nod firmly. "I'm sure."

I'm not sure. My wolf's prowling inside me, ready to bite off the head of the first West brother we see. I'm ready for him to do it too. All I hope is that my human side stays awake long enough to see it.

Typically, whenever my wolf takes over, I can see through his eyes for about five to ten minutes. Beyond that, I go to sleep inside my wolf until he decides he wants to shift back.

Even though Theo isn't a Detector, he senses that I'm lying. "It's not too late to back out, Jamie. If you don't think you can handle this—"

"I will keep him under control," I say with conviction.

"I'm not talking about your wolf anymore. I'm talking about *you*. It's been over a year since you've gone in. Are you *sure* you can handle this?"

I lick my lips and swallow hard as I remember how my last mission completely broke me. After clearing my throat, I push the traumatic memory aside. "Yeah, I can handle this."

Theo pats my shoulder twice. "All right then. Let's go fuck shit up."

Seventeen

COLTON

"Stop rubbing," Theo orders from the driver's seat of a black Escalade.

In the front passenger seat, I lower my hands from my face and glare out my window at the black sky. "It's irritating my eyes."

"I'm wearing contacts too, Jamie. You don't see me rubbing 'em."

"Fuck you. I haven't worn contacts in over a year."

"You told me you could handle this, so fucking handle it."

As much as I hate to admit it, Theo's right. If I stroll into the Wests' mansion constantly rubbing my eyes, someone might guess I'm wearing contacts. If they investigate and find out my nose is fake too, they'll blow my head off without question. I've gotta get myself under control.

Lamonte and Andre are in the car behind us. We're going in separately because it'll be suspicious if three men from the same group win all the first bids of the night.

Lamonte's voice bellows through my earpiece. "Andre, if you don't stop shaking your goddamn leg, I'ma do it for you by chopping the whole damn thing off."

"Sorry," Andre says from my earpiece. "I'll calm down once we're in there—once I see that she's alive."

"You better," Theo growls. "This is not a time for nervous breakdowns. We're coming up on the turn toward the mansion. Lamonte, take a loop around the neighborhood so we don't arrive at the same time."

"Got it, boss." Behind us, the bright lights of their Lincoln turn left and disappear into the darkness.

Theo makes a right down a paved road surrounded by thick dark woods. The farther we drive, the thicker the trees become. After a few more turns, we arrive outside a giant gate guarded by eight bulky men in suits.

One of the men steps up to Theo's window with a fireball in his palm. I know he's using it for light, but I also wouldn't be surprised if the fucker chucked his flames straight at my face.

As Theo rolls down the glass, the zense prickles in my chest.

"Name?" the guard asks from behind a pair of dark shades, even though the sun has been long gone.

"Peter Clark," Theo answers coolly.

The guard enters that name into a tablet, then eyes me. "And you?"

"Louis Henderson," I say.

He takes a moment to enter my fake name into his device. "And who invited you?"

"Drew Sporder," Theo says.

"Password?"

"Better than revenge."

The guard shakes his head. "That was the old password. We need the new one."

"The new one?"

"Yeah. The password was changed a few hours ago. Drew ain't tell you?"

Theo sighs and drags a burner phone out of his pocket. "That guy. I fuckin' tell ya."

The guard chuckles. "Yeah. He's a last-minute kinda man, ain't he?"

Theo pretends to go through his messages. "Hold on. He mighta sent me somethin'. Maybe I missed it."

From my earpiece, Lamonte says, "Taryn?"

Her voice responds, "Workin' on it." Barely two seconds later, she says, "Sporder's car accident happened before the password was changed. No one he invited should know the new password."

Right as she says that, another guard approaches our car, making my heart rate kick up a notch. "Did these guys say they're with Drew?"

"Yeah," the first guard says.

"Drew's in the hospital. He got into a bad car accident on the way here. None of his company will have the new password."

"Ah, I see. In that case, welcome in, Mr. Clark. And you, Mr. Henderson."

My thrashing heart settles a bit as the tall metal gate opens and we head up the long driveway. The driveway is so long, it takes about three minutes before a huge mansion comes into view. The building is so big, it looks like a fancy-ass private school.

Perfectly shaped shrubs decorate the perimeter of the estate. The ground-level windows arch upward so high, I'd need a long-ass pole to touch the top. The front doors are unnecessarily ginormous too. Usually, I'd see architecture like this and admire it, but knowing the Wests own it makes me despise every brick.

Theo and I join the back of the long line of expensive vehicles leading up to the double doors, waiting their turn for valet parking. It makes me sick to know how many men turn up to these sinister parties. How do they live with themselves?

Taryn's panicked voice comes through on my earpiece. "Abort. Abort. Jamie can't go in."

Theo locks his eyes with mine. "Explain?"

"I've been watching the Wests' staff hand out a drink to each guest. They're playing it off like it's a complimentary whiskey, but I just saw the bartenders crushing pills. I zoomed in on the footage. It's too blurry for me to tell exactly what it is, but I caught someone mentioning it's a transmogrifier. Looks like they're expecting us to crash their party, more specifically, Jamie."

Theo screws his face together. "What the hell is a transmog—whatever you just said?"

I answer before Taryn can. "It's a drug that forces Shifters out of their human form. If other Zordis take it, nothing happens. If I take it, I'll wolf up within seconds, and I'll be useless. It'll sedate my wolf for about an hour, and I won't be able to shift back."

"You've gotta be fucking kidding me." Theo pounds his fist against the center console. "Sorry, Jamie. You're out. Andre, Lamonte, and I will go in without you."

"Hell no! You're an idiot if you think I'ma sit out here twiddling my thumbs while my girl is in there."

"Tell me how you're gonna keep from blowing our cover the second you transform into a motherfuckin' wolf? The same wolf that Malik West has probably ordered his guards to kill on sight. You can't save your girl if you're dead."

"Easy: I just won't drink it."

"No can do, buckaroo," Taryn says into my ear. "Malik is making sure he toasts with everyone, especially the newbies. If you don't take a drink, he'll get suspicious."

"That's it," Theo says, "you're out, Jamie. End of discussion."

My wolf snaps at him at the same time I do. "Would *you* sit out?"

Theo glares at me as he pulls ahead in the line. He knows

I'm right. If it was me ordering him to stay back, he wouldn't obey. Not with Chloe in there.

"We're already through the gate," I say. "How do you wanna explain my sudden departure?"

"We'll say you're my driver and that we don't need valet because you'll be taking the car."

"If I'm your driver, then why the fuck am I not behind the wheel?"

Theo huffs. "Goddammit. We're six cars from the entrance, people. Think. Quick."

"There's an anti-drug," I say. "If I take that first, it'll keep the transmogrifier from making me shift."

"Will it keep your wolf from coming out at all? We're gonna need him tonight."

"The anti-drug only keeps me from shifting. My wolf will still be sedated for an hour, just on the inside."

Theo tosses his hands into the air. "Well, why didn't you say so sooner? Pull out the anti-drug and take it now."

"Oh, yeah, sure. Let me just reach into this suit pocket where I keep my stash of expensive pills at all times." I shoot Theo a dirty look. "Don't be a jackass. Obviously, I don't have any."

"Well, how the hell can we get some?"

Taryn's voice comes through my earpiece again. "I've got Keith on speakerphone. He might know a guy."

A male voice I've never heard before says, "Know a guy for what?"

"Any chance you know a drug dealer we can get an anti-transmogrifier from?" Taryn asks.

"Hmm. I think so, but he won't sell it to me. The dude hates my guts."

Theo groans from the back of his throat. "Can ya steal it from him?"

"Maybe if I knew where he lives."

"Give me a name," Taryn says. "That's all I need."

After Keith tells Taryn the drug dealer's name, Theo turns to me. "Let's keep you away from that drink for as long as possible. If for any reason Keith can't come through in time, you're gonna fake like you're sick and hide in a bathroom. When—and only when—I give the okay, can you come out and help us fight."

Reluctantly, I nod. I suppose that's a better plan than waiting outside.

When it's finally our turn at the front doors, Theo and I step out to be greeted by six guards in suits. One of them takes Theo's car keys. Another one offers Theo and me each a big fat cigar. We accept them, and I place mine into my inner jacket pocket. Then we head up the many stairs toward the mansion.

Once we're through the double doors, the smell of cigar smoke attacks my nose. I've never been a smoker, and I've always hated it. Smelling it now makes me hate it more. This is the scent of the people who kidnapped my bumblebee.

"We're coming up to the gate," Lamonte says into my ear.

A blonde woman in a tight red dress smiles at Theo and me. "Welcome to the West mansion. Would you like to check your suit coats?"

"No, thank you," Theo says.

"Me neither," I say.

"Great. Follow me then." Her red heels click with each step across the hardwood floor.

Theo and I follow her past a long line of busty women in skimpy dresses who are waiting to escort the next group of men into the party.

I try not to scowl at the women as they make my zense tingle and smile at me seductively. These ladies disgust me just as much as the men here do. They offer *willing* sex to the men who don't get off on the *unwilling* kind. It doesn't bother me that they sell their bodies. What bothers me is that they do it under this roof—the same roof that profits off torturing kidnapped women. How can they, as fellow women, be okay with that?

Red Dress Lady escorts Theo and me up a grand staircase, then down several wide hallways. The carpet looks fancy as fuck. Even while wearing dress shoes, I can feel how soft the fibers are. I glare at the plush floor once I remember how the Wests afforded it.

Down another hallway are gigantic portraits of each West man hanging on the walls. They begin with the men who've died and end with the West brothers I'm familiar with: Jamal, who's lying in a casket as of last year. Malik, the second oldest and the one my wolf almost—and should have—ended. Khalil, the third oldest and the biggest of the four. And lastly, Dom, the youngest, and known for being the cruelest.

I hate how they've got their pictures displayed on the walls as if their family is normal. This family is anything but normal. Generations of murderers and cultish behavior? *Yep, the typical American family can relate.*

"Miss?" Theo says.

Red Dress Lady turns her head but keeps strutting forward. "Yes, sir?"

"Where are the facilities?"

"There are some inside the playroom." It irks me how she can call it *the playroom* so casually.

"Is there a restroom I could use now?"

"Of course." She leads us down another wide hallway, then stops. "It's at the end of this hall, on your left."

"Thank you." Theo hands her a hundred.

She accepts it like it's a normal thing to be handed money for escorting men around this place. I guess to her, it is, which makes it more disgusting. "Thank you, sir. I'll wait here until you're finished."

I follow Theo to the end of the hall, where there's a single bathroom. While he goes in, I wait near a painting of a flowery landscape. In anyone else's home, I'd say the painting is beautiful. In here, it's fucking garbage. When Theo did research on the Wests in the past, he discovered that they use art to launder their money. All the paintings in this place are just more evidence of their culty crimes.

Theo's hushed voice comes into my ear. "Give me an update, Taryn."

"Keith just texted. He's got the anti-drug. Speeding back now. Might be another five minutes."

"Do we have five minutes?"

Taryn makes an *eh* sound. "Cuttin' it close. Lamonte, Andre, can you two stay outside for as long as you can? Keith says to roll your window down. He'll toss it into your car."

"Keith better run fast," Andre says. "We're only four cars from the entrance, and the line is moving quick."

"Just roll your windows down."

Theo stays in the bathroom for another three minutes. In that time, I count four other groups of men being escorted toward the party by dolled-up ladies in skimpy dresses.

When Theo steps out of the bathroom, I head in. My hands are shaky as I do my business.

"Keith's almost there," Taryn says.

I wash my hands for longer than usual. Then I dry off with one of the Wests' luxurious white hand towels as if leaving a single drop of water on my skin will be my demise.

When I come out of the bathroom, Lamonte says, "We've got it. Pulling up to the mansion now."

"Good," Theo says under his breath. "I'll keep soldier wolf from having a drink for as long as I can."

A moment later, my earpiece picks up a woman's voice. "Welcome to the West mansion, gentlemen. Would you like to check your jackets?"

"That's a beautiful painting," Theo says to Red Dress Lady.

"Thank you, sir. I'll pass your compliment on to the West family."

We follow her down three more hallways before we arrive at an elegant foyer with curved staircases on either side.

She gestures for us to enter. "Have a great time."

"Thank you for the escort, beautiful," Theo says and hands her another hundred.

With that, she leaves the way we came. Together, Theo and I join the crowd.

The air reeks of cigar smoke. Some glasses clink together over the sound of men chattering in little groups. Some guys look as young as nineteen or twenty. Most are in their forties and fifties. Every one of them looks like they own at least six cars, three vacation homes, and two private islands.

Several guards in suits are stationed along the walls. Each man has his eyes trained on the crowd. At the top of the staircases stand more guards—too many to count—and they've got guns. If I had to guess, I'd say those weapons aren't loaded with bullets. Zordinaries don't normally fight with bullets when our powers can do worse. Those guns are probably loaded with tranquilizers or perrizophine, a drug that blocks our powers from working.

I turn to Theo. "Security here is a little excessive, don't you think?"

"They're gonna need that many to take down your wolf."

I follow Theo toward the mini bar and see two guys standing nearby with fresh drinks in their hands. One is much taller than I am and looks like he spends as much time lifting weights as he does bleaching his asshole. As for the second guy, his height barely starts with five, and he looks like Lefou standing next to Gaston.

"I'll have a martini with your best gin," Theo says to the bartender.

"Got it," the bartender says, then turns to me. "For you, sir?"

Typically, I'd order an old-fashioned. That's Colton's favorite drink. However, tonight, I'm not Colton. I'm not

Jamie either. Right now, I'm Louis Henderson, a man from Pennsylvania who got his money through the stock market. What kind of drink does Louis like? "Same martini—dry with a twist."

"Comin' right up."

Theo nods his head at the two guys sipping their amber liquids. "Either of you a Pyro?" He gestures toward the cigar in his hand.

"Me," the tall one says. In an instant, a tiny fireball appears on his fingertip.

Once his cigar is lit, Theo turns to me. "You want yours too, or you still tryna quit?"

I'm glad that without me having to say it, Theo knows I'm not a smoker. I fake a smile. "Sorry, man. Still trying to quit."

The tall guy chuckles with his cigar hanging from his lips. "Good luck, bro. I've tried quittin' too. Many times. Wife even threatened to leave me over it. If you ask her, I've been smoke-free for two years."

The short guy laughs. "Like she's gonna leave you. Where the hell is she gonna go?"

"That's what I say too, but she assures me she's got options. I'm not tryna pay alimony, so it's easier if I just don't smoke around her. Keeps her happy. Keeps my boys happy too. They're at that age where they constantly remind daddy that smokin' ain't good for ya. Wanna guess the bitch who taught 'em that?"

The short guy shakes his head. "This is why I ain't ever gettin' married. Fuck that." He turns to address Theo and me. "You two married?"

Theo takes a long puff of his cigar, then blows out the smoke. "Was. Divorced now. Never again."

"I'm thinkin' about it with my current woman," I say. "Can't seem to bring myself to ask."

The tall guy waves his cigar at me. I hold in my cough.

"Here's some advice for you, man: Don't. Damn women only usin' ya for money anyway."

Loaded words from a guy at an event held solely to use women for their bodies.

"Two martinis," the bartender says.

Theo accepts his glass, then hands the bartender a hundred. I take my glass as well and offer the bartender the same tip. It's killing me that we're handing money straight into the palms of these monsters. However, Theo made it clear that we need to be believable. A couple of new guys with enough money to win the highest bids of the evening are the same guys who are willing to overtip the staff.

For the next few minutes, Theo and I make conversation with the tall-and-short duo. With every word that leaves their mouths, they make me want to obliterate the entire male species. I don't think I've ever met more vocally misogynistic men than these two.

I know Lamonte and Andre have entered the room when the background noise in my ear matches the noise around me.

A moment later, Lamonte's at the mini bar. "Scotch, please."

"Bourbon," Andre says.

The bartender nods. "Comin' right up."

Lamonte turns to me. "Martini, huh? Haven't had one of those in years."

"It's pretty damn good," I say and take a sip. *It's not good at all.* I'd rather be drinking an old-fashioned.

Lamonte thrusts a palm out for a shake. "I'm Jalen."

I take his hand and shake it. "Louis."

As we let go, Lamonte tucks a little pill into my palm. Resisting the urge to immediately pop it into my mouth, I casually keep my hand at my side.

Theo offers Lamonte his hand. "I'm Peter Clark. Nice to meet you."

Lamonte turns to the two guys I've been fighting the impulse to shove into an active volcano. "Jalen."

"Cornelius," the tall motherfucker says and shakes Lamonte's firm hand.

"Bobby," the short one says.

"Nice to meet you all." Lamonte gestures toward Andre. "This is my buddy, Timothy."

Andre offers everyone a head nod, then we all chat for a while. By that, I mean Cornelius talks and the rest of us listen. Apparently, the piece of shit has a misogynistic opinion about everything. Theo and Lamonte occasionally add in a few words, but they're not needed. Cornelius carries the conversation all on his own.

The motherfucker is in the middle of sharing a story about a time he was in the Maldives when Taryn's voice pops into my ear. "When are you gonna take that pill, Jamie? The z-net says the anti-drug needs at least ten minutes in your system to work."

"I already took it," I say under my breath without moving my mouth.

"What? I've been watching you on the cameras this whole time. How did I miss that?"

"I'm that good," I say behind a sip of my drink.

"Malik, six o'clock," Taryn whispers as if he can hear her.

The hairs on the back of my neck stand up as a deep voice bellows from behind me. "Looks like some of the newbies have gathered here by the bar. You boys forming a club, or somethin'?"

A man with tattoos covering his scarred face appears next to me. I barely recognize him. The only reason I know it's Malik is because his tattoos only hide so much of the damage my wolf left behind. In a diagonal across his face are three claw marks covered by tribal tattoos. He's also wearing an eye patch over his left eye. Looking at him now, I wish my wolf would have finished him off. Or at the very least, taken both eyes.

Cornelius laughs as he throws his hand out for a shake. "You must be Malik. I'm Cornelius. Heard lots about you from Sporder."

Malik shakes Cornelius's hand. "Ah, poor guy. Did you hear Drew got into an accident? Lost control of his car and went straight into a pole."

"Is that why he and his brothers ain't here yet? I've been lookin' for 'em."

"Yeah. They won't be making it. They're all in the hospital."

"Shit. That sucks. I hope they get better soon."

The pinch in my temples doesn't surprise me. I'm sure these guys secretly hate each other as much as they hate respecting women.

"Did you all come together?" Malik asks, pointing at the six of us.

"Nah." Cornelius slams a hand over Bobby's shoulder. "It's just me and Bobby."

Theo holds a hand out to Malik. "Peter Clark."

Malik makes his way around the circle and shakes everyone's hand. When he gets to me, I pretend like my wolf isn't barking like crazy, itching to tear his other eye out. "Louis Henderson."

"How often do you host these parties?" Cornelius asks.

Malik bobs his head from side to side. "Oh, we would like to do this at least a few times a year, but it's hard to put these on, ya feel? Invites always gotta be last-minute."

Does he really think *that's* what's hard about these events? What about the fact that he has to kidnap innocent women for this to happen?

Cornelius raises his glass. "Well, keep hosting, 'cause I'm havin' a great time already, and the show hasn't even started."

The show? God, I fucking hate this guy.

"Did any of you get your complimentary whiskey yet?" Malik asks.

Cornelius glances around the room. "Whiskey? Where do I go for that?"

Malik snaps his fingers at a woman in a lacey black dress. She appears moments later with a tray of lowball glasses filled with amber liquid. Cornelius and Bobby are the firsts to grab one off the tray.

Lamonte raises his scotch glass up. "I've already got a drink. Thank you."

"Nonsense!" Malik says. "Take a glass. We're gonna toast."

The woman makes her way around the circle, handing each man a glass. When she gets to me, I check my watch. It's been exactly ten minutes since I took the anti-drug.

Malik grabs the last glass off the tray, then raises it. "To more parties."

We all clink our glasses together, then take a sip. As I drink mine, I feel eyes on me. I glance up to find the guards around the room watching me—watching all of us. They've probably been ordered to keep their eyes on whoever Malik gives whiskeys to so they're ready to attack the second someone transforms into a wolf.

I wait to see if my body hums, but it doesn't. Inside me, my wolf falls onto his side and shuts his eyes. *Nap well, bud. When you wake up, this party is over.*

"Wow," Theo says. "This whiskey is amazing."

"Only the best," Malik says, still eyeing us. Eventually, when nobody turns into an animal, he lets out a sigh. "Well, I suppose I should go greet the rest of the newcomers."

A few minutes later, our little group separates to mingle with other people. Mostly, we separate because Theo and I hanging around Lamonte and Andre for too long might look suspicious.

We are in the middle of a lengthy conversation with a man

who looks like he could be my grandpa when I spot Malik stepping onto a small platform stage.

He speaks into a microphone. "Welcome, everyone!"

Within seconds, the chatter around the room dies, and all heads turn toward Malik.

"Good evening, gentlemen. I'm Malik West, your grateful host. My brothers and I are very excited that you're here tonight, because this evening is extra special. Not only is this our first party in over a year, but you will get to experience the West family initiation tradition."

The room explodes with the crowd's cheers.

I clap my hands together too, while I speak under my breath. "What the fuck does *initiation tradition* mean?"

From beside me, Theo speaks, but I hear his words better through my earpiece. "Not a goddamn clue, but if they're excited about it, I'm not."

When the crowd settles down, Malik continues, "You'll see around the house that we have thirty-five beautiful ladies you can enjoy. Pick any lady you'd like, and she will show you to a private room. For you more high-class men, we have three exotic ladies to choose from. First is a beautiful Chinese woman with long black hair you can twist and pull. Second, a gorgeous Black woman with skin so deep, you'll want to get deeper inside her. And lastly, an eye-catching Latina. At only nineteen, this one will have your mouth watering before you can even place your bid."

The crowd goes wild again. In my earpiece, Lamonte whispers, "Jesus, Jamie. You didn't tell us your girl is only nineteen."

"She's not," I whisper back. I'm not surprised that Malik lies about a woman's age to pique the interest of the older men. To these monsters, the younger, the better.

Malik continues, "Thank you for your enthusiasm! Now, if you haven't already, come see me for a complimentary whiskey. In the meantime, let's party!"

The crowd claps again, then a set of double doors swings wide open. All the men rush into the large dimly lit room, where upbeat music is blasting. Since Theo and I are in the back, we're some of the last to step inside.

I lose my breath once the doors shut behind me. Trapped in three display cases stationed around the room are the reasons why we're here. A bright spotlight shines on each woman. My Liz is in the middle, wearing a lacey white lingerie set that at any other time, I'd be happy to see her in.

If my wolf was awake, he'd be growling at the many men already surrounding her case. The bastards stare up at Liz with cigars hanging from their mouths and a filthy hunger in their eyes.

Eighteen

COLTON

"All right, boys," Theo says. "It's showtime. Perform like you're on a Broadway stage. Don't look mad. Look thirsty."

Since Chloe's display case is nearest the door, Theo and I head there first. She looks frightened, but unharmed.

Theo could be an actor. From the way he eyes up his wife in that red lingerie, I wouldn't think they're married. He looks at her like every other guy in here is, casually double-fisting drinks while examining the display cases like they're showing off precious gems in a museum.

"I'm bidding on this one," a voice says from behind me.

I turn to find that Cornelius fucker again. I've never wished for someone to catch Ebola and die before—until now.

"Why's that?" Theo asks.

"I've got a thing for Asians. I like the way they moan."

Seriously? If the universe could just get rid of this guy right now, that'd be doing the whole world a favor.

As if reading each other's minds, Theo and I don't say a word and head toward Liz's case.

In my ear, Andre says, "Take a sip of your drink if you

want me to end that guy. Take two sips if you wanna be the one to do it. Either way, this is that dirtbag's last night."

Theo clears his throat and brings his glass to his lips.

Then he does it again.

The closer I get to Liz, the more my lungs stop working. The crowd of men surrounding her is so large, I can't get within five feet of her. I'm not sure if I want to, anyway. Even from back here, I can tell she's scared out of her mind.

Through the glass, I examine her body. No cuts. No bruises. No bleeding anywhere. *Thank fuck.*

A sultry female voice comes over the speakers. "The show will begin in fifteen minutes."

I hate how well organized this whole thing is. It only reminds me that the Wests have hosted enough of these parties to have perfected every little detail from the music to the color of the balloons decorating the stage.

Malik's standing next to an extravagant balloon arch, talking to his brothers—the two who aren't dead . . . yet. With them is a teenage boy I've never seen before. Suddenly, it hits me what *initiation* means. I didn't realize their cult started so young.

After Theo and I take a few loops around Raven's case to make sure she's unharmed, we do it again with Liz and Chloe. The whole time, I try to make my face look like I'm enjoying this and simply deciding on which woman I want to bid on.

Eventually, the music volume lowers and a woman in a sparkly black dress offers to take away my empty drink glasses. The crowd claps as Malik and his brothers climb onto the stage with microphones. I force my hands to clap too.

"What do you think, gentlemen?" Malik asks. "Did we pick out some good ones?"

A round of whoops fills the air. Beside me, Theo joins in on the cheering. Again, the man should go into acting. He's not just clapping; he's getting into it, fist pumps and all.

The West brothers take turns introducing themselves, then they tell stories that highlight how rich and powerful their family is. After a while, I tune them out, mostly because my temples are aching from all the pinching.

Eventually, they invite the teenage boy onto the stage.

"You have all come on a special evening," Khalil says, wrapping his bulky arm around the boy's slender shoulders. "Our nephew just turned thirteen last week. Willie is now old enough to join the West family business. Tonight, you will witness his initiation into manhood!"

The crowd roars.

I can't decide what's worse: the Wests selling this nonsense as if it's the same as selling cookies at a family bakery, or all the men here who're happily buying it.

Dom raises a microphone to his lips. He's my least favorite of the West brothers because having a reputation for being the cruelest only puts you at the top of my shit list. "Most of you have probably never attended a West-style initiation night before. The last one was mine, and that was over ten years ago. Because of that, we didn't choose three random women for Willie. We picked three special ones. Why are these women special, you ask? You see, these are the bitches who belong to the men responsible for killing our eldest brother."

The audience erupts in boos.

Dom waits for everyone to settle, then he continues. "Jamal was Willie's father. Ever since his violent murder, my brothers and I have treated Willie like our son, because that's what a good family does."

Malik takes center stage again. "Many of you who host your own parties have your own unique traditions on initiation nights. Sometimes it's what you wear, what music you play, or the age of the women chosen. Our tradition dates back to my great-great-great-grandfather. He said it is a father's duty to teach his son right. Since Jamal could not be here, that honor has fallen onto me as the second eldest, and I shall do my brother proud!"

The excited crowd bursts into cheers again. They're all going to hell. Every. Single. One.

"Thank you for your encouragement," Malik says as he adjusts his eye patch. "This is not an honor I take lightly. On the same night that Jamal was stolen from us, the same men who killed him gave me these scars. Specifically, it was a Shifter."

The big dude next to me cups his mouth and yells out a loud *boooo!* Other men in the crowd join him.

Malik waits for the people to settle down before continuing, "Now every time I look into the mirror, I am reminded of what that Shifter did to me. What he did to my brother and his wife. He took away Willie's parents, along with my eye, my face, and any mercy I had left to give. Tonight, I shall get my revenge! Tonight, I will teach them to never fuck with the West family! Tonight, I will show Willie the way of the Wests, and I'm using the bitch who belongs to the wolf!"

The crowd goes wild again, hooting and hollering like they're cheering for their favorite football team. My body stiffens as Khalil and Dom roll Liz's display case onto the stage. It takes everything in me to remain where I am with a straight face.

Malik steps up to the glass, eyeing Liz with a sly smile. He presses his thumb against a fingerprint scanner on the side of the case. The thick glass door opens with a loud click.

My hands shake as Malik's younger brothers drag a screaming Liz across the stage. She shouts and kicks at them as they tie her wrists to a wooden post. As the men's hands touch hers, I wait for them to fall to the floor from her instant death touch. Unfortunately, they don't. I already knew an instant death touch isn't what Liz's body power is, but I sure as hell wish it was.

Sadly, even if that was her power, she wouldn't be able to

use it. Every woman I've ever rescued was drugged with perri-zophine. For about twelve hours, the injection renders all of a Zordi's gifts useless. I have no doubt Liz has been drugged too.

"Control yourself," Theo orders.

"What's going on?" Andre asks.

"His hands are shaking," Theo says.

I grit my teeth. "I can't help it. Malik is about to—" I stop because it's impossible for me to say those words out loud.

"I know, and I'm sorry," Theo says, "but I guarantee you this is his way of trying to flush you out. Look around. There's more of them than there are of us. Also, do you see those guys up there with the guns? I'll bet anything those are tranquil-izers and they purchased them just for you—your wolf. You'll be passed out before you can reach her. And once they kill you, the rest of us are fucked too—including the girls. Just stick to the plan. Wait until she's in the private room, where you can actually keep her alive."

I steal a quick look around us. It's not just the guards up top who have guns. Many guards on the floor have them too. And sadly, there are only four of us. Five if I count Keith, who's outside, waiting for the okay to speed in. Plus, without the pilot here ready to fly Liz away, doing anything now will risk her life.

"Also," Andre adds, "with your wolf still asleep, we don't stand a chance."

Andre's right, and I fucking hate it. Without my wolf, we don't stand a chance, and if I make a move now, we'll all die. More importantly, Liz will die.

I can't let that happen.

I won't.

Discreetly, I suck in a few deep breaths until my hands stop shaking. I picture Liz on my couch, cuddled up in my arms with a warm smile on her face. If I ever want to have that again, I need to be smart about this. And attacking now, while my wolf is sedated, is not smart.

It is hard though.

So fucking hard.

Especially as Malik grins and pulls his zipper down. Then he tosses his suit pants aside.

As Liz's screams echo through my ear, I silently vow to her that Malik won't live through the night.

Nineteen

LIZ

The thing about bad people is that they look like everyone else. An innocent trip to the mall can end with me walking past a guy who's soul smells like fresh vomit. Does the guy look like vomit? Of course not.

At a concert once, my seat was next to a dad of two cute little girls. While his daughters smelled of sugary cupcakes and lemon drops, the dad smelled of moldy onions in a dump truck. Did he look like a moldy onion? Not in the slightest.

There are bad people everywhere. By appearance, I can never tell who they are. They live amongst the normal, like the people who will occasionally park in handicap spaces or those who are too lazy to walk their grocery carts to the cart returns. Normal people do bad things, but they aren't bad people.

When I woke up on a private plane earlier, I had already been drugged with perrizophine. My hands were tied behind my back, my mouth was gagged, and I couldn't smell anyone's soul.

They've forced a second dose of perrizo on me since, but it's slowly wearing off now. A part of me wishes it wasn't, because this Malik guy wins the award for the most horrible soul I've ever smelled. The man reeks of a sewage plant mixed with burning flesh and a field of rotting dead animals. I'm already getting nauseous from being this close to him, and my gift isn't even working at full power.

Not only does he smell terrible, he looks it too. Malik's tattoos start at his forehead and go all the way down to his torso. I can only assume he got the tattoos in an attempt to hide his scars. A Zordi needs to be injured pretty badly for it to leave a scar. With a scar like Malik's, I can't imagine how bad his injury was.

I'd feel bad for him if he wasn't naked in front of me with a wicked fire in his eyes that makes me want to run and hide. I'd hide in a pit of vicious snakes if it meant I could get away from this guy.

I beg him not to touch me, but my words only light that fire in his eyes more. He starts by slapping my breasts and pinching my nipples through the lace lingerie so hard, I let out a high-pitched scream toward the ceiling. Tears drip from my cheeks to my bare feet as he makes his way down, pulls my panties aside, and shoves his fingers into me so painfully, it burns all the way up to my stomach. The more I scream for him to stop, the rougher he gets.

He only takes his fingers out of me when he wants to grab his erection with both hands. After giving himself a few long strokes, he grins at me devilishly, and that's when I know it's about to get worse. I shake my head and sob harder.

"Please don't," I beg between the hiccups of my cries. "Please."

With his damp fingers digging into my throat and a painful thrust of his hips, he's in.

My cries are stifled by his tight grip around my neck. No matter how hard I struggle against the ropes restraining my limbs, they don't budge. No matter how often I plead for someone in the crowd to help me, no one does. They only cheer louder.

When Malik finally pulls out of me, he's got a satisfied

grin on his face. Something wet drips down my inner thigh. I sob, feeling like a used and discarded piece of worthless scrap paper.

A woman comes out of nowhere with a steaming towel on a golden platter. As the foul man who just violated me wipes himself clean and gets his pants back on, the audience claps and hollers like we're on a game show and Malik has just given the winning answer. I'll bet anything all those men out there smell like acid, feces, and decaying skunks.

Malik's brothers untie me from the wooden post, only to drag me across the stage and lock me back inside my glass box. I slump to the bottom of it and let my tears fall harder as they roll my box to the side of the stage. Sadly, I feel safer in here than I did out there.

Fully redressed again, Malik spews bullshit into a microphone while I hug my legs to my chest and sob into my knees. I want to go home, where I can crawl into my bed, burrito myself within fluffy blankets, and never come out.

A woman's high-pitched screams make my head jerk up. Together, Malik's brothers drag the Asian woman I've been held in captivity with toward the stage. I haven't learned her name because while we were kept locked in the same dark room, we were tied up, gagged, and guarded by men who threatened to torture us with lightning balls if we so much as breathed too loudly.

I can't peel my eyes away from the poor woman as Malik's brothers tie her wrists and ankles to the same post I was just released from.

The moment thirteen-year-old Willie unzips his pants, I bury my head back between my knees. As the woman screams for help, I pray to any god who can hear me that someone will save her. However, if history is to repeat itself, no one will.

Based on the things I've been hearing around this place, I and the other two hostages are not the first people this has happened to. I'd like to know what happened to the others.

Were they killed once the night was over? Or worse, are they still here in this mansion somewhere?

Eventually, the screaming stops, and I'm able to look up again. I'm horrified by how roughly Khalil and Dom untie the crying Asian woman and throw her back into her glass box. Then they roll her box next to mine.

I want to comfort her. I'd offer her a reassuring glance to say everything will be okay, but the woman doesn't look up at me. She's too busy sobbing into her hands.

"Everyone, give Willie a round of applause!" Malik says into the mic. "Congratulations, nephew. You are now officially a man."

Where did these people get the idea that torturing women makes someone a man? I'm disgusted by the evil that exists in this world.

Malik spends the next few minutes explaining the rules of the "West-style auction." I have no idea what that means, and I'm terrified to find out.

After a bunch of nonsense about how to bid and process their payments, Malik says, "We couldn't be here without our loyal guests. The men who return every time we invite them. The men who bring their sons and friends to join us. Without you, we couldn't stay in business. That is why we're doing something special tonight to show you our gratitude. Each woman's first session is always the most coveted. There's just something about being the first man of the night, don't you agree?"

The crowd claps and hollers with vigor.

"To show our gratitude to you returning men, tonight, each woman's first session will be auctioned only to you. To qualify for this, you need to have attended at least one previous West party. As for the newbies in the house, don't you worry. You'll get your chance to play with these lovely ladies too. Now who's ready to get this auction started?"

The Black woman in the last box screams as Malik's

brothers roll her glass prison up to the stage. My heart thumps for her the heavy way it always does whenever I wake up from a night terror. I'd take a thousand nights of waking up from seeing other people's trauma over this.

"Isn't she beautiful, fellas?" Malik says. "If you're looking for a feisty one, this one's for you. She's a screamer, she's a kicker, and most of all, she'll make you want to buy her twice. Shall we start the first bid at fifteen thousand?"

Hands in the crowd shoot up. The auction goes on for a few minutes. Once a winner is finalized, the woman is rolled off the stage. She screams for help as two guards drag her out of the box and into a smaller room. I get a glimpse of a large bed right before the door shuts, muting her screams.

"How about the Asian next?" Malik says. As his brothers roll the woman's box toward center stage, tears fall from my eyes. "Long black hair for you to pull, gentlemen. As you saw earlier, she's also a screamer. Let's start the bid at fifteen thousand again."

Like before, a sea of hands shoots up. After the woman is bought, she is rolled off the stage, then dragged out of the box. Her screams are muted once she's behind a closed door of another side room.

Next, Malik's brothers roll my box to the front. I look straight into their faces, trying to remember as much about them as I can. If I ever get out of here, I want my descriptions to be so accurate, the sketch artist's drawings of them will look like photographs.

"This is the moment you've all been waiting for," Malik says. "At only nineteen, this girl is everything you've dreamed of. As you saw earlier, she's a struggler, and I can tell you from experience that she's tight. How about we start the bid at twenty thousand?"

I'm appalled by the mass of hands that flies up. Most of them belong to men in their fifties. I can't see the man who wins my auction. Whoever he is, he has promised to pay more money than I make in three years combined.

As Malik begins the auction for each woman's second session, his brothers roll me off the stage. Khalil unlocks my case with his fingerprint, then two bulky men drag me out of it. I fight with them as they carry me into a bedroom.

My shrieks are high-pitched as they restrain my wrists to the mattress. When their hands touch mine, glimpses of their worst memories shoot through my head. They're not full visions like the ones I usually get. With that bit of perrizo still in my system, their memories come to me in jagged, blurry snapshots.

From what I can see, one man was molested by his father. The other guy saw his brother get shot in the head, right outside a gas station. These are moments that they only had to live through once. When I go to sleep at night, I'll have to relive them over and over—that's assuming I'll live to see another night at all.

I sob as the two bulky men tie my legs down, then leave the room.

Panting from my cries, I tug at the ropes. They don't budge. The only thing I manage is more rope burn. I open my hands, trying to produce a water ball. I imagine the liquid forming in my palm and growing in size. The only thing that happens is a little trickle that falls to the white sheets. It makes me burst into a wailing sob. I want this to be over. When will this be over?

I'm alone for a while—so long that I begin to wonder if they forgot about me. I doubt I could be that lucky though.

Suddenly, the door opens. A pale-skinned man with salt-and-pepper hair enters the room. He shuts the door behind him, shrugs off his purple suit jacket, then kicks off his dress shoes. As he unbuckles his belt, he eyes me like he's about to eat the biggest, juiciest steak of his life.

"Please don't hurt me," I say through tears.

"Keep that up, sweetie pie. I like it when they beg." The man runs his grimy hands up my legs, then my inner thighs. With a grunt, he rips all the lace off my body. He grins deviously as he tosses the fabric over his shoulder. "Much better."

I screw my eyes shut so I can't see the way he's looking at my naked body. It's vile and inhumane. It's a type of evil I've never seen before, and that's saying something, considering I've seen many types of evil.

My tears fall harder as the man climbs over me. Not only do I feel like I'm suffocating under his thick body, but I can't breathe with the stench of his dark soul attacking my nose. He smells of dog shit and burning plastic.

No matter how much I scream, he doesn't stop. The more I struggle, the harder he goes.

When he's finally finished and slides off the bed to put his clothes back on, my throat is sore from crying. I cough a few times and try to swallow down the itchiness, but it's like swallowing tiny shards of glass.

I haven't had a drink of water since before I woke up on that plane. My mouth is so dry, it feels like sandpaper. My stomach is growling so hard, it hurts. I'm exhausted. My body aches. And most of all, I'm done. If this is what the rest of my life looks like, someone can kill me now.

I only get a few precious minutes alone before that dreaded door opens again. This time, it's a much younger man with short black hair and a scruffy beard.

He glances around the room for a moment, then stops when he catches sight of a camera attached to a corner of the ceiling. He drops his suit jacket to the floor, then unbuckles his belt. As he unties the laces of his shoes, I glue my eyes shut. I can't look into the eyes of these men anymore. The enjoyment in them destroys me.

I quiet my sobs to a soft cry as more clothes thump to the floor. I hold my breath as the man climbs over me because I can't take the smell of these men's souls anymore. Their scents are more repulsive than finding someone's diarrhea in my sandwich.

The man rubs his limp dick against my inner thighs, trying to get hard. He's less vocal than the first guy. The previous one kept calling me his *little whore* and asking me to beg him to stop. I did at first until I realized he was getting off on it. This time, I'm not going to scream, and I'm not going to resist. I can't give them that satisfaction. I won't.

I'm still holding my breath as the man runs his fingertips down my face and neck. Eventually, I can't hold my breath any longer. As I suck in some air, the man's scent rushes through my nose. His soul doesn't smell foul like I expected it to be. It smells like the ocean breeze and puppies. Lots and lots of puppies.

My eyes pop open. "Colton?"

The man's brown eyes go wide, then he smacks a hand over my mouth. Harder now, he rubs his naked body against mine, but not once does he try to put his dick inside me.

I steal a look at his torso. I recognize those abs. Those hips. That little trail of hair running from his belly button to his privates.

"Taryn," the man whispers in a husky voice, "tell them to hurry the fuck up."

The man's face—nothing on it looks like Colton's. But his soul . . . no two souls ever smell the same.

The man continues to thrust his limp dick against my inner thigh as he lowers himself to my ear. "Scream, Liz. And make it believable."

The second he removes his hand from my mouth, I let out a high-pitched wail to the ceiling. More tears fall from my eyes. This time, it's from relief. Colton's here. He's going to save me.

"That's good," he whispers. "Keep screaming until rescue comes."

Hearing the word *rescue* is like seeing a million little stars align. It's beautiful, it's perfect, and most of all, it gives me hope.

So I scream, and I shriek, and I struggle, and I yell for him to get away from me. The whole time, he doesn't stop thrusting against my—

"Fuck." Colton freezes.

"What?" I whisper.

"Our cover is blown."

Colton pushes himself off me. "When, Taryn?"

Suddenly, his eyes go wide, and he slaps his palms against my ears.

BOOM!

The bed shakes. Colton keeps his hands over my ears until the noise settles. Then he jumps off the bed and raises a hand toward the ceiling. With a strong gust of wind, the security camera crashes to the floor, smashing into pieces. Chaotic commotion rumbles from the other side of the door.

BOOM! Another explosion shakes the walls.

"How long until they can get Liz?" Colton says to nobody. Off the floor, he picks up his suit jacket and drapes it over my right hand. Then he fights with the ropes around my wrists. After he wins the battle, he drapes the jacket over my other hand and releases me from the restraints.

BOOM! This time, the explosion sounds closer.

With my hands free, I sit up. "Col—"

"Shh. Don't say my name." He rushes to my feet and tugs at the ropes around one of them.

I scoot forward to untie my other leg. Once I'm free, Colton helps me slide off the bed.

"There's no time to ex—"

The door flies open. A muscular man takes one look at me freed from the bed, then growls. A fireball appears in his palm. He launches it straight at us. Colton tackles me to the floor. Pain erupts up my tailbone as the fireball scorches the wall behind us. As Colton raises his arms, a little tornado of air spins the man out of the room. A second burst of air slams the door shut.

Keeping a hand pointed at the door, Colton helps me back onto my feet. "This won't keep them out for long." He aims his other hand at the carpet. Some air carries his dress shirt across the room until it lands in my hands. "Put that on."

I'm in too much shock to speak. I have so many questions. None come out as I shove my arms through the sleeves of his dress shirt.

Someone pounds on the door, making me jolt. "Motherfuckers!"

A loud crash comes from the room on the other side of the wall. It's the room the Black woman was dragged into.

"Liz?" My name leaves Colton's mouth like a broken plea.

I lock my eyes with his brown ones. "Yeah?"

"If I don't make it, I want you to know that I love you. I'm pretty sure I've loved you since the night we made wishes together at that fountain."

My eyes water. "I—"

BOOM!

The wall behind me explodes, and I fall to my hands and knees. Shining through the giant hole are the bright lights of a helicopter. Its whipping blades make it hard to hear anything else. I get a glimpse of the darkness outside, just as a man secured to a rope and harness leaps through the hole. A black ski mask covers his face. *Is this the rescue?*

The bedroom's door bursts open, then a naked Colton runs out, slamming the door behind him.

"No!" I shriek.

From the other side of the door, a loud and terrifying bark reverberates through my body. A man wails out in pain before suddenly going quiet. More barks echo in my ears. Running footsteps stomp in every direction, followed by blood-curdling screams and thuds.

Ski Mask Guy appears at my side, pulling me off the floor by my arm. "Come on! Helicopter's this way!"

I jerk my arm away from him. "But what about—" *Colton.*

"He'll be fine." The man grabs my forearm. "Now come on! We've gotta save one more."

I don't budge. "I'm not leaving without him!"

"The more time you waste, the more you're putting the other girls in danger. Now are you gonna come willingly, or am I gonna have to carry you?"

The man tugs on my arm again. This time, I let him.

Twenty

LIZ

The five of us barely fit in the helicopter. The pilot is in the front with the Black woman. The Asian woman and I are securely strapped to the two seats in the back. Ski Mask Guy has taken his mask off and is now sitting squished up on the floor between us. He looks Korean and like the type of guy who would offer you his ice cream because you dropped yours.

No one says a word as the helicopter coasts through the dark sky. I suppose if anyone tried to talk to me, I couldn't hear them anyway. I've never ridden in a helicopter before. I didn't realize the blades were so loud. I can't even hear myself think.

My stomach hurts like I've been slugged with a pillowcase of bricks. There's a sharp pain in my left side. I'm nauseous. My arms are numb. My head is spinning, and I feel like I could tip over and pass out any second. The other two women don't look any better. Actually, the Asian one looks like she's been electrocuted with lightning balls. Her hair is fried at all angles, and patches of it have fallen out.

I'm not sure how long it is before we finally land in an open field. It can't have been more than twenty minutes.

"I'm Elijah," Ski Mask Guy shouts over the helicopter's whipping blades as he helps me climb down from the machine. "My car's over there."

My gaze follows his pointing finger. A black SUV sits by the tree line. Without question, the other two women head toward it. Barefoot like they are, I follow them.

We all climb into the SUV as the helicopter takes off.

From the front seat, the Black woman asks, "Is Zach going back for the boys?"

How does she know the pilot's name?

"That's the plan," Elijah says as he shoves a key into the ignition. The engine turns on with a light rumble. Then he puts the car into drive, and we pull away from the trees.

"Where are the blankets?" the Asian woman asks from next to me in the backseat.

"Under you guys," Elijah answers.

From between her ankles, she pulls out a large blanket and wraps it around her shoulders, covering her entire body. The woman in the front does the same. I lean down, and sure enough, there's a blanket under my seat too. I unfold the fleece and drape it over my bare legs. My comfort level just went from a two to a three. Compared to how I felt in the mansion, though, I'm at a ten.

"There's Healing Water in the cup holders too," Elijah says.

I glance around, then spot a plastic bottle of lemon-lime Healing Water sitting in the door. I grab it and take a long-needed chug. The other women do the same with their bottles.

"I hope they're okay," the Asian woman says as she stares out the window at where the helicopter used to be.

"Don't worry, Chloe." Elijah waves a nonchalant hand through the air before slapping it back over the steering wheel. "The dream team is back. Theo, Andre, and Jamie have never failed a mission together. Well, except for the one."

Chloe's tone goes dry. "Thanks for the *highly encouraging* words, Eli, but Theo could be fighting alongside hundreds of men and I'd still wonder if he's gonna make it back home to me and the twins."

"He'll make it, Chloe. He's fighting for you this time. You shoulda seen how livid he was. He told the clan he was gonna tear apart every man in the West family himself. Andre and Jamie were pretty livid too, and you know how powerful they are. I would feel bad for the Wests, if they weren't such culty psychopaths."

A breathy sob comes from the front passenger seat. Elijah and Chloe turn their heads to the Black woman.

"Raven?" Chloe says gently. "Are you okay?"

Her shoulders shudder as she cries. "I—I just realized I don't feel sick anymore."

"What do you mean?"

Raven turns around, hiccupping. "You know what I mean, Chloe. You and I always get nauseous when our husbands go on these missions. The feeling usually fades as they make their way home, but it never just *stops*. Does your stomach still hurt right now?"

Slowly, Chloe nods. "Yes."

"And you're still nauseous?"

"Yes."

"Is your head spinning?"

"It's more like a pounding migraine."

Raven throws her head into her hands and sobs. "I'm not feeling any of that."

The car goes silent. Without saying it, we all know what has just happened. Suddenly, I'm grateful to have this nausea and the numbness in my arms. At first, I thought my body felt like this from the lack of food and water. Now I know better, and I hope this nausea doesn't suddenly stop.

For the rest of the long car ride, no one says anything. Raven cries softly and doesn't stop until we pull into the gravel driveway of a ranch-style house. The front door flies open as a woman with pink-and-blue hair dashes out.

"Chloe! Raven! You're alive!"

Chloe and Raven rush out of the car. Tears fall from their eyes as the three of them hug each other like they're best friends. Maybe they are. All these people seem to know one another—pretty well, too. I'd like to know how. More specifically, I'd like to know how *Colton* knows them.

"Are you bleeding anywhere?" Two-tone Hair Lady asks.

"No," Chloe says, swiping the corner of her blanket over her wet eyes.

"Me neither," Raven says through a tearful hiccup.

"Is the baby okay?" Two-tone Hair Lady lays a gentle hand over Raven's belly.

"I think so."

Jeez. I didn't realize she was pregnant. That makes everything the Wests did even worse.

"What about Jamie's girl? How is she?"

"You'll have to ask her," Chloe says.

"Where is she?"

Chloe waves for me to slide out of the SUV. "Hey, do you want to come inside with us?"

Inside where? I don't know whose house this is. I don't have a clue where I am. I don't even know if I'm still in the United States. No one's speaking in another language or accent, so I can only assume I'm still in the States. I can't tell which one though.

When I don't move, Elijah twists to face me. "So, uh, I don't mean to rush ya, but you've gotta get out. I have to go back to the field to get the guys."

Swallowing hard, I open my car door and step out. The sharp gravel jabs at my bare feet. I clutch the blanket around my waist as I follow the women into the house.

Any other day, I wouldn't be following three women I've never met into a house I've never been in, but from the scents

I gathered during the car ride, these people are good. Chloe smells of cherry blossoms and freshly brewed tea. Raven's scent is something like a sweet candle that's been burning throughout the house for a few hours. Elijah smells like soapy water on a baby.

"Where are we?" Raven asks as we assemble in the kitchen. I'm glad I'm not the only one who doesn't know.

"We're in Texas," Chloe says, then gestures toward the gray-haired woman cooking at the stove. "This is Betty. She's an old friend of Theo's."

Betty sets the pan of vegetables to the side and turns the stove off. "I've got clothes waiting for you three upstairs. Once you're showered and dressed, please come down to eat."

"There are only two showers here," Chloe says. "I'll let Raven and Jamie's girl go first."

If someone calls me *Jamie's girl* one more time, I'm going to flip out. "You two go ahead," I say. "I would rather sit down right now."

"Oh, sweetheart," Betty says with a hand to her chest. "Would you like me to show you to the living room?"

"That's okay. I can find it," I tell her.

The living room is just down the hall. It's dimly lit by a single lamp on a side table. Holding back tears, I slump onto the couch. With my knees pulled to my chest, I wrap the blanket around me, covering everything except my head.

My headache is fading. It's not suddenly disappearing, so I'm relieved about that. I can't fully process that I've found my soul mate, and I'm not sure if that's because of everything that just happened or because the glimmer is messing with my body. Trey told me the glimmer is both magical and conflicting at the same time. I didn't understand it back then. Now I can see why he described it that way. Couldn't there have been a more uplifting way for our bodies to tell us we've found our soul mates?

I'm only alone for about five minutes before someone steps

into the living room. It's that woman with the pink-and-blue hair. Her soul smells like a vegetable garden in full bloom. "Here. This will help with any pain you have." She holds out a bottle of berry-flavored Healing Water.

I pull the sleeves of Colton's dress shirt over my hands before accepting it. "Thanks."

She holds her other palm open. In it is a little white pill. "Take this too."

"What is it?"

"It's to make sure you don't get pregnant."

I eye the pill, then glance back up at her. My tone comes out gentle, but firm. "Sorry, I don't accept pills from strangers." It doesn't matter that these people smell trustworthy. Good people can still do bad things, and right now, I've had enough bad things happen to not want to take a risk.

The woman closes her palm and shrugs nonchalantly. "That's fine, but Jamie's not gonna be happy about that. And I can guarantee you he's gonna give *me* shit for it."

"Jamie?"

"Yeah. Your boyfriend." She sticks her fully tattooed arm out for a handshake. "I'm Taryn, by the way."

I stare at her hand, making no attempt to shake it. I might have if I was wearing gloves. This is the woman Colton was talking to at the mansion when it looked like he was talking to no one.

After a moment, Taryn draws her arm back. In the corner of my eye, I see her close her hand tightly. When she reopens it, a beautiful yellow daffodil has bloomed in her palm.

She sets the flower onto the couch cushion next to me. "For you, because daffodils symbolize hope and joy, and it seems like you could use some of that right now."

"I was told daffodils symbolize new beginnings."

"That too. These flowers are resilient. They can survive the toughest winters yet still bloom with bright colors in the spring, which is why they represent things like hope, joy, and new beginnings." With that, Taryn shuffles away. Just before leaving the living room, she twists around on her heel. "You hungry?"

I shake my head, not bothering to look up from my new flower.

"Do you want to shower?"

I shake my head again.

"You know, Liz, we're here to help you and make you feel comfortable. No ask is too big. If you need anything, just say so. One of us will get you whatever you want."

I crease my face at her. "How do you know my name?"

"Jamie told us earlier. All he said was that your name is Liz and that you're a dancer. I thought that was his way of saying he was dating a stripper, so I didn't think much of it. Then you came out of Eli's car, and I recognized you right away. I've been a huge fan of your band for years." She chuckles to herself. "Leave it to Jamie to find a mini-celebrity to date. That boy."

After Taryn leaves, she doesn't return for a while. When she does, she's got some clothes in one hand and a bowl in the other. She sets them down on the side table next to me. "I made you some soup. And by made, I mean I opened up a can, poured it into a pot, then heated it up over the stove. It's chicken noodle. Nothing fancy. If you want something else, I'd be happy to make it for you."

"I'm not hungry," I say somberly. Really, I just don't have the strength to move, and having to chew sounds like a lot of work right now.

Taryn grabs the empty Healing Water bottle from the coffee table. "Would you like another one of these? It could really help with your rope burns."

Under the blanket, I rub at the red marks around my wrists. "No, thanks."

"Mm-kay." With that, Taryn leaves again.

I stay on the couch, unmoving, until dawn creeps over the horizon.

Through the living room window, I spot the same black SUV from before pulling into the driveway. A bunch of men rush out of the vehicle, then the front door bursts open. Many pairs of footsteps stomp through the house.

"Chloe?" a man shouts. Since it's the first name he called out, I'm going to assume that's her husband.

"Oh, god!" Chloe says from the kitchen. "Your neck is bleeding!"

"Forget about me. What about you? Are you okay?"

I don't hear her answer because someone else shouts, "Where is she?"

My head perks up at the sound of Colton's voice.

"Where the fuck is she?"

"Calm your tits, Jamie," Taryn says. "She's in the living room."

Barely two seconds later, Colton drops to his knees in front of me. The only thing he's wearing is a pair of boxers. The scent of the ocean breeze and puppies greets me, and it makes me want to cry.

He's here. He's alive.

His fake beard is gone now, and his nose looks normal again. He's still got that short black hair and those dull brown eyes though. Cuts and bruises line his face and chest. A long gash on the side of his upper arm has streaks of dried blood running down to his elbow.

Colton's voice comes out broken. "Liz. Baby. Bumblebee. Are you okay?"

I nod weakly.

He cups my face, and I almost burst into tears. I didn't realize how much I needed to feel his touch. "Tell me yes or no. Are you okay?"

My voice barely rises over a whisper. "I'm okay."

He huffs out a breath, shaking his head. "Liar."

Roughly, he shoves my daffodil aside, then climbs onto the couch and yanks me against his body. I can't hold them back anymore; the tears gush from my eyes like a dam has collapsed.

The weight of everything that happened seems to fall onto my shoulders all at once: Waking up gagged on an airplane. Finding out I'd been sedated in my sleep and drugged with perrizophine. Spending hours upon hours tied up in a basement without any food or water. Being forced into lingerie and trapped in a glass box so men could look at me like I was an animal at the zoo.

Then there was Malik.

And the crowd of heartless men who watched.

All the cheering.

The clapping.

And that old guy who paid thousands of dollars to assault me too.

When I sob harder, Colton holds me tighter. He doesn't say anything. He simply caresses my arm and kisses the top of my hair. I'm not sure what I'm crying about the most—the trauma from what happened, the relief that it's over, or that Colton's alive. It's a mix of all three.

A shriek comes from the kitchen. "No!"

"I'm so sorry, Raven," a man says calmly.

"No!" she wails as she sprints out the front door.

Another man with a deeper voice says, "I'll go get her."

"No, Lamonte," someone says. It sounds like Betty. "I haven't finished cleaning your leg wound yet."

"The wound will still be there when I get back." A chair scoots across the floor, then heavy footsteps head out the door.

I tilt my head up. "Raven's husband is dead, isn't he?"

"Yeah." Colton swallows hard as he chokes up. "Theo ordered him to stay back, but Andre didn't listen."

More tears drip from my eyes. I haven't spoken a word to Raven, and I've never met her husband, but I'm devastated for them and their unborn child. "That could have been you."

He squeezes me tighter. "I know, baby. It almost was me, but I stayed back until the right time."

I glance at the wound on his arm. "You got hurt really bad."

"I'll have Doctor Betty look at it later. For now, I just want to hold you."

Colton keeps his arms around me as I cry. Letting it all out is making me feel a tiny bit better.

Eventually, my tears subside and my body stops shuddering. The house has gone quiet, with only the sounds of people shuffling around upstairs.

After a while, the front door opens again. A large Black man appears in the living room with a hiccupping Raven in his arms. "Where is everyone?" he asks.

"Upstairs," Colton says.

"Do you think there's a bed up there I can rest her on?"

"Probably."

A moment later, his heavy footsteps thump up the stairs.

Colton leans back, tenderly pulling some of my hair behind an ear. "Have you showered yet?"

I shake my head.

"Why not?"

"Because she refused to," Taryn says as she steps into the living room. She lifts a half-eaten sandwich to her mouth and takes a bite.

Colton crumples his face at me. "Why?"

I shrug.

"Wait. Are you still undressed under this blanket?"

I nod weakly.

He shoots a murderous glare up at Taryn. "Why the fuck has no one given her clothes yet?"

She throws her arms up in surrender, then points at the small table beside me. "I did. They're right there. She didn't want them. I wasn't about to force her into them. Or force soup down her throat. Or the pill. The only thing she took willingly was the Healing Water."

"What?" Colton gapes at me. "Babe, why didn't you take the pill?"

"I don't know these people. Why would I take drugs from people I don't know? Honestly, I'm questioning if I even know you, *Jamie*."

His face falls when I say his fake name. Or real name. I'm not sure which is which. For all I know, they could both be fake names.

He shoots another glare at Taryn. "I can't believe you. You've let her sit here for how long now without convincing her to take the pill?"

"Told ya he'd give me shit for it," she sings.

"Get me a fucking pill, Taryn."

"Already ahead of you." From her pocket, she pulls out the same little white tablet from earlier and holds it out to Colton. He accepts it from her as she takes another bite of her sandwich. "Also, it wouldn't hurt to say please."

Colton holds the pill out to me. "Please, take this, Liz."

"Not what I meant," Taryn says under her breath.

Colton ignores her. "Even though you're on z-birth control, you need to take this. Just in case."

I unfold my arms from under the blanket, and Colton drops the pill into my sleeve-covered hand. "Water, please."

Colton whips his attention up to Taryn. "Get me some water."

She plants the hand not holding her sandwich over her hip. Then she flashes Colton a motherly glare.

Colton sighs. "Please?"

"Better." Twisting on her heel, she exits the living room.

Less than ten seconds later, she returns with another bottle of Healing Water. It's the berry flavor again.

I place the pill onto my tongue, then chug the bottle.

"Can we get you into the shower now?" Colton asks.

Somberly, I nod. I guess a shower sounds good.

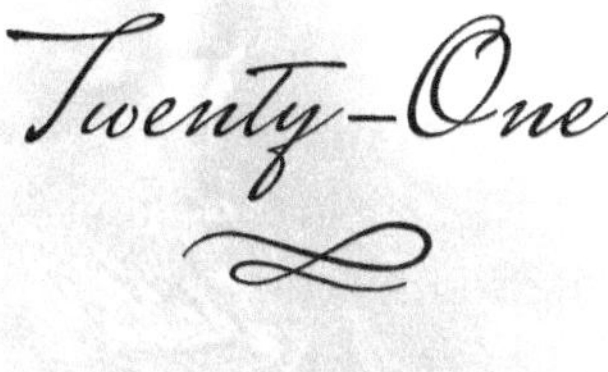

Twenty-One

COLTON

"Thanks, Betty," I say as she finishes wrapping my arm with gauze. We're stationed outside the upstairs bathroom, where Liz is taking a shower. I refused to be more than a step away from this door, so Betty was forced to bring the Healing Goo and first-aid kit to me.

"The goo will work within the next few hours," Betty says. "You might end up with a tiny scar, though, since the gash is so deep. If you can make your way to a Healer, that will help with scarring. In the meantime, get rest and chug lots of Healing Water."

Taryn's feet lightly thud down the hall. She's holding the shirt and jeans I came to Texas wearing. "I even washed them for you."

"Thank you," I say, taking my clothes from her.

"Here's your phone too." She holds out my device, which has been turned off since we left for the Wests' mansion. "Theo wants you to keep it off. He said something about getting you a burner phone to use for now. He also said he wants the entire team to get new phones once this is over. Ya know, just in case."

"Sounds good."

The ladies head back downstairs as I shove my legs into my clean jeans. I've barely gotten it buttoned when something collapses in the shower. My wolf pops up onto all fours. Shirtless, I rush into the bathroom. "Liz?"

She's crying behind the shower curtain. I peel it back to find my bumblebee hunched over in the tub with a steady stream of water falling over her body. She's got her head in her hands, and her shoulders are shaking.

I'm not sure if I should touch her or not, so I play it safe and don't. Instead, I kneel down, resting my hands over the side of the tub. "What's wrong, bumblebee?"

She says her words through tears. "So. Many. Men."

I'm not tough enough to say that some tears don't fall, because that is exactly what happens. For a few minutes, we cry together. I stare at my precious girl sobbing into her knees, wishing with all my heart that I had the power to take away her pain.

When I left this part of my life, I left because I couldn't handle how much it broke me to pieces. Now it's breaking Liz too. If I had known this would happen, I never would have pursued her. I would have stayed away from her. Far, far away.

My chest is heavy as I turn the water off, then aim a hand at the bathroom door that I apparently left open. A gust of wind closes it, giving Liz and me some privacy. I point my hand at the towel rack, and my air makes a towel fly up and hover in front of Liz until she takes it.

She dries herself off, still hiccupping from her cries. With the back of my hand, I wipe the remaining tears from my eyes, then hand her some clean undergarments.

Liz puts on the underwear, then the sports bra. I give her the leggings, then she pulls those on too. When I hold out a plain white T-shirt, she shakes her head.

"I want the dress shirt I was wearing earlier."

I don't need an explanation. I simply pluck the dress shirt off the floor, and she takes it. Once she's got the buttons done and the long sleeves folded over her hands, I rummage through Betty's drawers for a brush.

Liz is quiet as I lightly drag the brush through her curls. Droplets of water drip down her hair and onto the back of her shirt. In the mirror, Liz's face is unmoving and bleak. It eats at me. I'd do anything to erase the last day from her life.

When I'm done brushing her hair, she turns and crushes her face into my bare chest. I drop the brush, and it clunks to the floor. I don't even care, because now my hands are free to take her in. I squeeze my arms around her so tight, she lets out a strangled breath. I don't loosen my hold on her, though, and she doesn't seem to mind, only nuzzling in closer.

We stay like this for a while. With each passing minute, I'm more glad that my wolf finished off Malik. That pathetic excuse for a man did this to her, and he deserved what he got. Now he can never hurt another woman again.

"I'm hungry," Liz says into my pec.

"Let's go get you something to eat."

"Where?"

"Well, it's gotta be here. Theo said we can't leave until he's got the next step figured out."

"Oh." The way her face falls nips at my skin.

"You're safe here, bumblebee. I promise."

"I know. I just . . ."

She doesn't have to explain. If I were kidnapped, the last thing I'd want to hear is that I'm not allowed to leave a place until someone else says so. It's for her own safety, though, and I think she understands that without me having to say it.

I lead Liz down the stairs and into the kitchen. Taryn's sitting at the large table by herself, typing on her laptop. A pinkish apple is sticking out of her mouth.

"Hey, Taryn. Could you make Liz something to eat, please?"

She peeks up from her laptop and takes the apple out of her mouth. "Sure. What do you want?"

"Is that soup you made earlier still in the living room?" Liz's voice is soft and somber.

Taryn pushes herself away from the table and stands. "Yep. I'll heat it up for you."

"Thank you." Liz takes a seat at the table, staring at the wood with a desolate look in her eyes. I stare at her, willing that sad look to disappear. Something tells me it's not going away for a while.

I'm about to step out toward the living room when Liz's voice stops me. "Where are you going?"

I turn to find her with her eyebrows all screwed together. "I was gonna go ask Betty if she's got any gloves."

"Don't leave me."

Those three words slice at me more than she'll ever know. Within half a second, I've got my ass planted back in my chair. I give her knee a reassuring squeeze that says, *I will never leave you.*

Taryn reappears with a bowl in her hands. She puts it into the microwave, then presses a few buttons. From the fridge, she grabs two bottles of plain Healing Water and sets them onto the table in front of me. "Drink up, Jamie. Those cuts on your face don't look too hot."

I take my hand off Liz's knee so I can open one of the bottles. "Could you ask Betty if she's got any gloves?"

Taryn takes a bite of her apple. "What kind of gloves?"

"Any. Rubber, latex, boxing, winter, whatever. Preferably satin, but anything will do."

"On it."

Taryn isn't normally the one who takes care of the rescued women after we get them out; however, since the two women who normally do those duties are the ones we rescued, Taryn is stepping up. This isn't a job I'd want, so I commend her for doing it.

Theo's voice roars from the living room. "Those cock-sucking sons of bitches!"

I'm not sure what he's shouting about, and I don't care. Right now, my only concern is Liz. Inside, my wolf nods. He also feels the need to have Liz in our sight at all times.

The microwave beeps.

I offer Liz an apologetic look. "I'm gonna stand to grab your soup, okay?"

I only move once she gives me a nod of permission, then I immediately return to where I belong, with her warm bowl in hand.

Liz is blowing onto her spoon when Taryn returns. She's got a pair of rubber cleaning gloves and some green gardening ones. "This is all Betty's got."

"Which ones, bumblebee?"

Liz takes a glance at her options, then says, "Gardening, please."

Taryn sets the green pair onto the table.

"Thank you." Liz's shoulders relax once her hands are covered. I make a mental note to get her a better pair of gloves the second I'm able to.

Back behind her laptop, Taryn eyes Liz. "You know, whenever I watched your YouTube videos, I always thought your gloves were just a part of your unique style. Now that I know you're a Zordi, I'm beginning to think it's not."

Before I or Liz can respond, Theo calls from the living room. "Jamie! Come here! We've gotta talk."

I take a drink of the Healing Water. "You're gonna have to come to the kitchen. I'm not leaving Liz's side."

Footsteps thump down the hallway until Theo takes the seat between me and Taryn. Gauze is taped to the side of his neck where someone tried to slit his throat. Theo said my wolf ripped into the guy just in time. "Bad news."

"Hit me with it," I say.

"Remember when we looked around at all the bodies and couldn't find Dom or Willie?"

"Yeah?"

"Well, you said maybe your wolf pulled them apart so much that they were in unrecognizable pieces. Unfortunately, they're not. They're alive and well. I just finished going through the footage we have from Taryn, and I saw those two cowards dippin' outta there the second they heard the first explosion. And damn, they're out for blood."

"How do you know?" I ask.

Theo turns to Taryn. "You wanna explain?"

"Don't need to. I'll just play the video." She twists her laptop around for Liz and me to see. "This happened about an hour after the clan vacated the mansion." Taryn presses the spacebar.

Video footage of Dom and Willie in the event room plays. They're surrounded by bodies lying all over the floor in pools of blood.

"We're gonna get 'em for this," Dom says on the screen. "We're gonna find every single person on their stupid little team and kill 'em. Then we'll mail back pieces of their bodies to their families every day for the next year."

Liz's shoulders stiffen.

I put my arm around her. "Don't worry, bumblebee. I won't let that happen."

"Neither will I," Theo says. "That's why we're gonna find them before they can find us. Unfortunately, Dom and Willie found out that we hacked into their security system. They've since shut everything down and have abandoned the mansion. Keith is keeping watch around that area in case they return, but I have a good feeling they won't. That means we need to find out where they've run to before we make our next move. I'm not sure how long that's gonna take. Could be a few days, could be weeks.

"In the meantime, the clan is separating into small groups. Eli is going with Zach. Lamonte's taking Raven. I've got Chloe and Taryn. You're taking Liz. Taryn's in the middle of making fake IDs for everyone. I'll set you up with some cash and a credit card. Eli and Zach are out getting a vehicle for you right now. I suggest you bounce around some hotel rooms until we've located the remaining Wests. After that, we'll regroup and come up with a plan."

I nod. "Got it."

Taryn raises a finger into the air. "So, um, Jamie's dating a mini-celebrity. While I'm happy to make Liz's fake ID with her current picture, if someone recognizes her, that could be trouble. All someone has to do is post a picture of her with the caption, 'OMG I just saw Liz Hart in Arizona' or 'Spotted Liz from Flames in the Night at a Starbucks in Florida' and the Wests will know exactly where they are."

Theo turns to Liz, who's finishing the last spoonful of her soup. "You're famous?"

Liz shakes her head as she sets her spoon down. "Not really. My band is big on the internet, so some people know me, but I'm no Selena Gomez."

"But you're known enough to get recognized?"

"I can usually make quick trips into a grocery store, no problem, but I can't roam a mall without someone asking for a selfie."

"Hmm. That's a problem." Theo taps his chin. "Depending on what places you go in and out of, you may or may not get recognized. Are you opposed to cutting and dying your hair?"

"No."

"All right. I'll call Meera." Theo pushes away from the table and heads back into the living room. "Hopefully, she hasn't gone too far."

Taryn picks up her laptop and stands. "I'm gonna give you two some space while I work on these IDs. Holler for me if you need anything."

Once we've got the kitchen to ourselves, Liz asks, "Who's Meera?"

"One of Theo's disguise specialists."

"Is she the reason your hair is black and your eyes are brown?"

"Oh." I pop the contacts out. I forgot I was wearing them. I got used to them after a while.

Liz glances into my eyes and nods. "Better."

"How did you recognize me? In the mansion, your eyes were closed, but you knew it was me."

"Your soul's scent," Liz says as if I should know what that means. "It's my mind power. My brain can sense people's souls and tell me if they're good or bad by turning their soul's energy into a scent. Those doses of perrizo they shot into my bloodstream were wearing off by the time you got to me, so even though your scent was faint, I still knew it was you, because no two souls smell alike."

I've never heard of this mind power before. It must be pretty rare—like my Liz. "What does my soul smell like?"

"The ocean breeze and puppies, which makes sense now that I know you're an Aero and a Shifter wolf."

"Does that scare you?"

Liz shakes her head, and I breathe out in relief. "Despite the reputation Shifters have, it's not being able to transform into an animal that makes a Shifter bad. It's what's in here." She points a gardening-glove-covered finger at my chest.

"Now that I know your mind power, would you like to know mine?" I ask.

"I have a guess. Are you a Detector?"

I nod. "How long have you known?"

"Since earlier on the couch. It occurred to me why you needed to hear me tell you *out loud* if I was okay."

"You know all my powers now." *And I only know one of yours.* I really want to know what body power she has that makes her feel so uncomfortable without hand protection, but now is not the time to ask.

"And I don't even know your real name."

"You do, but around the clan, I go by Jamie."

Liz tilts her head to the side. "Why?"

"Theo says it helps keep our identities hidden from our enemies. This way, while we're on our missions, we'll never accidentally say each other's real names within earshot of the bad guys. Honestly, though, I think it's because Theo wants to make it easier for us to compartmentalize what we do here. It's easier to pretend we're not killers when we only kill as our alter-ego."

"So everybody here has a codename? Even the women?"

I let out a soft *mm-hmm*. "Chloe picked her name because it uses some of the letters in Theo. Raven did the same with Andre."

Liz thinks for a moment, then nods. "That's really clever. What about Taryn?"

"Taryn chose Taryn because the name means trespasser, which is fitting for the work she does."

"I see. And who are you people exactly?"

"We don't have an official name or anything. Theo just calls us *the clan*. We rescue Zordi women from sex crimes."

Liz nods like it's finally clicking for her. "How long have you been in this rescue group?"

"Technically, I'm not anymore. I left over a year ago. Before that, I was in for five years."

"How did Theo recruit you?"

"He didn't. Andre did. At the time, Andre and I were just work buddies. On the job sites, we always got along well, so we started hanging out after work too. Eventually, we became close enough for me to tell him that I'm a Shifter wolf. That's when he asked me if I'd be interested in meeting his friend Theo. All he said was that Theo would help explain his occasional sudden absences from work. I was curious, so I said why not?

"Later that week, I met with Andre and Theo at a secluded park, where Theo arrived with an extensive background check on me. At first, I was like, *what the fuck?* But once

Theo said the words *rescue innocent women* and *your wolf could be the advantage we need,* I was in."

I don't remember much from that secretive conversation. All I remember is how Theo made it a point to say, *"You know, I'll cover stuff like travel expenses and trips to a Healer, but this isn't a paid job."* I was a little offended by that, because not once during our conversation did I think about being compensated for saving kidnapped women.

The kitchen goes silent for a moment before Liz asks another question. "Are there more groups like this out there?"

"Yes. Two. They were started by people who branched off of Theo's original group. Two of his men didn't agree with the way Theo runs the show. One guy wanted to be a team that focuses on ending the lives of every single person involved with the sex crimes. That includes the hosts, the guests, the sex workers, and all the staff. He's got a pretty big team, and they end all their missions with a lot of bloodshed, even sacrificing the victims if they have to. To him, the sacrifice is worth it if it keeps more innocent women from becoming victims in the future."

Liz's scrunched face tells me she doesn't agree with that team's philosophy. Neither do I.

"The second guy is the opposite. His team focuses solely on saving the victims. They're stealthier and refuse to kill unless it's in self-defense. As for Theo, he likes to stay somewhere in the middle. His primary goal is to get the victims to safety. If it means ridding the world of some men who treat sexual assault like a leisure hobby in the process, he won't lose sleep over it, but he won't go out of his way to ensure that every single person involved is dead by the end of the night—except for tonight. Our goal was to get rid of *all* the West men, and we failed."

"You guys saved all the victims though."

"But because Dom and Willie got out alive, they could still

continue their culty bullshit, which means it's only a matter of time before more innocent women get hurt."

Liz stares at her empty soup bowl with a desolate expression. I can't imagine the trauma that's replaying in her head right now. I mean, I saw it happen, but it's not the same as being the one who experienced it.

"Bumblebee," I say, putting a gentle hand over her forearm, "I promise I'll make this right, okay?"

She continues staring at the empty bowl. "It's not your job to make this right. It wasn't your fault."

I take her gloved hands into my bare ones and squeeze them tight. "But if you weren't associated with me, they never would have kidnapped you."

"But how could you have known?"

She's right, I couldn't have. That doesn't make the guilt any easier to swallow.

I can't believe how forgiving she is when I still haven't forgiven myself. If I were her, I wouldn't want anything to do with me.

"The Wests took you because I took out their eldest brother last year and damaged Malik's face in the process."

"How did you do that?"

I lean back in my chair and let out a long sigh as flashbacks of that dreadful night come back to haunt me. This story won't be easy to tell, but Liz deserves to know what happened. I suck in a deep breath, mentally preparing myself to share the details of my darkest night. It takes me another three deep breaths before I'm ready to talk.

"About two years ago, the clan heard of the West family and how they were one of the best sex cult businesses out there." I put air quotes around *business*. "To me, having a rep for being the *best* makes them the *worst*. So Theo did some digging. It took a long time for him to find the Wests, but once he did, the clan made plans to take them down before they could host another one of their nasty parties.

"So a little over a year ago, the clan invaded the home of Jamal West with the intention of taking only him out. Then we planned to leave behind a warning note that if they didn't stop hurting people, we'd come after the rest of them.

"Sadly, our team severely underestimated how sick and twisted the West family is. Once inside their big-ass mansion, Theo, Andre, and I split up. The plan was for one of us to find Jamal, then wait for the other two to get there before making a move. Then we'd all attack him together and it'd be another great day of saving the innocent."

"Let me guess," Liz says. "That's not what happened."

"Nope. While Theo and Andre searched for Jamal on the main level and upstairs, I went downstairs. I snuck around for a while before coming to the end of a hall, where I heard a little girl screaming. And when I say *little*, I mean that she couldn't have been more than five or six."

Liz gasps. "No."

"Yes. They're fucking sick. Theo ordered me to wait until he and Andre got down there, but I lost control. My wolf couldn't stand hearing that little girl shrieking like that. He forced me to shift, and he went in for the attack himself.

"Since I can see the first five to ten minutes of what my wolf does through his eyes, the first thing I saw was him tearing through that locked door as if he was ripping through flimsy paper. Then I saw Jamal and his wife abusing and mutilating that tied-up little girl with knives and a bunch of other sharp things I can't even name. My wolf went insane. He attacked Jamal and his wife like it was his life's purpose.

"Unfortunately, before Theo and Andre could get down there, Malik did first. He was in another room nearby and heard the commotion. He stormed in, found my wolf, then shot fireballs at him. My wolf attacked him back, which is evident from what you saw."

I swallow hard as I prepare myself to say the next part. "A few of Malik's fireballs hit the little girl. Her hair lit up in flames, and her screams caught the attention of my wolf. He immediately tried to save her. However, in his panic, he—" I choke up, and the words get caught in my throat. *I can't do it. I can't say it.*

Liz places her gloved hand over my forearm and whispers, "It's okay."

"No. It's not okay, Liz. He killed her. My wolf killed her. He was only trying to put out the flames on her head, but he accidentally dug his claws into her instead. She was already dead by the time Theo and Andre got down there.

"When we looked it up later, the autopsy determined that she didn't die from the flames or sexual abuse, or even the mutilation. Her death was caused by the animal puncture wounds in her neck."

Liz takes one glove off to wipe away the wetness dripping down my cheeks. "Col—I mean, Jamie, it was an accident. You can't keep beating yourself up for it."

I despise hearing the name *Jamie* come out of Liz's mouth. She never should have had to use it. "I don't think you understand. I was supposed to *save* that little girl—not kill her. My wolf may be in control when he's out, but he's still a part of me, which makes him my responsibility. That's why I left the clan. I didn't want to be responsible for ending another innocent person's life ever again. I hate myself for it. I also hate myself for what happened to you."

I lower my tone, because I want her to hear how much I truly mean my next words. "I am so sorry, Liz. I'm sorry that you got roped into this mess, and I'm also sorry for slapping my hand over your mouth so hard back when we were in the mansion. You said my name out loud while the cameras were on, and I panicked. My only instinct was to keep up the charade until the helicopter arrived. I was afraid that if they saw that recognition in your eyes or caught you saying my name, they'd bust into that room and kill us both."

Liz's face drops. "Was I the one who blew your cover?"

"No, it was Andre. The monster who won Raven's first session was taking his sweet time getting into her room because he was too busy sharpening his knives first. Apparently, Jamal and his wife aren't the only ones who get off on mutilating people for fun. Andre was hoping the helicopter would get there before the guy was ready, but nope.

"As soon as Andre saw that man strutting into Raven's room with all that freshly sharpened metal, he rushed in to protect her. Honestly, I don't even blame him. If that had been you, I would have done the same."

Liz shakes her head. "But then you'd be dead—like . . ."

She doesn't need to finish her sentence for me to know her next word. If I had done what Andre did, I'd be dead like him. Watching Malik hurt Liz on that stage was horrifying, but I can see now that Theo was right: If I had reacted at that time, I wouldn't have made it out of there alive. Chances are, Liz wouldn't have either. I hate that Andre had to die for me to fully understand that.

"Anyway," I say, trying to shove all thoughts of Andre's death from my head, "once Andre rushed into Raven's room and killed the guy with the knives, our cover was blown. The Wests' guards rushed into action, and the guests started running away, thinking the party had been crashed by undercover Enforcers. Thankfully, Theo was already in Chloe's room and I was in yours. Andre fought a good fight, but in the end, he was killed by Khalil."

Liz bites down on her bottom lip, crinkling her forehead together. "So Malik and Khalil are dead, but Dom and Willie got away?"

"That's right."

"Who killed Khalil?"

"Lamonte. As soon as he saw Khalil drop Andre's lifeless body to the floor, he went ballistic. Within seconds, Khalil wasn't breathing either."

"Who killed Malik?"

"My wolf," I say, then take a sip of my Healing Water. "As soon as I left your room and shifted, Malik was the first person my wolf went after. And I'm not gonna sugarcoat this for you. He ripped into everyone on the way there." Because Liz's face remains impassive, I can't tell how she feels about knowing that a part of me is a vicious animal.

"Why aren't the Enforcers doing something about this?"

"Because when it comes to dealing with sex crimes, the Zordi police are as useful as a used match in a freezing rainstorm. I mean, they try—just not in the same way the clan does. Instead of focusing on saving the women, the Enforcers focus on making arrests. They care more about putting those bad men behind bars than they do about saving the victims.

"Theo's a former Enforcer who worked in the sex crimes department. After a year, he got sick of how often he saw more dead women's bodies than live ones. That's why he left the zovernment and secretly formed his own rescue team who would actually care about the victims—a team whose main priority is to get the women to safety, no matter what it takes." *Even if it means losing one of our own.*

That's something that sets Theo's clan apart from the Enforcers. He always reminds us before a mission that going in doesn't necessarily mean you'll come out. For years, Andre risked his life to save innocent women and never expected anything in return. I hope his baby grows up knowing their father was a hero.

I suppress my tears as I continue, "When Theo was an Enforcer, his uppers would order him and his team to get out whenever they were too outnumbered, which happened often, even if it meant leaving the victims behind to die. Theo became an Enforcer to serve and protect but left once he realized that the zovernment prioritizes serving and protecting themselves more than kidnapped women."

Liz shakes her head like a mother disappointed in her child. "What a sad world we live in."

A knock on the front door startles me.

On his way to answer the door, Theo calls out, "Meera's here."

A moment later, he strolls into the kitchen with Meera at his side.

"Ready for a makeover?" Theo asks.

Liz nods, but it's not eager. "Ready."

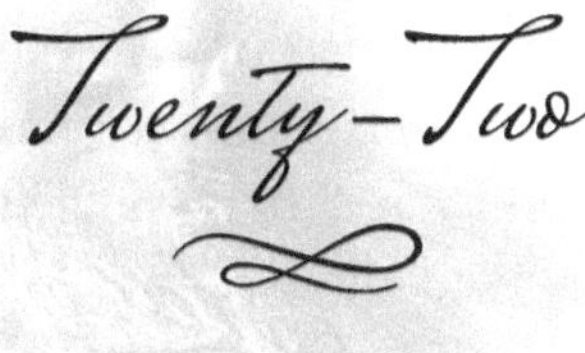

Twenty-Two

COLTON

Two hours later, most of the clan has already left in pairs to go into hiding. Theo, Chloe, and Taryn are the only ones left here. Betty, too, since this is her house.

Liz is upstairs with Meera, getting her hair done. Earlier, I insisted on being in the room with them, but Meera complained about me crowding her space. That's why I'm sulking in the kitchen by myself, waiting for them to be done.

When Liz finally returns downstairs, she's got straight blonde hair cut to her jawline.

"What do you think?" she asks, running a gloved hand through her new locks.

I prefer her cherry-brown curls, but I'm not about to say that. "You look different. Still beautiful though."

"I think different was the goal. Taryn already saw it since she had to take a picture for my fake ID, and she said I was mostly unrecognizable."

I gesture toward the corded item tucked under Liz's arm. "What's that?"

"A hair straightener. Meera's giving it to me so I can tame my curls while we're lying low."

"Perfect." I gesture a hand toward the large kitchen window. In Betty's driveway, a beat-up Honda Accord waits under the hot sun for us to climb into. "That's ours. Once Taryn finishes your ID, will you be ready to hit the road?"

"Yes."

Fifteen minutes later, Theo marches into the kitchen with a lightly worn backpack and hands it to Liz. "Here's a bunch of stuff you guys might need: hats, sunglasses, makeup, whatever. I've already thanked Betty for you, since this was mostly her stuff."

"Thank you." Liz accepts the backpack, then thunks it onto the dining table to stick her new hair straightener into it.

"Your IDs are in the front pocket, along with a burner phone, some cash, and two credit cards. Try to stick to the cash whenever you can. The cards are for emergencies. In the meantime, keep your personal phone off."

"Thanks, Theo," I say.

"No need to thank me. This is just what I do. Now remember, before you find a hotel, get out of Texas first."

I flash him a thumbs-up. "Got it. Anything else?"

"Nope." Theo sticks his palm out for a shake. "Take care, Jamie."

I take his hand and pull him in for a hug. As I pat him on the back, I say, "You as well. Don't let Chloe outta your sight."

He chuckles. "Don't worry. From now on, she's not getting away from me, even if she tries." With a warm smile, he turns to Liz. "You take care too."

Liz returns his warmth with a small smile of her own. "I will. Thank you."

After a few waves goodbye, we climb into the beat-up Honda, then pull away from Betty's house.

As I drive us down the gravel road, I say, "I called in to work already. I also called Dixie to let her know you'd be out for a week."

"What did she say?" Liz asks.

I drop one hand from the wheel and adjust my seat to get more comfortable. "She asked what I did to piss you off so bad that you decided to skip work. I played along and told her that we got into a huge fight."

"Did she ask you what we fought about?"

"Nope, she just went straight into threatening to shave off all my *precious blonde curls* if I didn't make it up to you."

Liz nods with her lips pursed. "Sounds like Dixie."

"I told her I am taking you on a weeklong vacation as an apology."

"Oh, I'm sure Dixie ate that up. She loves stuff like that. I swear, that woman reads at least three romance books a week."

"I believe that. She told me if you were still mad at me by the end of the vacation, she'd personally pay for us to go on another one."

The smile on Liz's face is faint, but it's there. "I love that woman."

"Is there anyone else we need to call for you so they don't worry?"

"No."

"Are you sure?" Because I can think of at least *one* person in Liz's life she should probably call.

"Yeah, I'm sure."

I make a right turn to get off the gravel road and onto a paved one. "What about Trey?"

Liz gazes out the passenger-side window with a gloomy look in her eyes. "He doesn't usually contact me until Thursdays, after his plane has landed."

"What about the rest of your band?"

"They'll be fine without hearing from me."

"Okay. What about your family?"

"Trey is my only family."

How can that be? I still don't know what happened between Liz and her sisters, but doesn't she have parents?

The car falls silent for a few miles. Every time I glance over at Liz, she's got a blank look on her face as she stares out the windshield. She barely moves. She barely makes a sound either. I wish I knew what she was thinking about, but I'm also too afraid to ask.

"Bumblebee?"

Liz keeps her stare out the windshield as she says, "Yeah?"

"Why don't you take a nap? I'm sure you're exhausted."

"I am, but I can't nap right now. If you want to nap, I'd be happy to drive."

"I'm feeling all right. You just sit back and relax, okay?"

A quiet hour on the interstate later, I spot a superstore just off the road. As I turn toward the exit, I say, "I'm gonna run in and grab some things we need. I think it's best if you stay in the car. I don't want to risk you being recognized, even with your hair blonde."

Liz nods her agreement. "What things do we need?"

"Lunch, snacks, water, clothes, toiletries, and a pair of gloves. Do you have any other requests?"

She could tell me she wants salmon and pickle-flavored ice cream, and I'd find a way to get her some. All she says, though, is "Nope."

"Could you put some sunglasses on while you wait for me?" I ask.

"Only if you wear some inside the store too."

"Deal." I rummage through Betty's backpack to find two pairs of sunglasses. I have Liz choose the ones she wants first, then I pop on the second pair. With a baseball cap over my black hair, I exit the car and make sure it's locked before I walk away.

Not long later, I return with a cart full of goodies. I dump most of the bags onto the backseat, then return to my spot behind the wheel with one plastic bag.

"Did I just see you pushing a cart?" Liz asks. "I thought you hate those."

"I do, but I had a lot of shit to buy and a basket couldn't carry it all. Besides, for you, I'd push a cart all day." That earns me a tiny smile from her.

Out of the bag in my lap, I pull three pairs of princess dress-up gloves, purchased from the girl's toy section. They were the only satin gloves I could find, and I figured the largest size would fit Liz just fine. "Cinderella blue, Aurora pink, or Belle yellow?"

"You already know which ones I want."

I set the pair of Belle gloves onto her lap. "I'll put the others in our backpack, in case you need them later."

After she yanks off Betty's gardening gloves, she slips into the princess ones. Then she looks up at me with soft eyes. "Thanks, Colton. You don't even know why I need gloves, but you feel the need to make sure I have some anyway. I appreciate that."

Hearing her call me by my real name makes my insides melt into a pathetic little puddle. I could listen to her say my real name all fucking day. I feel the urge to pull her in and give her a long, hard kiss. I don't, though, because I'm not sure where she's at with physical touch. Until she makes the first move, I'll keep some distance.

A few hours later, a giant sign on the side of the road welcomes us to Oklahoma. The sun is beginning to hide for the day, and Liz hasn't stopped yawning. My eyes are getting heavy as well, so it's about time we found a hotel.

When I pull into the parking lot of a crappy-looking motel, Liz says, "I'll need my own room."

I'm about to laugh and tell her there's no fucking way, then stop. Her refusal to sleep over with me, the way she said she *can't* nap, and her *need* for her own room. What isn't she telling me? "Could you explain *why* you need your own room?"

She doesn't look at me. "I just do."

"Liz, I'm not about to leave you *alone* for an extended

period of time with the situation we're in, so I'm sorry, but the answer is no."

She fidgets with the fingertips of her new gloves. "I'm not asking you, Colton. I'm telling you."

Liz has never spoken to me so demandingly before. Whatever her reason is, it must be serious. Unfortunately for her, I'm just as serious. "If the Wests find out where we are, I can't protect you from a separate hotel room. Is whatever reason you don't want to sleep in the same room as me worse than death?"

She aims her gaze out the window. "I guess not."

"That settles it then. We're getting one room."

Her attention falls to her hands in her lap, and suddenly, she looks sadder than she did earlier.

Lowering my tone, I say, "I'm sorry, Liz, but my number one priority is to protect you."

"I know."

I let out a little sigh. "Would it help if we got separate beds?"

"No," she says with a light huff. "If you're gonna be in the same room, we might as well share a bed."

All righty then. Now I'm even more curious to know what she's hiding. Why does she need walls separating us rather than a mattress? Normally, I'd ask, but Liz doesn't seem to be in the mood to explain.

The hotel lobby attendant barely looks at me as she hands me back my fake ID. While smacking loudly on her gum, she hands me a key card. "Second floor. Elevators are that way." She points down the hall.

Liz and I grab our backpack and grocery store bags, then head that direction.

Our hotel room smells of musty floor with a hint of cleaning supplies. The ceiling is yellowed like there's been a long history of cigarettes smoked in here. I don't care though. Any room with a bed is acceptable right now.

I rummage through our bags until I find the one with the clothes I picked out for Liz. "I got you some items I think you'll like."

Liz takes a seat on the edge of the queen-size mattress. "Let's see 'em."

The first thing I pull out is a yellow T-shirt with the words *bee kind* on it. The dot of the *i* has been replaced with a cute little bumblebee.

Liz nods her approval. "Nice."

The second shirt I pull out is also yellow, featuring the words *One Ring to Rule Them All* in black. "I didn't know if you're a *Lord of the Rings* fan, but I am."

"I am too, mostly because I love Aragorn."

"But he's not blonde."

Liz rolls her eyes, but a tiny smile cracks over her cheeks. "Contrary to what Dixie believes, I am attracted to men who aren't blonde. I love Aragorn because he's what every man should be: loyal, kind, and respectful to women."

Sounds like someone needs to introduce the West family to my favorite movie trilogy. They should all watch it and take notes.

Knowing that Liz is a *Lord of the Rings* fan only makes me love her more. I hand her the bag with the rest of her new clothes in it. "Sports bras, underwear, pants, and more shirts. I hope they all fit, because I guessed your size. Oh, and there are some pajamas in there too."

Liz digs through the bag until she pulls out a matching pajama set with sunflowers on it. Another hint of a smile appears on her lips, and it warms my soul. "Do you know why yellow's my favorite color?"

"Why?"

"Because yellow is bright and happy. Whenever I wear it, it reminds me to be a source of happiness for others in this world full of sadness."

I gaze into the eyes of the most amazing woman I've ever

known—besides my mother and Chrissy, of course. In my head, I tell Liz, *I love you.*

Back at the mansion, I said those words to her in the heat of the moment, just in case I'd never get the chance to. I think about saying it again now, but something tells me this isn't the right time.

Once we're ready for bed and Liz is in her new pajammies, as she calls them, we nestle under the covers together. I consider asking her to cuddle, but she turns over and falls asleep before I can gather the courage to. It doesn't take long for me to fall asleep either.

It also doesn't take long for me to wake back up to the sound of Liz shrieking.

Twenty-Three

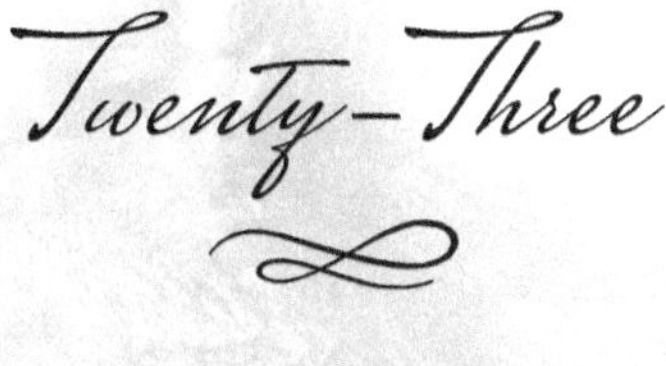

COLTON

She's flailing her arms. "Stop! It hurts!"

"Liz?" I spring upright. "What hurts?"

She responds with more screams.

I place a hand over her shoulder. "Liz, tell me what hurts."

"Don't touch me!"

I back off and slide off the bed. The blankets are already in a heap on the carpet.

Liz pants heavily with her eyes screwed shut. "Please, stop!"

Suddenly, it hits me: I see this in movies all the time. I rush back over the bed and shake her until she wakes.

With a jolt, she sits up and her eyes pop open. Her chest rises and falls with heavy breaths as her eyes dart across the room. She must realize she's safe, because after a few deep breaths, her shoulders relax. With her gloved hands, she wipes off her wet cheeks.

I want to hold her but don't, afraid I'll scare her more. "Are you okay?"

She swallows like she's got rocks in her throat. "How much of that did you see?"

"Uh, maybe just the last part, but to be honest, I'm not really sure what I saw. Zordis don't have dreams, and it looked like that's what you were having." I give her a moment to respond. When she doesn't, I scoot closer to her and tenderly wipe a tear off her cheek. "What was hurting you?"

"No."

I didn't ask a yes or no question, so . . . *huh?*

Instead of trying to get her to explain, I switch to comforting her. She seems to need that more than I need an explanation, so I lean back against my pillow, then pat my shoulder. "Come here, bumblebee."

She practically throws herself at me, and it makes my heart swell. It's a relief to know it wasn't *my* touch she was afraid of a second ago.

As soon as her head hits my chest, she bursts into tears.

"It's okay. I've got you." I hold her tighter against me and place a gentle kiss against the top of her hair.

She continues crying into my shirt, and for a while, I don't move. I don't talk either. I just hold her until her tears settle and her body stops quivering.

A digital clock on the desk across the room says it's 12:35 a.m. We barely got three hours of sleep. I need more, and I'm sure Liz does too. Also, my stomach is rumbling. We stopped for tacos on the way to the hotel, but they weren't that filling. I think about asking Liz if she's hungry but continue holding her instead. I don't want to break this sense of comfort we're sharing.

Eventually, she pushes herself off me and sits up with her legs crossed. "Could you just pretend like none of that ever happened?"

"Is that really what you want?"

"Yes."

Nothing pinches my temples, so I say, "Okay."

She raises her brows, giving me a wary look. "Really?"

"Yeah, really. If you're saying you want me to just forget it, then that's what I'll do."

Her jaw drops slightly. "How are you so accepting of me? Like without wanting any details?"

"Just because I'm accepting doesn't mean I'm not curious. Of course I want details, but if you're not comfortable explaining right now, that's okay. Although I do have a feeling that your surface want is for me to forget this, while your deeper want is something else."

Her expression slowly fades from shock to what looks like shame, which only confirms I'm correct. I don't understand though. She has no reason to be ashamed of anything. I'm the one who's got a shameful past. Not her.

Suddenly, an idea pops into my head. Before I can talk myself out of it, I say, "Could I tell you something terrible about me?"

Liz flicks her eyes up to meet mine. "Only if you want to."

I suck in a deep breath of courage, then blow out the apprehension. "When I used to do these missions with the clan, my job was just to get the women to safety. After that, I'd never see the women again. Chloe and Raven are the ones who'd comfort the victims and get them proper clothes, pills, and medical attention. Typically, the men would help out however they could, but after I helped a few times, I couldn't be a part of that process anymore. It was too hard for me—more specifically—my wolf.

"He couldn't understand why Theo would always order him to leave before he could rid the world of all those predatory men. Theo's rule is that once our first priority of saving the victims is achieved, our second priority is to save ourselves. Seeing all those women with bruises, rope burns, and sometimes mutilation marks made my wolf want to go back and turn those predators into prey.

"It put my wolf and me in a constant internal battle. I can't tell you how hard it is to have to reason with him, because honestly, there's a part of me that agrees with him. If we have the chance to stop those men from hurting innocent women in the future, why aren't we?

"Anyway, constantly fighting with my other half got to be too difficult, so I told Theo that once my part of the rescue was over, I had to go. I'm not proud of that, because it was selfish of me to put my needs over the needs of those women in pain. Theo and the rest of the clan were always so understanding, which only made me feel shittier for not sticking around to help."

Liz tilts her head to the side. "Why are you telling me this?"

"Because you seem to think that whatever battle you're fighting will make me judge you, when in reality, I'm too busy judging myself."

Her gaze falls to her hands in her lap. "I'm about to say something I think you'll judge me for."

"And what's that?"

"I want Trey."

Those three little words slug me right in the gut. I'm sitting right here, trying to take care of her and give her anything she wants, and what she wants is another man?

She keeps her attention on her fidgeting hands. "Like I said, I knew you'd judge me."

My wolf whimpers. Her words have wounded him too.

I lower my voice to speak as gently as possible. "Why do you want him?"

"I just want him to hold me."

Ouch. Electrocute me with a fucking lightning ball, why don't ya?

"Well, he's not here, but *I* could hold you?"

She shakes her head. "It's not the same."

I drag a hand through my stupid black hair, then sigh as I slide off the bed. With a huff, I grab the blankets off the floor and toss them back onto the bed. As I dig through our backpack, I say, "Do you know Trey's number by heart?"

I feel her gaze whip up to me. "You're actually going to call him?"

"Yeah." I can't hide the disdain in my tone. "He's who you want, isn't he?"

"Colton, it's not like that."

Well, that's how it fucking feels. I pull the burner phone out and tap the screen. "So do you know his number or not?"

Liz slides off the bed and comes to my side. She places a tender hand over my forearm. "Colton."

I don't look at her. I can't. I'm too hurt.

Her voice goes soft. "You don't have to call Trey."

"Well, you said you want him, so I'm gonna get him for you." *Because obviously I'm not enough.* I hate that my pain is coming off as anger right now. I'm not mad at her. I'm just mad about this whole situation.

"Why don't we get back into bed, and I can explain?"

Finally, I meet her gaze. "Explain what?"

"My nightmares, and why I wanted Trey."

Wanted. As in past tense. Does that mean she no longer— wait . . . did she just say nightmares, as in the thing only Ordinaries have?

It takes us a minute to settle back into bed together. Sitting with our legs crossed and facing each other, Liz takes another minute to stare at her gloved hands. I'm assuming she's trying to find the right words, so I don't rush her.

Eventually, she lets out a long sigh. "I know what you're going to say: Zordis don't have nightmares. Technically, my nightmares aren't nightmares. They're closer to night terrors, but even that term isn't accurate. When I touch people's hands, even if it's for a millisecond, I catch that person's most traumatic memory.

"At night, the memories I've caught always replay in my mind. Sometimes, it's a recent catch. Other times, it's a memory I caught years ago. Either way, it terrifies me so much that I usually wake up screaming."

Things are beginning to click together. "That explains why you're always yawning. You never get enough sleep."

"Yep, and because of that, I have to sleep every night."

"*Every* night? Like an Ordi?"

She nods. "I only get two to three hours of sleep at a time, so yes, every night. That's why I basically force Trey to cuddle with me whenever he stays over. For some reason neither of us can explain, when he holds me, the nightmares stay away. With him, I'm able to get a full night of rest."

Now I understand why she wanted him, and I'm less hurt by it. "So having night terrors is the *terrible* thing you didn't want me to know about you? This whole time, I honestly thought you turned into a hairy bloodthirsty swamp monster."

My joke draws a smile from her lips, but it quickly fades. "You know how Zordinaries are about this stuff. Our kind judges others for being the tiniest bit dysfunctional. People think I'm a disgrace to our kind. They say I shouldn't be allowed to have children so my bad genes can't be passed on. My last boyfriend told me I belong in a group home for the *defective*."

"What?" I screw my face together. "He actually used the D-word?" I could never fathom calling anyone the D-word. That's just wrong.

"Sadly, that's better than some of the things my sisters have said to me."

"The sisters you don't count as sisters?" I ask as a gentle invitation for her to tell me more.

She accepts the invite. "Yes. They're triplets, four years older than me, and they all treat me like shit. I've been wearing gloves for as long as I can remember. My sisters used to take them and cut the fingers off. The Pyro used to burn my gloves to ash in front of me. The Aero took pride in blowing my gloves into high places I couldn't reach. The Terra had a bad habit of burying them so far into the ground, it'd take me days to dig them back out. The shittiest part is they'd tell my parents I misplaced my gloves, and since it was three against one, my parents believed them. Eventually, my parents stopped buying me new gloves because I *couldn't be responsible* with them."

I shake my head in disgust. "I can see why you wrote off your sisters."

"Yeah, and sadly, my parents aren't any better. I was the accidental child they never wanted, and when they found out that my body power functions the way it does, they saw me as a *defective* burden—so much that when they put my sisters in ballet, they refused to let me join because I *wasn't worth the money.* I grew up watching my sisters dance from behind glass. I wanted to dance so badly, I taught myself. I'd memorize the moves I saw them do, then do them on my own later in my bedroom.

"In high school, I worked three jobs so I could save up enough money to move away and pursue a dance career. I wanted to prove to myself that I could do and be whatever I wanted, no matter what my so-called family said I was worthy of."

I lean back against the pillows so I can admire the strong woman sitting in front of me. "I have mad respect for you, Liz. Moving away at eighteen and making it on your own? That's huge."

"I didn't do it alone. I had a ton of help from Dixie. When I first moved to LA, I didn't have a job lined up yet. I had zero formal experience, so every application I sent in got denied. Instead, I walked into every dance studio I could find, asking them to hire me based on my skills. No one would take me up on it—except for Dixie. Barely a minute into watching me dance, she jumped up and screamed, 'You're hired!'

"At the time, I couldn't afford a Los Angeles apartment, so I hid the fact that I lived in my car. It didn't take long for Dixie to find out. Once she did, she convinced me to move in with her and crash on her couch. I did that until I was able to get my own place."

I already liked Dixie, but now I see her as a hero. "Do you ever talk to your sisters anymore?"

"Nope, and I don't care to. The last time I ever spoke to them was six years ago. I flew back to Chicago for Christmas and found out my mom never told my sisters I was coming. I overheard my sisters tell my parents how they didn't want their boyfriends to know they were related to a *defective* Zordi, so my parents told me to leave."

My jaw drops. "You're kidding. They told you to leave? On Christmas?"

"Yep. I sobbed the entire cab ride back to the airport, and I've never gone back. Not that they've ever invited me. Even if they did, I wouldn't go."

I can't imagine having a family so cruel and selfish. Yes, my dad left us, but at least I had my mom and Chrissy. Liz had no one, and all because of something out of her control? *Come on.*

I lean forward to cup Liz's fallen expression in my palms. "Do you remember when I told you I was suited up and ready to fight your battles with you?"

Her expression softens. "Yes."

"I meant it with all my heart. I'm here for you, baby. I'll spend every day making you feel loved and worthy, and I'll spend all my nights holding you until the nightmares stop. I won't judge you either, or run away, no matter the circumstances."

Liz's eyes glisten with tears. "That means a lot to me."

"*You* mean a lot to me."

She offers me a genuine smile, and it takes everything in me not to kiss her. "Do you think you could hold me now? I'd love to try to get more sleep."

It lifts my heart to know she wants to try that with me. I want nothing more than to be a safe haven for her, so I lie down, get comfortable, then tap my shoulder. "Come here, bumblebee."

Without hesitation, Liz snuggles her body against mine, then lets out a sigh of relief. I wrap a protective arm around her and pull her in closer.

As she falls asleep, I think of all the best nightmare-warding thoughts I can.

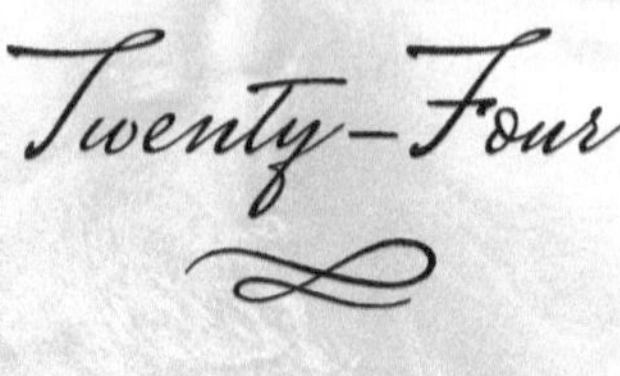

Twenty-Four

LIZ

"Liz, wake up!" Rough hands shake me.

I jolt awake, gasping for air. Images of my History teacher catching his wife getting fucked by his brother fade away.

I remember when I caught that memory. I was at school, on a day my sisters had stolen my gloves. My teacher's hand barely grazed my finger as he handed me some papers, and suddenly, I understood why he always had those bags under his eyes.

I sit up, letting the blanket fall down my chest. Sunlight shines through a crack in the hotel curtains. *How long was I asleep for?*

I glance at the digital clock on the desk across the room. It's just past seven thirty. That means I got about six hours of sleep. *That's incredible!*

I gape at Colton, who's staring at me with his eyebrows pressed together. "You did it."

He plants himself on the edge of the bed. "No, I didn't. You were having another night terror."

"But not for six whole hours."

He lets out a somber sigh. "Little wins, I guess."

My attention falls to his feet, and I scowl. "You're wearing shoes."

He hooks a thumb toward the door. "I didn't want to wake you, so I took Theo's phone call out in the hall. When I came back, you were screaming."

I don't think about my words before letting them out. "Trey never leaves me."

A wounded look flashes across Colton's eyes, and I immediately regret what I said. Before I can apologize, he says, "I couldn't have been gone for more than five minutes."

"A few minutes is all it takes."

"I'm sorry, bumblebee. I didn't realize I needed to stay until you woke up. You looked so peaceful, and the phone was buzzing, so I didn't think much of it."

"It's okay. I'm just thrilled to know you have the ability to keep the nightmares away too. That's never happened with anyone except Trey."

Colton's expression lightens up. "Tonight, I promise I won't leave you, even if someone's aiming a fireball at my head."

My lips perk into a smile. "I'd appreciate that."

"And if you want, I'll hold you every night for the rest of my life."

The rest of his life? Playfully, I narrow my eyes at him. "Mr. Finley, are you proposing?"

"Nah. When I do propose someday, I'll do it right. I'll have a huge-ass ring and you'll be standing somewhere much prettier than a hotel room with questionable stains on the carpet."

"*When* you propose? As in, you have definite plans to do so?"

"Of course. You're *my* bumblebee. No one else's."

No one has ever been so possessive of me before. It's refreshing compared to being treated like a flesh-eating worm that people can't get away from fast enough.

I tap my chin and pretend to think. "You know, I'm not sure if this'll work out between us. You don't like pineapple on your pizza."

He makes an *ick* face. "Because that shit's nasty. Name *one* person who likes pineapple on their pizza—besides you."

"Trey."

"Then he's just as gross as you are."

I let out a laugh for the first time in days, and it feels good to do so.

Colton smiles brightly. "I love hearing you laugh. It's so beautiful."

"Your laugh is too."

Suddenly, his smile falls. "You know, you're being extremely kind to me, even though what happened to you is because of me."

"I told you already, none of it was your fault." I slide off the bed before he talks more about what happened, because I have no desire to relive it right now. "I'm gonna go get ready. After that, maybe you can update me on what Theo called you about?"

"Of course."

After Colton and I are showered and have clean teeth, I work on blow-drying my hair while he packs up our things.

As I run the hot straightener through my dry curls, I scowl at my reflection in the mirror. I might adore blonde hair on men, but on me, it's out of place.

When I step out of the bathroom, Colton's got all our stuff packed and condensed into our backpack and one plastic shopping bag.

He hands me a pair of sunglasses. "Put these on. Let's get on the road, then I'll tell you about Theo."

We're a few miles away from the hotel when Colton takes his sunglasses off and drops them into the cup holder. I don't know where we're going, but I trust that Colton knows what he's doing.

"Theo said our homes were probably broken into." Colton flips the visor down to block the bright sunlight from his face. "He's got security footage of Dom and some other big men searching his house. Taryn is working on identifying the other men. Maybe that'll give us a clue as to where Dom is hiding. In the meantime, Theo wants me to leave you with someone who'll protect you so you'll be safe while the team and I go after the Wests."

I'm pretty sure I already know the answer, but I ask anyway. "Do you *have* to go?"

"I mean, technically, no one's forcing me to, but I want to. I need to help them end this."

"But you could get hurt again." I gesture toward his arm. After he removed the gauze last night, it revealed a tiny scar where his gash had been. The Healing Goo and Healing Water helped a ton, but he'll have a little reminder of this awful experience on his body for the rest of his life. Does he really want another? Or worse, what if this time, he ends up like Andre?

"The clan needs me, Liz. They're already down a man. I can't allow them to go into battle without my wolf. He's way faster and more agile than the average human. If the clan does this without me, it'll be suicide for them. Plus, we can't hide from the Wests forever. I'm doing this for *you* more than anyone."

I shift in the passenger seat to face him as I ponder that. I hate to say this, but . . . "I understand. I'd do the same if I were you."

He turns his attention away from the road just to gape at me. "You would?"

"Yeah. If I had spent over five years doing stuff like this for innocent people I didn't know, of course I'd want to do it now for someone I care about."

He offers me a grateful smile. "Thanks for understanding."

"So what's the plan now?"

"The plan is to drive until we get hungry. In the meantime, I think you should give Trey a call. He's the only person I can think of who'll protect you with his life while I can't."

I couldn't agree more. "Where's the phone?"

"Front pocket of the backpack."

I twist around to dig through the backpack and find the burner phone. After taking off a glove, I type Trey's number in and press the phone to my ear. It rings a few times before going to voicemail. I expected this, so I say, "T, it's Liz. Call me back ASAP."

With the blinker on, Colton merges the car one lane over. "He doesn't answer numbers he doesn't know, does he?"

"Nope." Seconds later, as expected, the phone buzzes in my hand. I put it up to my ear. "Hey, T-Bear."

"Did you get a new phone?" Trey asks.

"No." I know he'll want an explanation, but over the phone is not how I want to do it. "Are you home?"

"Yeah." In the background, a toilet flushes.

"Do you think I could come visit?"

He lets out a low scoff as a faucet runs. "When have you ever asked for permission to come here?"

That's true. Whenever I visit Trey, I usually just book my flight and tell him what time I'll be landing. "Well, I'm asking this time because I'll have Colton with me. We're on the road right now."

"Um, okay? When will you guys be here?"

I press the phone against my thigh. "How long do you think it'll take us to get to New York from here?"

Colton waggles his head from side to side. "If we don't stop much, maybe twenty-some hours?"

I put the phone back to my ear. "How's tomorrow morning?"

Trey pauses to think. "I mean, sure, but I've got a flight

back to LA around noon. Can't you just wait a few more hours to see me?"

In a whisper, Colton says, "I don't want you anywhere near your house right now."

Into the phone, I say, "Do you think you could cancel your flight, and we can stick around New York for a while?"

Trey lets out a long *uhhh* as he thinks, then says, "Do you plan to miss our shows this weekend?"

I glance over at Colton.

"I don't want you anywhere near the Soul House either," he says in another whisper. "Basically, I don't want you anywhere you're supposed to be until this is over."

"Yes," I say to Trey. "We'll have to miss our shows this weekend."

Trey's tone turns rough. "What's going on?"

I put on a fake cheerful tone. "What makes you think anything's going on? Why can't I just have an impromptu vacation in New York with my best friend?"

"Did that fucker hurt you?"

In the corner of my eye, I see Colton flinch. His hands slide down the steering wheel as he chews on his bottom lip.

"No, T. Colton didn't hurt me."

"Then tell me why you're driving to New York instead of flying, why you're bringing your boyfriend, why you want to miss our shows this weekend—something you never do—and why you sound so off."

I don't know why I thought I could have this conversation with Trey without him questioning everything. "Look, something did happen, but I'd rather explain it in person."

Trey goes silent for a moment, then lets out a long sigh. "Alrighty then. I'll cancel my flight and give our band manager a call."

"What will you tell her?"

"I dunno. She already finds any excuse in the book to yell at me. I'll just make some shit up."

"Thanks, T. You're the best." If I didn't already love Trey before, I do now. He's willing to accommodate my needs without any explanation. That's unconditional love if you ask me.

When I end the call, Colton rubs the back of his neck and huffs. "That man is gonna kill me."

"What? No, he's not."

"It didn't occur to me until you were on the phone with him that you'd have to explain to him what happened. Once he hears that you were hurt because of me, I doubt he'll allow me to walk away in one piece."

I slip my hand back into the glove I took off. "Once we tell him the whole story, he'll understand."

"Unlikely. If I were him, I'd just see me as the reason you were kidnapped and sexually assaulted. Seriously, Liz. How can you even look at me knowing I let that happen?"

"You didn't *let* it happen. Not only did you have no control over it, but you saved me."

Glaring out the windshield, he shakes his head. "That doesn't make up for what happened to you. Whenever I think about it, the guilt eats at me. Every time I look at you and you aren't smiling, I think about what I could have done differently."

As an attempt to lighten the mood, I say, "Well, I can't be smiling *all* the time."

"You used to. You're normally so cheerful. Now your joyful energy is gone."

He's not wrong. I haven't felt as cheery as I normally do. I don't even have the mental energy to fake it right now. "It'll come back over time. This chaos is just . . . a little fresh."

He places a tender hand over my knee and gives me a little squeeze. "You didn't deserve any of that, Liz. I'm so sorry for what happened, and I won't be able to apologize enough."

I place my hand over his. "You don't need to apologize, okay? I don't blame you."

"Could you please stop being so goddamn forgiving? I don't deserve you, Liz. Not one bit. But I can't stay away."

I give his hand a tight squeeze. "I don't want you to."

He takes his eyes off the road for a moment to smile at me. "Could I tell you something?"

"Sure."

"When we made wishes at that fountain, I asked the fountain fairies to make you fall in love with me."

My mouth pops open. "Really? That was, like, the second time we'd ever met."

"And it was all I needed to know I wanted you."

My heart does backflips in my chest. "Well, since the fountain fairies' magic worked on me, do you think they'll also help that homeless man find a nice home?"

Colton smiles, shaking his head. "I knew you were the type of person to make a wish to benefit someone else over yourself. You're making me look bad for being selfish."

Selfish? A man who spent five years risking his life over and over to save innocent women he didn't know is not selfish.

I lean over the center console to place my head against his arm. "I love you, Colton."

He kisses the top of my hair. "I love you too, Liz. So fucking much."

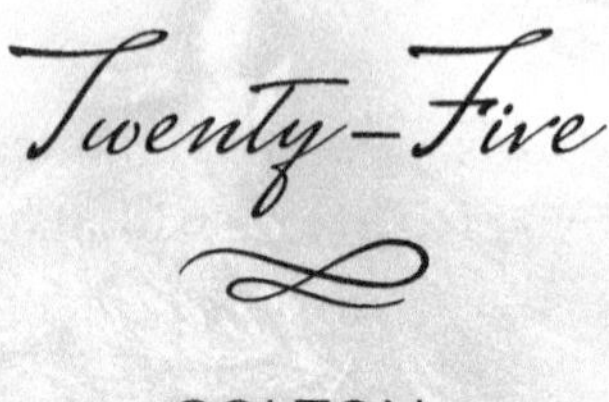

Twenty-Five

COLTON

"At least now we know that cuddling is the only method that works," Liz says as she glances out the car window at the midnight sky.

Because she wanted to make it to New York as soon as possible, she refused to allow us to stop at another hotel. Since I'm fully rested, I drove while she slept in the passenger seat. The plan was that I'd keep a hand on her arm as an attempt to keep the night terrors away. I didn't let go of her arm once, and I'm sad to say it didn't work. Her screams filled the car a minute ago.

"You made it almost three hours though," I say, trying to be positive.

"You're still not freaked out by me, right?"

Is she really still worried about that? Having night terrors isn't normal for Ordinaries. For a Zordinary, it's even more bizarre. Still, my feelings for Liz haven't changed. If anything, my feelings have grown stronger. "Like I said, as long as you don't turn into a swamp monster, we're good."

That puts a little smile on her face.

My stomach rumbles. "Since you're up now, would you wanna stop for something to eat?"

She nods. "Food sounds good."

"I'm guessing the only thing that's open at this time is a twenty-four-hour fast food joint. Are you cool with that?"

"It's not my first choice, but I won't be picky."

Within a few miles, we find an open drive-thru just off the interstate. Soon after, we've got two paper bags of food and two drinks in the cup holders. I pull our Honda into a parking spot and shut the engine off. Then I press the car ceiling light on.

The scent of warm fries fills my nostrils, making me hungrier. I waste no time ripping into my bag. I grab my burger out first and flip the top of the box open. From the bottom of my bag, I find a few packets of ketchup. I rip two open and squirt them into the burger lid. Then I find a packet of mayonnaise and squirt that over the ketchup. Next, I dig through my bag for the ranch I requested, then pour it over the mayonnaise. To finish things off, I sprinkle on some salt and pepper.

Finally, with two fries, I mix it all together until it forms a delicious pink sauce. I feel eyes on me, so I glance up. Liz's mouth has fallen open, and she's looking at me like *I* have turned into a swamp monster.

I freeze. "What?"

"Please tell me you're not planning to eat whatever weird concoction you just made."

"This is my special fry sauce." I stick the two fries I just used as mixing sticks into my mouth.

Liz gasps. "Ew!"

I let out a loud *ha!* "Bold reaction from someone who willingly eats pizza with pineapple on it."

"Pineapple on pizza is normal. This globby thing you just made is not. I don't know a single person who mixes their ketchup with mayonnaise, ranch, salt, and pepper."

"Don't knock it 'til ya try it." I dip a single fry into my special sauce and hold it out to her. "Here."

She jerks backward into her seat, glaring at the fry in my hand like it's an oversized tarantula with fangs. "Um, no, thanks. I'll dip my fries into unruined ketchup, like a normal person."

"Your loss." With a shrug, I eat the fry.

Because I know it'll get a reaction from her, I make a show of dipping a bunch of fries into my yummy pink blob, getting as much of it as I can. Then I shove all the fries into my mouth in the most unattractive way.

Liz half gasps, half laughs. "And you called *me* gross? You know that pineapple is a topping you can actually order, right? There isn't a single place on earth where you can order *that*."

"That's because I'm still working on my patent for this product. Once I release it to the public, I'll make millions. There will be a bottle of this stuff in every fridge. You'll see."

"Oh, you're *that* confident?"

"Yep," I say with a smirk. "I even have a great name for it."

She side-eyes me as she dips a chicken nugget into her boring ketchup.

I lean over and whisper, "This is the part where you ask me what the name is."

She rolls her eyes, but her lips curve into an unwilling smile. "What's the name?"

"Fry Lube."

As I intended, Liz bursts into a laugh. "Fry Lube?"

My goal of getting her to laugh is complete. "Yes. Fry Lube."

She continues to laugh, getting my wolf to perk his ears. "With that name, your product will be in the fridge at every frat house. That's for sure."

"And on the tables at every bar and grill."

She finishes her chicken nugget, then picks up another. "I hate to be the one to crush your audacious dreams, but I think you should go back to that detective idea. With your mind power, you'd be really good at it."

My mind power is part of the reason why I've always wanted to be a detective—besides solving crimes and helping the innocent, of course. "Maybe I'll do both. I'll become a detective while I market my industry-breaking Fry Lube."

Liz bursts into another laugh. "Oh lord. Stop saying that out loud."

I can't begin to explain how much I appreciate this moment. Being silly with Liz and making her laugh is helping me forget about how much I owe this woman for the shit she was put through because of me. Despite what Liz thinks, my saving her does *not* make up for allowing two men to violate her body. I still have a long way to go.

With all the tolls and stopping for gas and bathroom breaks, we don't make it to Manhattan until the late afternoon.

I dread every second as I follow Liz toward a towering apartment building near the Hudson River. I take a good look around and admire the busy city's beauty. This might be the last chance I get to see it before Trey murders me.

I don't know him very well, but I know he cares about Liz. She keeps assuring me he'll understand. To that, I scoff. I don't believe that one bit.

After Trey buzzes us into the building, the first thing I see are lush rugs under giant accent chairs and a chandelier above my head that probably costs more than a college tuition.

I swing our backpack filled with Liz's things over my

shoulder as she leads me into the elevator. "Renting a place like this can't be cheap."

"It's not." Liz presses the highest numbered button, then the doors slide shut.

"He lives on the top floor?" I ask as the elevator lifts us up.

"Yeah. One of the penthouses." She says that like it's normal to have friends who can afford penthouses.

"Damn. How much money does your band bring in?"

"Not enough to rent a penthouse. Trey's parents were murdered, so he inherited their wealth."

Murdered? And I thought Liz's past was bad. "Did his parents invent the z-net or something?"

"Actually, they were the inventors of healing products."

She's gotta be kidding. "You mean, like, Healing Water, Healing Goo, and Healing Spray? That was his parents?"

"Yep."

I blow out a breath. "No wonder the man can afford to fly across the country every week."

"Yeah. Don't tell him I told you about his parents though. He doesn't like people knowing he's rich or how he got it. He actually hid it from me when we first met. I only knew after I joined the band and found out he was financing the entire endeavor."

I almost groan out loud. Of course the man is generous *and* humble about being a multimillionaire. If I wasn't in this luxurious building right now, I probably wouldn't believe it. Trey wears plain clothes, rides a Harley, and plays in a local band for a living. Nothing about that screams, *I'm richer than most of the world.*

A soft *ding!* plays from the ceiling, then I step off the smoothest elevator ride I've ever been on.

Liz leads me to the last door at the end of the hall and knocks.

Seconds later, the door swings open.

I don't see it coming: My girl leaps into Trey's arms. He

catches her as she locks her legs around his torso like she's a fucking koala. My wolf growls through his teeth, battling with me to shift so he can claim Liz for himself.

I take a deep breath and try to control the vibrations humming through my limbs. *Don't take over. Not right now.*

Trey continues holding my woman against him. "It's good to see you too, Liz. But, um, why the fuck are you blonde?"

"Do you hate it?" she asks into his shoulder.

"With a passion."

"Me too. I want to get it out the first chance I have."

This is the first time I'm hearing that she *hates* her hair. Now I feel worse that she had to dye it.

Finally, Trey puts my woman's feet back onto the floor, where they belong. I resist the urge to pull her against my side.

"Why did you dye your hair?" Trey asks.

"I'll explain inside."

He waves us in. Liz and I slip off our shoes, then I place her backpack onto the kitchen counter—the fancy-ass kitchen counter. *Is that marble?*

The rest of his place looks just as expensive. The living room is filled with furniture I could never afford, and it faces a window that overlooks the Hudson River. The magnificent view looks like it belongs on a postcard.

"Make yourself at home," Trey says to me. "Liz always does."

Liz plops onto the ginormous couch and pats the empty spot next to her. "Come sit, Colton."

I obey as Trey heads into his kitchen with the pristine white cabinets and an island so long, it could seat at least eight people.

He opens the fridge. "I've got water or apple juice. I'd offer something with alcohol, but Liz poured my entire supply down the drain a while ago and forbids me from buying any more."

"And I have no regrets." Liz's lips spread into the most

genuine smile I've seen on her in days. Why can't I get her to smile like that? "I'll have some apple juice, please."

"I'm fine," I say, even though some water sounds great. I just don't want to be a bother.

Trey joins us in the living room with a glass of apple juice and two glasses of ice water. He sets one water in front of me on the coffee table, then takes a sip from the other glass. I hate that he went through the effort to get me a drink anyway. Kind gestures like this make it harder for me to dislike him.

I pick up my glass and down half the liquid in a few gulps. I was thirstier than I thought.

Trey takes a seat on one of the chairs across from us. "Sooo, should we pretend to make small talk, or can we skip that bullshit and get straight to why you're here?"

Before I can say anything, Liz blurts out "I was kidnapped."

Trey's in the middle of taking a sip, and he spits it out. Water sprays all over the carpet. "What?"

I slap a palm against my forehead. "Jesus, Liz. Way to ease into it."

With the back of his hand, Trey wipes off his lips. "You're joking, right? I thought you were coming to tell me you're pregnant."

I can see why he thought that. It's news Liz would probably want to share with him in person and with me in attendance.

Liz jerks her head back. "Pregnant? God, no."

I'm not a fan of the way she just said that, as if the idea of being pregnant is disgusting. I want to have a huge pack of kids in the future, and I see that future with Liz. Does she not want babies right now or not at all? Or is the thought of having babies with *me* unimaginable?

Trey slams his glass against the coffee table. "So you were actually kidnapped?"

"Yes, T. I wouldn't joke about something that serious."

Trey's voice lowers to a growl as his hands ball into fists. "Who the fuck kidnapped you?"

The more Liz goes into the details of how she woke up drugged on a private plane and all the horrible ways the Wests treated her, the more my heart breaks. No woman ever deserves to be slapped and dragged across a hard floor like that. I had no idea the Wests were that cruel to her, because she didn't have any bruising. The Wests were probably intentional about hitting the women just enough to get them to behave, but not enough to leave marks, so they still looked pretty inside the display cases.

Trey's expression is lethal, and Liz hasn't even gotten to the worst part yet. When she gets to the part where she finds out that she'd been taken because of a vendetta against me, Trey aims his deadly glare my way. I accept it with full remorse.

Liz doesn't. She leans over the coffee table just to smack Trey's chest. "Stop it. It wasn't Colton's fault. He didn't know. In fact, he was the one who saved me."

Trey looks like he's a second away from strangling me. "How?"

Liz turns to me. "Maybe you should tell this part."

After a deep breath, I explain to Trey how I used to be a member of Theo's rescue group. Trey's shoulders seem to relax—until the moment I say *sex crimes*.

"Wait." Trey throws a hand up, then pinches the bridge of his nose as he screws his eyes shut. "I swear to god, if you're about to tell me that anyone even *looked* at Liz in that way, I'm going to kill you."

I gulp—the kind of gulp that does nothing to settle the raging tornado in my gut. I knew this was going to be my end. When I come back as a ghost, I'll haunt Liz, screaming, "I told you so!"

When I don't respond, Trey aims his glare at Liz. "Tell me no one touched you."

She hesitates, and that's all Trey needs. He leaps over the coffee table and drives a hard fist straight into my face. My head snaps back as burning pain rips down to my neck. I groan and cup my probably broken nose. My hand is wet, and it's not from the tears forming in my eyes.

Trey hurls another fist into the side of my head. "How could you let them do that to her?"

I don't even try to fight back, because I deserve this. He's right, how could I let that happen to her?

"Trey!" Liz tackles him to the ground and tries to keep him there, but her attempts are fruitless. He easily pushes her off him, then gets right back onto his feet. He slams a firm punch right into my gut. I keel over, falling off the couch onto my knees, clutching my stomach.

"Trey! Stop!" A water ball appears in Liz's hand, and she launches it at Trey's head. It hits him, but he's unfazed by it. He simply swipes the water off his face, then drags me up by my shirt.

His elbow arches back, and I brace myself for another painful hit in the nose.

It doesn't come.

Liz gets between us and splashes another water ball into Trey's face. This time, he lets me go and coughs out the liquid. Then Liz shoves him backward and smacks his chest so hard, I almost feel it too.

"Don't you dare hit him again!"

Surprisingly, Trey stays where he is. I expected him to attack me some more.

Liz kneels in front of me still clutching my stomach, with a hand over my shoulder. "Oh, Colton. I'm so sorry. Are you okay?"

No. Not even a little bit. With my nose throbbing and the taste of metal in my mouth, I grunt out a little "Yep."

Liz flashes a deadly glare up at Trey. "Apologize."

He looks at her like she's crazy for thinking he would. "Hell no."

I don't want his apology anyway. We all know he wouldn't mean it. Even if he did, it wouldn't erase this agony in my face.

Liz gets to her feet. "Didn't you hear me? I said he's the one who saved me!"

Trey shouts back, "He's the reason you were kidnapped!"

My wolf snaps at him for yelling at Liz like that. Suddenly, my body hums again. I bring the bottom of my shirt up to my nose, then suck in a deep breath. I can't let my wolf out now. Liz would never forgive me for allowing my animal to eat her best friend.

"Like I said," Liz shouts, "it wasn't Colton's fault!"

"Seriously?" Trey runs a hand through his wet hair. "Are you actually going to stand there and defend this piece of shit?"

He's right, I am a piece of shit.

Liz squares her shoulders and crosses her arms over her chest. "If I remember correctly, Arella was also kidnapped because of you."

Trey's mouth drops. "That was a low blow, Liz. So fucking low."

She doesn't back off. "I thought if there was anyone who would understand Colton's side, it'd be you."

"I never would have allowed someone to *rape* her!"

"He didn't allow it! He didn't get there until *after* it had already happened."

My heart stops. Finally, it all makes sense: Why Liz was so quick to forgive me, why she's defending me, and why she doesn't blame me for any of it. She's got her facts all wrong.

Keeping my shirt to my face, I push off the floor and onto my feet. "Liz, that's not what happened."

She shifts to face me. "What do you mean?"

"I was there the whole time."

Her expression falls. "What?"

"Our original plan was to win the auction for the first private session so no one would even have the chance to touch you. Because the Wests did their bullshit initiation-tradition thing, I wasn't able to get to you beforehand. And when they allowed only returning men to bid on you first, my only choice was to win the second session."

"Wait." Liz shakes her head like she can't understand the language I'm speaking. "So you were there when they tied me to that post and Malik violated me in front of the whole crowd?"

In the corner of my eye, I see Trey's hands form fists again.

I ignore him and look straight into Liz's eyes. My voice comes out shaky. "Yes, I—I was there."

I see it—the moment Liz loses all her faith in me. Her jaw drops as she bursts into tears. "Why didn't you stop him?"

"I'm sorry. I wanted to, but I couldn't. Not without putting your life in danger."

Tears stream down her cheeks. "So you just stood there and watched?"

I gulp, but this time, it's in fear of *her* killing me. I doubt Trey would even stop her. If anything, he'd help her dispose of my body.

I say the only thing I can. "I'm so sorry."

With a shriek, she crumples to the floor with her head in her hands. I drop to my knees to comfort her, but Trey shoves me away. I fall onto my ass as my back hits the coffee table. Then I watch helplessly as Trey scoops up my bawling Liz and carries her into his bedroom.

I stay where I am, still holding my shirt to my bloody nose as Trey sets Liz onto his bed and covers her with a blanket. Every wail she lets out breaks my soul into pieces.

This whole time, I thought she knew. How could she think I'd only gotten there just before getting her out? Is it because she thought there's no possible way I would have been able to stand there and watch? I guess, from her point of view, that does make sense.

From my side, though, Theo was right. If I had done something at that very moment, we all would have ended up like Andre. The Wests planned that night the way they had as an attempt to draw us out. Their many guards were ready to murder us the second we revealed ourselves. They didn't think we would allow Malik to do what he did, but we had to. Waiting until Liz, Chloe, and Raven were in their private rooms was our best chance at getting them all out alive.

Fuuuck. I was a fool for ever thinking I could still have Liz after all that. I should have known she didn't have her facts right, because if she had, she wouldn't have been so kind to me. Or forgiving. Or accepting.

Trey steps out of his bedroom, shutting the door behind him. "Why the fuck are you still here?"

I stand up but don't move toward him. "I need to talk to her."

Still in his wet T-shirt, Trey stays in front of the bedroom door, crossing his arms like he's guarding it. "Over my dead body."

"Just let me explain the whole situation to her."

"Fuck no. There's no explanation for what you did. Now get out—before I blast you with a fireball."

For a moment, we just stare at each other. I think about barreling my way past him, then Liz's cries resonate from the other side of the door. That's all I need to hear to start shuffling toward the exit.

Twenty-Six

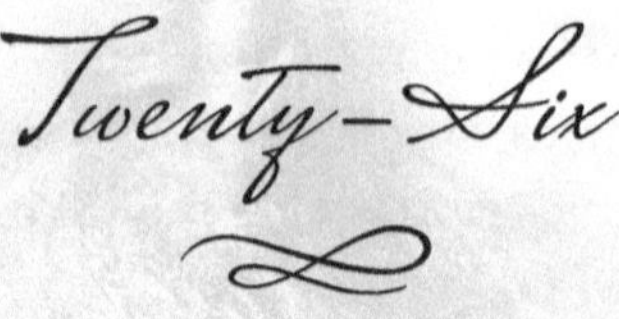

LIZ

It's been three days since Colton left, and my heart has never felt heavier. My mind is all jumbled. No matter what I do, I can't seem to unjumble it. I'm not even sure if unjumble is a word—that's how jumbled I feel.

I keep thinking that since it's April Fool's Day, someone might pop out and tell me this has all been a horrible practical joke. Sadly, no one's popped out yet, and Colton's still gone.

Trey hasn't let me out of his sight. As soon as I mentioned that the reason why Colton brought me here was for protection, Trey accepted his role as my bodyguard with full determination. Yesterday, he took me to a hair salon so I could get my hair dyed back to cherry brown. Then he took me to a Broadway show. At both places, whenever I said I needed to use the restroom, he came with me and guarded the door until I was finished.

Taking me to the show was Trey's way of distracting me from overthinking about Colton. He's also taken me shopping, out to eat at unique restaurants, and for walks around Central Park. For the most part, the distractions have worked.

Unfortunately, once Trey and I return to his apartment, my mind goes straight back to overthinking about Colton.

Where is he? What's he doing? Is he about to fight Dom West and his many guards? Is he going to make it out alive?

"Thanks, man," Trey says to the pizza delivery guy.

I'm on Trey's couch, staring out the dark window at the Hudson River, wondering if Colton's thinking about me.

Trey drops the pizza box onto his coffee table, next to my glass of lemon-lime soda. "You cool with eating on the couch?"

"Sure." I flip the top of the box open and waste no time grabbing the slice with the most pineapple on it.

Trey leaves, then comes back with some plates and napkins. Whenever we have pizza at my house, we usually put on a movie. Since Trey doesn't have a TV in his living room, we usually talk instead.

"Did you know that Colton thinks I'm the only person in the world who likes pineapple on their pizza?"

Trey wipes his mouth off on a napkin. "You are."

"Am not. You like it too."

"Do not."

I screw my face up at him as he takes another bite of the pepperoni-and-pineapple pizza slice in his hand.

"I don't *like* pineapple on my pizza," he says after he chews. "I tolerate it because *you* like it."

"What? If you don't like pineapple, why don't you pick it off?"

He shrugs and takes another bite. "Too lazy."

"We've been best friends for, like, six years, and we've gotten tons of pizzas together. You're only telling me *now* that you don't like pineapple on it?"

"Eh. It's not like I can't stand it. I'd just never order my own pizza with it."

I feel like an idiot. I thought I knew everything about Mr. Trey Grant. "You know they can make our pizzas with pineapple on just *my* half, right?"

"Yeah, but we're usually at your place. If I don't finish my half, it's not like I'm gonna fly back to New York with leftover pizza in my pocket. And if pizza doesn't have pineapple on it, you won't eat it, so I don't want it to go to waste."

I bite into my crust. "So when I'm not around, what kind of pizza do you order?"

Trey finishes the rest of his slice, then grabs another. "Meat lovers or buffalo chicken, usually."

"Huh. Noted."

The rest of our evening is pretty quiet—until I step into Trey's master bathroom and begin washing off my makeup. Out of nowhere, my stomach feels like it's doing flips inside my body.

I rinse the cleanser off and stare at my reflection in the mirror. *Was it the pizza, or is this the glimmer?* I wait a moment to see if any more symptoms occur.

"Trey?"

He answers from his king bed. "Yeah?"

"I—" The vomit rises up like a tsunami. I make it to the toilet just in time.

Within seconds, Trey is behind me, holding my hair back. "Jesus. What was in that pizza?"

My breaths come out heavy as I stare into the toilet bowl. "I don't think it was the pizza."

I wait a minute for the nausea to settle down, then I flush and grab my toothbrush.

Trey stations himself in the bathroom doorway with his eyebrows pressed together. "Don't take this the wrong way or anything, but are you sure you're not pregnant? It's fine if you are. I'll support you either way."

That's sweet of him, but "Yes, I'm sure. I'm on z-birth control. Plus, Colton pulled out. Both times." I say all that with my toothbrush sticking out of my mouth. This minty toothpaste tastes way better than that pizza did a second time.

"Then what could be the cause of—" Trey gasps. "Oh,

fuck." The look in his eyes tells me he just came to the same conclusion I did a minute ago.

I rinse out my mouth, then turn around and lean against the sink. "This is the second time now. The first time was after I was rescued and Colton stayed back to fight. I got all the symptoms of it: headache, nausea, numb arms, feeling like I was going to pass out."

"Do you feel all of that now?"

"Mostly the nausea, and there's a slight pounding in the back of my head."

Trey offers me his hand. "Come on. You should lay down."

I put my bare hand into his, then follow him into his dimly lit bedroom. The only light is what's shining through the window from the busy city.

Trey helps me into his bed, tucks me in, then climbs in with me. He props up two pillows behind him, then leans into them. His expression is bleak. He only ever looks like this when he's deep in thought.

"What are you thinkin' about, T?"

His stare remains blank. "Her."

I offer him a sympathetic squeeze of my hand. "Are you thinking about when you felt the glimmer with her?"

"Yeah, but I shouldn't be, so let's talk about you instead. Do you need anything? Z-meds? Water? A trash can in case you throw up again?"

"How about a trash can? Just to be safe."

With a wave of his free hand, a small plastic trash can flies up from the corner of his room. As he lowers his hand, the trash can stands upright on the nightstand next to me.

The room goes quiet as we both get lost in thought. The whole time, Trey keeps holding my hand, and I'm grateful for it. I really need his support right now.

"Do you think he's okay?" I ask, swallowing the dryness in my throat.

"Do you still feel sick?"

The slight pounding in the back of my head has turned into a heavy migraine, and my arms have also gone numb, so "Yes."

"Then technically, he's still alive."

I flash back to riding in the back of an SUV, hearing Raven's soft cries after she realized she didn't feel the glimmer anymore. A few hours later, it was confirmed that Andre was gone. I may feel like I have bad food poisoning right now, but at least it means Colton's breathing.

Trey gently pulls some hair behind my ear. "He'll be okay, Liz."

"How are you so sure?"

"Because after everything you've been through, it would be too cruel of the world to take your soul mate away from you now that you've found him."

Or it would be just my luck. It's terrible for me to think so negatively, but I've got a gift that functions like a curse, a family that disowned me, a community of people who think I'm defective, and I've just been through the most traumatic experience of my life. Colton's death would be the perfect cherry on top of this fucked-up sundae.

I almost say all that out loud, but in this relationship, Trey does enough self-loathing for the both of us. I don't need to add to it.

It takes a while, but eventually, my headache fades and the nausea simmers down. Thankfully, it never suddenly stops.

In the morning, my best friend makes me pancakes and eggs. Like usual, he covers his entire pancake stack with whipped cream until the pancakes aren't visible anymore. I, on the other hand, add an appropriate amount of whipped cream over my stack, like a normal person.

Trey's cutting into his pancakes when he asks, "Is it too early for a serious talk?"

I've got a fork full of eggs halfway to my mouth. "About what?"

"Five minutes ago, I got a text from that phone you and Colton were using."

My heart stops beating. "What'd it say?"

Trey picks up his phone, taps the screen a few times, then hands the device to me.

> Hi, Trey. This is Theo, a friend of Colton's. He asked me to let you know that it's safe for Liz to return to LA. She no longer needs to worry about the Wests. We took care of them all.

I hand the phone back to Trey. "Could you ask him if Colton is okay?"

Trey types out a message, then presses send. Barely three seconds later, his phone vibrates. I look over Trey's shoulder to read it.

> Colton is fine. Nothing some Healing Water and Healing Goo won't fix.

I let out a breath of relief. "That's great news."

My body already told me that Colton was okay. It's still good to get confirmation though.

"If you're ready to go home," Trey says, "I can look for plane tickets."

"Tickets?" A slow smile spreads across my lips. "Plural? As in, you'd fly back with me?"

"Of course. I can't let you travel alone. I'm your body-guard, remember?"

That makes me smile wider at him. "I love you so much, you know that? You go above and beyond for me."

"Everything I do is because I owe you."

"For what?"

"For being the best friend I never knew I needed. For always knowing the right thing to say to get me to stay sober. For always doing what's best for me, even if it's hard and I typically fight you on it. I could say more, but I'll sound sappy."

I let out a little laugh. "You do a lot for me too. You always pay when we go out, you treat me to the best birthday experiences, and you're always there for me when I need you."

"I do all those things because I'm selfish."

I pop some pancake into my mouth and chew. "How is any of that selfish?"

He ticks off each point on his fingers. "I pay when we go out because you're right, I do feel guilty when people spend their money on me. I buy you birthday experiences because material things don't excite you, and I suck at wrapping gifts anyway. And I'm there for you because I need you more than you need me. Returning the support you provide me is what keeps you around."

I roll my eyes as I stab my pancakes with my fork and cut off another triangle. "What about that time you bought me, Dixie, and Emmy tickets to One Direction *just because*? That wasn't selfish."

Trey throws his head back with a laugh. "Hell yeah, it was. I overheard you telling Kevin that you were going to ask *me* to go to the concert with you. I wasn't about to sit in a stadium for three hours, surrounded by screaming teenage girls, so I bought you and your other best friends tickets *just because* to get out of going."

I'll give him props, that was kinda genius. "What about that time you—"

Trey throws a hand up, palm forward. "I guarantee you, Liz. I did it because I'm selfish."

I eat some more eggs as I think. "You're offering to fly back to LA with me, and it's not Thursday yet. I know how you feel about being in LA for too long because you'll be too close to *her*. Are you saying that's selfish too?"

"Yes. I'm offering to fly back with you because, despite what Theo says, I don't think you're in the clear yet. If anything happens to you, I'll have no one. So, yes, my protection is selfish." He's grasping at straws. He just doesn't want to admit that he likes doing good things for people when he's also got a reputation for being a bad boy.

"How about your foundation that supports kids with deceased parents? Are you gonna tell me you started that out of selfishness?"

He pauses to think. "All right, you got me there."

"Also, you hold me at night, even when it's not your night to sleep. Are you saying you do that out of selfishness too?"

"All right, all right. So I do *two* selfless things."

I could mention more examples, but then I'd have to bring up *her*. Instead, I grin while holding up my invisible *winner* trophy. "I'll put this one on the shelf next to my others."

"Yeah, yeah, yeah." He rolls his eyes. "In the meantime, do you think you're ready to fly back home?"

Going home means facing reality. I'm not sure if I'm ready for that yet. However, the longer I put it off, the more I won't want to go back. I'll have to deal with real life eventually, so I might as well do it now. "Yeah, let's look at flights."

Twenty-Seven

LIZ

The only flight we could book tickets for at the last minute was an evening one, so it's pretty late when Trey and I arrive at my house.

In my bedroom, my phone is still sitting on my nightstand, plugged in and untouched for days. I've got a bunch of missed calls from Dixie, dated the day I was kidnapped. Other than that, I've got texts from the band and our band manager, asking if I'm okay. I don't know what Trey told our manager to explain our absence, but the texts make it seem like I was too sick to talk.

The oldest unread text I have is from Colton. My heart speeds up as I open his message.

> Hey bumblebee. Great news! I just called my boss to tell him that I'm resigning after this project. After our conversation last night about how I could be leaving the city soon, I decided it's not what I want. Staying here in Los Angeles with you sounds like a better plan. Think you can help me find an apartment near your place?

Trey steps out of my master bathroom, then freezes. "Everything okay?"

Instead of answering him, I hold out my phone, unable to speak. I've got a lump in my throat, and I'm about to sob.

He comes around my bed, takes my device from me, then reads Colton's message. "He quit his career just to be with you?"

"Seems so." I don't know why I'm surprised. Colton told me weeks ago that he would.

Trey sets my phone back onto the nightstand, then takes my bare hands into his. "Look at me, Liz."

I do—as one lonely tear rolls down my cheek.

"Tell me what you want. I'll make it happen for you."

"I don't know what I want."

"Do you want this man?"

My answer isn't a simple yes or no. I also can't make that decision while I'm still trying to recover from finding out that Colton was one of the men in that crowd who did nothing.

Trey sits on the edge of my bed and drags me to join him. "I've been doing some thinking about your situation. I understand how hurt you are, and from what you've told me, I also understand why Colton did what he did.

"Clearly, that man is in love with you. He's risked his life to protect you—twice. I can't imagine his decision to stand by and watch was an easy one. He must have weighed his options and went with the one that put your life first. Obviously, he made the right decision, because here you are, in one piece. If I was in his shoes, I probably would have made the same choice."

Trey must have done a lot of thinking to come to those conclusions. The only thing I've been able to think about is seeing all those men cheer as I was dragged across a stage back into a glass prison. I haven't stopped to think about how hard it must have been for Colton to see all that and not be able to stop it without putting my life at risk, along with Chloe's and Raven's lives.

Trey is right. If I was in Colton's shoes, I probably would have made the same choice. I realize that now.

I take my hand out of Trey's to wipe the wetness off my cheeks. "I find it interesting that you're defending him. I thought you hated him."

"I don't hate *him*. I hate what happened to you, but do you wanna know what I hate more?"

"What?"

"I hate knowing what it's like to lose my soul mate. You keep saying that I've been getting better, but to be honest, I'm not. I've only gotten better at hiding the pain. Every day I have to endure without her feels like a slow and torturous death. This sad existence is something I would never wish upon anyone—especially not you."

I picture the rest of my life without Colton in it. I see myself struggling to get through every miserable day the way Trey is. For him, moving on without *her* is one of the hardest things he's ever had to do. Some days, he's a barely functioning human. Other days, he's just faking it for the sake of everyone else. I've already done enough faking it in my twenty-six years. Do I really want to do more?

Trey tilts my chin up with a finger. "Just say the word, Liz, and I'll go find him for you. I'll knock him out and duct-tape him if that's what it takes to bring him here."

I offer Trey a warm smile. I may not have my family anymore, but at least I have him. "Thanks, T, but there's no need for that."

"You sure? I was gettin' real excited about the knocking-him-out part."

I roll my eyes. "You've punched him enough already. I'd actually appreciate it if you never do it again."

A scoff. "No promises." The air goes still for a while before Trey grabs my hands again. He squeezes them tight. "I don't wanna push you into anything you're not ready for, but if you want my two cents, I think you should call him."

"Why?"

"Because, speaking from experience, any amount of time you spend on this godforsaken earth without your soul mate is worthless. One of us should be with their person, Liz. And since it can't be me, it's gotta be you."

I swallow hard, not just for me but for Trey. If he thinks his life without his soul mate is worthless, how will I feel about my life without Colton? Trey's and my soul mate situations are completely different, but if I don't act now, could we end up in the same spot? Could I end up losing Colton forever?

I don't even know if he knows that we're soul mates. What if he's under the impression that I never want to see him again? I can't let him go on with his life thinking that's the case. If Colton and I are meant to be together, then Trey's right, I shouldn't waste any more time. It's already been four days. I should call him.

As if he read my mind, Trey waves a hand at my phone. It floats off the nightstand and straight into my hand. "Would you like me to step out?"

"No. Stay. I need your support."

As my finger hovers above the call button, I picture Colton sulking in his bed, waiting for my name to appear on his phone. That's probably not the case, but it's what triggers me to tap the call button.

I press the phone to my ear. It rings once, then a woman's robotic voice says, "We're sorry. You have reached a number that has been disconnected or is no longer in service." Then the call automatically ends.

All my hopes come crashing down. I don't know what I was expecting, but it wasn't that.

"Wanna try calling that burner phone?" Trey asks.

"Sure." I take his phone from him, then make the call.

For the second time, a woman's robotic voice says, "We're

sorry. You have reached a number that has been disconnected or is no longer in service."

My shoulders slump. "If I had to guess, I'm gonna say that after their mission was complete, Theo disconnected all of the team's phones so they'd be untraceable."

"Makes sense to me, but how are we supposed to get in contact with Colton now? Does he have any social media?"

"Not that I know of. He mentioned once that he hates social media, but now that I think about it, he probably doesn't have any profiles because of his past work with Theo."

"Again, makes sense." Trey hops onto his feet. "You know where he lives, right?"

I tilt my head back to gape up at him. "You want to go to his place?"

"Don't you?"

I glance at the time on my phone. "It's almost midnight. We can't just show up to his apartment this late, unannounced."

"Trust me, if that man loves you as much as I love *her*, then he's currently wallowing on the couch, waiting for you to show up."

"If that's the case, then why hasn't he tried to call me?"

Trey gestures toward my phone. "In case you forgot already, his phone was disconnected. Maybe he doesn't have a new one yet. How do you expect the man to call you when he doesn't have a phone? Besides, he probably thinks you hate him. Now go downstairs and put some shoes on."

"No. We can't."

Trey lets out a deep sigh and crosses his arms over his chest. "Do you really wanna do this the hard way?"

"What's that?"

"It's where I put you over my shoulder and toss you into the car. And if you refuse to tell me where he lives, I'll go knocking on every apartment door in this fucking city until I find him."

I wouldn't put it past Trey to do that, so with a huff, I slide off my bed. "Okay, but you're driving."

Trey grins, then holds up an imaginary trophy. "I'll put this on my shelf next to my *one* other win."

That makes me chuckle. "You only have *one* invisible trophy?"

"Yep. With you, I don't win often, so I've gotta be proud of all the fake trophies I can get."

"What was it for?"

"Remember when you said you didn't think Kevin and Bailey would get back together? I said they would, and they did."

"Technically, I said they wouldn't get back together within the week, and they didn't."

Trey shoots me a playful glare. "Hey, now, don't take that win away from me. It's fifty percent of my invisible trophies. Now hurry up. Let's go!"

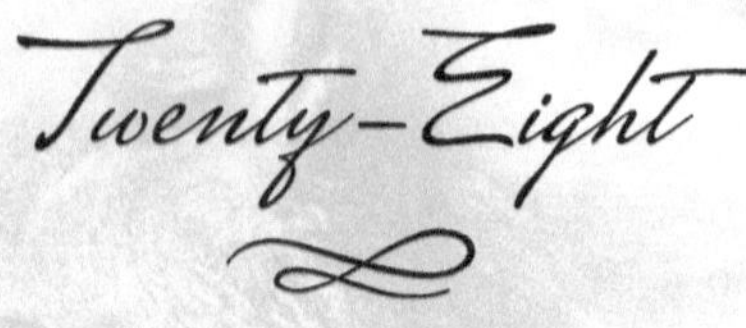

Twenty-Eight

LIZ

"Thanks for doing this, T," I say as he parks my car outside Colton's apartment complex.

The old brick building has seen better days. It needs a heavy power wash and someone to pick away all the weeds. A short, plump man is near the front door, smoking a cigarette.

"Don't thank me yet," Trey says. "We don't know what's going to come of this. Later, you'll either hug me or kill me."

I slip my hands into a pair of yellow satin gloves. "Will you come in with me?"

He gives me a monotone "Seriously?"

"I don't know if I can do this alone. I might chicken out."

With a sigh, Trey turns off my car and unbuckles his seat belt.

As we head toward the front door, I say, "Could you also turn down the intimidating big-brother vibe a notch? Or, like, seven notches?"

"I won't try to scare him off. I'm here to help you get him back, remember?"

We're about to reach the front door when the plump man puts out his cigarette and heads inside. Trey and I catch the door before it closes and step in behind the smoker, into a small room with lots of mailboxes.

Usually, I have to use the keypad on the wall to call Colton's apartment and ask him to buzz me in. As the smoker scans his keys at the second door, Trey and I simply stroll in behind him.

Together, the three of us head toward the elevators. The smoker presses the *up* button.

Ding! One of the four elevators opens up. Wordlessly, we step in, and the doors slide shut.

The smoker presses the 2 button. I press the 3. At the second floor, the smoker steps off, then the elevator shuts again.

Trey scoffs. "Jeez. We could have been serial killers, and that guy just let us in without batting an eye."

"But we don't *look* like serial killers."

Another scoff. "Neither did Ted Bundy."

The elevator opens up to the third floor, and I step out with my heart thumping wildly. I don't know why I'm so nervous. During the entire car ride here, Trey assured me that Colton probably wants to see me more than I want to see him. I hope that's true.

My breaths are short as we arrive outside Colton's door, because what if Trey's wrong? What if the real reason Colton disconnected his phone was so that I couldn't contact him? I mean, the last time we saw each other, my best friend beat him up. What if he hates me for that?

"Well?" Trey whispers. "Aren't you gonna knock?"

I shake my head and say in a low voice, "I don't think I can do this."

"We're already here. You can't back out now." He waits all of two seconds before saying, "Fine. I'll fuckin' do it."

"No!" I whisper-yell, but it's too late.

Knock-knock-knock.

With each second I wait for the door to open, my knees threaten to give out.

"Maybe he's asleep," I say. "It's well past midnight, after all."

"Actually, he's not home," Trey says.

"How do you know?" Once I ask, I realize it was a stupid question. Of course Trey would know.

He answers me anyway. "I can still sense people's emotions when they're sleeping, and I don't sense anyone inside this apartment."

I let out a huff. "Where could he be?"

"I dunno, but how about we come again tomorrow?"

So we do—at a more reasonable time. Trey and I arrive around three in the afternoon, and we let ourselves into the building with the help of Trey's telekinesis. He simply waves a hand at the bolt lock and turns it from the other side.

This time, I'm brave enough to knock on Colton's door myself. Unfortunately, the door never opens, and Trey confirms no one's home.

The next afternoon, we come back around five thirty. For the third time, Colton isn't home.

"Maybe he moved out already," Trey says.

"This would be a good time to have the gift of seeing through walls, huh?"

Trey wiggles his fingers in my face. "Just say the word and I'll get this door open for you."

"What? No! That's a violation of Colton's privacy."

"We're not gonna go in. We're just gonna take a quick peek to see if his shit's still here."

I debate it for only a second before my curiosity wins. "All right, but only a quick peek."

With a smirk, Trey wiggles his fingers at the doorknob and whispers, "Open sesame."

The bolt lock clicks, then the door swings open.

The late-afternoon sun shines through Colton's living room window, illuminating his pair of heavy work boots on the floor, his backpack hanging on the back of a kitchen chair, and an opened bag of chips on the counter.

"Looks like he still lives here," I say.

After Trey closes and locks Colton's door, we head down the hall toward the elevators.

"Where could he be?" I ask.

"Let's see, if I were him and I'd just lost the love of my life, I might be getting drunk at a bar, trying to bang the first willing woman I can find."

I slap Trey's arm. "I did not need a mental image of Colton doing that."

Trey presses the down arrow. "I'm just kidding. That's what old fuckboy Trey would have done. New Trey, the heartbroken one who can't get it up, not even with a hot bartender in his bed, would be sitting at home, waiting for a meteor to destroy the world. That's why I'm surprised Colton isn't here. He doesn't give me fuckboy vibes, and he's probably heartbroken. So why isn't he moping on the couch?"

Ding! The elevator arrives, and we step inside.

Trey presses the ground button. "Do you know of any places he likes to go?"

"Not really."

"Does he have a gym membership? A favorite coffee shop? A go-to restaurant?"

I think, then say, "Not that I know of. Whenever we hung out, it was always here. He'd make me dinner, then we'd just talk on the couch. He never mentioned any places he liked to go."

For the next few days, I feel like a stalker. Trey and I visit Colton's apartment once a day at various times. Every time, he's not home. In addition, Trey always uses his telekinesis to open Colton's door. Our quick peeks always look the same:

unmoved work boots on the floor, the same backpack slumped over a kitchen chair, and that opened bag of stale chips all remain untouched.

"I've already got a flight booked for this afternoon to head back to New York," Trey says as we leave Colton's apartment building on our eighth unsuccessful day. "Would you like me to cancel it so I can keep coming back here with you?"

My heart feels heavy as I climb back into the passenger seat of my car. "I appreciate the offer, but no. You've already stayed the whole week with me. I'll just come here on my own."

After we get lunch together, Trey drops me and my car off at my house, then I wave bye to him from my front stoop as he heads to the airport on his motorcycle.

For the first time since I was kidnapped, I'm truly alone. I'm not surrounded by scary men tying my wrists together. I'm not in a ranch house with Theo's rescue team. I'm not in a car with Colton, being grossed out by his infamous Fry Lube. And now I'm not with Trey either.

For a whole week, Trey made me feel safe when I needed it the most. Without him, I suddenly feel exposed and vulnerable, like anyone could kidnap me again. Like anyone could put their hands on me again.

I shove those terrifying thoughts aside as I enter my house, then bolt the front door. A few days ago, Trey installed a chain lock for me, so I secure that too.

In the kitchen, I recheck that the sliding glass door is locked, then I place a wooden plank at the base to keep it from opening. This was another of the many safety measures Trey added to my house. In addition, I've got a new home alarm system, paid for by Trey. He even went the extra step to install cameras outside my house.

With my doors now secured, I head to the couch, where I'll be sulking about Colton while watching a fast-paced action movie as an attempt to stop sulking..

My ass hits the cushions with a thud. I point the remote at the TV, and the screen brightens to life. I scroll through a few movie options, barely registering the titles because my mind is already wandering. *Where is he? Who's he with? Why has he been gone for so long?* I'm tempted to ask Theo if Colton really is okay. What if he's not? What if he needs help? Then again, if he was in danger, I would know. My body would——

A scratching noise makes me jolt. *What the hell was that?* I freeze and wait to hear if the sound comes again.

Scratch-scratch.

It's coming from the kitchen. It sounds like something's hitting the glass door.

I don't move. My heart does all the moving for me. It's thumping so loud, I can hear it. What if it's the Wests? Theo said I didn't have to worry about them anymore, but what if he's wrong?

Scratch-scratch-scratch. This time, it's accompanied by a whimper.

I'm too scared to check on it in person, so I pull out my phone and bring up the feed from my new security cameras.

The first footage is of my front door. No one's there.

I swipe and get a shot of the side of my house. Nobody.

I swipe again and get the feed showing my back door. I gasp. A huge dog is outside. As the dog lifts its paw against the glass, those scratching noises come from my kitchen again. Next comes the whimpering.

Curious, I set my phone down and rush to the door. When the dog sees me, he stops whimpering, only to jump around in a happy circle. Then he stops and stares at me through the glass as if waiting for me to let him in.

Jeez, he's ginormous. I mean, I'm assuming it's a male, by its size. His coat is a shiny golden yellow with hints of brown running down his back. His underbelly fades into white, and he stays white all the way to his paws. The more I look at him, the more I don't think he's a dog.

He scratches the glass, panting at me with a look like he's thinking, *Are you gonna let me in or not?*

I squint at the animal. "Colton?"

He barks once, then scratches at the glass again. I take that as a yes.

With a grin, I remove the wooden plank and unlock the door. The second I slide it open just wide enough for the giant furball to squeeze through, he tackles me to the floor.

I land on my ass and laugh as he licks my face. "Ew. You're so slobbery."

The animal doesn't care. He just keeps licking my cheeks. The familiar scent of the ocean and puppies sends a warmth down my spine. It really is Colton.

I stroke the top of the animal's head. "Lemme get the door shut, okay?"

As if he understands me, the dog—sorry, *wolf*—shuffles backward off me and stands aside. I push off the floor, then slide the door shut. The second the wooden plank is back in place, the wolf wastes no time reaching up to put his paws on me like he's trying to give me a hug. He's so big, he's almost as tall as me. Shamelessly, he pants into my face.

"Ew. Your breath is awful."

The animal doesn't seem to care.

"Is this why you haven't been home all week? You've been a wolf this whole time?"

He barks once as if to say yes.

"Do you actually understand what I'm saying?"

The wolf lets out another bark.

I look into his eyes, trying to find any hint of Colton in there. I don't. All I see are the eyes of a wolf. Colton mentioned that he can only see the first five to ten minutes of a shift. The rest of the time, his human side goes into hibernation.

"It's really nice to know you're okay, but could you get off me now?"

Like a good obedient dog, the wolf returns his paws to the floor.

I narrow my eyes at him. "So you really *can* understand me."

He lets out another bark.

In that case . . . "Can you shift back to being a human so I can talk to Colton?"

The wolf whines and huffs out a breath.

Oops. I didn't mean to make him sad. "I mean, I guess I don't need to see Colton at this very moment. You and I could get to know each other for a bit."

The wolf hops in a circle, then smiles up at me. His excitement makes me smile back.

I've never met a Shifter animal before. I don't know much about them. The few things I remember from Zordi school is that wolves are the most common Shifter animals and that even though the animal and their human are one being, each has a mind of their own. That's why the Zordi community views Shifters as reckless, uncontrollable, and dangerous.

I don't. Colton's soul smells good, and so does his wolf's soul. I'm certain that this animal would protect me with his life before he ever causes me any harm. *Wait!* This animal *has* protected me with his life—twice. Here's my chance to finally thank him for it.

I plant my ass on the floor to get closer to the wolf. As if reading my mind, he comes to me and nuzzles his face into my chest. Naturally, I pet him, stroking him from the top of his head down to his thick neck.

"Thank you for everything you've done for me, Wolfie." I might come up with a better name for him later. That's just the first name that came to mind. I kinda like it though.

The wolf continues nuzzling his face into my chest.

I tear up from the thought that this animal cares so deeply about me, even though this is the first time we've ever met. How can he be so protective of me already?

I push onto my feet and head into the living room. Wolfie follows and joins me on the couch, placing his head in my lap.

On my phone, I log into the z-net. I pet the wolf with one hand as I type with my other. After I've got my z-net credentials typed in, a search bar appears. I tap out two words: *Shifter wolf.*

After some light skimming, I learn that the Zordi community has stronger opinions against Shifters than I thought. I had no idea there are groups of people out there who believe that Shifters have no place in our community. Those groups go as far as hosting events where they get together to talk about ways they can eradicate the world of all Shifters. Now I understand why Colton was so quick to accept me for everything I am. He, too, understands what it's like to be viewed as unworthy.

Some other things the z-net tells me are that Shifter wolves are protective by nature and won't hesitate to kill anyone threatening the ones they care about. I suppose that's where the *dangerous* label comes from, but I see it as being misunderstood. If anyone posed a threat to someone I care about, I wouldn't hesitate to do everything in my power to protect them either. The difference between me and a Shifter wolf is that with their strength and agility, they're harder to beat. Now I see why Theo wanted Colton on his team. Having a wolf on his side is like having a secret weapon.

Back at the z-net's search bar, I type *how to get a Shifter to shift back into human form.* I skim three articles. Each one tells me the same thing: There's nothing I can do.

When a Shifter is in their human form, their animal side can sleep or stay awake inside them, which gives the animal the power to shift out if they really want to. However, when a Shifter is in their animal form, their human side is forced to sleep, giving the animal full control. Their human side can communicate with them before the shift about how long they want to be in animal form, but if the animal disagrees, the human is shit out of luck.

So that begs the question: How do I convince Wolfie to let me see Colton?

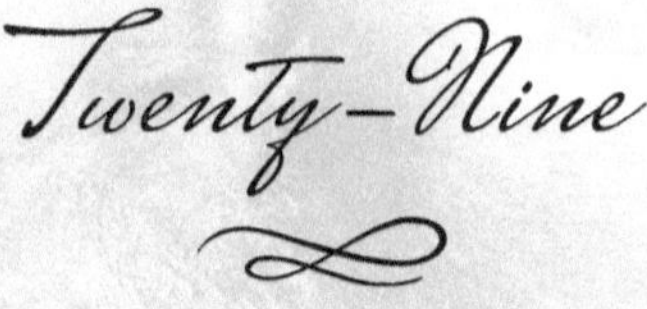

Twenty-Nine

LIZ

I'm in awe of how majestic Colton's wolf looks. He's got the most luscious golden coat and a pair of captivating brown eyes. His fluffy tail hasn't stopped wagging since I put my phone down and gave him all my attention.

The more I pet him, the more his hair falls all over my couch. I don't even care. Without Trey around, Wolfie's presence makes me feel safe. It's almost like he knew Trey left, so he came to protect me.

The size of him makes my big couch look like it was made for a children's playhouse. It's no wonder Colton survived five years of rescue missions with Theo's clan. If a wolf this size came charging at me, growling and trying to bite my head off, I'd be too frightened to move.

I scratch Wolfie behind his ears, making him fall onto his back with his limp paws in the air.

"I can see why the Zordi community sees you as a threat," I say in a cutesy baby voice. "You're just so damn vicious."

I scratch Wolfie's white belly and giggle as his tongue droops out of his mouth. He pants hard, looking up at me with admiration.

Yep. Vicious.

When I draw my hands back to pull some hair behind my ear, Wolfie cocks his head at me like *why'd you stop?* I return to scratching his belly until I find a spot that makes him do that leg-kicking thing dogs do.

"If I keep petting you this good, you're never gonna let me see Colton again."

Wolfie smiles at me guiltily, like I've just called him out on his plan.

We hang out on my couch until dinnertime, when I head to the kitchen in search of food to make. Wolfie trails me, never allowing me to get more than a step away.

I open the refrigerator to find some leftovers, a raw steak, and a half-eaten bag of broccoli. "Are you hungry, Sunny?" *Eh.* Now that I've said it, I don't like the name as much.

A bark echoes against my kitchen walls.

That's when it hits me that I have no idea what wolves eat. They probably eat meat, but what kind? Small animals like rabbits and fish? Or big animals like deer and elk? I guess it doesn't matter what the answer is, because I don't have any rabbits or deer in my fridge.

I unwrap the raw steak from its packaging and hold it out. "Would you eat this?"

Instead of barking his *yes*, Wolfie takes the steak into his mouth, then trots over to the table. Under it, he drops the meat onto the floor, then turns to face me. I wait for him to eat it, but he doesn't.

"Go ahead, Caramel. Eat it." I think my nicknames are getting worse.

Wolfie only stares at me, and I don't know why. He knew I was offering him the steak, and he took it, so why isn't he eating it?

After I toss the meat packaging into the trash, I pull out my container of leftover chicken tikka masala and pop it into the microwave. Three minutes later, it's steaming hot as I take it to the table.

Wolfie eyes me as I scoop up some basmati rice and eat it. Only then does he return the steak to his mouth and chew. Within seconds, the meat is devoured.

"That was sweet of you. I didn't realize you wanted to wait for me."

Back on my phone, I log into the z-net again. In the search bar, I type, *how much do Shifter wolves eat?*

A quick skim of the search results tells me that the average Shifter wolf will consume five to fifteen pounds of meat per day. However, with their flexible feast-or-famine lifestyle, they can go up to fourteen days without a meal. That steak I just gave him couldn't have been more than ten ounces.

"Are you still hungry?"

The wolf only stares at me. Since he didn't bark, I'm going to take that as a no.

After I finish eating, I head upstairs. Wolfie trots along behind me.

In my bedroom, I grab some pa-jammies, then step into my master bathroom for a shower. Wolfie follows me, planting himself next to the toilet.

"You can't be in here while I shower, Blondie." I shoo him with a hand. "Can you go wait outside the door?"

Wolfie whimpers, staying exactly where he is.

"I mean it, Fluffball." I step back into my bedroom and point at the carpet. "Come here."

He doesn't move.

I say it more sternly this time. "I said, come here."

This time, he obeys. Sluggishly, the wolf makes his way out of the bathroom.

I keep my finger pointed at the floor until he's at my feet. "Now sit."

He drops his booty onto the carpet, and I don't know why I'm so impressed. All evening, he's proved over and over that he knows exactly what I'm saying.

"Good boy, Dijon. Now you stay right here until I'm done, okay?"

I head back into the bathroom, expecting the wolf to follow me. He doesn't, so I shut the door. The second I do, he whimpers. It's so adorable, I almost cave and let him in.

As I get undressed, he scratches at the door and whines.

"Stop that. You'll ruin my door."

The scratching stops immediately. The whimpers don't.

"I'll only be, like, ten minutes, okay? Just chill."

As promised, I finish my shower within ten minutes. I step out with damp hair to find my uninvited but welcomed house guest lying as close to the bathroom door as possible, with his head slumped over his front paws.

"See? That wasn't so bad, right?"

He perks his head up and huffs.

Jeez. You'd think I had asked him to wait out here for ten days, not ten minutes.

I run a brush through my hair. "You wanna know what I was thinking while I was in the shower?"

He cocks his head at me.

"I thought of a bunch of different names for you, then came to the conclusion that I'm sticking with Wolfie. I like it the best. What d'ya think?"

Wolfie barks his approval.

A few minutes later, we get comfortable in my bed. I've got pillows behind my back and a romance book in my lap. As I read, Wolfie lays his head over my thighs. The calm and happy look on his face makes it seem like he's been waiting too long for this moment and this is exactly how he imagined it'd feel.

I finish fourteen chapters of my book before my eyes get heavy. "Are you planning to stay the night?"

Wolfie barks once.

I place my bookmark between the pages I'm at, then set the book on my nightstand. As I shuffle across the room to turn off the lights, Wolfie's eyes follow my every move. At this point, I *dare* someone to try to kidnap me.

When I return to bed, I don't have to ask Wolfie to cuddle with me. He simply tucks his head under my arms, then lets out a soft exhale.

I squeeze him tight. "Think of all the nightmare-deflecting thoughts you can, okay?"

He gives my cheek a lick, and I take it as an *of course I will.*

Four days later, I'm just leaving work when my phone buzzes in my purse. "Hey, T."

"Whose dog is in your house?" In Trey's background, Wolfie is barking in a manner I've never heard before. He sounds like he's ready to eat someone alive.

"He's *my* dog."

"When the fuck did you get a dog?"

I unlock my car and toss my duffel bag onto the front seat. "Technically, he's not a dog."

"He sure looked like one based on the two seconds I got to see him when I walked into your house and he tried to bite my leg off. I ran outta there and shut the door so fast, you woulda thought I was a Speeder. I'm about to go sit on your curb because he won't stop barking at me."

"Sorry about him. I was hoping to make it home before you, but Dixie really wanted my opinion on some changes we're making in the studio. Anyway, I'll be home soon. Could you just stay outside until—"

Trey gasps. "Oh my god. That's Colton, isn't it?"

"Yeah, but technically, it's his animal. Colton is in hibernation."

"Interesting. How long has his wolf been around?"

I was hoping to talk to Trey about this in person, but I'll settle for over the phone on my drive home.

I start by telling him that Wolfie showed up shortly after he left for the airport on Sunday. I share some of the information I learned about Shifters through the z-net and my experience with having Wolfie around lately. What I talk about the most is how Wolfie, without fail, has been keeping the nightmares away.

"I'm so well rested, I've only been sleeping every other night."

"Wow," Trey says. "Have you yawned yet today?"

"Not once."

"Awesome. Now, what's that you said about him refusing to leave?"

I knew Trey would get fixated on that detail. "Every day before work, I offer him the chance to leave, but he won't go. I even leave the sliding door half open for him while I'm gone, in case he needs to pee, or hunt, or whatever else it is that wolves do. But whenever I arrive back home, he's just laying on my couch, waiting for me. The only time he goes outside is when it's dark and if I'm with him. Even then, he just sniffs around the backyard, does his business, then trots right back inside." A part of me wonders if Wolfie can sense that I don't actually want him to leave.

A while later, I pull into my driveway. Trey's sitting on the curb, and there's still barking coming from inside my house.

"Has he not quit this entire time?" I ask.

Trey stands, shaking his head. "Not for a second."

I roll my eyes. "Lemme go in and talk to him first, okay?"

He gestures toward my front door. "Please."

The moment I enter my house, the barking stops, and Wolfie nuzzles his face between my legs like an innocent little baby.

"Hey there, you little shit. Are you not gonna let my T-Bear into the house?"

Wolfie lets out a little growl.

I drop to my knees in front of him and look him straight in the eyes. "Trey is not a threat to me, okay? He's just as protective of me as you are. Don't you think it'd be better if *two* of you were around to keep me safe?"

His growl turns quieter, like he knows I've got a point, but he doesn't like it.

"Can you be nice to Trey now?"

He stops growling, but it's not good enough for me. I need him to agree.

"Do you promise to behave?"

He lets out a reluctant huff.

Again, it's not good enough. "If you can't be nice, one of you has to leave tonight, and it's not gonna be Trey."

At first, Wolfie whines, then he lets out a reluctant bark.

I accept that as his agreement, so I stand back up, open the front door, and wave for Trey to come in.

"Are you sure it's safe now?" Trey hesitantly steps inside, eyeing the wolf, who's silently eyeing him back.

"Wolfie promised he'd be nice."

Trey slowly kicks off his shoes, never taking his focus off the animal. "You named him?"

"Of course. I can't just call him Colton. They're technically separate beings. Do you wanna try to pet him?"

Trey raises his eyebrows and widens his eyes. "Is he gonna let me?"

I bend to get on Wolfie's level. "Can Trey pet you?"

At first, Wolfie doesn't respond. After a moment of internal debate, he takes a step toward Trey.

Slowly, Trey reaches out a hand. "Please don't bite me. I have to play guitar on a stage tomorrow, and I'd kinda like to have all my fingers to do it."

Once Trey's hand connects with Wolfie's fur, Wolfie steps closer. Trey pets his head, down his neck, then all the way to his wagging tail. It's not wagging as much as it usually is, but at least it's wagging.

"What a good wolf." I beam, proud of how well he listens to me.

"Don't speak too soon, Liz. He could just be puttin' on a show for ya. The second you turn your back on us, he's gonna tear me limb from limb."

Wolfie doesn't. For the rest of the evening, he and Trey get along as we all have dinner and watch a movie. While I brush my teeth, they cuddle together in my bed. It warms my heart to see them like that.

As Trey and I get comfy under the covers, Wolfie settles on my other side. With them both here, there's no way I'll wake up with a night terror.

"So," Trey says into the darkness of my bedroom, "how long do you think it'll be before Wolfie shifts back into Colton?"

"I dunno, but I read on the z-net that some animals can stay in control for decades, especially if that's what their human wants."

"Do you think that after what happened to you, this is Colton's way of dealing with it?" Trey just came to the same conclusion I did a couple of nights ago. "Because if I was a Shifter and had the ultimate cop-out to avoid my human-related problems, I'd take it."

I think about that, then give Wolfie a scratch under his chin. "Wolfie baby, I want you to know that I forgive Colton. I forgave him a long time ago. If he's hiding from me, he doesn't have to anymore."

Thirty

COLTON

Someone pokes my arm. "Psst."

I slowly open my eyes, expecting to see a forest of trees. Instead, it's Trey staring back at me.

He whispers, "I never thought I'd ever have to ask you this, but, um, do you wear boxers or briefs?"

I spring upright to find that I'm sitting in a bed—Liz's bed. *What the fuck am I doing here? How did I get here? And, oh, god, I'm naked in front of her best friend.*

"You know what? You seem like a briefs guy." From a black weekender bag in the closet, Trey drags out a pair of blue briefs and tosses them at me. "Good thing you're my size."

I push my legs into the fabric. "Thanks. I really appreciate it."

"Don't mention it. Like, seriously. I guess you need some clothes too, huh?" Trey returns to his bag, then hands me a black T-shirt and a pair of basketball shorts.

"Thanks." I put on his clothes, then comb my hands through my messy blonde curls. "What day is it?"

"Sunday."

"I meant the date."

"May seventh."

"May?" My jaw drops. "Are you fucking serious? Last I remember, it was still April."

"Yeah. You've been a wolf for about five weeks."

I shake my head. If my wolf wasn't sleeping inside me, I'd berate him. This is *not* what we agreed on. I drove us all the way to the Sequoia National Park so he could run around for a week while I avoided reality. I specifically told him one *week*. Not one *month*.

"Liz is downstairs, making breakfast," Trey says. "She doesn't know you've shifted back. I was just coming up because I forgot my phone, and that's when I found your naked ass sleeping in her bed. I was wondering why your wolf wasn't at her side. Usually, he's never more than a breath away from her."

"Has my wolf been here the entire five weeks?"

"Only four weeks. We have no idea where you were the first week."

My guess is that as soon as I shifted in the middle of the forest, my wolf hunted, ate, then made his way straight to Liz. Chrissy told me he's got a good sense of direction and knows to stay hidden and to travel only at night.

Before Mom died, we lived out in the country. Chrissy used to let my wolf out on Friday nights, and he usually wouldn't come back until Sunday. That's something he and I would agree on, but five weeks? Come on.

Just before leaving LA with the intent to wolf up for a week, I resigned from my job, dyed my hair back to normal, then called my landlord to let them know I'd be taking over the rent from now on, instead of my company. Since I didn't plan to be gone for this long, I'm now late on rent. I guarantee it's the same story with my credit cards and car payment.

Oh, fuck. My car. I hope it hasn't been impounded for being abandoned for over a month at a national park. Internally, I sigh because I'll have to worry about all that shit later. Right now, my priority is Liz.

The last time I saw her, she was bawling. I thought going into hibernation for a week would help clear my head. Turns out, it was a huge mistake. Not only do I still have no idea how to fix things with Liz, but she probably thinks I'm a coward for avoiding her for this long.

Fuck, I have so much apologizing to do. Where do I even start?

"You're gettin' really fucking anxious," Trey says. "And I don't like it. Why don't you just go downstairs and talk to her? Ya know, rip off the Band-Aid and shit."

I suck in a deep breath, then blow it out. Trey's right. There's no sense in wasting any more time. Thanks to my wolf, I've already wasted enough.

As I head toward the hallway, Trey pulls out his phone and plops onto Liz's bed. "Come get me when you're done. I'm hungry, and I can smell the bacon from up here."

My heart pounds with each footstep I thump against Liz's stairs. Do I start by explaining that my wolf doesn't allow me to shift if he doesn't want to? Will she understand? I've wanted to talk to her since the moment Trey kicked me out of his penthouse. Walking away killed me, but I did it for her because she needed that space. Will she understand that, or will she think I didn't care enough to stick around?

I step into the kitchen to find Liz at the stove with her back facing me and a spatula in her hand.

"I'm making hashbrowns, T-Bear. Would you like an over-easy egg over yours again?"

The line comes to me easily. "How 'bout some Fry Lube?"

She gasps, drops the spatula, and twists around. "Ahh!"

I must be hallucinating, because she doesn't slap me in the face like I thought she would—like she should. Instead, she dashes across the kitchen, launches herself at me, and wraps her legs around my torso.

"You're back!" she screams into my ear. "You're finally back!"

I hold her tight so she doesn't fall—not that I need to. She's hanging on to me like she's a koala and I'm her tree. I fucking love it, because this time, her tree is me, not Trey. "I'm sorry I took so long. When my wolf is out, he's the one who—"

Liz crashes her lips against mine, stealing my breath away. I stumble backward into the wall but manage to keep her attached to me. I return her hard kiss with kisses of my own. I'm confused by her reaction, but I'm also not gonna stop her.

"I'm. So. Happy. You're. Back," she says between kisses.

Whatever my wolf did in those four weeks with Liz, I'm gonna have to thank him. She doesn't seem mad at all. I thought I was gonna have to work ten times harder to win her back than I had to work to get her in the first place. I mean, I was up for the challenge, but I don't mind this.

I set her feet back onto the floor. "Do you want to turn off the stove so you don't burn those hashbrowns?"

"Oh, shit! I totally forgot I was cooking." She rushes to turn the heat off, then runs straight back to me. In the sweetest way, she caresses my hair with her bare fingertips. I keep my hands glued to my sides to make sure they don't touch hers. "When did you shift back?" she asks.

"Like two minutes ago."

Her gaze pans down my body, then she giggles. "Are you wearing Trey's clothes?"

"Yeah. Whenever I shift back, I'm always in my birthday suit." Which reminds me, I'll have to apologize to Trey for him finding me like that.

"I have so much I want to tell you," she says as her face brightens. "But first, are you hungry? Breakfast is almost ready. I made tons of bacon, thinking Wolfie would have some, so there's plenty for you."

"Wolfie? I like that a hell of a lot more than Goldilocks."

"Lemme guess—that's what Chrissy calls him?"

"Yeah, and it took me a while to get used to."

Liz laughs, and the sound of it wakes up my wolf. He perks his head up, wagging his tail.

Hey, asshole. Five weeks? Seriously?

My wolf grins like he has zero regrets. Considering he spent most of his time with Liz, I can understand why.

"I'll go grab Trey," I say.

"No need." Trey strolls into the kitchen and plants himself into a chair at Liz's table. "I heard breakfast was almost ready, so I came down."

Together, we eat Liz's delicious pancakes as I fill them in on what happened with the Wests.

"Theo and Taryn tracked them down all the way to Colorado. Dom and Willie were hiding out with some of their other culty kidnapper friends. Smart move, because it meant they had extra protection. But also, dumb move, because it meant we could kill two birds with one stone. Since we'd be too outnumbered, Theo got in contact with one of his ex-clan members—a guy who leads his own rescue team."

Liz pauses with her fork halfway to her lips. "The one who goes in with the intent to kill everybody, or the one who refuses to hurt people unless it's in self-defense?"

"Well," I let out a humorless chuckle as I cut another triangle out of my pancakes, "it was Theo's wife they took and they killed Andre, so I'll give you one guess."

Liz nods her approval. "Good. So did everyone in the clan come back out?"

"Mostly."

She cocks her head to the side. "Mostly?"

I swallow hard as I flash back to the moment I shifted back to my human form and the first thing I saw was the inside of Keith's thigh. "Theo's Speeder lost a leg."

Liz's face falls. "Oh my god. That's awful."

"Yeah, but he'll be all right. Nobody on our side died, so that's a win in my book."

"What about the other side?" Trey asks. "Did you get 'em all?"

"Most of them. Dom and Willie are gone for good—we made sure of that—but some of their culty kidnapper friends got away. The moment they realized they were outnumbered, they ran off and left the battle up to their guards."

Trey scoffs. "Fucking cowards."

"Yep, but I don't expect anything else from people like them. Theo's planning to find them all eventually, but at the moment, he's down two men, so he needs to do some recruiting before the clan can get back out there."

Liz takes a sip of her pineapple orange juice, then sets the glass down. "Did he ask you if you would rejoin?"

I shake my head. "Nah, Theo knows better. I have no desire to ever live that life again. If it wasn't you I was fighting for, I never would have gone back in the first place."

She places a gentle ungloved hand over my forearm, then gives me a light squeeze. "Thank you for fighting for me, Colton." She pats my chest twice. "And you too, Wolfie."

Inside me, my wolf sticks his nose in the air and howls with happiness.

"So?" I say, ready to change the subject. "Fill me in on your adventures with Wolfie."

Liz perks up and starts by telling me about the week she spent coming to my apartment every day, only to find it empty. Then she tells me about Wolfie showing up at her back door and how he spent his days moping on her couch until she returned home from work.

"Wolfie and T are like best buds now," she says. "They even cuddle."

Wow. That's a change. Usually, my wolf is growling at Trey or huffing at the mere thought of him.

Once the three of us have finished our breakfasts, Trey

pushes his chair away from the table, then takes his plate to the sink. After he rinses it off, he dries his hands on a towel. "I think I'm gonna head to the airport early."

"You don't have to, T. You're welcome to stick around."

"Nah. You two have some making up to do—or making out. Whatever it is, I don't need to be here for it."

I stand and offer Trey my hand. "Thanks for the clothes, man."

He shakes my palm firmly. "Like I said, don't mention it. I don't even want them back."

I get that. If I were him, I wouldn't want my underwear back either.

Outside Liz's house, a motorcycle rumbles to life. Once the rumbles are out of earshot, the house suddenly feels too quiet. I've finally got Liz all to myself, and the thought of it is making me want to shift back into a wolf so I can curl into a little ball and hide for days. I feel so in debt to this woman. Assuming I can even make things right, where do I start?

Silently, Liz heads into the living room. Whether she wants me to or not, I follow her there.

She settles on the couch and pats the empty space next to her. "Come sit."

Grateful for the invite, I plop down next to her. I don't say anything, though, because I want her to be in charge of where this conversation goes. Whatever she needs me to do to earn her forgiveness, I'll do it, no questions asked. If, instead, she tells me she never wants to see me again, I'll leave, no questions asked.

I imagine myself walking out of here after she tells me to get lost. In reality, I don't think I could actually do that. This woman means too much to me. I can't just give her up. I'm willing to fight for her if that's what it takes to win her back.

"I got your text message," she says. "The one about you resigning from your position and staying in LA."

I barely even remember sending that text. So much has happened since then.

"I've been putting some thought into it." She pulls a curl behind her ear. "And I don't think you should get an apartment nearby."

My shoulders slump, and my eyes cast down. I knew I should have talked to her before quitting my job. Now I'm jobless, possibly homeless, maybe carless, and—

"I think you should move in with me instead."

My head pops up. *What?* My dropped jaw causes her to ramble off with an explanation.

"It doesn't make sense for you to pay for an apartment nearby when we're just gonna end up having sleepovers all the time anyway. I've got a spare room we can turn into a bedroom for Trey, then I'll rearrange my room to make space for you. Considering you have nothing for furniture, it shouldn't be too hard."

"But—"

She throws up a gloveless hand. "No buts. This makes the most sense, and it'll save you money. You won't even have to pay rent because I've got that covered. I would appreciate it if you pitched in for groceries though. Wolfie can eat over ten steaks in one sitting, and that shit adds up."

I'm so shocked, I'm speechless. Liz wants me to move in with her? Just like that? Don't I have at least six to twelve months of groveling to do?

Liz keeps going. "Did you know Wolfie's favorite steaks are T-bones?"

It takes me a second to find my words. "Yeah. Chrissy says he likes to chew the bones."

"He does. He's currently collecting them in a corner of my kitchen, and he refuses to let me throw them away. He whines if I try to move them, as if they're his emotional support pile of bones. Anyway, what do you think?"

"About what?"

"Moving in with me?"

"I—I'm not sure if I understand. I thought I was gonna have to beg for your forgiveness."

"I've already forgiven you, Colton. A long time ago."

"But how? I didn't do anything to earn it."

"It was Trey, actually. He said that if he had been in your shoes, he would have done the same thing. If *he* can trust that you made your decisions based on what you thought was best for me, then I can put that trust in you too. Also, Trey is miserable without his soul mate. I don't want to live my life the way he does."

My mom never found her soul mate, and Chrissy believes people can have more than one. I thought Hallie was my soul mate until I realized she wasn't. Ever since I broke off our engagement, I haven't thought much more about the soul mate thing. Now that I think about the way my wolf first reacted when he saw Liz, it's possible she's mine. "You think we're soul mates?"

"I *know* we are."

How can she be so confident? The only way to know would be—I gasp. "You felt the glimmer."

"Yep. Twice. And both times, you and Wolfie were fighting for me."

I think back to the day I found out Liz was taken and gasp again. "Wait! I felt it too! I was on my lunch break at work when I suddenly felt nauseous. I thought it was food poisoning. That must have been when you woke up on the Wests' private plane and realized you were in danger."

"Yeah, probably."

I fall back against the couch, in awe. I can't believe it. I've found my soul mate! And she's everything I've ever wanted: beautiful, honest, smart, and kind-hearted with an amazing sense of humor. Add in the fact that she can sing and dance, and it makes her the whole package. I can't wait to tell Chrissy about this. She's gonna be thrilled.

Oh, fuck. Chrissy is probably wondering where I've been. We don't normally go five weeks without talking. We rarely even go a whole week. Hopefully, she assumed my wolf took over. He's been stubborn about shifting back before.

I mentally add calling Chrissy onto my list of shit I need to do. But first, I'll need to buy a new phone. As a precaution, Theo asked the whole clan to change their phone numbers and get new phones. He's also helping everyone relocate if they want to. I told him I would take care of all that after my supposed *week*long mental break. Here I am, five weeks later, and still no phone.

"So?" Liz says. "What do you think?"

I offer her a warm smile. "I think you and I would look great together in a cozy six-bedroom home with many acres of land for my wolf to run around."

"Six bedrooms? Why would we ever need so many?"

"One for us, one for Trey, and one for each of our kids."

She lets out a loud laugh toward the ceiling. "You want *four* kids?"

"I want as many as you'll give me." Ideally, we'd have six to eight kids, but I'm willing to have fewer if Liz isn't up for that.

"Uh, how about we start with two and go from there?"

I grin. "Deal."

Liz doesn't return my grin. Instead, her face saddens.

"What's wrong, bumblebee?"

She doesn't look at me as she says, "I've been thinking a lot about this, and Trey has convinced me it'll be a good idea in the long run." It takes her a few moments to finally lock her eyes with mine and say, "I need to touch your hands."

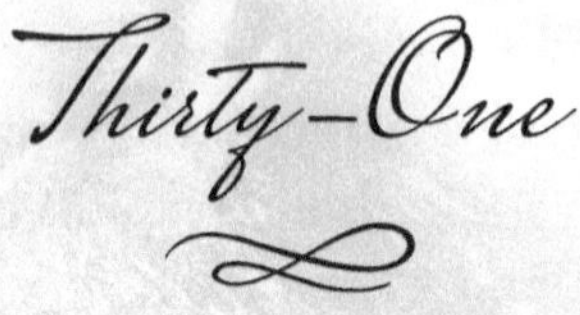

Thirty-One

LIZ

I wish I could say it's been easy, but it hasn't. I wish I could say it's been worth it, but it hasn't. At least, not yet. It took over three years of contact with Trey's hands before I saw nothing. It's now been over a year of purposely touching Colton's hands, and I'm still seeing his past trauma. Hopefully, I have only two more years to go—that is, if that's the way my body power works.

I have no idea if it's the length of time or how many times I need to touch someone's hands for their worst memory to stop invading my mind. It might not even be those factors at all. The nothingness could just be a fluke with Trey. Either way, I'm going to keep trying with Colton, even though it's more emotionally taxing with him than it was with my best friend.

The thing is, Trey's worst memory is seeing his parents get blown up. His parents were people I'd never met. Plus, all Trey saw was his house exploding with his parents in it.

As for Colton, he's got two traumatic memories, and I never know which one I'm going to get. Sometimes I see a bloody little girl screaming for her life while flames consume her head. The screaming stops once a wolf's claws puncture her neck, silencing her forever.

Sadly, I prefer that memory over Colton's other one: me wearing lingerie I was forced into, being tied to a wooden post against my will, and begging for someone to save me. Living that wretched moment was bad. Seeing it over and over is worse.

I didn't even know I could see two different traumatic memories from the same person. Then again, the only person's hands I've ever purposely touched this often is Trey's, and he only has one traumatic memory.

If someone else had this cursed body power and touched my hands, they would one hundred percent see me on that stage with Malik—and *only* that moment. I can't think of anything else I've been through that's more traumatic than that, which only adds to how hard it's been for me to go bare-handed around Colton. Whenever I question if I'm doing the right thing, I just remind myself that it'll be worth it in the end. *Hopefully.*

Tenderly, Colton caresses my hair with his fingers, then places a soft kiss against my forehead. "Is it over, bumblebee?"

"Yeah." Even though my vision of blood dripping from that little girl's body has faded from my head, I'm still breathing heavily. It doesn't matter that I've already seen this memory hundreds of times, it still affects me.

We're hanging out on the backstage couch at the Soul House, after one of my band's afternoon rehearsals. My bandmates left a while ago, so I felt comfortable enough to take my gloves off while Colton and I enjoyed a late lunch. Unfortunately, I accidentally made contact with his hand as we reached for the chips. Somehow, I managed to not drop my turkey club sandwich.

"What do you need, baby?" Colton asks with another kiss to my forehead. He's been gracious with me over the past year. He's patient, supportive, and does everything in his power to help me get through each unwanted flashback. "Cuddles? Ice cream? A walk? A walk to get ice cream?"

I offer him a reassuring *I'll be okay* smile. "A walk to get ice cream sounds nice. Let's finish our lunch first."

After our sandwiches are devoured, we exit the Soul House and head toward the same ice cream place we visited back when we first met. The summer sun warmly kisses my skin, which only makes me more excited to get some cold ice cream.

I take a hold of Colton's bicep as we stroll the sidewalk. Like the protective man he's always been, he switches sides with me to be closer to the road.

"Chrissy's planning to come visit soon," Colton says. "Would you be cool with her staying with us again?"

The last three times Chrissy came to visit, she's stayed in our spare bedroom. It used to be Trey's room, but he's since gotten his own place. Now the room is decorated with pink flowers and matching bedding.

"Chrissy is always welcome to stay with us," I say and mean it. She's become one of my bestest friends, and she talks to me more than she talks to her big brother nowadays. Whenever she's here, Colton becomes the third wheel. I'm surprised she hasn't mentioned visiting yet. She typically tells *me* before she tells Colton. "When does she wanna come?"

"She wants to come see me graduate from the academy."

Ah, that makes sense as to why she talked to him about it before talking to me. Six months ago, Colton started training to become a police officer. His graduation ceremony is next week. Eventually, he wants to be a homicide detective.

I'm proud of him for finally pursuing what he wants to do instead of only dreaming about it. It took a lot of encouragement from Chrissy and me. I also had to assure him that I could support us on my income alone. I've been able to do it comfortably, thanks to my band's successful third album and tour, which ended last month.

At first, Colton wasn't fond of the idea of living off my money, even if it would only be for six months. Once he came to terms with it, he dove straight into becoming a police officer with full force. He's even going back to school for a degree in criminal justice.

Every week, he shows me how grateful he is by giving me multiple foot massages and making sure I never touch a dirty dish or fold the laundry. I'm so used to it that at this point, I don't think I could ever go back to hanging my own dance skirts.

When the ice cream parlor comes into view, there's a short line snaking out the door. Colton and I eagerly join the back of the line, then peer through the windows to read the menu.

A few minutes later, we exit the cozy little shop with our ice cream cups in hand.

"You got any quarters in that little purse of yours?" Colton asks as we continue our walk.

"I do, actually."

Without him having to say it, I already know where we're headed. We haven't gone back to our fountain, as we call it, since the first time. We reference it quite a bit though. Whenever asked, Colton tells people that the night we made wishes at that fountain was the night he knew he wanted me forever. I tell people it was the night I knew he was crazy because he believed in fountain fairies.

"They're real!" he says, taking a bite of his peanut-and-fudge-covered sundae. "I wished for you to fall in love with me, and you did—all thanks to the fairies' magic."

"But I was already falling for you."

"And the fountain fairies sealed the deal."

I roll my eyes at him as we cross an intersection. "I'd like to think that I fell for you with my own free will."

"And I'd like to think it was partly that, partly the fountain fairies, and partly my ability to patiently impatiently wait through six weeks of dance lessons."

I laugh as I dig my plastic spoon into my cookies-and-cream yumminess. "You know what really sealed the deal for me? The way you can get me to come with your mouth in under ten minutes—sometimes five."

Colton grins with his nose in the air. "I'll make sure to tell our children that."

Lately, Colton's been bringing up the topic of kids quite often. He wants to have a large pack of little wolves running around, like six to eight of them. I only want two kids, *maaaybe* three. He wants to get started soon, while I still have so many things I want to accomplish before becoming a mother. My band is already working on our fourth album, and we're planning to tour again once it's done. I just don't see babies fitting into that picture.

Besides, I'd like to have kids *after* we're married, and we're not even engaged yet. Colton hasn't even asked me what kind of ring I'd like or if marriage is something on my radar. I understand that he's been focusing on finishing the academy and school, but to not even mention the *idea* of marriage? The closest he's been to talking about it was last week, when he casually mentioned that since he's been engaged before and it didn't work out, he's in no rush to get engaged again.

At first, I thought I was fine with that answer, but it's been gnawing at me ever since. It's not like Colton and I are just boyfriend and girlfriend. We're soul mates! Does he need more of a reason than that to pop the question? I'm not asking for a wedding to happen tomorrow. I'd just like to know that he's planning on it in our nearish future.

By the time we reach the park, Colton and I have finished our ice cream. We find a trash bin to throw our cups into, then head straight for the fountain. A couple with a stroller are sitting on the nearby bench that I once searched for coins under. Some other couples and families are resting on blankets in the grass, reading books, having a picnic, or simply enjoying the sunlight.

The closer I get to the fountain, the more the sound of the falling water drowns out the noise of the kids running around behind me. The fountain looks more majestic than I remember, although the last time I saw this thing was in the dark. With the late-afternoon sun shining down on it and all the leafy green trees and blooming flowers around, the fountain looks like a Hallmark movie set.

I unzip my purse and dig out two quarters, handing one to Colton. "Do you know what you want to wish for?"

"Yep." He turns his back to the fountain, closes his eyes, then tosses the coin over his shoulder. The metal makes a little *plop!* as it hits the water. With a smile, he opens his eyes and gestures toward the fountain. "Your turn."

I turn my back to the fountain. I don't have to think about my wish, because I already know what I'm asking these fictitious fountain fairies for, and this time, it's selfish. With my eyes shut, I say my wish in my head, then throw the coin behind me. I don't open my eyes until I hear the little *plop!*

"What'd ya wish for?" Colton asks.

"I can't tell you, remember? Then it won't come true."

"I'll tell you mine if you tell me yours."

I give him the biggest eye roll I can manage. "That line didn't work last year, and it's not gonna work now either."

"At the risk that it won't come true, I'm gonna tell you my wish anyway." Colton drops to one knee, making my heart drop with it. A gasp escapes my lips as he holds up a sparkly diamond ring between his fingers. "I wished for you to marry me."

I slap a hand over my heart as happy tears pool in the corners of my eyes. *Is this really happening?*

"I love you, Liz. You are my entire world. My soul mate. The love of my life. My bumblebee. My everything. Now will you also be my wife?"

I throw myself at him, wrapping my arms around his shoulders. "Yes! Of course, yes!"

He stands, keeping me tight against his chest. Our lips meet in a passionate kiss. When he tries to pull away, I yank him back and keep his mouth against mine. Our tongues dance together naturally, the way they always have. Every moment I've ever spent with Colton has felt right, from the second I saw him walk into my ballroom to now. And I wouldn't have it any other way.

Eventually, I allow him to step back.

With the biggest grin I've ever seen on him, he pulls out a pair of black satin gloves from his pocket. "I brought these so I could put your new ring on you."

I stick out my bare left hand with a grin wider than his. How did I get lucky enough to find someone who cares to think about the little things?

Once the ring is on my finger, I hold my hand up toward the cloudless sky to get a good look. "Wow! It's so beautiful." The rock sparkles in the sunlight. It's a modern and elegant ring design I definitely would have picked. "You wanna know something funny?"

"Sure."

"I wished for you to ask me to marry you."

Colton smirks. "See? Now you can't tell me that fountain fairies don't exist. Their magic just keeps on working."

I side-eye him skeptically. "I thought you said you weren't in a rush to get engaged again any time soon."

"That was a lie to throw you off. I've actually been planning this proposal for months."

My brows shoot up. "You have? This wasn't just a spur-of-the-moment thing?"

"Not at all. See?" Colton gestures toward the trees behind me.

I twist around to find Trey and Chrissy hiding behind some bushes. Both of them are holding up their phones, capturing this special moment.

I run toward them, holding out my left hand. "Look! Look! Look!"

Trey and Chrissy come out from their hiding spots and meet me in the middle.

Trey gives my hand a once-over, then nods his approval. "It shines more on your finger than in the box."

"You've already seen it?"

"Yep. Saw it months ago. I was the one who helped Colton pick it out."

Colton joins us and gives Trey a hard slap on the back. "Thanks again, man. I had no idea what I was doing, so it was nice to have someone with experience there."

"Well, *I* haven't seen the ring yet," Chrissy says, slipping her phone into her pocket. Without reaching for my hand, she gazes at the diamond. "Wow! It's so perfect for you!"

I wrap my arms around Colton's shoulders, already thinking about the engagement celebration fuck we'll be having later. "He really is."

Thirty-Two

COLTON

The fountain-fairies thing started as a joke to get Liz to laugh, but now I'm starting to believe they actually exist. In the past four years, I've returned to our fountain to make a wish three times. Each time, my wish has come true.

My first wish was made a few months after I proposed to Liz. On a dark December night by myself, I tossed a coin over my shoulder into the fountain and wished for Liz's mind to stop seeing my memories whenever our hands touched. It was killing me to see her go through that pain every day, and I figured why not give the fountain fairies' magic a shot?

The next day, while we were cuddling in bed, Liz's hand came in contact with mine and she finally saw nothing. It's been like that ever since.

My second wish was made the following April, during our wedding. We held a cozy ceremony at our fountain. Trey was my best man. Despite how I felt about him in the beginning, now I can't imagine my life without the bastard. I would trust him with my life. Liz chose Chrissy as her maid of honor, who went all out helping us plan the wedding. My sister cried happy tears every step of the way, from ordering the flowers to the moment I kissed my new wife.

Dixie, who claims to never cry, also cried. She cried when she saw Liz in her flowy white dress. She wept when I read my vows, and she practically sobbed when I mentioned that I had plans to have as many babies as Liz would give me.

After Dixie wiped away her tears using the bottom of her bridesmaid dress, she said, "If you wanna get kinky in one of my ballrooms, just make sure you turn my new cameras on first."

"You mean *off?*" I asked.

"No, no, Mr. Finley. On." Then she smirked and flashed me a wink.

At the end of our beautiful ceremony, we encouraged our guests to toss coins into the water and make a wish. I wished for the fountain fairies to give my bride some intense baby fever.

Within seven months, Liz secretly got off birth control, then surprised me with a positive pregnancy test. Nine months after that, we brought home our baby boy, August.

We didn't plan for Liz to get pregnant again right away, but four months later, when she surprised me with another positive test, I was thrilled.

We were in the midst of moving into a new house when our second baby boy came home a week early. Samuel looked almost identical to his big brother.

My third wish was made three months ago, after my bumblebee told me she was finally pregnant again. It had taken us several months of trying for baby number three, so I exploded with excitement. At the time, our boys were having a night out with their Auntie Chrissy, so I scooped my pregnant wife into my arms, carefully dumped her in the passenger seat of my truck, then drove us straight to our fountain to wish for a baby girl.

Today, during two-year-old August's birthday party, Liz

and I stood next to our fountain and cut into a cake that read *Boy or Girl?* in frosting. The moment I saw that pink butter-cream inside, I shamelessly teared up in front of all our friends.

After all that, how can I not believe in fountain fairies?

"Maybe this time, you should wish for a million dollars," Liz says, fiddling with the coin in her gloveless hands. While August plays in the grass with Trey and his wife and daughter, Liz and I are staring at our fountain, debating on what we want to wish for.

I adjust our cooing Samuel to sit more comfortably in my arms. "I'm not tryna be greedy, babe. The fountain fairies might sense that vibe and stop granting me all my wishes."

My wife—I'll never get tired of calling her that—lets out a chuckle. Like usual, the sound of it gets my wolf to perk up. He wags his fluffy tail, staring deeply at Liz. I've been married to her for three years now, and my wolf still looks at her with hearts in his eyes—as do I.

Liz flips her coin in the air and catches it. "I'm just saying that if the fairies really wanna prove they exist, making a million dollars appear in our bank account is a good way to do it."

"They've got nothing to prove. Besides, every single wish I've ever made at this fountain has come true, so they've got *me* convinced."

After another minute of pondering, my wish finally comes to me. I turn my back to the water, visualize what I want, then toss a coin over my shoulder.

When I open my eyes, Liz has hers closed. She, too, has her back to the fountain, then tosses her coin behind her.

"What did you wish for?" she asks when she opens her eyes.

I gape at her and scoff dramatically. "Excuse me? You know the rules, Mrs. Finley."

"I'll tell you mine if you tell me yours."

Unlike Liz, I have no self-control. "All right, fine. I wished for you to name our daughter Sophia."

"Sophia?" Liz gazes at the coins at the bottom of the fountain and thinks. "Hmm. I really like that."

"You do?" I'm shocked, because every single name I threw out for our boys was turned down. I liked Lex, and she said it reminded her of the villain from the DC world. I suggested Bart, and she said it sounded too much like fart. When I said, "How about Tucker?" she said the kids at school would call him fucker.

"Yeah," Liz says. "Sophia's a cute name."

Samuel coos some more as I hold him tighter against me. "I'm glad you like it. Now tell me what *you* wished for."

Smiling up at me, Liz takes my free hand into hers. I relish the feel of her bare hand and admire her shiny yellow nail polish. They are two things I'll never take for granted. "I wished for you to choose a good name for our daughter."

I pause. "Seriously?"

"Seriously."

I pull her into me and kiss the top of her hair. "Never doubt the fountain fairies."

Secrets Trilogy

Read Trey's story: a slow-burn tale of forbidden love, filled with crazy twists and so much emotional damage that it needed three whole novels.

Acknowledgments

*To **Chris***:
I dedicated this book to you because you're my ride-or-die guy
bestie the way Trey is to Liz. You've been my friend the
longest, and I've always loved the kind and intelligent person
that you are. I hope we continue to have adventures together,
especially the ones in tandem kayaks.

*To **Sara Bendickson***:
Whenever we are in a tandem kayak with Chris, I hope your
paddle always goes *bloop!* in the water. Thanks for being my
ride-or-die girl bestie, behind-the-scenes helper, and event
assistant. I love you!

*To my **husband, Joe***:
You were my inspiration for the "Fry Lube" scene in chapter
twenty-five, because that type of banter is sooo us! And yes,
the spicy scene in chapter fourteen is also inspired by you. ;)
Please see the last three words of said spicy chapter.

*To my **beta readers***:
How did I get lucky enough to find a bunch of ladies who just
get my humor? Thanks for always telling me which parts are
funny and should stay in the story! Kaycee Racer, Priscillah
Bancy, Kelsey Davis, Whitney Tanner, Atima Kim, Annie, and
Sara T.

To my **readers**:
If you're here after reading the Secrets Trilogy, thank you! Liz is my favorite character from those novels, so naturally, she got her own book. I hope you continue to read my writing, because I've got so much more in store for you!

To **Enchanted Ink Publishing**:
Natalia, Stephanie, Christian, Lisa, and Greg.
It says a lot about your team when an author chooses to stick around throughout four novels and beyond. Each of you set high standards for the craft you specialize in, and I'm so grateful to have you!

To my **Secret Keepers**:
My cult—I mean, street team—is a collection of completely unhinged romance lovers. Whoops! Did I say unhinged? I meant normal! Completely normal. And no, they've never made a dick joke in our group chat or threatened to hold me hostage in a basement. Nope. Never.

To the **Swifties**:
Did you catch all the subtle Taylor Swift references in this book? What if I told you none of it was accidental?

To **anyone who society deems "unworthy" for something out of their control**:
Your differences make you unique, so don't allow anyone to take that away from you. Like Liz, you deserve love and respect too.

About the Author

Melissa Lam loves reading and writing romance books that take the reader on an emotional roller coaster full of mystery, suspense, and heartache.

As an extroverted introvert who doesn't like to leave the house (because it requires wearing pants), Melissa enjoys playing strategic board games and taking long showers. When she does find the will to put pants on, she can be found traveling, enjoying bubble tea, or experiencing the world through food.

TL;DR I like to eat and write about heartbreaking shit.

Website: authormelissalam.com
Instagram: instagram.com/authormelissalam
Facebook: facebook.com/authormelissalam
Newsletter: authormelissalam.com/newsletter